Ó mo chara aindiach Jim:

Beannachtaí Dé ort

Jim

Leave of Absence

About the Author

Jude Collins is a university lecturer, a columnist with the *Irish News* and a regular contributor to BBC Radio Ulster, BBC Radio 4 and BBC 5 Live. He has written two collections of short stories, *Booing the Bishop* (Blackstaff, 1995) and *Only Human* (Blackstaff, 1998). His first novel, *The Garden of Eden All Over Again* (Simon & Schuster/TownHouse, 2002), received the McCrea Literary Award.

Leave of Absence

Jude Collins

First published in 2005 by

TownHouse, Dublin
THCH Ltd
Trinity House
Charleston Road
Ranelagh
Dublin 6
Ireland

www.townhouse.ie

A CIP catalogue record for this book is available from the
British Library.

ISBN: 1-86059-238-4

Cover design by Sin É Design
Typeset by Typeform Ltd.
Printed by Cox & Wyman Ltd, Reading, Berks

For
Maureen, Phoebe, Patrick,
Matt and Hugh

Chapter 1

THE END

Somewhere outside, maybe quarter of a mile away, dogs were fighting. Their barks sliced and tore at the morning air. A thin high yip, a deep-chested bark, then a flurry of snarls and slobbers as they got close to each other. The sound rolled up the length of the chapel, along the top of the altar, over the lilies in the vases and up to the stained-glass window that showed St Joseph the worker, wooden hammer in hand, about to hit something. Bounced back from the strong reds, blues and yellows of the window to the rows of seats that banked up to the right of the central aisle and to the left, where the chief mourners and their families were seated. Children peered along the pews at each other, giggled when they heard the dogs, glanced sideways towards the church door, which Andy the caretaker had propped open with a wedge of wood.

In his seat to the right of the central aisle Dr Diarmuid Monaghan closed his eyes, loosened his Clarks Active Air shoe to ease the throbbing in his right foot, and told his worries to line up for identification. Worry number one: this year's timetable (big) and promotion prospects (small). Worry number two: funerals – three and a half months ago Mammy's, now this one. Worry number three: Mammy's will and what to do about Uncle Dan. Worry number four: Mammy's will and the shingles-itch to punch Paul's mouth every time he said 'Let's try to

1

concentrate on what she'd have wanted.' Worry number five: Frances and her friends Joy and Mairead, and the ache to scream when they started talking about organic food or house upkeep – and sometimes when they had stopped talking about organic food or house upkeep, or were getting ready to talk about organic food or house upkeep, or were just glancing at him eating or, more likely, drinking inorganic things or not keeping up the house, and pursing their mouths so that little vertical wrinkles showed like three hens' arses turned towards him. Worry number six: the 'God Lives!' column and the tapeworm that burrowed deeper into his stomach each week when he sat down to write it. A couple of other worries were shuffling up to join the queue but they got elbowed out of the way as a single image, like a slide in full colour, filled centre screen.

In it Professor Claire Thompson was alive again, behind her desk as she'd been last Monday, fingering an earring the size of a sanctuary lamp, one calm blue eye and one calm brown eye studying Diarmuid as he gabbled on the other side of her desk. Beauty and the blabber-mouth. And behind her the computer, with its cordless mouse and its sideways-fanny drive; and inside the computer's little sideways fanny, a disk, his disk; and on the disk a file called 'Broadcast' but that was a bad name for it, because inside the file marked 'Broadcast' was also a seven-page document that should have been on a separate file called 'Little Known Facts' but somehow had... Diarmuid put his face in his hands and suppressed a groan. Only four days ago. And now look. Claire in her coffin and that bastard Terry with his skinny body and Dick Nixon jowls out there somewhere, getting ready to read, if he hadn't already read, the Little Known Facts section of the Broadcast file, and when he had it read to pass it on to God knows who. Diarmuid put his palms between his thighs and squeezed. All right, Terry wasn't actually out there; he was at home in bed with the toothache, one of the other secretaries had said, left early after his interview with the cops, in agony apparently. And if he was at home in agony with his teeth he wouldn't, couldn't be at the funeral.

So. Think of something calm. The dogs, try the dogs. Maybe those yelps and growls and yips were doggy sounds of pleasure, telling the world and themselves how good it felt to be alive, grinning with their doggy faces, wrestling in the sunshine, sticking their bits into each other for a few minutes of jiggling delight before death. How long did dogs live? Eight years? Twelve? Did they have moments like this to look back on or forward to as the years unfolded, or did their lives resemble his own, a one-way tunnel smelling of regret and fear?

The image of a dog having a piss at the edge of a dark underpass was shattered by the noise of car doors slamming, gravel crunching and voices in the porch. The congregation glanced discreetly towards the entrance. The undertaker, grey hair and pink face, backed his way into the church, hands waving like someone directing a car from a driveway on to a main road. Then the front of Claire's coffin came into view, carried by six young men with fair hair and big round faces, resembling hers but distorting her beauty into plainness. Country cousins, probably, hurley players from Meath or Louth or some southern wildness.

They moved cautiously up the middle aisle, faces tense, the coffin biting into their shoulders. At the altar rails the undertaker touched the prow, steady and all together lads, hold her carefully, lower at the same time... That's it. Claire's final vehicle sat on a little wheeled contraption, brass coffin handles winking in the morning sun, pale coffin wood undisturbed by what it contained.

The congregation looked down at the coffin, across at each other from opposite sides of the aisle, coughed and settled back in their seats. Near the altar on the left the relatives sat. Near the altar on the right, two rows of university colleagues. Not the Vice Chancellor, of course – Claire had been only a head of department – but the next rank after that. The Dean of Lifestyle and Learning, pale tight face and pink-rimmed glasses turning to look up and down the chapel. The Chief Examinations Officer in a yellow floral dress, her new hairstyle making her look even more like Michael Douglas than usual. In front of her Warwick and Crompton from Cont Psych, heads inclined towards each other as they whispered; along the seat from them some office staff from the Women In New Developments (WIND) Project. Considering it was early August and most university staff had used the summer to put as much distance between themselves and Belfast as humanly possible, a respectable turn-out.

A gong sounds in the sacristy and Dr Fr David Hillocks, assistant chaplain and head of Historical Pedagogies emerges led by two altar-girls, both taller than him. His little round face, half smiling as usual, looks to either side of the congregation, nods with each step. As he passes near the front row he stops and whispers something to a woman. Claire's mother, probably. Head bowed, a hanky balled up in her fist, ready to punch away any tears that might try to escape. A younger woman puts an arm round her. Claire's sister almost certainly: the one who had phoned Claire that evening, Claire with her hand cupped over the mouthpiece, eyes pleading: 'Could you just give me a minute, Diarmuid? My sister...' Now Dr Fr David has left the woman and is facing the congregation, fingertips on forehead, the altar almost level with his chest: 'In the name of the Father.' The Mass begins.

They had got to the Confiteor when voices sounded at the back of the church and two women entered. The smaller, stocky one wore blue denims turned up at the bottom, the taller a pair of beige-coloured jeans with pockets down each leg. The stocky one scratched her frizzed ginger hair and glared towards the altar. Her companion shifted from foot to foot, glancing sideways at the coffin, arms hanging awkwardly by her sides. Joy and Mairead! What were they doing here?

Then a secretary from the WIND Project waved the two women towards her and Diarmuid remembered. Six months ago Claire had asked Joy and Mairead to address her WIND people. The gardening and handiwork duo had jumped at the chance of free publicity, talked for a full hour, Frances said, about how they, two mere women, had set up their own business, had coped with male negativity, had become successful, blahblahbloodyblah. Frances had been there too, and loved them so much she'd arranged there and then for them to landscape the front garden. Two weeks later they'd half clipped the hedge, pseudo-mown the lawn and placed a small wooden cart filled with earth in the middle of it. In spring, they assured Diarmuid and Frances, the cart would convert into a cascade of daffodils and tulips – and cast a really nice shadow over the lawn in the evening, Mairead added. May came and still not a single flower. On his third gin one night, Diarmuid asked Frances if Joy and Mairead shouldn't be giving *them*, Diarmuid and Frances, two hundred pounds, rather than taking it from them, for having ruined their front lawn? She hadn't spoken to him for several days after he said that.

Then, almost immediately after the two women had settled in their places, the chapel door opened again and Terry Prundy, in a cream-coloured suit and a black tie, entered with, two paces behind, as usual, Hazel Ward, the department's only full-time Master's student. For a moment they stood, Terry with hands in pockets, his treacle-ball eyes checking for a vacant spot, Hazel blinking apologetically at his elbow. Diarmuid put his hands over his face and prayed: Please, God, I don't want to talk to anyone but especially not Terry about our late department head nor Hazel about her dissertation *or anything else*.

Then the congregation sat down and a music student stood beside the organ and began to sing 'The Lord is my Shepherd'. The notes rose sweet and mournful, deepening the sombre mood as people tried not to think of being dead but of the Lord being their shepherd and making them down to lie and refreshing their spirit.

During the last verse Dr Fr David approached the coffin and a server held up a brass bucket into which he dipped his sprinkler and sent spots of holy water flicking on to the pale wood. His lips moved in prayer, telling God to give Claire a safe passage and eternal peace. Then he stood before the lectern, dabbed his mouth with a white hanky.

'Brothers and sisters in Christ.' His gaze took in the relatives, the colleagues, the children. 'Welcome, all, to St Ultan's Church here in the parish of Dunbeg. A special welcome to Claire's mother, sister and other relatives who have come some distance to be here this morning We gather to receive the mortal remains of our sister in Christ, Claire, and to support her with our prayers to her final resting place.'

There was silence for a moment, the hum of distant traffic filling the space. The dogs had moved on.

'For those of you who don't know me, I'm Dr Fr David Hillocks, a priest and a colleague of Claire's at North-Eastern University. Death is a deep and difficult mystery at any time, but particularly on a morning such as this, as we try to cope with the fact that someone in the prime of life such as... Claire' – for a moment it seemed as if he might have forgotten the name – 'should have reached the end of her journey so soon. A week ago, a mere seven days, I sat at an inter-department meeting with Claire, planning how my Historical Pedagogies people might work with her Learning Outcomes people for a productive academic year.'

The coffin sat in the aisle, framed by the seats on either side. On top of it was a raised crucifix – Christ on the cross – thrust clear of the wood, arms wide. Christ the gymnast, energetic and flexible through the ages. Light brown coffin, its grain flowing and fixed at the same time. Strange to think that one day somebody had planted a tree that was fated to be felled and then form Claire's coffin. She might have found that tree and tried to uproot it, but that would have been futile. Death would still have come galloping after her, caught her, squeezed her into another coffin pretty much the same as this one. Diarmuid looked at his hands joined in front of him, the pudgy veins, the overlong nails. Where was his tree? Leaning over a stream somewhere, trunk thrusting into the sky like a giant's dick, waiting for Diarmuid's death shudder.

Dr Fr David's voice was slower now. Claire's suffering was past, he said. We must mourn her loss but we must also come together and rejoice in the gift that had been her life, a gift shared by her university colleagues, her family, the wider community. And now Claire's sister Angela would say a word.

She came to the lectern in a calm, unhurried way, a woman of maybe forty, in a black overcoat with a silver-coloured scarf tucked inside the throat. Body plumper, face a little flatter than Claire's. Not as beautiful.

'Claire was many things to many people. For me she was a sister – my big sister. When I started school, she showed me my classroom and my teacher and the toilets. All the essentials of living for a five-year-old.' There was a whisper of laughter around the church. 'When I got old enough to go to discos, Claire showed me who and what to look out for, what things to tell our mother, what not.' She smiled briefly towards the older woman and leant forward, elbows on the lectern. 'I wouldn't pretend she was perfect. Claire could make demands, hold a grudge, just like the rest of us. Lose her temper, even. When I think of her now, she's as likely to be doing something silly or petty as she is to be doing something nice.' A pause. Hair flicked back impatiently from her face. 'She was a human being, jostling her way through life. Just like all of us.'

She drew in her breath as if about to continue, then instead crumpled her notes and hurried back to her seat. Dr Fr David, blinking quite a lot, said Dean Saddington would now address the congregation. The Dean moved carefully to the microphone, a light from the stained-glass windows briefly turning his cropped white hair pink.

This was a sad day for many people, the Dean said. First and foremost for Claire's family and friends. Then for colleagues, current students, former students who'd been touched by her energy and dedication down the years. His voice, grainy like Richard Burton's, rumbled round the church. 'As Dr Fr David has indicated, NEU – our university, yours, mine – today confronts loss. One week from today, I would have met with Claire and her department, to prioritise teaching and research strategies for the months ahead. Now we will face an empty chair. Someone else will pick up the torch that has fallen from her hand. But regardless of who does so, one thought gives us comfort: Claire's achievements will remain undimmed in our hearts.'

The Dean returned to his place and two children carrying lilies were prodded towards the lectern. At the offertory the gifts included Claire's briefcase and a Trócaire collection box with the face of an African child on its side. Dr Fr David held up the Trócaire box which made a chunking, almost-full sound, and told the congregation that somewhere in Africa hundreds, maybe thousands of children were alive today because Claire Thompson had not passed by on the other side.

At the Sign of Peace the priest moved along the front row, pausing for a special two-handed clasp with Claire's mother, seated beside the sister Angela.

Communion time and Hazel joined the queue waiting to receive the Body of Christ. Her partner Terry stayed in his seat, eyelids droopy, glancing resentfully at the congregation. Diarmuid watched from between his fingers. Of *course* he'd talk to Hazel, maybe even Terry, but not yet, not today, not while everything was so *raw*... He bent forward and pretended to tie his shoe. Terry might not even have found the disk: it might still be sitting undiscovered in Claire's computer. The uniformed pig-cop with the Moneymore accent, what was he called, Dalton, no Dover, no Dixon, that was it, Constable Dixon, dick's son if ever there was one, Constable Sonovadic – he would have mentioned it if he'd known, wouldn't he? And he hadn't...

'And did discussion between yourself and the deceased lady centre around a particular topic at all, sir?' Voice like a bumble-bee circling a flower.

'Discussion with the deceased lady centred around her granting me six months' study leave.'

'I see. Study leave. Right. I see.' Sonovadic adjusted his cap on his knee, then wrote slowly in his notebook.

After Mass it was like coming out of a cinema in the afternoon. People blinking at the daylight, the sound of traffic from the road mixing with the voices of the choir as the priest and coffin led the way to a convenient cemetery just twenty yards from the church side door. Not having to walk half a mile probably meant more to most of these people than Claire's death. At the cemetery edge, a big beech tree with crows' nests in its upper branches. People pushing against each other to see the priest sprinkling and praying. Claire's mother, tired and unsteady now, supported on one side by Angela, on the other by one of the fair-haired cousins.

Diarmuid watched the brown wood being lowered and the green pretend-grass carpet covered in flowers draped across the hole. It was terrible but it was bearable, because this was Claire's and not Mammy's coffin that was vanishing from the world forever. You could sense the relief when the prayers ended, people turning to each other, smiles and exclamations breaking through. Thanks be to God, we're still alive. She's down there but we're up here. The family moved a few yards back from the grave, as people formed a queue to offer sympathies. Diarmuid joined it. What to say? what to say? She was more than a colleague... Claire was a person of... yes, right. Positive, P for Positive, smiling, S for Smiling, vitality, V for Vitality. PSV.

'Mrs Thompson.' He held her hand between his own. 'I'm Diarmuid Monaghan, a colleague of Claire's, Dr Diarmuid Monaghan, and I want to tell you your daughter Claire was a person. A person who was p—' Something seemed to have lodged in his throat. A plum, maybe, or a tennis ball. 'She was...' It was as if the connection between brain and tongue had been severed. Claire's mother stared at him, one hand clenching the handkerchief, veins like tiny red lightnings in her eyes. If he stood there looking at them and trying to speak for another two seconds, he was going to start bawling, howling like a child. What about? For God's sake, this was... He bent his head over Mrs Thompson's hand, clenched his teeth. 'Hard times, Mrs Thompson,' he whispered.

Then another hand took his. Smoother than Mrs Thompson's, warmer. He looked up into the face of the woman who had given the speech, her head to one side, studying him. Blue eyes, mouth above the silver scarf plumper than Claire's. His own mouth pressing down on it, her stomach warm and alive against his, her leg hooked over his back – oh, Jesus shut up, you disgusting *brute*.

'I'm Angela, Dr Monaghan – Claire's sister. Thank you so much for coming.' She tucked the scarf tighter round her neck. 'There's a cup of tea for everyone in the Tuttyglass Hotel after – we'd love if you could come.'

Diarmuid nodded and, detaching his hand, hurried past the remaining three relatives, head down. Dug into the breast pocket of his suit for a half-cigarette and, miracle, three matches. Out of the graveyard, down the path back towards the chapel. He paused and blinked through the smoke. A crow came parachuting into the branches leaning over the cemetery wall. Above ground, nest-building, starting again; underground, Claire, held in the darkness, finished, last page of her story.

Diarmuid stood in a corner created by a buttress. How amazing, the way birds and lambs and dogs went on nest-building and barking and peeing, not moved in the slightest by humans and their crises. Maybe he'd use that for the 'God Lives!' column this week. When all others forsake us, we have God, the Rock of Ages, cleft for us, to rely on; with his rod and staff to support us, we fear no evil... Except we do, we fear it like nobody's business.

Beyond the graveyard wall, two black Mercedes with tinted windows sat parked on the street. Should he hang around, confront the grieving family a second time before they climbed on board? Approach them with shoulders back, dignified blub-free expression: 'Dr Diarmuid Monaghan. Meant to say to you earlier when we spoke – that I'm so sorry.' Odd, really, the way some people face death with resolution. Leaving others like himself to choke and slobber if it came within an ass's roar.

He'd almost finished his half-cigarette when the graveyard gate opened and two figures started to move down the path. In front, head bent, bobbing towards him like a wind-up toy, Terry.

And a couple of steps behind him, moving neatly by comparison, Hazel. Was she going to approach him about her damned dissertation? He'd sent an email only yesterday telling her it'd be a few more days before he could get back to her on the methodology chapter. Too late to make a run for it now, and anyway the way his foot had begun to throb, running or even trotting was out of the question.

Terry's Dick Nixon chin had two pimples in its cleft. Behind him Hazel, her little face occasionally coming round her partner's shoulder, nose bent slightly to the right, smiled foolishly.

'Terry – and Hazel – good to see you. Toothache cleared up, Terry? Good man, that's good news. Hazel, I keep meaning to contact you – that chapter, I'll have it back to you ASAP – bogged down at the moment, as you can imagine.' Diarmuid paused, nodded solemnly. 'Such a tragedy, really.'

Terry drew a line in the gravel with his heel. 'A sad end that shouldn't have happened. That's the tragedy of it. Should never, not ever, have happened.' The soft Birmingham whine, like tinfoil on the teeth, irritating beyond belief.

'Well, none of us knows what's round the corner.'

'Cause and effect, things done and things happening. That's the way I see it.' Terry's hands, deep in his overcoat pockets, banged against his thighs. 'Somebody must have known about that lift!' He took out a dark red hanky and blew his nose, closing his eyes to get better power. 'And now the Dean decides we're to have faculty meetings next week, as if nothing had happened... I don't know. There should be more respect than that.'

'There's a divinity that shapes our ends.' The phrase jumped out of Diarmuid's mouth and hung awkwardly between them. 'I mean, perspective – that's the one thing we don't have. And sometimes it takes time for the pattern to emerge, Terry, so that events can merge into a mature perspective.'

Terry's whine grew thinner, higher. 'I don't have that kind of time and, I'm telling you, divinities have nothing to do with

11

what happened. It was because somebody did something they shouldn't have done, or didn't do something they should have done, in connection with that lift. That's what cost our poor sweet DH her life. Not your divinity.'

'She was a dote,' Hazel said, coming round Terry's right side. 'She told me my dissertation could make a real educational difference. Not many people go to the bother of being as supportive as that.'

Terry's gaze twitched from gravel to tree to church roof. 'Somebody's bound to have spotted something. There are, I don't know, *dozens* of people, staff and students, going up and down in that lift every day. Somebody was *bound* to have spotted *something*.'

Diarmuid looked away. Something. Like a shuddering when it began to rise. Like a bleeping sound halfway up, and then a sort of swoosh that brought it to the top and left Diarmuid panting as he got out. But his panting then hadn't been as hard as it was now, as he raised his head and saw the pimples on Terry's chin and the way Terry's shoulders sloped rapidly away from his neck, like a giraffe's. Waiting for Diarmuid to say something incriminating.

'Except...' Diarmuid paused, tried to get the phrasing right. '...except maybe people didn't notice any signs that it would. You know. Give trouble.'

'If that was me, I'd have fainted straight off,' Hazel said. 'In Austria two years ago at a conference, I actually did pass out – got sick in a lift and then fainted. It was awful.' She smiled tearfully.

'What puzzles me,' said Diarmuid, 'is not the lift so much, it's that she should have, ah, suffered fatally.' Keep going. 'Because I mean, she seemed... Did she ever complain that—'

'No.' Terry's whisper rose to a hoarse rasp. 'Complaining, about her health or anything else, wasn't DH's style. I mean, if I'd thought for one instant that she was under the weather in any way that evening I'd have done something. *Something*.'

'Don't blame yourself, Terry.'

12

Terry looked up, glared. 'I'm not blaming myself – believe me. My consolation is that she's at peace.' Then, without a pause: 'So what did you and DH talk about that last evening?'

Diarmuid felt his heart lurch. He should have run when he'd had the chance. The sneaky little bastard, daring to ask a question like that. 'Afraid I can't tell you that, Terry. Confidential discussion, I'm afraid.'

'Well, the police asked *me* what I talked about.' Pause. 'So I naturally assumed they asked you the same thing.'

You bet your life they asked. For over an hour. The uniformed ape from Moneymore, sitting back-straight on the sofa, taking notes. Had he taken the lift, why had he taken the stairs, did he usually take the stairs, two at a time, is that a fact, and no one had seen him, that was a pity, everybody else using the lift, of course, and that was why his not taking it and going by the stairs was— No, no, not unacceptable. Just a bit of a... surprise.

'Well, there you are, Terry,' Diarmuid said. 'Police asked me to keep matters confidential. I expect they have their reasons.'

'The other thing they asked me about was computer files.' Terry's eyes flicked up to Diarmuid's, then away. 'They wanted to know if any of the files in DH's room were mine. So I said, "Well, I don't know exactly who owns everything in there, but none of those things, files and that, are mine. I have all my stuff in my own office next door."' Terry pulled his shoulders up as if to touch his ears with them. 'That's what I told them.'

A pain travelled up Diarmuid's leg to his groin, then shot through his chest and into his head. *The little scoot of shite. He'd been stringing him along, so he could get him lulled into a false sense of safety and then hit him with the computer thing when he wasn't expecting it. 'Computer files,' he'd said. The shifty giraffe-shouldered little wanker.*

'So in the end the police told me to just keep an eye on DH's office. They'll be doing a proper inventory next month, they said. So I told them that seemed a long time to wait, and it is, it is. But they said it was standard. With their stretched resources, they said, it's the best they can do.'

As they left, Diarmuid assured Hazel that he'd definitely be addressing her work inside twenty-four hours. He watched them, Terry's bobbing back, Hazel's fat little behind, pass through the gate that led to the street. And now the funeral congregation had begun to move down the path in threes and fours, the women linking each other. Claire's mother and sister were visible among them.

A month's reprieve. Was Terry telling the truth? He could have made the whole bloody thing up. Or maybe the cops had decided to let Diarmuid sweat, see if he cracked. In which case he should contact them now and come clean, shouldn't he? Look, I actually did go up in the lift but when I was leaving I walked down, well, I panicked when I was asked, I suppose, don't know why I felt, you know, guilty. Thing is, I heard this noise – in the lift, going up – only then in the excitement of the discussion with her, with Claire, my department head, yes, of course, I forgot to tell her. Just as I forgot to mention it to you when you interviewed me first. That's all. Of *course* I forgot – I told you – I was *frightened* and *confused*. And I feel terrible about it. No, it never crossed my *mind* that Terry Prundy would be leaving later, might get into the lift and find himself stuck halfway down. Of *course* I didn't want something like that to happen to him, much less Claire. Or anybody at all. For God's sake... The disk? The Little Known Facts file? Simply notes for a novel I'm thinking of writing. That's all. Little Known Plot Facts, you see. Creative jottings. Imagination. *Fantasy*.

Diarmuid checked inside himself. He really shouldn't be thinking so much about himself and not feeling anything much at all for poor Claire. Despite all his worries, he was lucky compared to her. At the same time being alive had its disadvantages because it meant he had to cope with and worry about *the fucking file and the damned, damned, fuckingdamned stuff in it. Oh, GodGodGod*. Somehow or other he had to get that file back.

And yet, four days ago, there hadn't been a hint of any of this.

14

Chapter 2

UP AND DOWN

Halfway up in the lift, there was a bleeping noise and the machinery shuddered, seemed to pause in the shaft for a second, then the hum resumed and the glass box moved on to the eighth floor. When the door opened, and again when it closed behind him, it repeated the bleeping sound. Panting, Diarmuid stood looking down the corridor. There'd been a story of the lift and all its buttons jamming when the Chief Administrative Officer was in it, and when they finally got the door open two hours later her hair was like Phyllis Diller's rather than Michael Douglas's, and she was half in and half out of her huge bra, some said because it had got so hot, others that she planned to use it to climb through the glass ceiling to the next floor. But that had been over three years ago and was probably malicious lies. At the same time, he must remember to mention the problem to the Physical Resources people.

He moved swiftly down the corridor, trying not to think about the way the dark-green carpet was spattered with yellow and the strip lighting made everything look like a hotel where rooms were rented by the hour. He checked his watch: quarter past four on a Friday. The only time someone like him could be fitted in.

The door to the Learning Outcomes office stood slightly open. The screen-saver with the fish riding a bicycle was on, the chrome fan on the window-sill was revolving – or was that oscillating? – a Cellophane-wrapped box labelled 'Omega Zip Drive' sat beside the mouse mat, but no one was on duty. Then, as Diarmuid leant across the desk a rump rose from behind it, pushing against the inside of a pair of light brown trousers. The rump's owner followed, a floppy disk between finger and thumb.

'Ah, Terry. Herself in?'

Terry slid the disk into the computer and started typing. He hated when anyone referred to his boss as anything other than 'Department Head', and especially when they said 'Herself'. Little slopy shoulders resentful, little dirty-brown eyes locked onto the screen. 'We've set up a booking system for interviews – haven't you heard? Department Head and I find it works much better all round.'

'Yes, but Herself and myself only arranged this meeting yesterday, in the corridor. There wasn't time.'

A muscle twitched in Terry's cheek as he took the desk diary with the brass corners from a drawer. 'Out of my hands, I'm afraid. Let's see… Wednesday next, would that suit?'

Diarmuid felt his right foot begin to throb and his voice rose. 'No it wouldn't suit. Because I don't want Wednesday next, Terry. I have arranged *Now*.'

As he spoke the door to the inner office opened and Claire emerged carrying a bundle of papers. Her blonde hair was skewered in place at the back of her head by what looked like a strip of leather and a knitting needle, and she was wearing a blue shirt open to the…first, second, third, fourth button – omiGod – and, and, and a pair of cream trousers that were tight at the hip and loose at the ankle.

'Oh no, I don't believe it, it's Diarmuid!' Her mismatched eyes shining, a dab of high colour on both cheekbones. 'What with this meeting with the Dean to get ready for and all kinds of other stuff as well, I completely…' It was a sign of insanity, Frances claimed, having one duck-egg blue eye and one chestnut brown. Except if you were a dog.

'If it's difficult, Claire, I can come back...'

She closed the door and stood with her back to it. Diarmuid would have to barge through her heart-stopping breasts to get out. Her mouth puckered up at him. 'Nooo, Diarmuid, no Diarmuid. In we go.'

Terry, sidling up. 'Department Head – would you like double space or single on this document? Or subheadings only?'

'Double, Terry. But not now – please? It'll keep till Monday. Shoo.' She waved Diarmuid into the inner office ahead of her, closed the door. Was that a roll of the eyes? 'Terry's a – have a seat, you must be – Terry really is, you know. There's no other word for him. A dote.' She bustled in behind her desk and leant back in the black leather chair. 'Anyway, I know how busy you are, so thanks for cordoning off these few minutes. Everything under control?'

Control? Let's see. I've been at my salary ceiling for eight years, you gave me an extra ten hours a week on my timetable this year. I write a 'God Lives!' column every month, two thousand words for twenty-five pounds even though I've stopped believing half of what I write. I've applied twice for study leave in Boston to finish my pamphlet on Gaelic games in Protestant schools – and, yes, yes, which would also have given me a chance, an outside chance but a *chance,* to become a Reader and so have less bloody teaching and more time to, well, not teach. Except my line manager – that's you – keeps blocking my chances. Aaaand... Let's see. I hate my brother and miss my mother, my wife has started not sleeping with me, in forty years I'll be either dead or eighty-five. And you ask if my life is *under control?*

'Oh, yes, fine. Things are grand.'

'Good, good. By the way – I fully intended to email you – I read that column you wrote about the child amputee and the mother washing the socks. Marvellous, really. *So...* authentic. Right. What I'd like now though is a word about this radio discussion, which is coming up...coming up on the... remind me.'

'Friday the seventh of September and Friday the fourteenth of September.' Claire nodded at him, each eye beaming its own encouragement. Go on, go on. 'They are both two-man panel discussions lasting fifteen minutes each. The first will be about universities and global links, the second about effective school experience for student teachers. In the first I'm going to stress our international dimension – the link with Boston College, that sort of thing. In the second I'll be explaining the philosophy that underpins our *150 Essential Skills for Student Teachers*.' He reached into his jacket pocket. 'I've got the whole thing outlined here on a floppy disk... Only I was wondering because, you see, I'm a bit concerned about Boston. You see—'

'No need for concern, I promise you Diarmuid. You've talked to me about the outline before, and I just know—'

'It's not the outline. I'm talking about my application for a study-leave semester in Boston. That's what I'm concerned about – my application. Because this will be my third time applying for study leave to Boston, you know. And it's a bit discouraging.'

Silence. Claire picked up a paper knife and began to dab gently at the heel of her left hand. 'Do you know how often I've been to the Far East in the past year?'

'No.'

'Three times, Diarmuid. Car horns and hotel rooms the size of a shoebox and rib steaks the size of a tennis racquet. *And* they work twenty-five hours a day.' She reached inside her blouse and tugged at a strap. 'Travelling abroad, let me tell you, is *no joke*. In Asia or the States or anywhere else. But let's the two of us rehearse this radio discussion first, shall we?'

Diarmuid looked away and tried not to think about the word 'rehearse' or look at the painting of Icarus that hung in the corner of his department head's office. (Don't try to fly too high with me, buster.) He took out a floppy disk labelled 'Broadcast'. 'I'll start by underscoring the international thing. Then remind them of our cross-border links, how we were the first institution to have an external examiner from the south.'

'Mm. When was that?'

'Nineteen eighty-nine – Frank Murphy. Corduroy trousers, beard, from Limerick. Remember?'

'Of course! My God. He was – I nearly said a *complete* disaster, only nothing, really, was complete about Frank.' She laughed and crossed the room to her computer, a faint trail of perfume drifting behind her. 'Let's perhaps steer a discreet path around Frank, shall we?'

There was silence. Diarmuid was the one who had identified Frank, argued with his colleagues for his selection as examiner, canvassed votes for him, said he had country ways but a sharp mind. 'That's fine. No problem. Skip Frank. That's very helpful.'

Diarmuid joined her at the computer and pushed the disk into its little sideways fanny, brought the cursor awkwardly up to My Computer and clicked. Her perfume was musk. Clicked on 3 1/2 Floppy. 'Broadcast', there it was. Or maybe violets. Click once more and here's the document, headed 'Broadcast Outline' and scroll down and you have. Oh, God. Scroll to fuck to the top again, *QUICK*.

The phone on Claire's desk rang, the noise slashing like razor-wire along his nervous system. Claire reached behind her and picked up the receiver. 'Hello?...Well, I... No, I'm sorry, I really... Listen. Just a second. Just a second.' She cupped the phone with her hand. 'Could you just give me a minute, Diarmuid? My sister...'

'No problem. I'll be next door.'

In the outer office he sat in Terry's seat, put his elbows on the desk and his burning face in his hands. Little Known Facts. It was on a disk safely locked in the little metal box, wasn't it? At home. It wasn't here. It couldn't be here. Not in Claire's computer. Not with Claire looking over his shoulder at it. *Not in there with Claire maybe reading it this very fucking minute as she talks on the phone.* Burst in and hit her on the head? Set fire to the office? When he squeezed his eyes shut, he saw blobs of red drifting through deep-green darkness.

He'd started composing it nine months ago, last January, after a particularly protracted Friday afternoon meeting. When at last it had crawled, fluttered, squirmed and slithered to a weary end, he'd gone straight to his room, locked the door, started typing. Slow at first, then faster and faster. Constructing a report on the meeting that changed all the contributions, the ideas and resolutions-passed into something wilder and more libellous. Ending with a grovelling apology from Claire as chair for having kept them so late. When she was seventeen, she informed the meeting, her old schoolmaster had stopped her one hot June afternoon and asked her what she intended to study at university, and she'd told him Russian, and then he'd told her he always knew she had a first-class brain, she'd go very far, there was no doubt about it, and a first-class body, come to that, and then he'd asked her if she'd like to come for a drive with him to a remote area near Lough Neagh because he was in for the Photograph of the Year competition with the local paper and he had a definite notion that if he got a picture of her with no clothes on against a background of rhododendron shrubbery, he'd be in with a shout, and was she game? So she'd thought for a minute about how much she owed this man, how he'd laid her educational foundations in her early years and without him she'd have got nowhere, and they'd gone to the spot by the lough where she'd folded her clothes neatly at the foot of an oak tree and he'd taken twenty shots of her in ballet poses, then said she was the best girl he had ever taught or taken a picture of for that matter. But by the time she got home she was a full hour late for her tea, and that had been the start of her habit of letting things go on too long and she'd never been able to break it.

Somehow just writing it down had smoothed in part the irritation and fatigue that had built up during the meeting. Soon Little Known Facts became a habit – a release, a shout of defiance after meetings, but also a store of amusing, satirical and sexually explicit reports on colleagues, featuring cupboards, donkeys, French maids, a trapeze and, in the case of the Dean, a boa constrictor.

And then, two Sundays ago, the thought had struck: *what if*

Little Known Facts gets a virus? All that artistic effort, crafted with such energy, style and *joie de vivre*, slithering into oblivion?

Breathing fast, he had created a copy of LKF, put it on a disk, hidden the disk at the back of the bottom drawer of his desk at home. And then, just to be doubly sure, he'd made a *second* copy. So now there were three – grandfather, father, son, wasn't that what they called them? Ironic, given that he and Frances hadn't achieved anything along that line... And then last week he'd made the mistake. In a hurry to get to class, he'd saved the final three entries of the grandson copy on the Broadcast disk. A temporary arrangement, soon to be rectified. And what was in those final three entries? Oh, nothing much. Just one on the Chief Administrative Officer and one on Hazel, the dissertation student, and another in the Claire-and-the-old-schoolmaster series. *'As I lay on the P5 floor with a hurley stick between my knees, he climbed on a desk and looked at me through the camera. "I'll just try an F11 for this," he said, and his face above me seemed funny and twisted.'*

Mother of God – supposing the Sunday tabloids got hold of this? 'God Lives! Man Prince of Porn'; 'Don't say lecturer, say lecher.' He forced himself to take slow, deep breaths, count the number of pens and pencils in the purple mug Terry kept beside his computer. Eleven. Fragments of conversation drifted through the closed office door.

'Well that wasn't my intention... Yes, I *know* she's sensitive... Oh, for God's sake, grow *up*, Angela!'

Diarmuid swivelled round in his chair, tilted back, glanced at the compressed-peat crucifix hanging above the door leading to Claire's office. There'd been claims that Terry had emailed the Dean to have it removed – shouldn't be allowed under the Flags and Emblems Act, he said, because although it was above *her* door it was, strictly speaking, in *his* office, and people might think it was *his*. The Dean had emailed back, he quite understood, embarrassing indeed and not the sort of thing anyone would want to happen *but*—

'I'm sorry.' She stood at the door, gesturing him back in. 'That

21

was my sister – doesn't believe in letting the sun go down on her anger... Anyway. International links. Right. Let me show you something.'

She lifted a bulging folder from the filing cabinet.

'Know what that is? *One tenth* of our international contacts. I've established a number of them myself, but you can see that they do need careful screening, otherwise we'd simply drown in all the... Right. This is your Broadcast Outline here, is it?' She bent towards the screen.

Diarmuid nodded, hoped she couldn't hear his heart. *Talk*. 'The radio discussion series has a different theme each week.' He pointed to the screen, willed his finger not to shake. 'Our week – my week – the topic is education and inclusive outreach, widened access in the north of Ireland. Myself and one other guest.'

'Why do you call it that?'

'Call it what?'

'The north of Ireland. The name of the place is Northern Ireland. Or Ulster.'

'Well, I— '

'Anyway.' Her pink fingernail tapped the screen. 'Professor Tiedt – I know him. Dublin, isn't he?'

'Not sure. That's why I'd like to be fully briefed.'

He looked up. Tough sister, under all the eyelashes fluttering and oh-you're-so-good-to-spare-the-time. On the wall to her left Icarus plunging into the sea, with a ploughman at work ignoring him. Wasn't there a poem about that? How nobody would give a damn if you were to bleed to death on the pavement or fall from the heavens with melted wings or mislay some intimate and semi-erotic pen portraits and, God God *God*, let me get *out* of here...

'Did I mention?' Claire checked each earring in turn. 'On the study-leave front. Harold rang this morning.' Diarmuid stared. The Dean. The Dean had phoned her. About study leave. And she was only mentioning it *now*. She was playing him like a... 'Not official so don't jump to conclusions. But we believe there's a chance that by January there may be an extra study-leave berth.'

'Bub. When?'

'January to July.'

'Bub. D'you mean study leave in Boston?' After so long a drought, the gushing of hope.

'Well, it could be Boston or... The Dean will probably confirm it one way or another, when he meets with us next week. Meanwhile let's crack on with what we have in hand, shall we?' She picked up her pen and tapped his shoulder with it. 'You know our department can do itself a lot of good with this broadcast, raise our profile, or, *or*—'

'I know. Do damage. It's OK – I did that TV interview the time the out-centre in Tandaragee was opened, remember.'

'Well, yes. Except that was over eight years ago. And it's closed now.'

Bitch. 'As long as I'm fully briefed, it'll be no problem.'

'We need to be one hundred per cent sure nothing goes wrong.'

'Of course.'

'And what we say, and who says it, must carry maximum wallop.' *Who says it?* '*The Sunday Times* had a feature article last week – maybe you saw it – about appearing on TV. The single most important quality – guess what? Being *natural*. People with a lot of experience of TV – 'chat-show tarts', the article called them, ha-ha – guess what? They're hopeless. Every drop of naturalness drained out of them because they've had experience.' *What was she getting at?* 'And the odd thing is. At least according to the article. Or maybe not so odd when you think about it. But the people who have *never* been on TV – media virgins, the article called them, I mean they really have a nerve... Anyway, these people bring this, well, *freshness* with them.' There was silence. 'Take me, say. Would I fit?'

Diarmuid felt a depth charge begin in the area of his navel and go shooting up his body, not in a straight line but weaving from side to side, crashing off the inside of his rib-cage, scraping against the inside of his throat, until it burst into his head. *Take me?*

'How do you mean? I'm not...'

She smiled, teeth white and regular, as if his six words had been so witty she couldn't possibly explain how much she admired him for speaking them.

'Well, we're agreed this could indeed be a defining moment in our department's history.'

'Absolutely.' When had he started using that fucking word?

'So. For all our sakes, it's *imperative* we make a strong showing.'

We again. We must make a strong showing. The depth charge turned round in his head and began its journey down his throat, headed for his scrotum.

'Do you mean – were you thinking that...maybe you should come on the...radio programme as well?' Oh, shite. Now that he'd said it, it became more fixed. Erect a roadblock – *quick*. 'Because, in my experience, producers are strict about numbers. Real life, yes, you could have a hundred people in a discussion in real life. Well, maybe not a hundred, but you know what I mean... But more than one person speaking for the same institution on a radio discussion – that just wouldn't. You know. Work.'

She looked thoughtfully at her left arm and pushed a silver bracelet further up it. A delicate silver bracelet with a little chain dropping from its catch point. 'I wasn't thinking of having two of us on the programme.'

He knew what she meant. But she still must say it. 'How do you mean?'

' I thought it might actually be better if I, as head of Learning Outcomes, were to do it myself. At the end of the day. What do you think?'

He felt his fingers tighten on the cap of his pen. Squeezing, pushing, as if it were her windpipe he had between his fingers, or the windpipe of all the people who'd ever buggered up good things, good opportunities that had happened in his life. Ping!

the pen-cap said, cartwheeled over the computer and struck the wall, then vanished behind the desk.

'My goodness!' A flashbulb smile and she was squatting, bent forward and underneath the desk. 'Flying pen-tops – ah! Think I have it...' Diarmuid turned sideways as she straightened, to show that he hadn't been gawking at her bum and the edge of pink knickers that showed above her slacks waist when she bent down. Which he had been. She passed him the pen-cap and he screwed it on tight. There was a knock at the office door and Terry's head appeared. 'Department Head, I—'

'*Terry.* What are you doing here still? No matter what it is, no. Go home. Go home *immediately.*'

'I forgot my keys.' Terry held them up as if to prove the truth of what he said. Peep-tom bastard.

'Well, for goodness' sake, *shoosh* this instant.' The door clicked behind him and Diarmuid remembered the lift. Should he call Terry back, mention the way it had squeaked? Too late now – he was gone.

Claire stood staring at the door that had closed behind him. 'Poor Terry. I sometimes think he's...' Her voice trailed away. 'Anyway. Where were we?'

She's going to take my place. 'The radio discussions.'

'What I mean is, I think I should pick up on this one. As DH. For all our sakes.' Her face hot and her little triangle nose shiny. 'The one thing that's vital in these things is continuity, isn't it? And if the extra study-leave place did emerge and you found yourself in Boston, then continuity would be out of the question, wouldn't it?'

The bad news: with one hand she was slamming the radio door on him and nailing it shut. The good news: with the other she was offering him Boston. A pure and simple, totally easy-to-spot trade-off. No broadcast: Boston. Broadcast: no Boston. Well, great. Except if he was in Boston from January until June, how would he be in Belfast for the annual round of Reader interviews in April? And yet if he turned up his nose at what was on offer, he'd *never* get a job as Reader. Marked to attend ball-

cracking meetings and give lectures on the Senior Teacher as
Communication Nexus, and Management Teams in League
Tables forever... He leant back in his chair, gripped its arms,
tried to smile, did a little rock of frustration. It Just. Isn't. Fair.
Backwards and forwards, *backwards* and forwards. It *just.*
Wasn't—'

Crush.

Even before the biting pain started, he realised what had
happened. His left foot had been curled under the chair, in foetal
position, the chair castors had rolled back, and one had steam-
rollered his toenail with all his weight on top of it *and, Jesus, he
was in agony.* He pitched forward in the chair, face against his
knees, moaning.

'Is the pain in your... Loosen your tie. Here, let me.' He could
smell her perfume, definitely musk, glimpsed the pink of her
scalp where her hair parted and framed her face. He tried to
imagine his finger touching the pink line on her skull, his hand
cupping her hot face... anything to distract from the jack-
hammer pain that was stabbing into his toe again and again.

'Castor – rolled over my, oh, Jesus...'

'Poor *you.* I thought it was your – OK, let's get that shoe off
quick, sock too – your heart, maybe.'

She untied the shoe, lifted it forward carefully clear of his toes
without bumping. As her fingers supported the sole of his foot
he closed his eyes. It was like when you fell and your mammy
picked you up, mmha, mmha, kiss the sore place better, good
little boy.

Blinking back tears, he opened his eyes. The toenail was
white, and so was the rest of the toe – as if the pressure of the
chair had forced every drop of blood out of it. He could feel it
throbbing violently and yet there was no sign of bruising or cut
skin or damaged nail. Internal injuries. He closed his eyes again
and watched behind the lids as green and red blobs swam into
each other.

'Can you move it?' she asked. The toe refused. Refused again.
Then it gave a micro-twitch, a fraction of a millimetre. 'That's

good. That means it's probably not broken.' She took out a little hanky, corner embroidered 'C', and bound it round his toe. The one in his pocket was crisp with snot. 'OK – let's slip the sock and shoe back on. That's it. I don't think it's broken but you can never be sure. Unfortunately I have to give this talk in Banbridge tonight, or I could have driven you home. Will you be all right?'

He wanted to thank her – for Boston, for the hanky, for having two contrasting eyes with such beautiful whites round them, for having an arse that being close to, touching, would erase all pain, all other sensation, maybe life itself. But the throbbing in his toe clamped his teeth together.

Anyway, her driving him home was out of the question. Frances glaring at her as she oxtered him up the driveway. Frances saying little until Claire was gone, then starting one of her repeater phrases – damaged prospects when damaged toe, damaged prospects when damaged toe, when do I get a chance to do something, when do I get a chance to do something – until he wanted to take the poker and beat her parrot skull into watermelon mush. No, somehow or other he'd get home by himself.

'I'm sorry.' His voice was a hoarse whisper.

'Don't talk nonsense. Now see to it you get that X-rayed first thing tomorrow – promise me?'

He tried not to groan as he limped down the corridor. What was it they called the condemned man's walk? The green mile. For a moment he was tempted to take the lift, then thought, No, bad enough having a crunched toe without being stuck in a lift as well. On the stairs he paused to lean against the wall and catch his breath. It wasn't until he reached the bottom that he remembered he'd meant to tell Claire about the lift making funny sounds. And it wasn't until the next day, when Dr Fr David rang to tell him some bad news, yes, afraid so, very bad in point of fact, brace self, Claire in stalled lift, stuck between floors, probably there three hours anyway, no one around Friday evening, stroke, we think, unspeakable indeed, we're all devastated, tragic indeed, yes, dead, afraid so, a history of high blood pressure, no, no one seems to have known but doctors say, yes, that's how it was, may God be good to her and give her repose, that he remembered he'd left the disk with the LKF file sitting in her machine. *Oh, sweet, holy, suffering Jesus.*

Chapter 3

CLOSURE AND COMMENCEMENT

'I wasn't at her funeral, so what would I be doing at this do? I don't even know half of them,' Frances said from behind the *Radio Times*. 'And don't say for me to network with them, you're the one's supposed to be networking, not me. I'm not the one looking for a change of job, it's you. Put it to UK Gold, would you?'

Diarmuid clicked the red button. The new wide-screen TV gulped and went blank. He punched the green at the top of the remote. The screen crackled and lit up again.

'Twice – that's how often I met her, and both times she was busy rolling those two weird eyes of hers at any man that would look near her. And you should be at home with that toe.'

'She was OK. As a department head she was OK.'

Frances pulled her blue cardigan over her fat breasts. 'You're some innocent gom. If she'd given you promotion I wouldn't mind, but she was playing you like a *céilí* fiddle – getting you to do this, that and God knows what. That's not UK Gold, by the way.'

'A Closure and Commencement Evening' had been the heading on the Dean's email message. He hoped all Lifestyle and Learning staff would be able to come to the meeting, which he had originally arranged for two o'clock in the Brian Faulkner

Room; but now planned to conduct at seven, at his, the Dean's, house at 19 Oak Drive. He felt confident that attendance would reflect the esteem in which the late head of Learning Outcomes had been held, as well as commitment to the coming year's work.

'You're the one who's always going on about money and career advancement,' Diarmuid said. 'You're not going to have that if I don't get to Boston.'

Frances's eyes came over the top of the *Radio Times*. '*I* won't get career advancement? I beg your pardon. It's your career, not mine. I'll still be stuck here trying to grow something in the garden so I can get the basis of a business going, that's all I'll be doing. And, anyway, the last time I was the only spouse in the room, apart from the Dean's spouse on one side of me and some psychologist woman's spouse with a beard on the other – and all he did was burp and fart and all she did was talk. And when I mentioned that I was hoping to set up in commercial organic gardening, they both couldn't wait to get away. There, that's good, keep it *there*.' On the screen Frank from *Some Mothers Do 'Ave 'Em* was falling through a ceiling and landing on the bed of a woman wearing a hairnet.

'There's the matter of showing respect for the dead,' Diarmuid said. 'And the matter of the Dean wanting to talk to you about my study leave. That's all. If you're not there it'll look funny.'

'The Dean wants to talk to *me* about *your* study leave?'

'It's no big deal. I mean, do you want me to get to Boston or not? And stop repeating what I say, would you?'

'What kind of a question is, do I want you to get to Boston? If your death's head Dean asked me why you aren't applying for the job of head of Learning Outcomes, I could talk to him about that, could talk for *hours* about that. Isn't your man a scream? He's worth five million, you know.' Frank was now standing on a roof trying to fix an aerial.

It was almost nine o'clock the next evening when Diarmuid lifted his finger from the Dean's front-door bell.

'Midnight at the latest,' Frances whispered. 'I need to be up early for Joy and Mairead to help them with the cauliflower implants. And I hope you realise I could have been at home watching *Who Wants to be a Millionaire?* instead of this. Twelve o'clock.'

The Dean's wife opened the door. She was wearing a thin dress that showed the outline of her underwear. 'Welcome,' she said, reaching behind her to tug forward a sulky-looking girl of about sixteen with badly plucked eyebrows and a left hand that curled against her middle, as if she were carrying something. 'This is Rosalind and she will look after you. *And* you'll have a chance to try her *amazing* desserts later on.'

The girl led them with overlong strides to the kitchen. A swing band was playing from a hi-fi near the sink. Rosalind, avoiding eye contact, took their coats over her right arm and nodded towards the table. 'Have a drink. The rest are inside.' She slouched from the room.

From the hi-fi Frank Sinatra sang that someone did something to him. Diarmuid poured whiskey into two glasses and was adding some ice when the squat figure of Billy Warwick from Cont Psych appeared in the kitchen doorway. His untrimmed ginger beard clashed with the red sweater he was wearing. Under it you could see the swell of his little round belly. 'By heaven, if it's not the Monaghan Two. Welcome to the house of tears.' He reached up and put his left hand on Frances's shoulder. 'You're looking more fetching than ever – no, ravishing, that's the word that throbs for release. Ravishing. You're beyond ravishing, in fact.' He glanced towards the hi-fi. 'Isn't that the most appalling brain-damaging cacophony?'

Frances stared at the squat figure and removed his hand. 'I don't think I've met you.'

'In which case, truncate my greeting to a simple "You're looking fetching-slash-ravishing." I'm Billy Warwick, Cont Psych.' He grasped her hand. 'You, of course, are Frances – the man in your life has been known to breathe your name.' He held on to her hand. 'What do you do, Frances?'

'I'm a housewife and I do organic gardening. What are you?'

'I'm an educational psychologist,' Warwick told her, 'and I swindle big companies.'

Frances giggled. 'Swindle?'

'Trick them, then. Into giving me lots of money to do Contemporary Psychological research that has no conceivable application. I don't tell them that, naturally. I tell them that my research is of pressing contemporary importance. Amazing how many of them take me at my word.' He peered at her more closely. 'You really have the most sensuous ears – has your husband drawn them to your attention?'

'No.'

'Not even in moments of intimate passion?'

'Not even then.'

'How odd. They make me want to ravish you.' He crossed to the kitchen and began opening cupboards. 'Word to the wise, incidentally – the Dean's wine is of the don't-work-this-horse quality. My consolation is that this allows me to win ten pounds from my friend Crompton, who foolishly put his faith in the Dean's good taste, which of course is the proverbial broken reed and tinkling cymbal. And right now I am on a mission to get a splash of Coke for my rum.' He opened another cupboard.

For a moment Diarmuid thought of saying something about the way Warwick had referred to Frances's ears and the stuff about ravishing, but the words wouldn't assemble properly. He nodded towards the living room. 'Sounds like a good turn-out this evening.'

'As we both know, when the Dean says come, they cometh. Lest their career perisheth. I've just been trapped into spending half an hour listening to the Chief Examinations Officer talk about a recruitment visit she made to Borneo last year. It was like having one's head punched for half an hour, gently but firmly, by Mike Tyson. Somewhere, I am sure, there is a less attractive female than our Chief Examinations Officer, but where, I wonder?' Warwick broke off and glared at a speaker on a shelf above him. 'If this caterwauling continues, I may be driven to violence.'

'I like Frank Sinatra,' Frances said. 'Francis Albert Sinatra. He sings as if he means the words.' She paused. 'Has anyone applied for the head of Learning Outcomes job yet?'

Warwick didn't seem to hear her question and turned to Diarmuid, his back to her. 'Three guesses regarding who's here.'

'I have no idea.'

'Terry. Sloping-shoulders Terry, in snooping mode. There is not one other secretary here. This is supposed to be an academic gathering, and yet Whispering-blue-chin-giraffe-form Terry is here. I was told he was stricken with toothache.'

Diarmuid shrugged. 'He attends all meetings of the department.'

'Yes, to take minutes – that's what secretaries are for. Not swanning around drinking and mixing with his betters. *And* he's brought that droopy Nuts woman with him.'

'Hazel.'

'How are we supposed to have a meeting when there's a student called Nuts listening to our every word?'

'She's a Master's student,' Diarmuid said. 'I'm her supervisor. And I might be asking you to act as internal examiner for her dissertation, by the way.'

'My God, you are a cruel man.' He sipped his drink. 'Do you think the unspeakable Terry is sleeping with her? Or merely employing her as arm candy, as our American cousins call it? You'd be surprised how men are that way – give them a woman somewhere near, somebody soft and cheerful to break up the scenery and look up to them, and that's all they want. Majority of men aren't half as horny as they pretend.' He swung round to face Frances. 'Would you share my analysis?'

'Pass.'

Warwick turned back to Diarmuid. 'Crompton says he met a chap at one of his sad golf-club dos last month, and it turns out he actually *taught* this Nuts girl. "Not Special Needs but near enough", was his judgement. And now she's our Master's student.' Warwick raised his glass and drank most of its contents. Wiped his ginger beard and burped. 'Is it true you were the last one to see her alive?'

'Claire, you mean? Well, yes.'

'So did she... Did she give any, um, indication that something was about to happen – a sign, maybe?'

'Well, since she didn't know in advance that the lift was going to stick, she'd hardly have done that.'

Warwick combed his beard with his fingers, first with his right hand, then the left. 'Yes, but people like her sometimes do get a... get a sense of foreboding about these things. Besides, she was a pray-er.'

'A prayer?' said Frances.

'No, not a prayer – a pray-er. One who prays. I'd come into her office and she'd be poring over this Jesuit website. Supposed to be running the department, but spending half her day communing with her Maker via the Jesuitical Internet. Odd.'

'I see nothing odd about it,' Frances said. 'And I don't think you should talk that way about somebody who's just died.'

Warwick draped one leg over the corner of the table, leant towards Frances. 'How long should I wait, would you say? A week? A year? And what will have changed in the interval? Although I will grant you, since she died, I've become aware of the possibility that... How can I put this? ... That she may be *monitoring* us. Listening in. After all, she had a humungous crucifix hung over her office door. Are you that way inclined? Towards religion?' he asked Frances.

'Not really.'

'You see? That's another thing we have in common. G.K. Chesterson got it right: if people believe in God, they'll believe in anything.'

'For a start,' Diarmuid said, 'it's Chesterton, not Chesterson. And for another, his aphorism actually was, when people stop believing in God, they don't start believing in nothing, they start believing in anything.'

'Exactly what I said. Anyway, the point is, she now *knows*. If there's an answer to the mystery of life, she now has it. Extraordinary when you consider that, wouldn't you say?'

Frances said something that sounded like 'Doodledaddle,' and walked towards the living room. Warwick watched her leave. 'Your wife cuts quite a...figure, really. Claire had one too – remember that arse of hers? I used to dream about Claire's arse. Lying in bed at night, I'd see it come at me out of the darkness, like a sort of pear-shaped meteor. One of the few things I admired about the woman, actually, her hindquarters. Very like your wife's. Not that I let my personal feelings interfere. Claire was a ghastly department head but her arse had nothing to do with that either way.'

'Glad to hear it,' Diarmuid said.

Frank Sinatra told someone to fly him to the moon.

'She was a compulsive go-getter, as I'm sure you know,' Warwick said, scratching his thigh. 'That was the problem, really. A gal who could not say no. She'd visit these places, in Japan or China or wherever, and they'd say something like: "Fifty of our teachers want to do an online diploma in Philosophical Athletics, and they'll pay for it. Does your university offer a diploma in that?" And she'd say "Oh, do you know, it does!" And then she'd come back and get people like myself writing night and day to construct a diploma that could be driven through Validation in three weeks, only it wouldn't work, and the Validation people would piss on it from a height, and the whole thing would fall through and all our work would have been for nothing and she'd have alienated another sizeable chunk of the population of Asia. And then when things got too hot for her, she'd lock her door and start praying to her computer.'

'Well, I know what you mean. But still, she was all right. She was going to support my application for a semester in Boston College – did you know that? If this...tragedy hadn't happened I'm sure it would have come off OK.'

Sinatra said that what he really wanted was someone to hold his hand.

'Perhaps. Or perhaps not. Perhaps you *thought* she was going to support it. Perhaps your academic judgement was dazzled by the glory of her arse... I think we've had quite enough of this wretched Eyetie, don't you?'

Warwick picked up what looked like a remote control from the counter and pointed it towards the hi-fi. Nothing happened. He peered at the buttons. 'Oh, I see, very clever. A cordless phone that looks like a remote control – what a jolly, jolly piece of designing fun.' He tossed it onto the counter, where it skidded along the granite surface and into the half-filled sink with a soft plop.

'Watch out – the water will ruin it. *Quick*!' Diarmuid called.

'All these gadgets are waterproof nowadays,' Warwick said, sauntering towards the sink. 'I'm sure I read that somewhere.' He rolled up his sleeve and retrieved the dripping phone.

Diarmuid patted it with a dishtowel and held it to his ear. 'No dial tone. It's wrecked.'

'How I loathe technology. Perhaps if we...' Warwick took the phone from Diarmuid and opened the microwave door.

'Don't put it in there, Billy! That's not going to help. Tell them – the Dean's wife, maybe – what happened. It was a simple accident, that's all.'

Warwick placed the defunct phone on the microwave turntable, closed the door and set the controls at two minutes. The microwave lit up and hummed. 'My dear Dermot—'

'Diarmuid.'

'I've told you, my limited Manchester tongue cannot find its way round your wild Celtic syllables. So, my dear *Dermot* – If I were to make a clean breast of my involuntary misdemeanour, the daughter with the eyebrows would start bawling, the mother with the underwear would come at me carrying a kitchen knife at chest height, and old Deany-Meany-Miney-Mo would call a meeting of Senate to have my balls nailed to the Senior Common

Room wall using a ceremonial mallet. But have no fear – our technological tool will be dry in a jiff.'

It was more than dry. When Warwick took it from the oven, the 2, 3 and 9 buttons on the phone had melted.

'Well, penetrative congress with an aged goat, how unfortunate.' Warwick took out his hanky and spread it on the counter. 'Stop looking at me that way. The clanking of your moral judgement is deafening.'

'There's such a thing as honesty, you know.'

Warwick took a paper towel from the counter and wrapped the phone in it. 'Honesty, eh? Very well – let's be consistent. Pop inside to the drawing room, there's a good chap, and tell the Dean about the futility and pointlessness, not to mention upper-strand mismanagement you believe to be at the core of our faculty's work. "Meaningless, Dean old dog, it's all meaningless and futile." He'll like that, I'd say.'

'Very funny.'

'Simply pointing out the difference between you and me, Dermot, my old pork-sword. You keep wanting things to achieve significance. I'm content to get by.' He slipped the phone into his trouser pocket.

'What are you going to do with it?'

'Dump it in the nearest rubbish-bin.'

'I really think you should tell them.'

'They'd blame me for damaging it. Maybe sue me.'

'But that's what you did. An accident, I know, but you did damage it.'

'Yes, I know... Oh, please, Dermot. Or should that be Dare-not? You look as if I'd evacuated my bowels on the table. It's merely a phone. These things happen at the best-run parties.'

Frank Sinatra announced that he had done everything while standing tall and doing it his way.

'He was impotent, you know – Sinatra,' Warwick said. 'Mia Farrow had an appalling time trying to tickle his trombone.' Whistling silently, he strolled towards the main room.

Diarmuid was about to follow him when his mobile rang. 'Diarmuid?' It was Brother Ambrose, his voice blurred because, as always, he was speaking too close to the mouthpiece. 'No, no, no, you're grand, we don't go to press until tomorrow evening, as long as we get it in time... Indeed. Trust in the Almighty but keep an eye on circulation, ha-ha. What we need is more staff, Diarmuid, every night I'm praying to the Almighty to send even one more hand to the pump... Anyway, grand job, Diarmuid. Look forward to the column – and mind you keep it the right side of heresy! Ha-ha. God bless.'

Diarmuid switched off his phone and moved into the livingroom, which contained more noise and colour than seemed right on an evening like this. The Dean sat a little apart, glasses glinting, his large head white and bony against the upholstery of a wing-back chair. A glass of whiskey sat on the table beside him. Laughter and shouted conversations came from a cluster of people gathered near the door.

'Or it could say "This certificate acknowledges that Joe Slobberdedog, property developer, has paid the requisite sum for this degree"?' The crowd parted to reveal the faculty's Chief Examinations Officer wearing what looked like a blue silk tent. 'Have you any thoughts on the subject yourself, Dean?' she called across the room.

'On?' The Dean spoke the word as if it had two syllables.

'Honorary degrees. We noticed that the university plans to award another two over the next month. Might there be a danger of degree inflation?' There was a subdued chuckle.

The Dean drew a fingertip gently along the line of his chin. 'Honorary degrees get my vote of approval. They at once provide an acceptable forum for the recognition of achievement and remind the wider community that we exist. As well as acting, I rush to concede, as a source of revenue for the university, through donations from grateful recipients.'

The Chief Examinations Officer leant forward in her seat. 'I notice the one in two weeks' time – a doctorate – is to the First Secretary at the US consulate in Belfast, a Mr Kaminski. In an idle moment some days ago I conducted an Internet search and it seems Mr Kaminski was a sausage-maker in Chicago who left school at fourteen. Very much an American dream success story, of course – but is a doctoral degree in exchange for pork-sausage money what this university should be about?'

The Dean sat up straighter in his chair and his voice hardened. 'Mr Kaminski has indeed business interests in Illinois. He also – and I don't expect any of us needs reminding of this – has brought significant US investments to this province. Our own all-weather hockey pitch was not a product of beneficence by hobgoblins, you know.' A small whisper of amusement rippled through the listeners. 'There is even a possibility he may help us establish Dufferin House as a doctoral-studies centre, which would be a truly...' he looked up, showed his teeth in what passed for a smile... 'ground-breaking event. As for sausages, I confess to a soft spot for them. Something inherently, hmm, plucky about their plumpness.'

His wife appeared at the door. 'Do be sure to help yourselves to drinks when the need arises,' she told the company. 'Just nip into the kitchen and—' The doorbell sounded and she hurried from the room.

'Terry.' At the sound of the Dean's voice Terry gave a little jump. Beside him Hazel smiled and pushed her thin black hair behind her ears. 'As a non-academic and probably therefore a sensible person, how do you view this honorary-degrees affair?'

Terry addressed his feet and the others had to strain to hear him. 'Have to say, in the light of recent events, who gets or doesn't get an honorary degree seems...irrelevant.' He ran his finger round the rim of his glass.

'Yes, but that wasn't the question,' Warwick said. He straightened up from where he'd been resting an elbow on the mantelpiece. 'The Dean asked you what you thought about honorary degrees.'

'All I know is, my head of Learning Outcomes was an outstanding human being. A twenty-two-carat person.'

'Indeed,' the Dean said, nodding. 'By the way, did you get

that zip drive I resourced for you? Claire mentioned it so I had it fast-tracked.'

'Thank you, yes, indeed, Dean. I haven't had a chance to unpack it yet in the stress of events. But I hope to use it in the near future.'

Hazel peered over Terry's shoulder, little bent nose resting against his shirt. 'She used to ask me to go for coffee with her. She could have gone with anyone, but she went with me.'

There was a silence, punctuated by gasping sounds from the Chief Administrative Officer, who appeared to be getting ready to stand up.

'I, too, find it difficult to accept that Claire is gone,' the Dean said. 'We all do. And, yes, as you intimate, Terry, it does make discussion of other issues seem, um, almost heartless. But discuss them we must.'

'Attention, everyone!' The Dean's wife, standing in the middle of the room, clapped her hands twice. 'Sorry to cut in, sweet soul.' She angled a brief smile towards her husband. 'But I'd like to introduce three people, although some of you may know them already. First we have' – she went back to the door and drew into the room by the arm, miGodalmighty, Diarmuid thought, the woman with the soft hand – 'Angela Passmore, Claire's sister. Many of you will remember her from the funeral. And the gentleman behind her is her husband Tom, Mr Tom Passmore. The medical consultant.' A man with receding fair hair, brown eyes and a very muscular neck gave a small wave. 'And behind him' – she pointed to a woman in a red wool dress – 'is Dr Jean Rafferty, a friend of Tom and Angela's.'

The Dean touched Angela's upper arm as they shook hands. 'Such a blow, the loss of your sister. For us all.'

Tom put his arm gently around his wife, nodded to the Dean over her shoulder. 'I was actually in the States when I heard. Just half an hour from delivering a keynote paper at a medical conference in Chicago. I remember looking at the delegates – three hundred of them at least – and thinking: "None of these people know this, or would be interested if they did know it, but my sister-in-law Claire is at peace now." That's what I thought, and I was very grateful to be able to think it.'

Warwick stood and addressed Angela. 'Sit you there – my posterior is in the fifth state of numbness.' He turned to Tom. 'So you didn't make it back for the funeral?'

Eyebrows raised, Tom glanced at him, then turned to the Dean again. 'A wonderful people, the Americans. But their can-do reputation is perhaps exaggerated. Three national airlines and *not a single one* could get me home in time.'

Jean, long-necked and erect, perched on the arm of Angela's chair. 'When Tom rang me at work, he was *incandescent*. "It's their attitude!" he kept shouting. "Their patronising attitude!" I had to hold the receiver away from my ear!'

'Oh listen, listen!' Warwick called. He turned to Crompton, who had just entered the room. 'Tell her that joke.'

Crompton ran his finger round the neck of his black polo-neck sweater. 'I don't know what you're talking about.'

'Yes you do – the golf-club one, about the man at the airport.'

'Oh, that one. What do you want me to tell that one for?'

'Because we've been having a conversation about airlines. And it's funny.'

Crompton glanced round the room. 'Are you sure?'

'Perfectly. Listen, everybody.'

Crompton set his drink on a small table and put both hands deep into his trouser pockets. 'Weeell, OK... OK. This guy, this guy is in an airport bar, waiting for a plane, and he notices this stunning woman next to him. And he's keen to chat her up, so he thinks, "She must be an airline stewardess, with looks like that – wonder what airline she's with?" So he leans towards her and whispers the American Airlines slogan: "Something special in the air?" The woman looks at him, what is this, and he sees he's got it wrong. So then he tries the British Airways slogan, says to her: "Flying the flag?" And he gets the same blank look, and he's starting to feel a bit of a prat. But he decides he'll try just one more – the Air France slogan. "Making the sky the best place on earth?" he says. And the woman turns to him and she has her teeth gritted, eyes popping out of her head with rage. "What the *fuck* do you want?" she yells at the top of her lungs. And the guy leans back, folds his arms and smiles. "Ah!" he says. "Now I have it. You're with Ryanair!"'

There was a moment of silence. Then Frances said 'Would it have been equally funny if the attendant had been a man?'

'No.' Warwick said. 'Because then the man in the bar would have had to be gay.'

'That's not what I meant,' Frances said grimly.

'I had one crumb of comfort,' Tom said, turning towards the Dean, his back to Crompton. 'A thought that helped me cope with the whole ordeal, actually, and which I passed on to my wife and other relatives when I met them. It's this: it's very very difficult to die of asphyxiation. I held on to that thought over the week that followed. Shock, yes, you could die of shock, but not asphyxiation, or at least not in a lift. And the good part about shock is, it's quick. Lift sticks, panic, stroke, end of story. I mean, how long would you say, Jean, from start to finish?'

'Oh, I would... Five minutes?'

Warwick drank and wiped his mouth with the sleeve of his sweater. 'So. Our department head was *lucky*. Only had to suffer for five minutes... I expect she found that a relief.'

Tom glanced at him again, then away. 'Non-medical folk often have these false perceptions. Want dramas of all sorts. Well, that may work with *ER* and *Casualty*, but medicine in the real world is ninety-five per cent undramatic. So it's a mistake – essentially immature, to be honest – to try dramatising what is inherently undramatic.' He put his hand on his wife's shoulder and squeezed gently.

'Right,' Warwick said. 'You're incarcerated in a lift, you die of a stroke, but that's acceptable, even desirable, because the doctor says it's undramatic.'

'Oh, for heaven's sake.' The Chief Examinations Officer's blue dress made a lot of noise as she shifted in her seat. 'Must you always be quite so contentious, Billy?' She turned to Tom.

'I've often wondered – how exactly does a layperson recognise a stroke?'

Tom shrugged. 'Subject collapses. Follow-up symptoms – loss of movement, speech impairment very often. And/or death, of course. That's it, really.'

Diarmuid felt Frances's voice warm in his ear. 'Midnight, remember. At the latest.'

The Chief Examinations Officer pushed away a strand of hair that hung in front of her big, handsome face. 'But collapse tells you nothing. There could be half a dozen reasons for collapse, other than shock or stroke. There'd have to be other symptoms.'

'Colour,' Jean said. 'The skin, particularly around the face, develops a bluish tinge, then closer to black.' She glanced at Angela. 'But perhaps it's time to change the subject.'

Diarmuid turned towards the kitchen and almost walked into Brian Crompton. He seemed totally unfazed by the reaction to his joke. 'The very man,' he said, gripping Diarmuid's lapel between finger and thumb. 'Any tickets for the game tomorrow? A few regulars at the golf club swore they'd have me one but you know what golf-club regulars are like… I know I'm going to end up watching it on TV. And did I tell you I have a ten-pound stake that could net me over eighty quid? No, I'm not kidding. For a scoreless draw – Ireland Nil, Portugal Nil. Plus – no, hold on. Plus, plus. Plus Figo has to have three shots on target – on the Irish goal – in the first half. Well, it could happen. He'll have at least that number, I reckon. Warwick was going to stick a tenner on too but the old bugger chickened out in the end – he thinks Ireland is going to win.'

'Excuse me.' It was Frances, standing the other side of Crompton, a large glass of red wine in her hand. In the black dress with the scoop neck she looked almost nice. 'A man over there says you're president of that golf club out the Killyleagh Road – the Morton Club?'

'Well, yes, I am president this year, for my sins – missed the first three months more or less, because I was ill and—'

'How come you don't allow women members?'

'Well, we do, actually.' Crompton smiled down at her. 'Any lady can become an associate member – or she can just use the club if she—'

'But not a full member.'

Crompton raised his eyebrows. 'Well, no. It – it's just one of these, you know, traditions. A lot of us wish it was otherwise, of course, but tradition, whee – it's a hard one to crack... Do you play yourself?'

Frances took a quick sip, shook her head. 'Two friends of mine – women friends – told me they were going to put in a bid for the maintenance of the garden at your clubhouse. And then they heard it barred women.'

'And do they play golf?'

Frances lowered her glass, eyed Crompton for several seconds. 'You're missing the point. The point is, they refused to have anything to do with—'

From the kitchen came the sound of a spoon being banged on an empty glass and then the Dean's wife and daughter wheeled in a trolley. Its upper section carried three trays of dessert: on the right a huge dark-chocolate gateau, on the left some form of apple crumble, and in the middle an oval dish with a top layer of custard decorated with dabs of cream. The trolley's lower section held a range of cheese and biscuits.

Mrs Saddington raised her spoon and glass and was about to strike them again when a smiling Dr Fr David Hillocks, head of Historical Pedagogies, entered the room, wearing a light grey suit, a blue shirt and yellow tie, with a small silver cross in his lapel. The Dean's wife waited until he was seated near her husband, then rapped spoon against glass.

'Ladies and gentlemen, just a word before my husband speaks. We have some light refreshment for you – I don't know if you're going to allow them to eat before you speak, dear, or after? Very good – all the more enjoyable for the wait! But I should tell you that all three desserts you see here were produced by the effort and talent – the *sole* effort and talent – of our daughter Rosalind. Who is sitting her GCSE in Home

Economics at the end of this year and who, I must tell you, locked myself and my husband *out* of the kitchen for much of the afternoon, so even *we* were not allowed to *look*, for goodness' sake, until she'd finished her work. I know you'll find one of the three dishes to suit your taste, and I'd just like to say how proud I am, we both are, of our lovely daughter!'

Mrs Saddington put an arm round the girl's shoulders and kissed her. Rosalind made a face, then she sat in a chair and hunched forward, eyes on her feet.

The Dean stood up. 'Colleagues and friends, I'd like to start my remarks near home – in fact, let's be honest, *at* home, by echoing my wife's words and thanking Rosalind for her culinary efforts on our behalf this evening.' He began to clap and everyone joined in. Many smiled and nodded towards the Dean's wife and daughter.

'"Closure and Commencement", I titled my email to you, because tonight we look back and remember Claire Thompson, a colleague, an inspirational head of Learning Outcomes, a friend. Let us now take a minute of silence to remember her, each in his or her own way.' He stood with bowed head. From the corner of his eye Diarmuid could see Warwick, moving his weight from foot to foot. Near him Crompton looked as if he was trying to suppress a smile. At last the Dean's head came up again. 'And to mark this occasion we'd like to present a small memento to Claire's sister Angela. If you would be good enough to step forward, Angela, and accept a token of the esteem in which the faculty held your dear sister.'

Angela opened the parcel presented to her.

'A faculty scarf,' the Dean said, pointing. 'Do you normally, ah, wear a scarf?'

'Not as a rule.'

'Perhaps you will now begin.'

Tom put an arm round his wife and led her back to her seat.

'And so, to the second part of this evening – Commencement. At this juncture I want to thank our acting head of Learning Outcomes, Dr Fr David Hillocks, whose cover appointment in that role, combined with his normal duties of head of Historical Pedagogies, I'm happy to announce will extend for a further month, thus allowing us to arrange for a permanent appointment in Learning Outcomes. David?'

The priest smiled and stood, little legs apart, hands in his trouser pockets.' Well, really you know, briefest of words. First and most important, Claire – keep her and her family in your prayers, won't you? This night and in the days and nights to come. Second, if I might move to professional matters. Let me be frank: my ambition is strong, but not for myself – it is for the Learning Outcomes department, alongside my own. Working together, I hope we can build on Claire's many achievements. And, third, if I could share some news just in. After considerable negotiations and contact and, in my own case, interminable form-filling, ha-ha, the World Bank has finally decided to support our doctoral programme with a spend commitment of a quarter of a million pounds over the next three years – *if* we can indicate that in staffing and physical-resources terms, we are prepared.' There was a murmur through the room. 'That is a truly generous gesture and one I am sure we will publicly acknowledge. It is also a challenge to which I know we will rise. Thank you very much.'

Right, Diarmuid decided. That's what I'll do the 'God Lives!' column about. God is for all mankind, no, humankind, not just some; he is for organisations great and small; he is found in all locations, not just some. Maybe work up a last line pay-off: 'God lives, not just in the church tabernacle but in the vaults of the World Bank as well.' Oh, *Jesus*.

The Dean raised his fingers, a little like the Pope about to give a blessing, and silence fell again. 'One other brief matter, housekeeping you might say, but urgent and related to the World Bank generosity. Last year, colleagues, you'll remember we had a, mm, spirited debate about the possible future development of Dufferin House, revolving around its designation as a doctoral centre. David, you, along with many others, saw it as an important part of our development as a faculty. Say a word, maybe?'

Dr Fr David nodded. 'Indeed. Doctoral work is where the gravy is, if you'll permit me the vernacular. As the World Bank offer clearly indicates. We know that there are students out there – particularly in Borneo, a recruitment area we've been targeting – who would be happy to register on our doctoral programme. The truth, however, is that we simply haven't the teaching accommodation – the seminar rooms, the offices – to cater for them.'

'And, like me, you feel Dufferin House would fit the bill,' the Dean interjected.

'Indeed. It's an elegant building, admittedly in need of some refurbishment, but nothing insurmountable.'

'Thank you for that, David. Brian, did you have something to suggest?'

'No, no, no.' Crompton shook his head, folded his arms and leant against the mantelpiece. 'Nothing to say.'

The Dean stroked his cropped grey hair lovingly. 'Any other, um, thoughts?'

Warwick set his glass on the coffee table. 'These Borneo people we're hoping to recruit – what level of language skills have they?'

The Dean looked again at Dr Fr David.

The priest smiled and pushed his glasses higher on his nose. 'Well, they're not here yet, and we haven't got our centre. However, I'm given to understand their mastery of English is impressive. They all teach at third-level institutions in their own country, and that suggests some fluency in speaking the language, since instruction is in English in most of these places.'

'With respect,' Warwick said, 'I didn't ask if they could speak English. I asked had they the language skills to embark on a doctoral-level programme?'

The Dean raised his open palm, quelling further discussion. 'These are matters for the future, perhaps. The point Dr Fr David is rightly making is that each of these people will bring with him or her a full registration fee as a foreign student. As I understand it – and David can correct me if I'm wrong – '

'No, no,' Dr Fr David murmured. 'Absolutely right.'

' – were we able to muster accommodation, we could take between twenty and thirty of them tomorrow. And if you do the calculations, the World Bank has made a commitment to support their professional development as third-level teachers, so each student would bring some fourteen thousand pounds with them. Conceivably twice that, in practice.' A collective sigh, laced with soft whistles, went round the room. 'Solving at a stroke the financial problems under which this faculty currently groans.'

'Except that Dufferin House is derelict, we have no money to develop it, and our proposed students may not have a level of English that would allow them to embark on an A-level programme, let alone a doctoral one,' Warwick said.

The Dean glanced towards Angela's husband and Jean. 'I suspect we may be boring our guests with protracted shop talk. So can we take it that most of us are in favour of further exploring this topic at the next faculty board meeting?' There was a murmur around the room. 'Good.'

'Borneo – isn't that where they've the head-hunters?' Crompton whispered.

The Dean cupped a hand behind his left ear. 'I didn't quite catch that, Brian?'

'I said, isn't the dessert trolley just heavenly scrumptious?'

'Indeed. Banish all cholesterol-tending thoughts, everyone.'

Rosalind's mother moved around with a pen and pad taking orders, starting with the Chief Examinations Officer and Dr Fr David, who were now seated on either side of the Dean. The list of orders was taken to Rosalind, who cut and spooned the selected dessert, using her left hand. There was a great deal of 'Mmm-hmmm!'-ing and 'Ohmygoodness!'-ing as each plateful was tasted. The central custard-topped dish was scraped clean within minutes.

Terry, on a stool beside Diarmuid, lifted a spoonful of apple crumble to his mouth, chewed briefly and swallowed. 'Department Head started those World Bank links, you know. She was the one who made the contacts, laid the foundations. Whole thing would have been impossible without her.' Fragments of food shot from his lips as he spoke and landed on his knees and the fly of his trousers.

'What I'd be anxious about,' Diarmuid said, 'is how many of these Borneo people have a proper first degree. We can't just collapse the university standards because we're anxious to sign up doctoral candidates.'

'What *I*'d be anxious about,' Crompton said, in a low voice, 'is how many of them are still head-hunters. I don't want to look up and see some bugger coming to discuss his mark with a machete in his fist.'

'Don't worry – you won't have time to look up,' Warwick told him. He put an arm round Diarmuid's shoulders. 'Dermot Dare-not, old son – relax those moral sinews, would you? Consider the last grant I got, from Paleothon, the American crowd in Craigavon. They provide software for weapons systems in the States – it's a verifiable fact, I promise you, read their annual report. But does that small blemish mean I'll reject their money, tell them it has blood on it? One must be practical.'

'That's exactly what you should do,' Diarmuid said. 'It'd be different if the research actually *did* something for people.'

'Research doesn't do, it *is*. The bigger the grant, the better the research – that's the rule. Even Homer Simpson works with nuclear power.'

'Homer Simpson is make-believe – he's a cartoon, for God's sake.'

'Yes, but your problem is, you expect life to be like a *Simpsons* episode. Beginning, middle and happy ending. A causes B, B is the reason for C, and so on. Well, forget that. Because things just happen. And if you insist on thinking otherwise, you'll end up trapped in a web of agitated self-righteousness.' Warwick sipped his drink slowly and smiled.

'That was good, wasn't it? 'Agitated self-righteousness'. Write that down, quick, Terry, or we'll forget it.'

'My late Department Head lived her principles – that's what made her special,' Terry said, to no one in particular.

'That and her arse,' Warwick said softly. He headed towards the kitchen.

There was an awkward pause. Diarmuid turned to Terry. 'Terry, tell me this, Claire's office, is it accessible to staff members yet?'

'The police said it could be used as a working office, as long as I kept a record of anything added or taken away. Which I'm doing.'

'The place is full of files of all kinds,' Hazel said, emerging from behind Terry. 'We took hours yesterday making a list of what's there – didn't we, hon-comb?'

'Department Head's first commitment was to her students,' Terry said, ignoring Hazel and wiping his mouth with a blue check hanky, 'not administration. Students were nearest her heart.'

'I think at the end of the day she was tired,' Hazel said. 'She told me one time it was like rolling a stone up a hill, fighting for the students against the institution. It wore her down.'

'The one thing I do appreciate,' Terry said, 'is the way the Dean has given me custodianship of DH's records. 'You are the gate-keeper,' he said to me. 'Claire's legacy is in your hands.' I found that quite moving.'

Hazel patted Terry's sleeve, then his shoulder. 'We mustn't miss the last bus, hon-comb. I'll get my coat – won't be a tick.' She headed for the hall.

Diarmuid took a deep breath, then said to Terry, 'Nothing of mine in Claire's office, I suppose.'

'Not in the paper files. Electronic files have still to be checked.'

'Well, I'd appreciate being kept informed on anything that might turn up, OK?'

'You'll be the first to know.'

Diarmuid stood looking around the room. People were eating and talking energetically, some holding a loaded fork in mid-air as they made yet another point to their listeners, others swallowing quickly so they could make a witty reply. A few isolated figures admired several paintings of beaches and whitewashed cottages that hung at the far end of the room.

Diarmuid was wondering if he should have offered to share a taxi with Terry and Hazel, keep them sweet or at least not too sour, when the sound of a breaking plate came from the kitchen. There was a silence, then a high-pitched squeal, followed by raised voices. As people looked at each other, clearly wondering if they should start talking again, Rosalind emerged from the kitchen, her left hand to her mouth. She said something to Dr Fr David and her mother, then ran up the stairs. They seemed to be about to follow her but stopped as Crompton emerged from the kitchen with a beer in his hand, smiled and walked over to the bookcase, which he began to examine carefully. A few moments later Warwick appeared, hands in pockets. Dr Fr David and the Dean's wife descended on him and began to talk vigorously, especially the Dean's wife, who pointed up the stairs and then at Warwick's chest. Warwick looked at her, listening calmly to the outburst. Eventually he shrugged, said something and strolled into the living room to join Crompton.

'What was all that about, Hazey?' Terry asked, when Hazel returned with her coat. 'Did something happen?'

Hazel leant into them, blinking rapidly, her voice low and rapid. 'Apparently the girl, Rosalind, was sent to the kitchen – you know Rosalind their daughter, the Dean's daughter – with some empty plates and to get drinks. And when she went there, she says, the girl says, Rosalind says, there were two people standing leaning against the counter. And she says they had their arms around each other and were, you know, sort of *snogging*. And that's when she dropped the plate she was carrying. And squealed.'

'Snogging?' Diarmuid said.

'You know. Hugging and kissing and... Pretty heavy, too, apparently.'

'Who was? Who was snogging?' Terry asked.

'Well, that's the *thing*. According to Rosalind, it was Crompton and Warwick. Snogging in the kitchen *with each other*.' She paused as the others digested this. 'And she says, when she dropped the dish Warwick just laughed. And next thing he came over and put his arm round her and said did she know her right ear was gorgeous, that he'd never seen anything like it. And then Crompton came round the other side and said he'd never seen anything like her left ear. One on either side, an arm each round her, talking about her ears—'

Hazel broke off as the conversation hushed again.

People watched as the Dean crossed the room, then spoke quietly to his wife and Dr Fr David. That done, with most of the guests trying to look away and watch at the same time, he went upstairs.

Mrs Saddington turned towards the guests, her voice wobbling only a little. 'Another drink, anyone?'

'I'll keep you posted,' Terry told Diarmuid quietly, helping Hazel into her coat, 'if anything of interest turns up in Department Head's office.'

'That'll be grand.' Diarmuid said. But as he watched Terry leaving he was thinking Terry could go to hell. He'd skin this particular skunk himself.

The Dean didn't come downstairs for fifteen minutes, although it seemed much longer. People glanced at each other but went on eating and talking, elbow on mantelpiece, backside propped against piano edge, back sunk into a sofa. Outside, through the patio window, Crompton could be seen standing on the lawn smoking, staring at the night sky. Warwick crossed the living room, carrying a fresh glass of wine, and sat on the couch beside Frances. Leant his head close to hers. 'How is my favourite faculty wife enjoying the show?'

'Very interesting. From what I see *and* hear.'

Warwick took a spoonful of his dessert, a sip of his wine. 'In that case, let me round things off with a tip that could make you over eighty quid.'

'Needn't bother – your friend Crompton's already given it.'

'Please,' Warwick said, pretending to shudder. 'Brian Malachy Crompton has never put his size eights inside a bookie's in his life. Knows nothing about betting, principally because he's too busy contemplating his own back passage. He thinks he has cancer, you know.'

'Crompton?' Diarmuid said. 'Crompton thinks he has cancer?'

'Indeed. Where are you going?' Warwick asked, as Frances began to move away.

Frances didn't reply but walked down the room and stood considering the watercolour paintings. Head to one side, she was staring at her third whitewashed cottage when Mrs Saddington approached, touched her arm, led her to the Dean.

'What was that about Crompton being ill?' Diarmuid asked again.

'He thinks he's dying of cancer. Nonsense, of course, but he thinks he is.'

'What makes him think that?'

'Rectal bleeding.'

As if he had heard the words, Crompton crossed the room and joined them.

'We're discussing your anus,' Warwick told him. 'We've agreed you should show it to the lovely Dr Jean – she might have something interesting to say. Or is it too late for that?'

'More pointless than late. I had a barium enema two days ago,' Crompton said to Diarmuid, 'And a major X-ray. Waiting for results.' He put a cushion on the floor and sat carefully on it, back against the wall.

'What exactly happens with a barium enema?'

'Don't ask,' Warwick told Diarmuid.

'It's where they give you a major X-ray,' Crompton said. 'And the day before, you have to take this fizzy stuff that cleans out your digestive tract. Tastes like sink water and acts like carbolic soap.'

'Then the nurses get you to put on a green paper gown,' Warwick went on. 'And they shove this tube up your servants' entrance and pump stuff into you. Air and some sort of fluid that inflates the passage. Crompton liked that part best. Didn't you?'

'No, I didn't.'

'A certain person of my acquaintance – no, not Crompton, perish the thought – this person was lying on the table with his paper gown open at the back and a tube inserted some distance up his posterior, waiting for what seemed like hours for the examination to start. Eventually the theatre door opens and this specialist, from Eastern Europe or somewhere – they've no choice but to get them from there, not enough being trained here – he comes in and says to him, in this Croatian accent, "Are you happy and relaxed?" This unfortunate man, remember, has a tube up his Chunnel, is waiting for a cancer check to be done, and this anal-department star wants to know if he's happy and relaxed. "I think it's safe to say neither of those adjectives apply," the man on the table managed to say. Did anyone ask you if you were happy and relaxed?'

'No,' Crompton told him.

'But they did put a tube up your botty?'

'Yes,' Crompton said. 'They did.'

'Did they grease it at all before inserting?'

'Maybe we should change the subject,' Diarmuid said. 'What happened in the kitchen?'

'And they bullied him into taking an organ-donor card – didn't they?' Warwick slipped Crompton's wallet from his hip pocket and extracted a small red card. 'Look. "I hereby give permission for… any organs required, including heart, kidney, lungs, eyes, to be used to help others for medical purposes in the event of my death." You were pressured into signing this, weren't you?'

Crompton took the card, replaced it in his wallet. 'Not so much pressured as—'

'There's not a profession on earth in the same league as medicine when it comes to moral stink,' Warwick said. 'They give you medical treatment that is so successful you die, then slice you open so they can scoop out a handful of organs and shove them into some other poor unfortunate and make more money out of him before it's his turn and the cycle starts again. The Borneo head-hunters are the soul of compassion in comparison.'

'You're twisting everything,' Crompton said. 'It's an act of charity – all sorts of people do it, all sorts. You see them on billboards. Famous people, like Rosemary Farquhar in the BBC. She's donating her organs.'

'Know that ad for Viagra, with Sir Stanley Matthews in it? I was at a conference in Brazil, and three independent sources told me that, far from having an erectile dysfunction, it took men throwing buckets of water over Sir Stan at regular intervals to get him to stop. Anyway, I'm not sure I'd want Rosemary Farquhar's spare bits, even if I lost my own. Never know where they've been.'

'The thing that would worry me would be if they made a mistake,' Diarmuid said. 'Started cutting bits off while I still wasn't dead.'

'And what about the titles they use?' Warwick continued. 'Dr this and Dr that. And then the *consultants* – "I'm *Mr* Tom Passmore, because you see I used to be a doctor, but then I went so high in the medical ether, my Dr bit fell to earth and my Mr bit took over." There's only one word for what the medical profession does, and that is it sucks. Sucks money out of us all, and sucks full stop.'

'Really.' Dr Jean was standing in the doorway, head tilted on her long neck. 'I take it, then, that if I were to spend the next ten minutes bad-mouthing *your* profession, you'd have no objection?'

'Be my guest.' Warwick smiled, as he poured what remained

of the wine into his own glass. 'It sucks too.' Crompton struggled to his feet and picked up the cushion. Past Warwick's shoulder Diarmuid saw the Dean laughing at something Frances was saying, his shoulders heaving.

'Well, first of all, I find your remarks grossly offensive,' Dr Jean said, her face quite pale. 'But, then, I'm not particularly surprised, in the light of what I understand occurred a few minutes ago in the kitchen. An incident that I understand verged on *child abuse*. So I probably shouldn't be surprised.'

'Shoosh-shoosh-shoosh.' Mr Tom Passmore stood beside Dr Jean, an arm at her back. Where was Angela? 'The empty vessel makes the loudest noise, Jean. Besides, libel cases pay very well these days.'

'Slander, old chap,' Warwick said. 'It's slander, not libel. If it's written down, it's libel. Spoken is slander. Important to get these things straight.'

Mr Tom smiled, an elastic-band smile. 'And since I was talking about both written and spoken defamation, "libel" is actually completely accurate. Besides, how anyone with an ounce of self-respect, let alone respect for the dead, could act as you have acted on an occasion convened to honour the memory of my late sister-in-law, I really...' He paused, head bent. 'Quite amazing. Not that I'm surprised.' When he raised his wine to drink, his hand trembled.

'So you're amazed and not surprised at the same time,' Warwick said. 'That's a good trick. Can you teach it to me, or must I have a doctorate in medicine first?'

The Dean's wife appeared, tapped Diarmuid's shoulder. 'He'd like a word with you now, if you're not totally caught up,' she whispered.

The Dean was putting a fountain pen and a small notebook back into his jacket pocket. 'Ah, sit down, Diarmuid.' There was no sign of Frances. 'Good to see you. Have a pleasant evening?'

'Well, yes. It's... it was... very—'

'These informal occasions, I find, can be most agreeable. And informative. And then, of course, the World Bank support is good news.'

'Absolutely.' *Bollocks.*

'It's just unfortunate that something, um, avoidable has been allowed to sound a somewhat jarring note…' He glanced away for a moment, sipped his whiskey. 'But let's not consider that now. Did I notice you favouring one leg as you approached?'

'My foot, gave it a little, you know, twist. That's all.'

'Too bad. Still, could be worse. Now, I've received two pieces of information about you recently, one rather sad in nature. I believe your mother passed away. A few months ago. What age was she?'

'Eighty-three.'

'Well. Distressing, but she had a full life, I'm sure.' Diarmuid tried not to think about his mother's face on the pillow without her false teeth. 'The second matter points to the future. I gather you're to be our, um, spokesman on some upcoming radio discussions. That's good. I sometimes think it's the most spiritual of the media, radio.'

'Well I – yes, when you think of it. Absolutely.'

'It's a gift, I always think, to reach beyond the loneliness of the airwaves and connect with a hidden listener. Has the matter for discussion been decided?' Diarmuid began to explain, but the Dean raised a hand. 'Save it for the broadcast. And, remember, your department is behind you on this venture. *I* am behind you.'

He was turning away again when Diarmuid's voice stopped him. 'I was wondering, Dean, if anything had, ah, transpired on the Boston study leave. Or when you would expect to know about that, ah, side of things. The late DH was, as I think you know, supportive.' His voice sounded louder in his ears than he had intended.

The Dean turned back, took off his glasses and cleaned them methodically on his hanky. 'As it happens I was talking to your wife about that very thing. She, it hardly needs repeating, is also supportive of your application for study leave. Although she does at this moment remain uncertain about her, um, capacity to accompany you during your tenure.'

'Well I'm sure when the time— '

'Which is good to know, of course. Because, as it happens, we have a fall-back position. By an odd coincidence, Dr Fr David has himself been developing a research proposal that would involve *him* taking up residence at Boston College – indeed, it *is* a small academic world. But if he were able to avail himself of this opportunity to spend the second semester there, it would go some way to consolidating a linked international programme, exchange of students, etc., etc., etc. Someone of his calibre *in situ*, in such a prestigious institution, it's precisely the level of input that our faculty needs for growth and development.' The Dean nodded agreement with himself, dipped the tip of his little finger into his whiskey and sucked it.

Germs, Diarmuid thought. Where had that finger been? 'Oh, well, yes, of course. In need indeed.' For fuck's sake.

'And when last heard from, the Pope had yet to sanction nuptials for his celibate clergy, so Dr Fr David does not have, what shall we say? The *complication* of a wife. Ha-ha, I'm joking, of course.' The whiskey in the glass swirled and curled as he made a chuckling noise. 'Well, I'm happy you see it the same way. Boston, incidentally, will be hosting an education conference in November – Dr Fr David is on the editorial panel so you may wish to submit a paper. The faculty would naturally fund a visit by any staff if they...'

The Dean's words trailed off and he stared past Diarmuid, eyes bulging behind his glasses in a way that reminded Diarmuid of a hen he'd once seen laying an egg.

Diarmuid turned in his seat and followed his gaze. He saw Crompton bent sideways on a couch at the opposite side of the room, mouth open, face pale. He appeared to be looking at a pancake on the cushion beside him.

'Good God!' The Dean stood up and crossed the room hurriedly. 'The fellow has vomited on our new couch.'

Other guests who had been sitting or standing nearby had got to their feet. Warwick brushed past them, sat on the arm of the couch, put a hand on his friend's back. 'You OK?'

'Too much drink,' someone said.

Crompton, eyes closed, shook his head. It was impossible to tell if it was his illness or that he was disagreeing with the suggestion. Slowly, cautiously, he opened his mouth and spat some more yellow into the pool of food on the couch. Wiped weakly at strands of spittle that hung from his lips.

'Oh, my God,' the Dean said. Then, louder, 'This is unacceptable conduct. Please stop immediately.' He flicked the back of his hand against Warwick's shoulder. 'Take him home, can't you? In the name of God.'

Crompton belched and spat a second time. A half-mouthful of red joined the pool of yellow.

Mr Tom was down on one knee, looking into Crompton's face, then at the pool of vomit. 'Well, now, let's see what we have here. Mmm.'

'Has he an ulcer?' Frances said. 'A bleeding ulcer? Maybe he's allergic to custard and his ulcer reacted.'

Then, with the guests gathered round flinching and saying, 'Oh, Christ Almighty', 'Oh, for God's sake' and 'Gross, disgusting', Warwick put his hand into the pool and, with his finger and thumb, removed something. 'Well now.' He produced a white handkerchief, then wiped the custard and blood off something shiny. It was about an inch long and immediately recognisable as a shard of glass.

There was a surging babble of voices. Several could be heard urging that a doctor be sent for.

'We have a doctor, we have *two* doctors, for goodness' sake,' the Dean's wife said. 'Two.' Her face had turned a light grey.

'If you could maybe clean off the couch?' Mr Tom said.

The Dean's wife ran to the kitchen, came back wearing rubber gloves and carrying a towel and a bowl of water. Soon the offending area had been sponged down and a clean cushion from another chair put on the damp spot.

Mr Tom sat down carefully beside Crompton. 'Now. Just

open nice and easy, let me have a look in there.' He put a hand gently against the side of Crompton's face, but the injured man gestured towards the door.

Warwick put his hand on Mr Tom's chest, eased him back. 'Brian would prefer you did not touch him – I do read you right, Brian?' Crompton, the hanky pressed to his mouth, nodded several times. 'Will I take you to the hospital? Is that what you want to happen?'

Crompton nodded again.

'Let me see the sliver of glass, please,' Mr Tom said, reaching forward.

'I think...' Warwick wrapped it carefully in his handkerchief, '...I think I'll hang on to this, if you don't mind.' Arm round Crompton's shoulders, he headed towards the door.

Mr Tom took a step after them. 'You know you're being very silly refusing treatment. The first need is to staunch the bleeding—'

'Would you like me to call an ambulance?' the Dean called, his voice hoarse.

'Ah, no. Excuse us,' Warwick said. The two friends, arms round each other, went out into the darkness.

In the kitchen Diarmuid reached for the gin bottle. Empty. The beer seemed to be finished as well. A search of the cupboards produced a quarter-bottle of vodka and a can of Schweppes. He gulped the mixture back, felt the alcohol seep into his bloodstream.

Back in the living room, nervous, whispered conversations were being held around the room.

'I stuck to the gateau.'

'How do you know that was OK? She could have put something into that as well.'

'Of course it was an accident. A young girl wouldn't do the likes of that deliberately. Have sense.'

'What difference does deliberate or accident make? It's still glass. Your stomach doesn't care if it was meant or not.'

'You'd have noticed it. You couldn't be eating glass and not notice what you were doing.'

Diarmuid felt Frances's hand gripping his sleeve. 'Did you take dessert?'

'No.'

'Neither did I. And it's now five to twelve.'

There was the banging of a spoon on glass. Deathly pale, the Dean and Mrs Saddington stood on either side of Mr Tom. The consultant spoke. 'I'm convinced there's no cause for alarm, but, but, *but*. Just to be on the safe side, if anyone who had dessert – *any* dessert – were to drive by the City hospital for a brief, very brief, diagnostic procedure, I think that would be good. It's ninety-nine per cent likely to be unnecessary, but it's best to have peace of mind on these things. There's a place in my car for anyone who needs a lift.'

'And,' said the Dean loudly. 'I would appreciate if everyone here treated this incident in confidence. *Strictest* confidence.'

Diarmuid felt a sudden need to pee. He left the room and mounted the stairs.

From behind a closed door at the top, the sound of clothing being adjusted, a flushing toilet. Angela Passmore came out, straightening her dress. Her eyes glinted in the semi-gloom.

'Oh, my goodness. It's… Dr Monaghan, right?'

'That's right. Diarmuid, though – please. I met you at the…funeral.'

She nodded, her eyes moving round his face as if in search of something. 'Yes. We missed you at the lunch.'

What did she mean by that? That she'd noticed he hadn't been there? Or that she'd missed him at the lunch and ever since, been pining and pensive in her bedroom, thinking about him…? Shut up – what sort of crack-brained fantasy is that? She's speaking again. 'Did – did you help pay for the scarf as well?'

'No, no. They've a gift fund for that sort of thing.'

'As long as they don't think this will somehow stop our claim on behalf of Claire. My solicitor says they're using every trick in the book to make it difficult for us – me and my family – to bring them to court.'

'The university, you mean?'

'That's why the Dean was so chummy-wummy earlier – thought maybe a scarf would be cheaper than a court case. Especially when their defective lift was what caused her death. And now they could have a second legal front opened up after what happened this evening.'

He looked at her carefully – at the dark shininess under her eyes, at the soft line of her jaw, at the way little bits of spit gathered at the corners of her mouth when she smiled. 'You didn't take dessert, then?'

Her hair shimmered as she shook her head. 'Watching the weight.'

He felt a brief impulse to put his arms round her, but said instead, 'You're the one has a right to be upset. I mean, your sister died and everything, and yet everybody here has virtually ignored you.'

'You're forgetting my lovely present.' She smiled, then looked away, fiddled with an earring. 'By the way, did somebody tell me you were the last to see her?'

'You're the second person tonight to ask me that. I probably was, but—'

'Angela?' The call was from the hallway. Tom's voice, full of reasonableness. 'Can you come on now? We're giving the Dean and his family a lift to the hospital.'

She touched his arm. 'What's your number? Quick.'

'I'll write it down.' He scribbled at lightning speed. She smiled, tucked the scrap of paper into a tiny breast pocket and went downstairs, her wedding ring making a clicking sound on the banister.

Diarmuid locked the bathroom door behind him and raised the toilet seat. Below, the sound of cars heading for the City Hospital filled the night air.

'I thought I'd never get out of that madhouse.' Frances looked out the taxi window at the darkness. 'First Warwick with that ears stuff – I could have him up for sexual harassment, you know. And then that other creature throwing up on the couch, all that bleeding and so on – you can get little capsules, phials, things in joke shops that look just like blood, then you bite them and pretend... Joy and Mairead were at a party where they had them one time. *And* I don't believe that necking-in-the-kitchen nonsense – putting on an act, the pair of them. Just looking for attention.'

Diarmuid imagined himself grabbing the lapels of her jacket and pulling her face close to his so he could yell into it and tell her that swallowing glass was not a matter to be taken lightly. But instead he spoke quietly and carefully. 'Listen. Did the Dean talk to you about my leave of absence?'

She took out her house keys and rezipped the bag before she replied. 'I couldn't care less if the pair of them are gay or bisexual or whatever. Doesn't give him the right to talk like that – I mean she's only a *child*. Him and his ears. Know what I think? He put that glass in the food himself. Not saying you could prove it but I bet that's what happened. To get off the hook over what happened in the kitchen with the girl.'

'Did the Dean ask you about my leave of absence?'

'Oh, for God's sake. It always has to come back to you, doesn't it? Yes, he did. All right? He asked me how I felt about spending time in the States. That's all. I asked him if he was making an offer I couldn't refuse. Thought he was going to have a seizure, he started laughing so much.'

'That was all?'

'He asked me if I wanted to go to the States. I said it depended who was taking me, and he said it'd probably be you. That's all. That was the whole conversation.'

'And you said nothing after that, when he said it'd probably be me?'

She turned towards him, chin up. 'I just said I could think of other things to do. And that I didn't understand why women in the States had to wear stretch pants when most of them had backsides the size of an end gable. He laughed at that too.' She rubbed mist from the side window and stared out. 'Was I supposed to tell him lies or something?'

'I distinctly said to you before we left, I said the Dean is keen on wives going on study leave too. Thinks it keeps the husbands happier. I mean, for fuck's sake.'

'Well, excuse me. Does he think this is the nineteenth century? Chinese women doing rest-and-recovery duties for Jap soldiers, is that along the lines he's thinking?'

'What has the war in Japan got to do with...' Look. He simply thinks it makes sense, and the fact is you've told him you're not interested in going and now he's turned down my application.'

She stared at him, frowning. 'He's not going to let you go because of what I said? That's ridiculous – bet you there's some other reason. Did he say you couldn't go?'

Diarmuid saw himself pushing her half out of the car and banging the door on her head. 'There's no other reason.'

'That's rubbish. You're talking pure rubbish.'

In bed, turned away from each other, in the silence, he thought of Claire in the lift. The small squeal as the system jammed. Her calls, her hammering. Then her face changing colour – what was it, white, blue, black? Her cheek jammed against the lift wall where she fell, mouth open. If he'd mentioned the noise he'd heard in the lift, she might never have got into it. So the least he could do now was tell Angela about the noise: it would strengthen her family's case against the university. Right, great. And then, under intense questioning, someone would ask why he hadn't mentioned the noise to Claire, and he'd have to say he forgot, that because he had a sore toe, he had, oopsadaisy, forgotten something that could have saved his department head's life.

He went to the toilet again. The street lamp shining in the window meant the bathroom light was unnecessary, but he switched it on anyway. Checked the toilet bowl as he peed. Pale yellow. He washed his hands, thought of that Edward Albee play where the man went into the toilet and started to scream when he saw the blood. 'This is my death warrant!' Even being stuck in a lift would be better than that. Less time to worry.

Back in bed, she was asleep. Her mouth was open, and there was a tiny rattle in her throat every time she breathed. She'd scuppered his chances of getting to Boston but it didn't seem to get between her and a good night's sleep. Her tongue had wagged and his hopes had toppled. Once upon a time she'd put that tongue into his mouth, and one or two other places as well. No wonder the unionists wouldn't shake hands with Gerry Adams: think what other things that hand had done, what other places it had been. But, then, everybody was the same. 'I wiped my arse with this hand half an hour ago. Put it there.' And what about where Warwick and Crompton put theirs? Maybe Crompton would bleed to death and the Rosalind girl would be charged with his murder. Maybe half the guests were bleeding internally at this very minute. Maybe, even though he hadn't touched any of the dessert, he was bleeding internally at this minute...

He tugged the duvet around his backside, let his feet jut over the edge of the bed. His toe was throbbing but he forced his mind to turn to Claire in heaven, looking down, watching everybody, seeing who was upset and who wasn't. Did he really believe that stuff? Most dogs and seagulls deserved eternal life more than most human beings. And yet what about the sun and the moon and the earth circling like dancers, and all the molecules and gravity, and everything, doing their stuff for centuries and thousands, millions of years, keeping every single human being and all matter and all the rest of it going? Then why hadn't he gone to Mammy's funeral, brought flowers to her grave? All from the Big Bang, the scientists claimed. A big bang and that set everything going. Big Shag, they should have said. More creative, Shag. And as he tried to think what that would look like, and imagined his article with the heading 'Cosmic Screw – or God?', he slipped into space over the edge of a cloud bank, fragments of words twisting and falling around him like ticker-tape, Claire's cries for help turning into Angela's whispers of regret that he hadn't spoken up, which in turn became notes on a wild and beautiful flute echoing across the waters of a moonlit Boston harbour.

Chapter 4

CUT OFF

He was wakened by the sound of birds, fluttering and arguing in the ivy beneath the bedroom window. Eyes closed, he felt cautiously with his leg across the bed. She was up. She couldn't bear to lie on in the morning, especially in a bed that contained him. And after the argument over what had been said to the Dean last night, it was a wonder she'd even got into the same bed in the first place. He lay back, felt his morning erection collapse, disappointed again. From the kitchen came the rattle of saucepans and the sound of running water. Maybe that was what he'd do the column on this week. Skip philanthropic banks, write instead about the renewal each day brings when we turn the tap on and make a cup of tea, or take our first bite of a piece of toast. Head it 'Morning Has Broken'. Not that they ever used his headlines.

He must have drifted off because suddenly it was brighter and car doors were slamming, questions being shouted, instructions called. Diarmuid got out of bed, went to the window, gripped the sill and peered out. In his driveway, covering the patches of moss, a white van. 'Handywomen!' it said, in blue letters, on the side. And underneath, in joined-up handwriting, 'Joy and Mairead!!', and underneath that, 'Sisters Go Gardening and Maintaining!!!' It was almost twelve o'clock. Joy and Mairead had arrived.

He showered. His injured toe was still completely white, looking like something undercooked beside the others. He dabbed it with a towel, as he might have dried the body of a sunburnt baby. Never mind Crompton's arse – maybe he should have shown his toe to Mr Tom or Dr Jean last night, stepped out into the garden, slipped off a shoe, got a diagnosis. Or even just gone to his GP. Yes, but what if the doctor took one look, turned pale himself? Yelled exchanges between Joy and Mairead were audible from the garden. Had they brought their dog? They sometimes brought Princess – a bitch with two bitches.

After breakfast he took yesterday's paper and went quietly back upstairs. The toilet seat was chilly at first on the backs of his thighs. He started at the back page ('Mick's Men Face the Final Hurdle') and read to the front ('President Bush to Visit Europe'). That done, he tiptoed back to the bedroom, where he lay on top of the bed and reread an article about how student fees made sense. He must have dozed off then because when he looked at his watch it was five past one. Just over half an hour until the Final Hurdle.

He rose and peeped out the window. In the farthest corner of the garden, the seat of Frances's brown corduroys bobbed up and down as she worked on the organic fruit and vegetable patch. For an instant he remembered their honeymoon, when she'd lain with her face in a pillow, her bum in the air, pretending at his request to be Bo Derek. Better go down and talk to her.

'Hard work,' he said. Silence. 'Those raspberry roots – they must be halfway to Australia by now.' Nothing. 'Don't know why they haven't a good crop. The way you protect them from all that pesticide, they should be the size of footballs by now.' More silence. 'Although I read somewhere, if you were to give them just a little bit of a spray, nothing much, just a touch, they might have a better chance to – fffffhhh.' He sucked in his breath as, without warning, the pain exploded in his toe. Then, as quickly, subsided. What was going on? Was he having a stroke in his leg?

She dug the trowel into the earth. Didn't look at him, didn't speak.

'You know, if we could sit down maybe and work out this Boston thing. Talk it through. Because what I forgot to mention last night was, the Dean said—'

'Aaah, bollocks!' The yell of frustration came from the kitchen. 'I can't possibly do this thing on my own.'

Frances glanced up. 'That's Joy.' Then she crouched forward and stabbed at the soil with renewed viciousness.

There was no point, he realised. She was still mad with him for saying she'd buggered up his chances of study leave. The fact that she had buggered them up made it an even bigger crime for him to have mentioned it. The way her shoulders were raised, the defensive curve of her back told him it'd be some time before she loosened into half-friendliness again.

He turned and walked towards the house, masking his limp as much as possible. Joy was on her hands and knees in the patio, struggling violently with a roll of transparent sheeting. The legs of her jeans, even when turned up several times at the end, accordioned on to her shoes.

'Ah, Joy. Saw you at the funeral – didn't get a chance to chat. Very sad, wasn't it?'

The sunshine caught a hint of ginger stubble as Joy tilted her chin towards him. Her hair was pulled back from her face and held in place by a rubber band. 'The past's the past.'

'Well, that's true...'

'What I'm wondering now is why you let your hothouse sheeting get in this rotten state. Poor way to help your wife develop an organic garden, letting her good sheeting get in a rotten state.'

Then, before Diarmuid could say, 'Yes, but, you see, it's my property, my garden, so I can do what I like with it, so *shut your gob, bitch*!', she had raised the electric blade and started to cut the sheeting along lines marked in black felt-tip. She kept going, shoulders vibrating, as the blade moved down each line in turn, shoulders like the horses Seamus Heaney's da sent down that ploughed field. Diarmuid shielded his ears from the noise and moved past her to the kitchen.

Through the far window he could see Mairead. As usual she was wearing her size-five pink trainers. Her feet were size eight, but she always wore size-five shoes in the belief this made her feet look small. Now, constricted feet apart, electric screwdriver in hand, she positioned a white shutter to the left of the living-room window and groped for a screw in one of the twelve pockets down the side of her biscuit-coloured jeans. Whiiiiine. Diarmuid waited until the noise died down, then gave her a thumbs-up. Hard to tell if her response was a grimace or a smile.

In the corner of the kitchen where neither of them could see him, he poured a gin. Lifted yesterday's newspaper from the floor. Headlines explaining how Mick's men would today be facing the Final Hurdle. At two forty-five. Half an hour to go. He picked up *The Code of the Woosters*, located his turned-in page and sat reading and sipping.

Ten minutes later Joy entered the kitchen, cutting blade in hand. 'I need somebody to help me with the sheeting for the hothouse.'

'What about Mairead?' Diarmuid suggested. 'And Frances is in the garden somewhere—'

Joy's hand came up like a traffic cop's. 'Your wife has her plate overflowing, getting those raspberries established. I'd have thought a partner's job was to help her with her whole organic venture.'

'What about Mairead? *Your* partner. Would she not help you?'

'She can't. Mairead's working at the shutters.' Joy stared at the glass in his hand. 'How long until you're finished there?'

'Hard to say.'

'I'll wait, in that case.' And she sat in the chair by the cooker, frizzy hair flattened against the chair cushion, watching Diarmuid read. 'What's the book?'

He held the cover towards her briefly without speaking.

Joy crossed her legs, right over left, then reversed that, left over right. 'I think I read it one time. Is it any good?'

'It's OK.'

Tap-tap of fingers. 'If it's the same one, it's about butlers and aunts and all sorts of codology.' Cracking of fingers. 'Mairead has dozens of books at home. Keeps them in a built-in bookcase we have at the head of the bed. Probably hundreds, actually. She reads them at night – used to keep me awake for hours. Now, though, I'm so used to it I don't notice. She's probably read more books than you have.'

Diarmuid tried not to think of Joy and Mairead in bed. 'What sort of books?'

'That woman from the north of England – Catherine Cookson. She hardly reads anything but Catherine Cookson.'

There was a pause while Joy cracked her remaining knuckles. Then, 'You don't know how lucky you are.' Diarmuid looked up slowly. 'Having a garden this size. Mairead and me have only a hanky patch out the back. We were thinking of getting an allotment, but then you'd need to be sure you had a market for all the organic stuff you'd produce. Because not that many people are prepared to buy the organic. You'd be surprised the number of people don't see they're being poisoned by supermarkets.'

Diarmuid held in mind an image of pouring a lethal cocktail down Joy's throat, then went back to reading.

'Tell you another way you're lucky. You're lucky that we got here at all – because we nearly didn't. Princess had a runny right eye. Mairead wanted to take her to the vet, but I said we'd leave her at home, take her after instead, since we'd promised Frances we'd do her stuff for her today. That's how we've won our reputation in the business community, you know – particularly the organic business community. We say we'll do something and then we do it. Mairead comes up with the ideas, how the thing will look when it's finished and so on. I'm the one that looks after the business end. But we both stick to our word, which is why we've got a reputation in the gardening and maintenance field.' Pause. 'Although we'd still need to be finished by mid-afternoon, or we could miss the vet. Poor old Princess needs taking to the vet.'

Diarmuid put a fist over one ear.

'I heard somebody got a lump of glass in their food last night. Funny sort of monitoring system your university must have. We monitor all our work down to the last T.'

Diarmuid groaned, tapped his teeth, turned his back, but Joy went on talking, the chair creaking as she adopted yet another position in it. Three minutes later Diarmuid closed the book and stood up. 'OK. What is it you want done?'

On the patio, she produced a three-litre tin marked 'Premier Hothouse Adhesive' and levered off the lid with a screwdriver. 'Now,' she told Diarmuid, 'take this brush and slap it on.'

He worked from one end of the sheet while Joy worked from the other, moving slowly closer, until they both had to step off to allow the middle section to be smeared. He held the edges while she applied the gunge. Her brush plopped down again and again so rapidly that both his hands were spattered. As he stared at them, the phone rang. 'If you'd used your common sense you'd have known to put on a pair of gloves,' Joy told him.

'That's the phone. I'll just—'

But as he approached the kitchen door it stopped. He returned.

'If you were to get cancer then you would have a problem,' Joy told him. 'This stuff can give you cancer, remember. Don't say I didn't tell you.'

When they went to erect the sheeting over the metal framework it was even worse. She got him to climb the ladder and position himself at an intersection. Then she passed the smeared strips up to him and shouted instructions – move back, keep it flat, to the side, more than that – while she scrambled into position at the other side and pulled the sheeting taut. What if the hothouse frame collapsed under him and he hit the ground twelve feet below, still astride a metal strut? What if he lost balance and landed on his neck on the bare earth below? Crack, choke, the end. When he looked to his right he could see Belfast Lough stretched out in afternoon sun, a white super-ferry inching its way up the channel to port. At last, the final sheet in place and tightened, he descended the ladder. Immediately the phone began to ring again.

'Easy knowing a man who's not used to work,' Joy said, half jumping forward to block his way at the bottom of the ladder. 'I don't know why you can't do your share about the place. That's not how Mairead and me operate, I may tell you.'

I'm a grown-up man, Diarmuid thought. My Dean has asked me to go to Boston and deliver a paper at a conference. Six months from now I could be a Reader. Yet I am standing outside my house, being lectured by an overweight lesbian with stumpy legs who has been hired exclusively to fix the hothouse covering in place, then fuck off and take her long, skinny friend with her. Lectured about my relationship with my wife while the phone is ringing and not being answered. As he thought this, the phone stopped.

'That's what makes businesses not work,' Joy said. 'When people won't shoulder responsibility.' She folded the ladder and tucked her tools tightly into a roll of khaki cloth. If she'd been a man, Diarmuid might have gone for a pint with her. Or maybe not.

He waited until she was on her way to the van, then went inside, poured himself a double and limped into the living room. Pointed the remote at the TV. The screen burped, crackled into life. Generous, startlingly clear picture. He should have ignored Frances's complaints about expense and got the twenty-eight inch flat screen years ago.

Oh, thank God, not too late. Twenty minutes gone and still Ireland Nil, Portugal Nil. Crompton's bet could still come off. Although, with the cut-mouth incident, the two of them had probably forgotten about it.

Only right now the Portuguese were running things. Dark-eyed, sweaty heroes, straight from the pages of a Hemingway novel. Or was Hemingway Spain? Whatever, they were heading for the Irish goal like a plague of bloody locusts.

Off camera, Mick McCarthy is doing his thoughtful tactician bit: they've muffled his words but you can still guess them: 'Get it. Fucking. OUT!' But it's a waste of breath, because here's that brilliant bugger Figo coming through the middle, picking up a rebound and LASHING it straight for an empty net – OmiGodomiGod – the upright, the blessed upright saves us... Would the upright be considered on-target for Crompton?

At half-time Diarmuid limped into the kitchen, added a splash of tonic, tasted, added a slug of gin, and was about to hobble back to his chair when the phone rang.

'Do you never answer your phone?' His brother's voice, tight and irritated. 'I've been trying to get you all day.'

'I do when I get a chance.'

'Presumably that means something. Anyway. Can we go over there today, please? I've checked everything but it'd be better for the two of us to do the final sweep together. Can't postpone and postpone. I mean, it's only a house.'

Diarmuid heard the crowd roar as the teams emerged for the second half. Paul never watched football. Had never even played it. 'Can't make it this afternoon, I'm afraid. Frances has me helping with some DIY. I'll ring you, OK? The minute I'm free.'

'When will that be?'

'Next week. Are you around on Tuesday? OK, let's say Monday around four. Or failing that Tuesday. Monday at your place except there's some cock-up, in which case we'll go for Tuesday... Look, I have to go. Talk to you soon.'

Diarmuid hobbled back to his chair, propped his right foot on a cushion on top of the footstool. Set the gin on the floor beside his seat, folded his arms and took stock. Foot: a bit sore but could be worse. Disk: bad situation – Terry as good as said he had it, as good as said that if Diarmuid wanted it, he'd have to... On the screen, a girl with black hair and a tight green T-shirt that stopped two inches above her navel waved at the camera and bounced up and down. Diarmuid thought about sitting at the match beside her. Hugging her when Ireland scored. Or when Portugal scored. Or just hugging her. Or even sitting beside her, smelling her warmth, within touching distance of her jiggling green. *Peep*. Second half kicks off.

Forget the bloody LKF file. Forget it and Mammy's will and missing her funeral, it was no big deal, if you're sick you're sick, let the dead bury their dead, *and* the paper for the Boston conference and 'God Lives!' and all that other stuff. Do your work when you're at work, stop thinking about your work when you come home. You think Figo bothers with football outside work? Look at him – my God, don't back off, *don't back off*. Figo again, sets it up – shoooooots. And it's—

There was a loud hiss of what sounded like boiling water being released from a vat and the screen went from Figo and the green of the turf and hardened, energetic players the colour of teak, to a jumble of sideways stripes. Hissssssss.

Diarmuid grabbed the remote control, jabbed the 1, the 2, the 3. Hissss all the way to ten. Above the hisss the sound of an electric hedge-clipper outside the window. Wielded by Mairead. Could she…?

He stumbled to the door, pain shooting from his toe. It should be better by now, he was *sick* waiting for it to mend. Rammed his hands into his pockets, arm-locked a smile into his face. Strooooolled out towards the corner of the house – no, don't limp. Right, there she was. Keep a safe distance from her – lop your mickey off, given the chance, look at that Bobbitt guy.

The aerial must be somewhere… Here it is, and its lead disappears into the prickly bush growing against the wall. And Mairead, the upper part of her feet bulging out over the edge, is whacking chunks out of the bush with her machine. A bit like cutting hair, except you wouldn't get an aerial in the middle of your hair. Damn it – this was his house. His aerial. Why was he afraid to ask the woman if she had in fact damaged HIS AERIAL?

He approached the bush. Raised a hand in silent greeting to Mairead while the electric trimmer roared on. Touched the aerial lead, which instead of being taut and heading firmly along the wall and into the living room, did a flaccid, useless swing the moment he touched it. Perfectly sheared in two.

'You've. Cut. It,' he mouthed, holding up the sheared end and pointing. 'Fucking cut it!' he wanted to add, but didn't dare. Mairead took her finger from the trigger of her trimmer. 'What did you say?'

'I said the TV aerial. You've – it's been cut.'

She stared at him, forehead creased in concern. 'How did that happen?'

'Your trimmer, maybe. These things can be very sharp.'

'Don't see how that could have been me. I would have noticed if it had been me.'

'Probably because it was in the bush. The wire, I mean. That's the difficulty. Hidden. Maybe if I could shove the two bits...' He rooted in the bush for the rest of the lead, scratching his arms and hands. Mairead stared at him briefly, then went on trimming.

It took about three minutes to locate the other part of the lead. Then another three minutes at least, pulling back the copper-mesh stuff and the outer rubber coat and exposing the core wire, then linking the two sheared bits together. Squeezing them tight with the pliers, blood on the back of his hands where they'd been scratched. All the time pushing aside images of the Portuguese forward line slicing through the Irish defence. Then rushing inside to see what the reception was like. Hiiiisssss. Collapsed shadowy figures. The occasional twisted roar of the crowd. Time to face the facts: the skinny, long-faced tart had ruined the match. Because he was a kind and affable person, because he didn't lay down the law, she'd combined with Joy to ruin the match – *his* match. Two lesbians, or probable lesbians anyway, buggering up the little bit of pleasure he had. My God, Portugal could have put three in the net by now. Not to scream, not to shake his fist under Mairead's big dumb-fuck nose and ask her what she thought she was playing at. Try instead to accept gracefully. In movies, the woman could slap the guy on the face and he'd do nothing. In real life, Diarmuid saw himself scream, pick up a pillow, put it over Mairead's face and sit on it until she stopped squirming and lay lifeless, realising too late what a stupid and selfish thing she'd done.

He switched off the TV. Without the hiss the room was suddenly silent. Tick, tock. The clock on the mantelpiece, below the oil painting of three horses in a thunderstorm. Tick, tock. Close eyes and breathe to the dregs-bottom of your lungs, say ooohhhhhmmmm. And have a large drink of—

His fingers touched something wet on the carpet. He peered over the edge of the chair's arm at his glass, which lay on its side, empty, the carpet around it sogging. Inside, he felt as empty as the beached glass: 'Oh, for Jesus's *sake!*'

At the same moment Frances entered the room. She was carrying a bunch of yellow flowers. He watched her arrange them in a vase and position them on the small table inside the door. What a contrast between the open mouths of the flowers and her tight-stitched lips. Even her breasts looked over-big and torpedoey, like those of the woman who ran the sweet shop opposite the local school. Time was cruel with women, when you thought about it. To start with, it made them soft-mouthed and attractive, driving men mad with desire, then hard and stitched-up, driving men mad with disappointment.

'How many of those have you had?'

Those drinks, she means, only she won't say it. Attack. Best means of defence. 'Have you any idea what bloody-well happened? Have you?'

She moved the two Hummel angels slightly further apart on the mantelpiece. 'Well, I thought you were watching the match. Joy said you were complaining about missing it, when she asked you to hold the hothouse sheeting for a minute. And you said you'd be out to help me with the raspberry beds, but of course you didn't materialise, but I said nothing, I thought, He's maybe contacting his brother to sort out his mother's affairs. Or ringing his colleagues, to see if they're all right after last night. But no. You've a match to watch. That's your idea of using your time –

sitting in a darkened room, on your own, watching other people doing things.'

He felt a stab of pain go up his leg. How could he begin? Where could he begin? Fuck Handywomen. Fuck the sisterhood. *Fuck this.* 'You'd think I was a voyeur or something, the way you talk.' He closed his mouth, breathed slowly through his nose. 'First, your chum Mairead buggered up the TV. In the middle of the game. Or, at least, just past it. In the... fourth sixth of the game. She's supposed to be doing the garden and instead she's buggered up the TV in the fourth sixth of the game. Didn't even say she was sorry.'

Frances stared at him, eyes two grey marbles. Then lifted the cushions on the couch, punched them gently and put them back carefully.

'First she had to take the bloody hedge-cutting machine' – why couldn't he remember what it was called? And should that have been second, not first? – 'and she created an *insane* racket outside the window. I could hardly hear myself think when I was trying to watch the match.'

She produced a yellow cloth and polished the mirror above the fireplace, even though it didn't look like it needed cleaning. 'News to me that watching football required thought. And is that wet on the carpet beside your chair?'

'All right – I could hardly *hear* – OK? I could hardly *hear* the TV. Next thing, pppsssssst, cwwwkkkkk, she's cut the wire. Cut the bloody wire, the aerial to the TV. I mean the wire that goes to the aerial.'

'I would still like to know what that is on the carpet beside your chair.'

'Her and bloody Joy with their bloody van and bloody silly signs – couldn't cut a pack of cards between them, never mind a lawn. 'Dykes cut wires!!', that's what their van should have. 'Buggering Up Games R Us!!!'

'*What. Did. You. Say?*' She stood in front of the fireplace, arms folded, very still.

Speak slowly. Distinctly. 'That is – was – a drink. It got spilled because one minute it was on and the next minute it was hissing and gone. The TV, I mean. All because of that damned pair of... lezzies. I've had bloody well enough.'

There was a silence, during which she looked away from him, out the window; then slowly back with a stare that had deepened its stoniness. 'Well, as it happens, so have I. There was a time, once upon a time, when I'd have put my head down and made excuses for you, said you were always a bit immature, or that you were under stress, any excuse for you. Although, God knows, you're probably the most immature person I've ever met in my life. So I accepted that you could live any way you wanted – drinking evening after evening, watching TV, wanting to get away from me to Boston, *cut off*. I even accepted your evaluation of me, which was worse, that I could do nothing on my own. And since then I've been struggling to get this organic-produce idea going. I've accepted that I'm never going to get any help from you. But I'm not going to accept verbal abuse. Oh, no. I've learnt better about that kind of thing. That's over.'

'Look – it's not the bloody Holocaust or anything, Frances. All I said was—'

'Bogman, stone-age talk – I'm not going to accept that. Because I'm tired listening to it, so now you listen to me. Either you make it clear you're prepared to accept categorically that you owe them an apology – an apology each, two apologies – or that's that, as far as I'm concerned.'

'That's that? What does that mean, that's that?'

'He doesn't understand the Queen's English now. Well, start learning fast, mister. Because you've just given me the – hiss, hiss – straw that bu-bu-broke – the camel's – baaaaccckkk.' The last word she wailed, leaving it floating behind her as she slammed out the door and ran up the stairs. Like the Dean's daughter, except... He could hear her struggling not to cry, her breath coming out in suppressed coughs.

He sat looking at the grey screen sizzling like an electronic fry. Or scrambled eggs. Was that why they talked about scrambling the data? Or was that something to do with wartime pilots? The minute he'd seen her in the garden, he'd known she was still seething from last night. After eleven years of marriage you can smell it. Like two electric wires, live but separated. They come together and...kah-BOOM. 'Contact,' he said softly, and sighed.

Of course, Joy and Mairead would have got her up to it. Feminist bastards who impinge on people's lives, poison: first they drip-drop this phrase, and then that slogan and then another, and in no time the woman has a whole vocabulary, a whole grammar, and is being twisted and manipulated out of all her femininity, and for what? So that all the happiness that she *did* have and didn't know it, all that's polluted into some sort of ball-slicing, *dick-amputating* agenda. He tried to think of Frances and himself in the days before Mairead and Joy had appeared, but he couldn't remember what it was like.

And now they were trying to pull Frances into their bloody dyke net. Sticking fingers and God knows what up each other's God knows where. Was the world gone mad? And then that thing about Crompton and Warwick snogging in the kitchen. And then the glass in the food – that girl hadn't looked right in the head from the start, the way she said, 'Have a drink,' and slouched off. Diarmuid drew his hand across his eyes, pinched the bridge of his nose and tried not to think about Frances on a bed with the two women, all three naked, their knees apart, their cheeks hot, giggling and groaning in turn.

The door opened and Frances entered, followed by the gardeners. All three fully clothed. Joy was wearing her cutting-up gloves and Mairead was holding the electric trimmer.

'I've explained to Joy and Mairead what occurred.' Diarmuid could tell from the way Frances spoke that she'd memorised what she was saying. 'And because they're grounded, generous people, they've agreed to overlook the matter. I'm just flabbergasted that people could be so forgiving, but they're probably more in touch with themselves than I am.'

There was silence. Joy took off her gloves, stood staring at Diarmuid, hands on hips. Mairead, standing on the other side of

Frances, touched the trimmer blade with the fingertips of her right hand.

'Touching that thing – dangerous,' Diarmuid said.

'Touching what?' Joy demanded, scratching her frizz of hair as she spoke. 'What're you talking about, touching that thing?'

Diarmuid felt a shiver move down the left side of his chest, across his belt and down his right leg. It must be a mini-stroke. 'I was talking to Mairead. Your friend Mairead. Suggesting that she – Mairead – not mess with the – the – the thing she has in her hand. Accidents do happen. Best safe than sorry.'

'Better,' Joy said 'Better two, best more than two – that's what I was taught at school.' She looked at Frances, then Mairead, then back at Diarmuid again, and smiled. 'So it should be "Better safe than sorry." I'm surprised someone who teaches in a university didn't know that.' She stood at an angle to Diarmuid, arms folded, right foot tapping noiselessly.

Diarmuid could hear heavy breathing and it seemed to be coming from inside his nose. 'Well, then.' He heard his voice come crackling out with a jagged edge. 'Do your eyebrows with it if you like. Trim your nails with it, curl your hair. But don't say I didn't warn you when you get electrocuted.'

'It wasn't a warning we came for.' Joy stroked the back of one glove with the palm of the other. 'It was to make a proposal.'

Diarmuid glanced quickly at Frances. For an instant, behind her red-rimmed eyes, he thought he spotted – what? An appeal, maybe? To be a man, to assert himself, look after her.

'Not a marriage proposal, I hope. I'm afraid I'm already spoken for.' He smiled broadly at Frances, who didn't respond.

Joy stroked her chin. 'No, we were thinking of your mother's house. That house belonging to your late mother. Grand big house, basically. We passed it last week, Mairead and me, so we stopped and had a peek in the window. It's been let go to unbelievable rack and ruin, you know. Which really is a shame. A house like that could be made very liveable. Mairead and I told Frances and then we did a quick costing and – roughly speaking, mind, but thereabouts – we're talking under three thousand, maybe less. We could have exterior and interior shipshape again inside what? Five, six weeks? Seven at outside. Paint, windows, plastering, the lot. Leaving you with an eminently rentable property.'

'We'd see it as a challenge,' Mairead said. She rose briefly on to her toes, then down again, as if to ease the pain of her feet's constriction in the tiny trainers. 'That's basically what we'd see a job like that as. Never done as big a job as that before, you see. And it'd really be good with a house like that, because it has character and what-not. And it gets the light in the evening, with a garden at the back to pick up the shadows.'

'I told them you might want to think about it before you committed yourself,' Frances said. She looked at her husband, anxious, waiting for his answer. Joy turned up one leg of her jeans, Mairead touched each blade of her hedge-cutter with the tip of her finger. Watching him. Waiting for his response.

'That's a tempting offer.' Diarmuid's voice was soft and affectionate. 'A very tempting offer, girls.' 'Girls'. That was good. 'Or, at least, it would be, if I was the kind of person who didn't care what became of his mother's house. But, you see, I do care about her house, actually her home, and what was my home at one time. And I have by now missed' – he looked at his wristwatch – 'the first one third of the second half of the game, maybe even part of the fifth sixth of it. That's because my aerial, that I paid for and had installed, cost fifty-five pounds plus VAT, was sliced in two by that instrument of destruction you hold in your hands. Yes, yes, take your word for it, it was an accident, but it still deprived me of the game. So no, no, *no thanks,* I'm not really keen on having people go into my mother's house and tart it up and make it look pinky and brothelly, because what I'm looking for is maybe a *bit more quiet* to be exercised around this place. If you know what quiet is. So I can sit with a small drink for a little while, reading my book, in my own bloody living room, with nobody bothering me, *if that's all right.* Because, you see, I have a sore foot – a *damned* sore foot – I'm tired, and I'd like a little peace in *my house.* If that's all right. So, if it's not asking too much, before something else gets vandalised, why don't the two of you pack your electronic kit and throw it in the back of your van with the bone-brain slogans on the side of it and you know, piss off home to hell out of here?'

Joy tapped her right foot, then changed her weight to the other leg and tapped the left one. 'Some things never change. The eternal male.'

'Oh, for God's sake – *shut to fuck up, you*!'

He half shouted the final five words over his shoulder as he pounded up the stairs to the bedroom.

It was a pointless thing to do, because when he got there he had nowhere to sit and relax, any more than in a hotel bedroom. And the words couldn't be taken back. Because it was too late now.

He lay on the bed, gripping a copy of *The Economist*, trying to read. Below, he could hear a murmured, intense conversation between Joy, Mairead and his wife. They didn't sound as if they were talking about things. They sounded as if they were talking about people. About him, to be exact. It seemed maybe he'd misinterpreted Frances's look – she'd have preferred if he had agreed, accepted the offer, hadn't been such a real man. On the dressing-table the photograph of Frances as a girl, standing at the gate of her house, looked at him. Seventeen, with her thick brown hair curling over her shoulders and around her face, her mouth open as if she was saying something to the person photographing her. Why did things never work out?

Suddenly, the jangle sending a jolt through his body, the phone on the bedside table rang.

'Hello? Who's there?'

'Ah. Hello. I was looking for Dr Dermot Monaghan...'

'Your search has ended, my good man. Except it's Diarmuid.' It seemed a wonderful little success, that the call should have been for him and that he should have got to it before Frances or, worse still, either of the harpies below could intercept it, and that he should have had such a witty thing to say when he did speak. Even as he thought of it, there was a click from the downstairs extension.

'Hell – *lo*? Hello, can I *help* you?' Frances's voice sounded strained.

'It's… Frances, I've got it. OK? Get off the line, would you? Sorry about this. Frances, I said I've *got* it so get *off* the *line*.' Sounded a bit bossy. 'Get OFF the LINE' – but it was a business call and he did need to. There was a click and the echo was gone from the call. 'Right, that's that,' Diarmuid said. 'Can I help you?'

There was a nervous laugh. 'Jonathan Wilmslow, BBC in Belfast, here, Dr Monaghan. I just wondered what were your initial thoughts for our live discussion in, what is it? A week or so from now.'

'Pre-planning,' Diarmuid said. 'Except there's many a slip 'twixt pen and tongue and wee timorous programmie.'

Jonathan laughed again. 'Well, indeed. Absolutely. Only not too timorous, I hope. I just wondered if there was a particular line you were thinking of taking? I mean—'

'Least resistance. That's the line I'll be taking. Experience has taught me that's usually best. In the end. Although I may also be taking a week in the US in November as well. To escape the hell of tedious teaching. And attend a conference, of course. That's why I'm going to the States.' There was silence from the other end. 'Of A,' Diarmuid added. 'US of A.'

'Indeed. USA. Super. Um…maybe if I call you back in a day or two, Dr Monaghan, we'll both have had time to develop these initial, you know, exchanges into something more um, expanded, when there's space to do so and we're not, eh, distracted. All right?'

'Most good ideas only need three minutes – read that somewhere.' Diarmuid listened to his own voice speaking, was struck by how pleasant and intelligent it sounded. 'May not apply to every idea, of course – for example, Einstein's theory of relativity – but seventy-five per cent would be not bad, if you ask me. That's why the *Reader's Digest* does so well. Like a telescope

– it can be made big or small, whichever way you like it best. As the bishop said.'

That last bit sounded slightly risqué – hadn't meant it to be.

'That's fine.' Jonathan didn't seem to have noticed the rudeness. Phew. 'Thursday morning I'll call – mid-morning probably.'

'Great – I'm all a-tremble.'

Jonathan laughed again when Diarmuid said that, then hung up.

Breathe deep. Put down the mag, take long, slow breaths, like the Tranquillity website said. Let the breathing in and out, the life coming and leaving your body – only temporary, don't panic. Let that tide drown the anxieties, leave the body filled with carbon dioxide, or was it monoxide? No, that was when you tried to kill yourself in a garage.

Maybe he fell asleep again or had just begun to think of something else, but next minute Frances was in the bedroom, tugging open drawers, piling underwear and skirts and blouses into a suitcase open on the floor, making an awful racket. His mouth felt dry and his big toe felt as if someone had pushed a sliver of bamboo under the nail and ignited it.

'What are you doing? Listen, I'm not feeling that well... And did you know I had a phone call? That was the BBC, arranging with me about my talk. I need—'

She stopped and stood looking at him, arms folded, head to one side. '*You* need? *You*'re not feeling well, *you* keep thinking about things? No, let's try something different: *I* need. Me. *I* need someone who's willing to support me in my business. *I* need someone who doesn't think of themselves all the time. I need someone who's half grown-up. But, above all, what I feel a need for right now, *I* feel a need not to talk to you. *So shut up, please!*' She went on packing.

Diarmuid thought of telling her that he'd been going to say, 'I need to think about this offer the Dean has made to me. Would I consider giving the key – yes, *key paper* at this conference coming up in Boston. Is that grown-up enough for you? I need to

think about this offer. And I need to not think about my mother.'
But he didn't. Because all he could think about was this woman
who was his wife, she hadn't asked about what it was the Dean
had offered *after she'd buggered up his leave of absence,* she
hadn't asked about his sore foot either, granted he hadn't told
her about it but a sensitive person would surely have noticed by
now, and it ached terribly and he needed a drink of something
and he generally felt like shite, and why couldn't somebody nice
share his dreams and stay in bed with him in the morning, and
when you thought about it, wasn't life from start to finish one
big disappointing scab on a rat's arse, and what was the point of
it all anyway?

Chapter 5

DISK LOCATION

Joy and Mairead didn't come inside again: they waited in the white van until Frances came out carrying her suitcase. Then Mairead jumped out of the passenger seat, opened the back door, and swung the case in alongside the lawnmower, the electric trimmer and the tub of stuff that gave you cancer. Diarmuid sat in the living room, his foot propped up on the window-ledge, watching the van disappear in a trail of light blue smoke.

She had left him. Upstairs the hot tank gurgled. In the back garden a thrush, excited by the digging Frances had done, was yelling its head off. On the TV, nothing, because Mairead had buggered it up. Frances had left and life wobbled on.

His left foot felt bloated and when he leant his weight on it, pain shot up as far as his knee. He limped to the kitchen and poured another drink. He really should see a doctor. But then again these things often fixed themselves. Wait and see if there was an improvement during the time it took him to have a drink or two. And if a man didn't need a drink or two when his wife had left him with two lesbians – no, not with, *for, for* two lesbians – when did he?

Diarmuid stopped, put down the glass, pinched his lip. Hold on, *ho-o-old* on, Tonto. Maybe this was a time for action, not drinking. He thought about the different worries that needed attention. The conference paper in Boston – have to wait for the Dean to confirm it was going to happen. Mammy's house – there'd have to be a showdown with Paul pretty soon, high noon, eyes narrowed against the glare, slap leather, yuh ornery varmint... Which reminded him of Frances. Frances, Joy and Mairead and the way they'd sounded, stamping out of the house. He heard himself start to laugh, listened in a half-detached way as his voice filled the room, shouted out the ah-ha-*HA* pattern again and again. 'No good laughing over split-the-scene lesbians,' he gasped. Which left, after the laughing had faded... Of course. The LKF file.

If he was going to recover it, liberate it, OK, OK, OK, steal it, there was no question of having a drink, let alone two or three. Now that the IRA had packed it in, the cops were everywhere with their breathalysers; and if they didn't ambush you, some bugger in the university would smell the booze on your breath and start telling people how he came on you wandering around campus three-quarters-plastered. He'd have to wait an hour at least – and without a drink. But it'd be worth it.

Provided, that is, his foot held up. He tested it on the kitchen floor. Maybe the drink was working. Maybe he should have some more and it would feel even better? On second thoughts, no, don't be stupid. Sober up. Rest for a while. And sober up.

He went into the kitchen and made a big mug of black coffee, took it to the living room and lay on the sofa. What a contrast there had been between the thickness of Angela's husband's neck and the thinness of her arms in the half-light outside the upstairs toilet and the wideness of her eyes as she spoke to him. Her husband must have trapped her into marriage – got her drunk, got her pregnant, married her. Bastard.

At eight o'clock Diarmuid went to the kitchen again, got more black coffee and an organic rice-cake with lots of organic butter and a big spoonful of organic honey spread over the pitted surface. It tasted so light it was like chewing air. Then he went upstairs and checked his email. Nothing except 'Gain Length and Mass Fast' and 'Get It Up'. Gain Length showed a doctor in a white coat checking his clipboard and said it was doctor approved; Get It Up showed a couple laughing in bed and promised the World's First Penis Enlargement Patch would add three plus inches today.

In the living room he sat at the piano and played 'Imagine', swaying his body the way he'd seen Phil Coulter do on TV. He'd played for two American presidents, Coulter. What was the reason they gave for Coulter's music always playing on Aer Lingus planes before take-off? Ah, yes. After you'd listened to that for ten minutes, you wouldn't care if the plane crashed or not. Ha-ha-ha, not bad. He closed the piano lid and sat looking at the damp stain on the wall, then out the window. Odd that Frances laid such emphasis on the garden and didn't seem to care an awful lot what the inside of the house was like, whereas Uncle Dan was the other way round – continual plans for redos of kitchen and bedrooms and study, but the garden left a jungle of wild grass and cat shite. Too busy checking his investments on the Internet to care what was happening outside. Investing and sneezing. Although it was Carmel, not Dan, that was behind the push for renovation indoors. Left to himself, Uncle Dan would have had inside the house a jungle as well, asking nothing more than a clear path to his computer and a hanky to catch his flying snot.

He went upstairs again and sat at the computer, hammered his knees with his fists as he tried to think of an opening sentence for the column. 'Every day is a gift, because even when we wake up and it's raining, we should thank God'? Too long. 'Ever watch a child greet a new day?' A bit better. He began to type, trying not to think how bad he felt about the words appearing on the page. 'Every day is a gift from God, full of beauty and promise. Consider His handiwork – the trees, the grass, the flowers – His Blood upon the rose, as the great Irish poet and patriot Joseph Mary Plunkett put it.'

He sat back and scratched his balls. Tapped his index finger against his lips. Tried to fart. A small peeping one. *Un pet Jesuit.*

Did Jesuits fart more than other religious orders? Or just French Jesuits?

'But in some parts of the world the Maker's handiwork is being ignored. Worse still, we're defacing it. Sacrilege is being committed.' Go on, shove in a comparison. 'It's as if the sponge of vinegar that was pushed into the face of the dying Christ was being shoved again into the beauty and awesome power of His creation, as immeasurable tracts of rainforest are mutilated and the ozone layer thickened.' Or was it thinned? And if they couldn't measure the rainforest, how did they know it was shrinking? 'Like a mindless child, Man is pulling God's creation to destruction and sealing his own fate as he does so, like a schoolboy pulling the legs off a spider.' Something wrong with that last bit. Too many 'likes', maybe.

He reread what he'd written, drew back his lips until they left his clenched teeth exposed, then whispered, 'You fucking prostitute!' That was what it felt like, grinding this garbage out every week for twenty-five quid, saying things he only half, quarter believed. But the money was such a comfort when it came, and there was something sad and moving about the letters people sometimes sent to him, on blue-lined notepaper, in old-fashioned writing: 'Dear Mr Monaghan, I am in my 70s now and a fan of your column in *St Jude's Almanac*, I wouldn't miss it.' 'Diarmuid *a chara*, My mother is an invalid and I care for her, so I don't get much opportunity to get out and socialise much, and your column is a ray of...' But it was still prostitution, and he felt the way the girls in the movies said they felt after being raped – scrub the prints from his fingers, scrub his hands down to a stump, end this pious claptrap, these weekly candyfloss lies that he maybe never *had* believed but definitely didn't believe now.

'There is a lesson in all this, if we have but the wisdom to receive it,' he typed, and kept typing, face contorted, for another ten minutes. Eight hundred and seventy-four, the word count said. Near enough. He read it over again, added a final three lines: '"Praise for the sweetness/Of the wet garden," the hymn tells us. What timeless wisdom! Let's stop complaining about the dark clouds that hang over our selfish lives and praise God for the part those clouds play in the daily refreshment of our earth.' Did the word 'refreshment' make sense there? Was that not ice-cream and sweets and popcorn?

At twenty-five past eight he gargled with mouthwash twice, put on his trainers (making sure to tie the right one loosely, foot feeling not too bad), his coat and the New York Yankees baseball cap, then went out to the car.

As usual there was no light at the big grey house that contained the office of *St Jude's Almanac*. He rang the bell, listened to it jangling like a lost leper in the darkness beyond the front door.

Finally Brother Ambrose appeared, the front of his soutane flecked with what looked like gravy drops, a cigarette in his right hand. 'Ah, good man. *Semper fidelis Josephus.*' He took the two sides of A4 and glanced at them. 'Mm – hmm – yes... Oh, by God... Powerful stuff, Diarmuid. Top-notch as always.'

'You're a powerful flatterer, Brother Ambrose.'

'Not one bit of me, not a smidgen of an inch of me.' He reached with his free hand and gripped Diarmuid's arm. 'Do you know there are people buy the *Almanac* just to read your column? That's the God's truth. There are people out there, and I'll tell you, their eternal salvation hangs on what you write. Now. And I wouldn't be exaggerating either, I would not, for to say that the circulation of the magazine – the *survival* of the magazine, for feck's sake – is largely in your hands. Not solely, of course, for we are a team, but in considerable measure. So now. Never underestimate the importance of what you're doing, Diarmuid – d'you hear me? Good man. *Ad majorem Dei gloriam.*' He passed Diarmuid an envelope containing the twenty-five pounds, gave a wave through a cloud of smoke, and closed the door.

There was a sizeable crowd of people coming and going to the university sports centre, especially since it was, what? A quarter to nine at night. Diarmuid stopped some ten yards from the entrance to the staff car park, watched the Dean's 4x4 reverse its way out. He waited, face averted, as the stupid fat-wheeled truck with the cow-catcher on the front swung past, then drove in and took a space as far from the Dean's reserved bay as he could get.

Lock the car and walk briskly, look as if you are going to do something *official*. Head down, hands in pockets, he almost collided with Warwick at the entrance to the tunnel.

'You're either coming from robbing a bank or are on your way to an erotic assignation. I've seen your wife, so my bet is you're fresh from robbery with violence.' He was wearing a purple zipped jacket and a red tie, the knot obscured by his ginger beard. 'Correct?'

Diarmuid looked down at the teeth pushing clear of the wet mouth. 'Collecting assignments from my office, actually... Any word on Crompton? That really was a terrible affair at the Dean's.'

'He's on antibiotics and nothing but liquids for the next week. Doctor's orders. It's a blessing in disguise, actually – he's so preoccupied with his stomach or maybe his mouth, he can't decide which, he's stopped bleating about his rectal bleeding.'

'Did he get the results of his X-ray?'

'Piles, apparently. He was bitterly disappointed.'

'That he didn't have cancer? Come on – for God's sake.'

'Well, you see, he thought the effort he had put into *worrying* about cancer had rather *earned* him something serious. I did what I could to highlight the absence of link between worrying about something and it happening. "Shit happens," I said to him. "That's all there is to it. No cause and effect. The trick is, not to be in the wrong place at the wrong time." Anyway, we – which in effect means I, since Crompton finds concentration beyond five minutes difficult – I am putting together a legal case, two legal cases, actually. The glass thing and the Dean's wife's defamation-of-character thing.'

'She defamed him?'

'Didn't you hear her? In front of witnesses she declared myself and Crompton to be a pair of queers who had assaulted her daughter.'

'So is that what you're in here about?'

'Well, no, actually. My computer at home is down so I'm checking the state of some shares. A fatherly piece of advice: avoid shares. Property is where it's at. Shock-proof investment.'

'Yes. Although with so much homelessness around, I think I'd feel guilty doing that. Being a landlord.' Shut up, Diarmuid told himself. Skip the social analysis and *let him get on.*

'They do these things so much better in South America – round the bastards up every six months and shoot them. The homeless, I mean, not the landlords. Speaking of bastards, did the Dean's wife contact you? Apparently she was ringing round to see if anyone knew the whereabouts of her missing phone. Happy to say I didn't hear from her so mum's the word on our little kitchen misadventure.' Warwick looked at his watch. 'Must dash – told Crompton I'd pick up *Wall Street* from the video shop.'

'Do you really think you can win those cases? Against the university?'

'We can but try, with the breastplate of righteousness in place. Shoulder to shoulder, as it turns out, with Mr Tom's lovely wife – the late DH's sister. She's going after the university too, over its faulty lift. She won't win, alas, because the confounded lift was serviced only three months before it stuck and they've almost certainly got a record of it. Shame, really. But you have to admire her spunk.'

Diarmuid hurried on, feeling as he usually did after a conversation with Warwick, confused. The man seemed to have no moral compass of any kind, and yet there was something almost thrilling about the way he talked.

The service tunnel grew dimmer as he moved further into it, keeping carefully on the thin strip of footpath. Place of fluttering pigeons, overhead pipes, lorry fumes, the occasional cat scampering into the shadows. This was the university's gut into which nourishment flowed each day and from which no-longer-needed materials were expelled. Since last year, all academic staff below the rank of professor were required to enter their offices by way of the tunnel – something to do with personnel congestion, the email had said. Professors and higher ranks continued to have access by the main entrance. In a way, that was what Diarmuid liked most about the tunnel – no deans, no chief administrators, no Physical Resources *Oberführers*. Approaching the basement door to Block A he felt an affinity with the pigeons and cats that cooed and miaowed down there, hiding away from the information-grubbers above.

Pull open the door to the block. The sound of a child yelling from a distant corridor. Better not take the lift – might meet someone else, give them the chance to ask where you're going. Not that he had anything to hide – or, at least, not much. Only a devouring need to get his hands on what belonged to him by right.

He climbed the concrete stairs until he stood at the entrance to the eighth floor. No sound. Ease open the door, slip inside, let it sigh closed behind. Total darkness now, apart from the faint glow above the EXIT sign. He should put on the light – there was a switch along the wall here somewhere. Normally it was in the down position, but tonight it wasn't. That meant someone had turned off the lights at the other end. Slowly, carefully, hands in front of him, he moved down the corridor.

It felt as if the air in front of him and all around had substance – like a black soup that wasn't wet, didn't make contact with his body, but still drowned him. In the distance a child's feet clattering downstairs, jumping the last few. What was it Pascal had said about faith? 'A leap in the dark.' Suck your breath away, just thinking about doing that.

A new sound: from a few floors lower down, men's voices. Shouted instructions, or was it goodbyes? Now the voices had stopped, been replaced by an individual's footsteps. Coming steadily up the stairs at the other end of the corridor. One of the security guards, doing a walk around. Well, what about it? Oh, nothing. Just that he was standing halfway up a corridor with no light on, at nine o'clock at night, so what the hell was he doing that for, and how would he look when the guard put the light on and saw a stupid buck rabbit with gawking eyes, blinking and blinded, blabbering excuses? Get out of here quick. *Anywhere.*

He turned, shuffled down the corridor, his right foot big and awkward, feeling the wall with his hand for an office door. Got one. The door-handle, where the hell was the... OK, got it. Turn it, *turn it.* He tried, but it wouldn't budge. Locked. Damn. Key in his pocket would open it probably, but there wasn't time for that now. Hurry, hurry, toilets at the end of the corridor, no lock on their door, *hurry.*

Behind him he could hear the outer door opening at the top of the stairs. Ten more paces would take the security man to the inner door... Gritting his teeth, Diarmuid sprinted the last few metres, feeling with his trailing right hand for the metal rectangle on the outer door of the toilets. There it was, stop, stop. Inside quick. Switch off the light at the outer door. Now get a cubicle – where are the cubicles, damn and blast them? Jesus the pain, the knee on his good leg had hit something... At last he stumbled inside one, rammed the bolt across, crouched on the toilet seat so his feet didn't show at the bottom and his head didn't show at the top, and tried to hold his breath.

In the dark the cistern hissed. No sound from outside. Had the security man given up, gone off? Or was he crouched outside the toilet, waiting for Diarmuid to give himself away? No, here he was. Fat slapping footsteps on the corridor, jangling keys, whistling 'Return to Sorrento'. Near the toilet door the whistling and the footsteps stopped. Silence. A long, tapering fart, and the footsteps and whistling resumed, mixed in with humming, now heading down the stairs, slowly, leaving stale air threading through the metal banisters at the top.

Better sit tight. Diarmuid lowered himself carefully on to the toilet seat, slipped off his right shoe. The tiled floor felt cool through his sock. Nine twenty on his watch. Take ten minutes, give the whistler time to find another place for gas release.

Speaking of which: Diarmuid loosened his belt, unzipped his trousers, settled on the plastic seat.

Funny how people were programmed to do the same thing every day. Talk, eat, shite, sleep. Caught in a cycle out of which there was no escaping. Think more about these things when you got to Uncle Dan's age, probably. Wake at night, stare into the darkness at the crack in the ceiling, wonder if it would be here, now, tonight. Or blot it out with thoughts of money in the bank and shares and colour-coordinated home improvement. Or God. To cease upon the midnight with no pain. Seventy-three, seventy-four, the average man copped it If each decade was a day of the week, he was now approaching midnight on Thursday. Above him, the cistern gave a brief gasp. Although ten years, thirty years, forty years – the difference not worth noticing. 'He died in 1914/ He died in 1934' – a decade or two was nothing, certainly when you looked back. Or someone *else* looked back. The thing was, what lay ahead? After your death day. Only two questions worth asking: what use am I making of this tiny life of mine, and what happens to me when it ends?

God: What use did you make of your tiny life, Diarmuid Monaghan?

DM: During most of my tiny life I was a university lecturer in education.

God: Which involved?

DM: Which involved giving lectures about education, visiting schools, pretending to know what I was talking and writing and reading about.

God: Why on earth did you choose such a pointless existence?

DM: No idea. Bad companions, maybe.

You'd think, with life being such a disappointing, third-division product, dying would be a minor inconvenience. But no. People would do anything rather than think about the groan or twitch or scream that would mark their end. Except for people like Brother Ambrose – him and the other Brothers in the house – oldish, old and very old men, bent and wheezing, on the last lap to eternal reward. Death for them would be the thing that made sense of their lives. Dying – would the pain be worse than a toothache? Would you come out of a blackness like this? Run down a tunnel towards the people you'd known and loved? Or maybe just go out like a lightbulb or a bubble – ping!

Give it two more minutes, then try Herself's office. Could be the authorities had set the whole thing up, an elaborate sting. Some fill-in person sitting there behind the desk, snap their fingers, two RUC baboons leap from behind a door, throw you on the floor, clip the cuffs on behind your back. Gotcha, you thieving Fenian bastard.

Suddenly, with no warning, his bowels began to empty. The waste left his body in a nose-tweaking stream, splash splash splash – no wind, just steady emptying. Until finally it ended, leaving him bent forward, panting. That was the second time this month. Maybe there was something wrong in there, worse than his foot. Him and Crompton, terminal twins. And what about the knee? No, knee OK. He felt for the roller. Oh my God. No. Toilet. Paper. Nothing but the cardboard core. Check in his wallet – all those useless receipts, bound to be some of those he could use. He felt in the dark for slips of paper... Stopped. He couldn't do that. He'd kill himself if he wiped his arse with a tenner.

Holding his trousers around his knees, he undid the lock and shuffled into the adjoining cubicle. Felt carefully... Oh, thank-thankthankyou, God. A full roll on top of the cistern. He waddled back, locked the cubicle door behind him again. The ease, the heart-filling, hole-plugging handfuls of it. In where was it? Indonesia, China, they used the hand – *only the hand*. And then wiped the hand, presumably. Washed it. Scrubbed it. But still there'd be gunk and God knows what under the nails, wouldn't there? That time he'd seen those Chinese men outside the BBC in Belfast – clearing their throats and spitting on the pavement – they didn't look as if they'd bother much with antiseptic soap.

Should he flush it? Risky. But if he left it they could trace his DNA. He pulled the handle, listened to the Niagara roar crashing around in the pipes. Why couldn't they make them silent like cars – cars had been noisy once. He opened the door of the cubicle with great care to make up for the splashing, rattling racket. Then felt his way in the darkness to the washbasin and ran the tap quietly, eased the soap-dispenser forward and back, the foam thickening between his fingers and palms.

He had rinsed his hands and was about to tug the roller towel when behind him the door opened. He stood frozen, holding his breath, waiting for the light to click on. Now. All right then – *now*. In that case, definitely NOW… But it didn't. The light stayed off. Instead, through the darkness, a sound. '*Mmmmmnnnnhhhhh!*' Like someone with masking tape over their mouths trying to shout, or someone being smothered. Or someone having an orgasm. Then the door banged shut and footsteps hurried away down the stairs.

Hands dripping, heart thudding, Diarmuid shuffled back into the cubicle, locked the door carefully, crouched on top of the toilet seat. *Mnnnnhhhh*. The cattle in the field he passed on the way home from the cinema as a child used to make that noise. *Mmmmmnnnnhhhhh*. Going up the scale at the end, on the *nnnhhhhhh*. But you couldn't have a cow on the eighth floor.

Ten minutes later, hands dried on toilet paper, he tiptoed out of the cubicle. Eased open the outer door. No sound, corridor light on. *Run*. But where? To Claire's room, of course, at the top of the corridor. The whole purpose in coming here was to resolve the disk thing: there'd be no point *at all* in funking it again. Face your fear. Get into the office, close the door, get the disk, open the door, get fucking out. Simple.

Ribs sticky with sweat, he took out his office-door key and shoved it into the lock of Claire's door. One size fits all. It opened. Lock the door from the inside and sit for a minute until the throbbing in the foot died down and the heart stopped thumping. OK, now switch on the light. *Eaaaasy*.

The office wasn't much different from the last time he'd been here. No Claire, of course, and no bastard Terry either. At least... Diarmuid stood with his ear to the door of Terry's office next door. No sound. He eased it open. Nobody. Semi-darkness. Fan off, computer off, new zip drive gleaming on mouse mat. He locked the door from the inside and surveyed what had been Claire's room. The spotless, organised desk. The Maori warrior figurine on the filing cabinet. The Icarus painting near the window. What would happen to these things now she was gone? Maybe her sister would collect them, arrange them over her fireplace, on her mantelpiece... But no time to dawdle. The disk, where was the disk? Right there, in the sideways fanny. He hurried over, pressed eject, and out it popped.

Only it wasn't his disk. It was a disk that said 'First Year Course Lists and Details' in Claire's neat handwriting. His disk wasn't on her desk either. Or in the first drawer at the top. Or the second, or third, or bottom. Or on any of the bookshelves, or between the pages of a book... In fact, the fucking thing. Was. Gone.

Except... He lay on the floor, peered with one cheek against the rough blue and green splashed carpet, under the desk, under the bookcase, behind the computer where Claire had peered that night. Everywhere. No trace of it. He lifted two empty chalk boxes, a tin container that had once held a bottle of Jameson's whiskey, a transparent plastic bowl. He lifted everything that could be lifted and a few more that shouldn't have been, but it changed nothing. *The bastarding LKF disk wasn't there.*

The police. They'd come in, taken it down to the police station and marked it 'Exhibit A'. Evidence of what? What crime had he committed? Don't worry about that, sir, we'll think of something.

Terry. The slopy-shouldered bastard had spotted it and lifted it when the cops weren't around. Read every entry, cut and pasted all the juicy bits into one place. At this minute he was at home, or in Hazel's apartment, getting her to help him prepare a ransom note.

Or maybe the Dean had it. He'd been concerned to salvage as much of Claire's materials as possible, to pass to Dr Fr David. He'd come on the disk and pocketed it, forgotten to check what was in it. But he would eventually, maybe was doing so at this very minute.

Diarmuid eased a trainer off and cuddled his sore toe, felt his fingers throb in time to his pounding heart. What had he been thinking of, imagining it'd just be a matter of collecting the disk and that'd be the end of it? People like him didn't get off as lightly as that, not a chance – the forces ranged against him had him in their sights.

He slipped the trainer back on, tied with the loosest of knots, and had his hand on the doorknob, about to leave, when he glanced back and seemed, for a moment, to see Claire behind the desk, smiling, earrings wobbling, and... Oh my God! There it was. On the window-sill, half blending into the blackness of the blind. Was it – surely it wasn't *his* disk? He moved cautiously across the room, telling himself not to hurry, not to grab it too quickly, don't let it see you're full of hope – if it notices that's your game it'll trip you up.

He lifted the disk from the window-sill. Turned it over.

It was his.

At the same moment that his brain took in the fact that he'd found it, he heard the noise of the handle in the door to Terry's office being turned, then the noise of the door being pushed. Locked. While the noise of a key being inserted was still happening, Diarmuid slipped the disk into his jacket pocket and leant forward, pretending to read a document on Claire's desk. When, a half-second later, the door to Terry's office opened and Hazel stood staring at him, Diarmuid was able to look up, surprised. She was wearing a cream polo-necked sweater and a black skirt.

'Oh, my God.' She took a step back, touching her breastbone with three fingers. 'Didn't know there was anybody here.'

'Well, I don't usually work this late, but Claire had some international contacts documents stored here and I really do need them for a meeting next week, so...' He raised his eyebrows, felt pleased with how lazy his voice sounded. 'What about you?'

Hazel smiled, bobbed her head from side to side like a boxer ducking punches. Maybe that was how she'd got the bent nose. 'Well, the two of us *were* on our way for a meal in Villa Italia, only then Terry took one of his toothaches – he's *tortured* with them, poor thing. His teeth get so *hot*, he has to get a drink, water or anything, to cool them off, they're that bad. So I said to him, 'Dr Fr David said he'd leave my essay on women in nineteenth-century national schools in the postgrad tray in your office after work. Why don't we collect it now, and you go off somewhere and use a tap or water fountain, cool your sore little mouth off? So we did, and that's where he is this minute.' She took a deep breath. 'Only I can't see my essay anywhere. Do you think did he mean he'd leave it in here and not in the tray in Terry's office?'

'Well,' Diarmuid glanced around, 'hard to say, really.'

'The other thing I was wondering was,' She smiled hard, teeth showing, the skin on her cheekbones and chin tightening, 'I'd like to hand you in my dissertation next week.'

Diarmuid swallowed as discreetly as he could. 'Well, naturally you can hand it in at any stage, Hazel. Although I *will* be able to get that methodology chapter back to you inside the next few days at most. Apologies for that – it's just that I've been incredibly busy, what with, ah, one thing and another.'

'Yes, but you see, I think I should.' Hazel's bright smile grew tighter still. 'Been working really, really hard. And the thing is, I feel it's pretty well finished now. From A to Z.' She leant her face towards him, evidently willing him to agree.

'That's good to hear. Though by the same token, if *before* you hand in, you feel you'd like me to give you some feedback...'

'No. Better hand everything in now and be done with it.'

'Yes, well, naturally it's your decision.'

Hazel laughed rather loudly. 'I've been over it and over it and I don't see any major problems. It's not perfect, but—'

101

'She's being modest.' Terry's voice was even more Birmingham whiny than usual as he stood in the doorway behind her. 'Both of us read it last night – in bed, actually. It was *good*.' He pressed Hazel's shoulder, turned to Diarmuid again. 'So what did you – I mean, were you looking for something in particular here?'

'Claire mentioned some international contacts to me that time we were talking... Said I could use them when I felt the need. Now I need them for next week. So I came in. To check for them.' It sounded jerky and lame.

Terry eased past Hazel and moved slowly a round the room, hands behind his back like the Duke of Edinburgh inspecting bare-breasted Maoris. Stopped near the window. 'It's hard to keep track of everything, isn't it? Disks, now. I could have sworn there was a disk sitting here, on this window-ledge.' He sucked air into his open mouth, blew it out quickly again. 'Except maybe I've mixed it up with another disk. You know what they say – you see one floppy, you've seen them all. Besides, no telling when something's going to go missing, right out of the blue, when you're least expecting it.' He turned again to Hazel. 'You've arranged a day with Dr Monaghan for bringing in your dissertation, haven't you?'

'I could do it Monday or Tuesday or whenever. Whatever suits.' She touched Terry's arm. 'Is your mouth still hurting, pet? I can tell it is, you poor little—'

'Well, of course, it isn't me you hand in to,' Diarmuid said. 'I'm only the supervisor. It's the Registrar's office you hand in to. Open nine to five.'

'I'll do that, then.'

'Assuming, that is, you're happy to submit at this stage.'

'Oh, she's happy to submit all right. Aren't you, Tufty?' Terry took a strand of Hazel's tired-looking hair and smoothed it over her collar. 'It's quality work – I'm sure Dr Monaghan will spot that immediately.'

'Well, certainly, if the work—'

'I must remember to check my records for that disk. It's like an itch, isn't it, not being sure if you have something or not?'

'Come on, hon-comb,' Hazel said, hugging his arm. 'You need something stronger than paracetamol and water for those teeth.'

Terry let her lead him to the door, where he turned briefly. 'Lock up when you're leaving, OK, Dr Monaghan? I have to caretake until the police investigation next month.'

When they had left, Diarmuid sat down. Looked at his hands resting on the desk in front of him. They were still shaking, but the amount of perspiration dripping from his oxters was easing off.

Mmmmnnnhhh. The sound of a man suffering toothache pangs, but no conscience pangs about blackmail. Was this the way the entire world worked – through blackmail? Move and counter-move, block and tackle. First Claire, with the broadcast as counterweight to the trip to Boston, then the Dean with the conference paper to balance the loss of the Boston study leave – even Brother Ambrose telling him that if he stopped writing the column he'd be sending people to hell. And now this bastard Terry as good as saying 'Fix things so she gets a high mark if you don't want me to tell them you stole your filthy pornographic disk from the office.'

Diarmuid switched off the light, pulled the door shut and locked it. He couldn't arrange for Warwick to give Hazel a high mark just because he needed to keep the LVK disk private. And even if he could arrange things, that'd be to cave in to intimidation, and how unprofessional was *that*? Besides, there was always the possibility that Warwick and the external examiner might think her work good on its own merits, in which case there'd be no problem And anyway – *anyway* – his heart lifted as the thought hit home and he felt his pocket: *he had the incriminating disk now, not Terry*. So why should he bother hinting to anyone that she should get a high mark? In fact, he'd hint that she should get a bit *less* if he took the notion – hah!

That bugger Terry should have hidden the disk better than he did, if he'd wanted to have bargaining power.

He stifled an urge to do a few dance steps as he walked back down the tunnel. In the pipes above his head some roosting pigeons called: 'Roook. Rooook. Roooook.' Diarmuid smiled up at them. 'Teach us, sprites or birds, what sweet thoughts are thine,' he whispered.

It wasn't until he was driving from the car park, with Ricky Nelson singing 'Poor Little Fool' on Radio 2, that a second thought struck: Terry was a creep but he wasn't a stupid creep, *which meant he had almost certainly made at least one copy of the contents of the disk*. Diarmuid checked that there wasn't any traffic coming and nobody in a parked car watching, then hit his forehead once, twice off the steering wheel and groaned as loud as he could. 'Damn and blast and fuckfuck*fuck*!'

Chapter 6

THEY REMEMBER MAMMY

The rolled-up *Belfast Telegraph* was lodged in the mouth of Paul's letterbox. Shuffling footsteps from within, the door opening, then Anne's bald head, looking oddly obscene as she bent to retrieve the newspaper. No smile as she straightened up. 'Paul said you were coming tomorrow and now you turn up today, I wish people would make themselves clear. He's upstairs.' She turned back into the kitchen before Diarmuid had time to ask her how she was keeping.

'Hello!' he called as he neared the door of his brother's study. An image of Paul, aged six, smirking in Daddy's arms as Daddy got ready to swing him round and round and Diarmuid stood pretending to be too old but aching for the strong-arms intimacy of it. His brother was all grown-up now, cropped iron-grey hair, frowning over a manuscript.

'Ah, Diarmuid.' He eased the manuscript to the side of the desk, glasses flashing. 'Didn't hear you. Just doing a quick proofread of our new A-level anthology. Sit ye down.'

'Anne let me in. She says you told her I was coming tomorrow.'

A sad headshake. 'Those new drugs can knock her off a bit occasionally.' He picked up a piece of paper from his desk. 'The hospital gave a double prescription – pick up a second month's worth when and if the first works out OK. We're keeping our fingers crossed they'll make a difference. Take a tip – don't get ill. An expensive business, I can tell you.'

'How is she? '

'Oh, good enough form. The hips continue to be a nuisance, of course – a pain, you could say. She's down for a double op – do both together, it's a new technique. Catch is, with present waiting lists she'll be lucky to get done before 2010. Meanwhile Anne is Anne and she copes.' He looked at his watch. 'So. You're no doubt pressed for time as I am myself. When would you like to go over there?'

' I didn't say I'd like. I said I'd go.'

'Oh dear. Like that, is it? In that case, let's get it over with.' Paul stood and shrugged himself into his jacket. At the bottom of the stairs he called towards the kitchen door, 'Back in an hour, pet!'

Anne's head appeared. 'You mean you're not waiting for the tea I'm hardly finished making? What's so important all of a sudden?'

'Well, we were about to go to check the things in Mammy's house and then maybe call in at the solicitor's. But if you would—'

'No.'

'Because it doesn't matter to Diarmuid or me. Right, Diarmuid?'

'No, no,' Diarmuid said. 'Doesn't matter to, ah, to us.'

Anne looked away, the top of her head glinting in the hall light. 'It's a pity people can't say what they mean and mean what they say, because if they only could for *once* do so, just once even, it'd simplify life for the rest of us *considerably*.' She closed the kitchen door with a slam.

On the way to the car and afterwards Paul didn't speak. Switched on the CD player: the sweet piercing notes of 'O Dry the Glistening Tear' filled the confined space. Just like in school, when the whole Gilbert and Sullivan chorus came dancing out, dressed as girls, the music filling the hall with its sweet, swelling grandeur.

'So how're tricks in the wacky world of educational publishing?'

Paul lowered the volume. 'Less than wacky and something more than tricks. We're halfway through assembling – *actually assembling* – second-level textbooks for 2002–3. You have to keep that far ahead to meet orders, otherwise it's hopeless. Not that the schools – the *clients* – help a lot. What is it – what in heaven's name *is it* about educators, that you must never be wrong? Did the school get their order in on time? Oh, definitely. Definitely. Even when I've got in my hand documented evidence that they did nothing of the sort. Lost the ability to distinguish between myth and reality, that's what it comes down to, I'm afraid.'

Diarmuid swallowed and imagined himself swimming naked in a lake with soft clouds and a yellow sun. When Paul had annoyed him as a child, it had been simpler: sit on his chest, thump his face. Not now, more's the pity. How did Anne stick the bastard?

'She's heroic,' Paul said, as if reading his thoughts. 'Chin up every day, never complains. Abandoned the wig permanently now, as I expect you've noticed. If she only had the hips fixed, I'm certain the other end of things – the alopecia – would soon sort itself out. But going private, that's prohibitive.' He sighed. 'Anyway. What about your end?'

'Fine – apart from Frances leaving me for two lesbians,' Diarmuid felt like saying. But he didn't. 'Great, great... Although we lost our department head last week.'

'*Lost* him?'

'Her. In the lift. Took a stroke, dead when they got her. Last week. Very sad. Only thirty-eight. In a lift.'

Paul whistled through his teeth and turned off into a side road. 'That's rough... But is it possible that, you know...the ensuing upheaval may be the wind beneath your wings?'

'I doubt it. Not yet, anyway.'

'Well, of course. But at the same time, it's important to be alert should something arise. Thing is, you *do* have a tendency to let opportunities float past because you're thinking of something else. The money they pay you for that "God Goes On" column or whatever it's called. That's buttons, really, isn't it? Must be some way you could be making better use of your time and energies than *that*. We make our own luck, you know.'

Past Mick the Snipe's shop, past the petrol pumps, past the place where the thatched cottage had been and the woman with the squint had leant on the half-door, butt in hand and turban on head, watching the world parade past. Then the drive up the side road to the house, high hedges on either side cutting off the world, crunch to a stop outside the green door and the six dark windows. Paul clicked the central locking on his car. 'I spent an hour over here on Saturday on my own. Totally depressing experience. Have you heard from Uncle Dan?'

'No.'

'I rang twice but he – they – were out. Thought of leaving a message on the answering machine but decided not to. Her ladyship has the feet run off him, checking every décor place in Belfast. Or certainly the expensive ones. '

The grass in the garden was overgrown and somebody had written 'The IRA's' above the words 'Private Property' on the sign. Indoors, Diarmuid half expected her to be sitting in the big armchair at an angle to the fireplace. What was it? The smell of powder? Or of the pee that sat in her adult nappy those last months, until the County Care team came to change it, led by a young skinhead guy with a stud in his ear. When he smiled at her she didn't respond, or to queries about how she was today – just stared at his head. The same way she'd stared at Anne's bald head, the first time she'd come without the wig. Paul had stayed in the kitchen pretending to be washing dishes, which meant Diarmuid had to explain that Anne's head was a disease, that alopecia was something you caught from stress or maybe tiredness or maybe a virus. But then he'd made the mistake of mentioning Sinead O'Connor's head, and Mammy had frowned and tugged at the tassel on the arm of her chair. She didn't like Sinead O'Connor, not after what she'd said about the Pope.

Now Paul was in the middle of the living room, writing in his little notebook with the gold-edged pages. 'Let's see. Television – you could hardly give away a black-and-white telly these days. Two china shepherdesses – who'd want the likes of them?' That's what he'd said when he'd visited Diarmuid the day after Mammy's funeral, talking about two silver candelabra that he had wrapped in newspaper and put in the boot of his car: 'Who'd want the likes of these?'

In the living room, they listed the TV, the shepherdesses, two holy pictures. Then on to the bedroom where she'd died, twelve hours after managing to suck the Precious Blood through a straw. The instant her breath had stopped, the nurse had grabbed her false teeth from the glass and rammed them into her mouth before it stiffened. Ninety minutes later the undertaker asked Paul and Diarmuid to help carry her to the hearse – neither of his helpers had turned up. Diarmuid remembered the terrible feeling of her legs through the body-bag thing, like a bird's, all the way out to the hearse, then the undertaker driving off to prepare her so he could bring her back for suitable display at the wake.

'Stamp on the passport is for 1962,' Paul said. 'He'd have been... fifty-one then.' He flicked to the photograph. Daddy, big jaw stuck out and staring eyes. Hair salt-and-pepper, arrowing to a point on his forehead. The cleft in the chin looking down at you, breathing pipe tobacco, telling you to get up for school this minute or you'd be late. 'Which means she'd have been forty-two.' Her hair was dark, curled around her face, and she was smiling.

'Nineteen sixty-two,' Diarmuid said again. 'What did they need a passport for in 1962?'

'Don't ask me – I wasn't born.'

'Oh right – the Fatima pilgrimage. Now I remember. They sent me to stay with Auntie Nellie and the night I arrived I told her I'd have liked it better if Uncle Dan had looked after me because he didn't smell as funny.'

Paul took out a tissue, licked it, and ran it along the top of a picture frame, cleaning off dust. 'Remember the story she used to tell about looking for a toilet in Fatima? Asked three different people and all they could do was jabber at her like a monkey, only Our Lady must have been looking down, for a wee nun from Tipperary came along, took her by the hand and led her to a cubicle, even though it was only a hole in a board. A miracle, she said. An angel from heaven, not Tipperary at all, who knew where the Fatima lavatories were.'

They laughed and looked at the woman who had carried them both inside her body, had drawn strength from every part of that body to push them out into the unpredictable world. And now the body and all its parts were lying buried on a country hillside four miles away.

'Do you want it?' Diarmuid said. 'The passport?' Go on, say you don't. Surprise me, this once.

'No, I'm not pushed about it. Certainly not the passport. But the photo would be nice. She looks terrific in it, doesn't she? Take it out, get it enlarged and framed.'

Paul rummaged through the long flat drawer. Produced a set of imitation-pearl rosary beads and a glass sphere containing the three children of Fatima and Our Lady. When you turned it upside down, all four were enveloped in a snowstorm. He put it back into the drawer, pulling a face. 'Very elegant.'

There was a brooch the shape of a bear which she had worn to Mass on Sundays, and a powder compact, and a letter from Daddy's sister, the nun in Boston, urging Brigid to put her trust in God – she felt sure the Almighty would come to her assistance and Tom's, and that things would be a lot better in the New Year. It was dated 15 December 1959.

'What happened in 1959?' Diarmuid asked.

'No idea. Doubt if anyone ever will now.' Paul poked at the contents of the drawer. 'Want any of the stuff in here?'

'I hate the way everything that happened gets lost. As if it had never been.'

'Anne can't stand clutter and there's nothing I'm too keen on anyway. You'd be well advised to grab your share before Dan and Our Lady of Mount Carmel arrive and start stripping the place.'

The bottom of the wardrobe in the second bedroom held old copies of the local newspaper. Underneath them the torpedo-shaped vacuum-cleaner she'd hung on to even after Diarmuid had bought her a new one. 'A great old warrior,' she called it. Which, by an odd coincidence, was what the doctor had called her after she had had her second stroke.

Paul tapped his notebook with the pen. 'Right, I'll put one column D for Dump, and another K for Keep. Vacuum-cleaner, D. Right? '

In the end nearly everything got a D – vacuum-cleaner, the pile of newspapers, the two holy pictures ('Do you plan to hang them somewhere? Right, D'), four boxes of pills, a tin of Elastoplast, a brown delft teapot, and a parchment saying that the marriage of Thomas Paul Monaghan and Katherine Dolores Torney had been blessed by His Holiness Pope Pius XII. Her wheelie-bin had been taken away long ago, whether by the council or vandals wasn't clear, so they put everything in black plastic bags and carried them to the boot of Paul's car. It got so full they both had to lean on the lid to get it closed.

'OK – let's check with McAleavy and see if there's anything needs signing, while we're at it.' Paul stood at the door, key in hand. His cheeks had more colour, his eyes were brighter, now that it was time to go.

'Hold while I visit the toilet,' Diarmuid said.

Paul clicked his tongue. 'Anne is on her own. Lock the door coming out, then – and switch off the lights.'

There was a brown stain in the throat of the bowl. Couldn't be shit – rust or something, probably. Her brown eyes staring at the carers as they removed the soiled wads. Diarmuid stood peeing, facing the frosted-glass window. A bird fluttered in the undergrowth and shouted a warning. Maybe she'd heard a bird like that when she lay in bed at night, unable to sleep, thinking about her two childless sons, neither of whom could quite find room for her. Granny flats? What an excellent idea. Mammy coming to stay with us? Um, pass.

The car horn honked impatiently. Diarmuid washed his hands, took a deep breath on the way to the front door. The smell of loneliness.

'Do you know what I was thinking?' Paul said, turning on to the main road and towards the town centre. 'We don't see enough of each other. No, seriously. Anne and I were talking the other day and we were saying, "Why don't we ask Diarmuid and Frances if they'd like to come over for— *shite*!" A tired-looking woman with a baby buggy stood in the road inches from their bonnet. Her eyes, staring at them, were round and angry. Then she called something and finished crossing the road.

'Did you see that? She just walked out on the road. No pedestrian crossing, nothing. Half-wit – she could have got herself *killed*! And the child!'

Distract him, before he remembers what he was talking about before. Quick. 'Has your man – McAleavy, the solicitor – has he been paid?'

Paul clicked his tongue, tapped the steering wheel irritably. 'Yes – in 1984. Not since.'

'You mean he doesn't send bills?'

'Oh, he sends them. Every six months. Just that Mammy ignored them. 'Bad scran to him – he has enough money.' Bad scran... remember that?'

Diarmuid tried to smile but it was hard. He could feel weariness, bone-cracking weariness, overpowering him, its knees on his chest, its thumbs on his windpipe. He murmured responses as Paul continued about Mammy's bills, the cost of living, the cost of car insurance, single mothers who walked in front of cars.

McAleavy answered the bell himself, big fleshy neck bulging over his shirt collar each time he nodded. 'Well, boys, good to see the pair of you. She was a powerful woman, and may God be good to her. Come in, come in.'

His office was hot and airless, and he closed the door quickly behind them as if to prevent ventilation entering. At his bidding they took off their coats and sat down.

Paul pointed to a framed photograph on the lawyer's desk. 'Is that your little girl? The last time I saw her she—'

'Natasha herself, the apple of my eye, and the plum too. Three years ago that was taken, she'd have been…ten.'

'She's a lovely child,' Paul said, passing the picture to Diarmuid. 'Isn't she?'

It was a school photograph, with Natasha dressed in uniform. The child had the same tight eyes as her father, the same strong eyebrows, the same plump neck.

'The spit of you,' Diarmuid said. 'God bless her.'

McAleavy took the photograph, breathed on it and polished it with the sleeve of his jacket, then repositioned it on his desk. 'That's what it's all about – family and loved ones. You've no children yourselves?'

Paul shook his head. 'Sadly, no. My wife suffers from arthritis.'

McAleavy nodded, as if this explained it. He looked at Diarmuid, eyebrows raised. One two, one two three, Diarmuid counted silently. If you're looking for an answer, then don't look at me. He focused on some bird-shit that streaked the window behind McAleavy's head and thought about swimming in a mountain pool. Sipping an iced drink poolside, while McAleavy sank to his death in an inverted pyramid of bubbles.

Eventually Paul spoke. 'The pair of us did an inventory an hour ago. Everything is sorted. The question is, now what should we do?'

When McAleavy leant back in his chair, you could see where he'd nicked himself an inch below his ear, a patch of stubble left growing round the cut. 'Advertise the property locally, that'd be my advice. You'd have bidders, no question. Many's the envious eye has been cast on *that* property over the years.'

'So, you say it'd be better put it on the market?'

McAleavy tugged at the back of his collar. 'Well, now, Paul, there is definitely a lift about things these days – a body couldn't

113

miss it. Right across the province, you'll find, they're fired up to invest in things. Seller's market.'

'Really?' Diarmuid said.

'End to end, up and down.'

'You think a buyer might come in from Donegal, then?'

The solicitor stared at Diarmuid, then put back his head and laughed. He'd once played the Ghost in the school production of *Hamlet*, although no one else in the room knew that, and the laugh was something he'd first used in that production. The reviews had called it infectious. He shook his head now and laughed again, his face reddening and sweat shining on his forehead. 'By God, not much gets past you, Diarmuid. Six Counties, of course you're right, that's what we should be saying. Them and their bloody province.'

'Please,' Paul wasn't smiling. 'Let's postpone the linguistics seminar. You think selling now would work – rather than in, say, the spring?'

Before the solicitor could answer, the phone rang. McAleavy picked it up. 'Yes... Yes... Well, what's wrong with that? Well, I could but I'm... Oh, all right, if you... Send her over in a taxi.' McAleavy touched his forehead, looked at the dab of sweat on his middle finger, wiped it dry on the sleeve of his pinstripe suit. 'The wife. Giving me a lock of child-minding duties. Where was I?'

'Selling the house,' Paul said.

'Right, surely to God. Your best price for the house will come – no, no, don't let me say that. Your best price is *likely* to come from a party that doesn't want it. Isn't that the odd thing?' He tugged the end of his nose with his finger and thumb. 'You see, the party in question owns maybe ten acres of land to the right of your house, OK? And he also owns maybe five acres to the left of your house, OK? Ten and five makes fifteen, and the four acres your mother's house stands on. That's nineteen acres. Nineteen acres fronting on a good busy road. It'd be my guess that this particular party, with nineteen acres, the first thing he'd want to do would be tumble the house and put up a whole new development. Maybe a Spar or a VG or a showroom. Which would be right up our alley, because it'd mean we'd be getting prime development prices for the property. D'you see what I mean?'

Diarmuid saw the hill behind the house, rolling gently up and then sloping gradually down to the river. Saw the anglers in their waders on summer evenings, standing like statues in the water, coming to life as their reels made a corncrake sound, the invisible hook curling into the shadows beneath a tree on the far bank. Saw an Easter morning, when he and Paul had sat in their Easter house, made of meal bags draped on sticks, sipping nettle soup and choking on the smoke from the fire. Saw and felt the world spin in a green bumping blur as they rolled downhill, because it was there, because it was good to be able to change the world, or at least how you saw it, by just climbing a small hill and rolling down.

'I wouldn't want that.'

As McAleavy began to reply, the office door burst open and Natalie entered. Behind her she dragged a bulging schoolbag. 'The girl herself!' He called. 'Come you and sit at this side of the desk. OK? How was school today?'

'All right.' The child tossed her bag onto the floor and sat in a chair beside McAleavy, her chin sunk in her chest, staring at Diarmuid and Paul over a pair of black-framed glasses.

'Now, isn't she great?' McAleavy said to his visitors. 'Sit you and amuse yourself and Daddy will be finished in two skips of a lamb's tail.' He consulted his notes, nodding as he did so. 'The fact is, we sometimes have to do the right thing for business interests to succeed. I don't know if you're fully taking that into account, Diarmuid.'

Paul touched Diarmuid's arm and addressed McAleavy. 'To be honest, I feel much the same myself.' The solicitor started to speak but Paul raised a traffic-cop palm. 'Except. We have to deal with present realities. The real world. You can imagine what our mother would have said if she were here.'

'"I thought I was dead," Diarmuid said. 'Do you think? "I thought I was dead."'

Paul didn't smile.

McAleavy leant back and felt under first his right armpit, then the left. 'Your mother, God be good to her, had a head on her shoulders. It'd be a lie to say anything else. At the same time, people feel what they feel, and only a gulpin would pretend they don't.'

The child sighed and turned to her father. 'Are you going to be long, Daddy?' she asked.

McAleavy produced his Hamlet laugh again. 'Not at all, child. Read you your book or something for a minute. Attagirl.'

Diarmuid leant forward in his seat. 'What's that supposed to mean – about people feeling what they feel? Does that mean you don't want the house to be bulldozed? Is that what you're saying?'

'Bulldozing... I don't know why you put it like that, but if that's what you call it, bulldozing would be the last thing, the *last* thing, any of us would want.' Paul stared at McAleavy, then at Diarmuid. 'But we all must bend to events. Life intrudes.'

McAleavy slapped the desk with the flat of his hand. 'That's it exactly! You've put the whole thing in a nutshell, Paul – life intrudes. At the same time, mind, it'll take your uncle Dan to be a party to whatever's decided. He's a beneficiary too. Don't you forget because he won't, and I can tell you he's one man with an eye for business. Not much passes the same boy.'

In the end McAleavy had to cut the meeting short because Natalie was making faces and clutching her stomach. 'Don't feel well,' she muttered. 'Think I'm going to be sick.' The solicitor hastily ushered her out of the room, calling over his shoulder to Diarmuid and Paul that they'd maybe leave it at that, the other papers could wait a while but the family would need to have a decision made soon if they wanted to catch the boat, for the interested party might just go on to other things.

Outside, the night air felt like chilled champagne after the heat of the room. As he swung the car towards home, Paul whistled – something from an opera, full of frilly bits, drumming occasionally with his fingers on the edge of the steering wheel. When they got to the main road he glanced at Diarmuid. 'Maybe it'd be better if we talked honestly. Straight talk, no varnish, cards up on the table.' He wiped his mouth with the back of his hand. 'In my opinion – *my* opinion – it was a mistake for us not to have sat down and discussed it first, the two of us. Washing the family linen in front of the likes of McAleavy was not a good option. Just as your not being at the funeral – her funeral – wasn't a good option. We show disunity in public, we'll be the ones to suffer.'

Diarmuid looked out the side window. It was hard to keep his voice steady. 'Are you saying if we'd talked, or I had been at the funeral, which I couldn't be at because I was sick, you wouldn't be voting to see a big bulldozer come in and smash the floor and sink and wallpaper and fireplace and every fucking thing Mammy worked all her life to build up? Is that what you're saying? *Is it*?'

'I'm saying nothing remotely like that. But facts are facts. And that sort of crude language won't change them.'

'She used to start washing the curtains – the lace ones – at around nine o'clock on Christmas Eve. Couldn't bear to see anything not spotless and in its right place. Now you're for putting a bulldozer through her house.'

'Oh deary me.' Paul sighed. 'The house is empty, ready for selling, a customer is interested, but... but no, that'd be too straightforward. It has to be melodrama, string orchestra, heavenly chorus. It has to be Little House on the Prairie, Mother's memory, holy ground.' He glanced sideways, his face red. 'For Heaven's sake, Diarmuid! What about growing up for once?'

That's what the art teacher – his favourite teacher – had said when he caught Diarmuid with the sketch of the vice principal, naked except for a crab clinging to his private parts. 'What about growing up?'

Now Diarmuid thought about jabbing a fist into Paul's face,

even though he was driving. 'In that case,' he said, trying not to let his voice wobble, 'you tell your plans to Uncle Dan, right? Or, better still, Carmel. See what real melodrama looks like after you've had an extended chat with her.'

'I repeat,' Paul said, sighing, 'it is our house – yours and mine, and maybe, *maybe,* Uncle Dan's. But certainly not Carmel's. If she wants to do up *his* house, fine. If he wants to let her, fine. But this place of ours, it has nothing to do with her. And maybe not with him either.'

Diarmuid hated being in the car like this with Paul. Sitting close to him, surrounded by his gear-stick and his floor mats and his dashboard and his sticker stuck on it showing a cigarette with a red line through it. 'He's in the will. A will is a will, and Uncle Dan's in this one.'

Paul glanced towards Diarmuid, a twitch flickering at the side of his eye. 'And a contested will is a contested will! Do you really think Mammy would have signed that clown into it if she'd been thinking half straight? A corner-boy who rolls into town two months before she dies and does the I'm-your-baby-brother routine, and then calls up McAleavy – we need you round here, she wants to change a few things. I mean, come *on!* – Mammy didn't even *like* him. "Lowest of the low," remember? She'd say it and she'd look past you towards the wall, as if she could barely bring herself to think about him. The fact that he's been able to salt away sufficient of his ill-gotten gains to keep half the décor shops of Belfast happy changes nothing. She thought he was the lowest of the low and she definitely wouldn't have wanted a third of all she had to go to the lowest of the low. Not if she had her wits about her.'

'But she did.' Diarmuid tried not to think about Mammy blowing worms and soil out of her mouth so she could contradict Paul. 'That's why she put him in the will. What's more, if you try keeping what is his from Dan, you'll end us both up in court. And court, in case you haven't noticed, costs money.'

'So does giving away a third of your rightful inheritance.'

'Oh Christ... All right, all *right*. We'll talk to him – I'll talk to him. Will that do?'

Paul rubbed the windscreen with the back of his hand. 'I wish you luck. Personally I'd prefer trying to locate Howard Hughes – considerably easier prospect.'

Diarmuid sat listening to the whoosh of traffic going past as the truth struck home: my brother is afraid. He's afraid Uncle Dan will agree with me and not him, and that he won't be allowed to bulldoze the house. That's why he doesn't want him contacted. *Bastard.*

Paul kept his eyes firmly on the road as he spoke. 'You think I'm heartless, and maybe I am. But don't forget, heartlessness comes in different forms. At least my conscience is easy about her funeral.'

'I said already, I was sick. Every time I got out of bed, the room started spinning. *I could not walk.*'

'And the next day, when the funeral was over, it stopped spinning. And you could walk.'

'Exactly. Because I was better.'

'So how often have you been to her grave?'

'What's that got to do with it?'

Paul's shoulders came up in a tiny shrug. 'Since we're discussing heartless.'

'You really are something. Look, Mammy's dead, OK? If I had played ping-pong on her grave or lit candles every day, it doesn't make a dot of difference.'

'I'd have thought respect for the dead made a difference.'

'How the hell can you show respect to a dead person? Anyway, nobody said anything about you being heartless – you're the one brought that up. All I said was, I don't want Mammy's house bulldozed.'

'And you think I do? Look – all I want is to get my hands on the money from the sale of it, that's all.' He pinched the space between his eyes. 'Because these days, for a private hip operation you pay eight thousand pounds. Two of them, even with discount, fourteen thousand. Meanwhile my wife is in pain. I see it and hear it every morning she gets up, and I see it and hear it every night she lies down, and I see it and hear it frequently at times in between. You *bet* I want the money.'

They didn't speak for the rest of the journey. As soon as they pulled up in front of the house Anne came shuffling awkwardly down the path, smiling, put both hands on Diarmuid's arm. Her earlier mood seemed to have lifted. 'You. Are coming in. For a cup of tea. This minute.'

But Diarmuid took her hands carefully away – always be gentle with someone on medication. Thanks, but no thanks. If he sat across the table from Paul, it would mean thinking about what a bastard his brother was, the way he'd talked about the house and about Mammy, and about not being able to contact Uncle Dan, and about Diarmuid not having been at the funeral and not having visited the grave. What was more, sitting across the table from Paul and Anne would mean thinking about Anne's hips, and how he, Diarmuid, was blocking her chances of being relieved from pain and how that made *him,* Diarmuid, the bastard, not Paul.

Get out quick then, now, immediately. 'See you soon!' Hand raised in smiling goodbye as he swung his own car on to the road. When he was a hundred metres from the house he stopped at the kerb and sat taking long, deep breaths that filled his body from top of skull to soles of feet, life-giving breath, making him slightly dizzy but protecting him, renewing him, pushing back the seeping poisons all around.

Too many things piling up too quickly.

Chapter 7

DOG SITTING

Frances came back, of course. Just when he'd begun to get used to walking naked from the bathroom to the bedroom, an extra beer in the evening, farting at will, she came back. In some ways he'd missed her. The house seemed bigger, and when he'd sat down to his evening meal – steak, frozen peas, boiled potatoes – he'd heard the kitchen clock ticking. But when he switched on the radio he stopped hearing the clock, and it was nice to be able to prop up the paper and read as he ate. It reminded him of his tiny student flat – alone but not lonely.

On the Friday he went into the university, even though he had no lectures. The morning was split between marking, writing final notes to himself about the broadcast, and looking at Educational Studies on the Boston College website. Just after lunch he got an email from Hazel, saying she had submitted her dissertation, that the Exams Office would be sending him a copy and was that OK? He typed a one-sentence reply: 'I look forward to receiving your work.' Detached, cool, professional. Maybe her dissertation would be brilliant and he wouldn't have to struggle with his conscience.

At half past three the sky through the office window looked so blue and hopeful that he went on a slow walk around the university's artificial lake, watching the birds tumble and swoop above it like curved knives in the sunlight. This time on Friday next they'd be back doing the same thing and he'd have the broadcast over. What would they be doing during the broadcast? Eating, probably – or mating. When he was making his most telling point, thousands of pairs of ears hanging on his every word, the birds – maybe thousands of them – would be bringing their feather-framed sexual parts together. Or did they go in for that sort of stuff in the autumn? He must remember not to think of birds humping when he was speaking. Distracting image.

But then, as he approached the artificial jetty with the little blue rowing-boat moored to it, his foot began to feel thick and awkward again. It was as if the blood in the rest of his body had decided to head for it and, having arrived there, to expand very rapidly. He sat on the mooring point beside the jetty, his leg stretched out in front of him, and thought about visiting the doctor. Saw the doctor frown, shake his head, whisper to the blonde nurse, her eyes widen and the doctor comes towards him, serious-faced, but then the pain receded and the blood in his leg seemed to be pumped back up into the other parts of him. He got to his feet and moved with hardly a trace of a limp, the quarter-mile back.

When he got home and went into the kitchen she was standing at the sink, drying cups. There was a dishwasher the size of a tank under the counter, less than four feet from where she was standing, which Diarmuid had been going to load that very evening to have his first proper dishwasher wash. But she had beaten him to it and stood with a rack full of gleaming cups and plates, knives and forks, which she seemed to have washed by hand. Now she had started to dry and stack them in the cupboard. Saying nothing. The little groove down the back of her neck looked tanned and delicate above the pink blouse

'Hello!' he said. 'I'm making a cup of tea – want one?'

'If you like.' She didn't look around. Just said the three words in a toneless voice, then walked into the living room. He poured the tea, arranged biscuits on a plate and brought them in. Sipped his own, watched as she dipped a biscuit corner into hers, stared out the window. When the phone rang in the kitchen, she didn't move. He went out and picked it up.

'Hello – who's that? Hello?' Joy's voice, grainy and resentful. Pretend you don't know the bitch. Blame technology.

'You're very indistinct – it's difficult to hear you. Can you hear me? If you could move your mouth back from—'

'This is Joy. Give me Frances. Now.'

'My goodness – it's your friend Joy!' Diarmuid called, smiling to show he was glad she'd rung. 'I hardly knew her voice at first.'

Frances hurried past him, took the telephone with trailing cable to the opposite end of the kitchen. Back in the living room Diarmuid could still hear her.

'No, honestly, I didn't think... Well, naturally, if I *could*, but... OK. No, of course I don't mind... I'll talk to you then.'

She hung up. The utility-room door opened, closed, and the vacuum cleaner started up. He followed her into the hall. 'I've already done that!' he called above the din.

She switched it off. 'What did you say?'

'I've already hoovered – no need to do it again.'

'Could have fooled me.'

After she'd suctioned the living room, the kitchen and the three bedrooms, she started to make the evening meal, chopping mushrooms with a new sharp knife she appeared to have brought back with her. Later, as they sat at the kitchen table, eating, she propped the *Radio Times* against the radio, turned its pages without looking up.

'What's Joy planning?' he asked eventually.

A pause. 'They're going on a workshop weekend to Inishgorm. A body-soul weekend.'

'Uncle Dan was talking about body-soul at one point, wasn't he? Furniture lay-out and colour selection and that kind of thing. Is that what it is?'

'It's physical and spiritual synergy. Jorg Doherty, he's the original founder of the body-soul system, will be doing the

Inishgorm weekend.' Pause. Her voice became quiet, almost reverent: 'He's meant to be amazing.'

Supposed to be amazing – *supposed, supposed, supposed.* 'And so Joy and Mairead are into that too, eh?'

'Of course. If any of us gets bent under too many material things, our spiritual posture becomes deformed. We need a human balance. It's obvious.'

'I suppose it is, when you think of it… Did they ask you to go with them? For the weekend?'

'Yes.' An image, vivid and horrible, of Joy and Mairead in a room, and Frances coming into it, all three women unbuttoning their blouses. 'Only I can't. Besides, I told them I'd look after Princess. And before you start, she'll be no bother – I'll slip her into the utility room. You won't even know she's there.'

Yes, he would. The Dobermann Pinscher's big, thrusting head and naked arse below the docked tail. Her nerve-jangling whine. He'd know all right. 'Why did they invite you to go with them if they needed you to look after their dog?'

She raised her eyebrows, lowered them, continued eating. Afternoon sunlight in Sorrento, their honeymoon, eating ice-cream at a pavement café, a five-minute sprint from the hotel bedroom. Then the idea came to him.

He brought two more mugs of dark tea and set them on the table. Sat down. Sounded casual. 'You know, I could look after Princess. You could go on your weekend and enjoy yourself and I could look after her.'

'That wouldn't work.'

'Of *course* it'd work. All you have to do is tell me what needs done, when she's to go out on a walk and so on. I can manage that.'

'No, no. They asked me. I'll look after her.'

'Yes, but they *also* asked you to go to Inishgorm.' He took his mug over to the window. 'It'll do you good.'

'Yes, but that'd mean you looking after yourself *and* the dog.'

'Yes it would. But I'm smart, remember. I passed my eleven-plus.'

A near smile. 'Well...if you're sure. And your foot is up to it.'

'All my bits are up to it.'

He could hear Joy's voice squawking when Frances phoned them back to make the suggestion.

An hour later the two women arrived with the dog, Joy hurrying ahead, tugging Princess on her lead. Joy was wearing blue jeans that fitted her fat little thighs like tights. 'No off-lead activity in any public area,' she told Diarmuid, thrusting the end of the lead into his hand. 'And remember she's still got a cold – see that snot in her right nostril? Means she could have a bit of difficulty smelling her food, and if she can't smell it properly she won't eat it. Hold a bit in your hand and pretend to eat it yourself – that usually works. Then walk her within half an hour of giving the evening feed. Put out a fresh bowl of water before bed. And brush her coat as well.' Joy stared hard at him. 'Are you listening to all this? Animal care involves serious responsibilities. Don't take it on if you're not up to it.'

Eventually Diarmuid waved them off, and when they'd turned the corner, he went into the house and closed the door. The silence felt like an old friend, except for Princess whining in the utility room. He poured himself a good-sized whiskey, so he wouldn't have the bother of pouring a second too soon. Then he put on a Chopin CD to drown Princess and sat in the living room, feet propped on the footstool, half reading *Changing Places*. The pain in his foot started again as he reached the mid-point of the second whiskey, but he felt good. In control.

It was almost a quarter past ten when he turned off the hi-fi, switched on the TV and limped to the utility room. Princess looked up at him, pink-rag tongue flopping from one side of her mouth. He took the food pellets from the cupboard and shook a small helping into her dish, poured some fresh water. The dog glanced at it and turned back to him, whimpering, jelly-snot splashed around both nostrils now.

'Here, girl. *Nice* pellets – Mmmmmh.'

The dog looked up at him, twitched her stump, whined.

Diarmuid crouched forward until his face was level with the dog's. 'Look, Princess. Look – *yummy*.'

He held the handful of pellets under the dog's nose, then moved them slowly towards his own mouth. The dog stretched her neck forward. When Diarmuid made a sucking noise and pretended to chew, the dog barked and her stump wagged. But she still didn't eat. In the end, Diarmuid had to lean his face into the dish and scoop up two pellets with his tongue and actually – *oh, God* – pretend to chew. Only then did the dog give a bark, thrust her nose in the dish and start to eat noisily, her stump twitching like a stripper's tassel.

Diarmuid closed the door, took a pint glass of water and rinsed his mouth out three times. then did the same with a mouthful of Listerine in the bathroom. After that he poured another big whiskey and took it to watch *Newsnight* where Bríd Rodgers, the minister for agriculture was telling Jeremy Paxman that she and her team were doing a very good job under terribly, terribly difficult circumstances. Diarmuid felt the whiskey surge through his body, removing the taste of dog pellets, softening all pain. 'Me too,' he told Jeremy and Bríd.

As he descended the stairs next morning, feeling the tiredness in his head like an upturned can of paint, he heard the dog. It was making a small whining sound, like a pornographic film he'd once ordered up electronically in his Manchester hotel room during a conference on Special Needs. Meee. Mmmeee. Mmmmmeeee. In the pauses, the scrabble of claws. Diarmuid approached the utility door carefully, the tiles cool against his soles. His foot felt... OK, really. Warm rather than aching.

He checked that the doors leading out of the kitchen – into the hall, into the street – were closed, then gripped the handle of the utility-room door, eased it open inch by slow inch. There was no sound. Maybe the dog had got tired of thrashing about, was lying back having a snooze. Smoking a post-coital cigarette.

Carefully he put his head into the room. Immediately something warm and heavy hit his thigh, the scrabble sound became hailstones on a roof, and Princess skittered across the kitchen, reared up on her hind legs and clawed at the kitchen door, leaving deep black scratches on the white wood. At the same moment the phone rang. Diarmuid stood staring from the dog, which now appeared to be trying to eat the bolt at the bottom of the door, to the phone, and back again. He limped across, made a half-kick with his good foot. 'Stop *that*, you bare-arse bugger!' The dog ignored him.

'Hello? Hello?'

'Dr Monaghan? Jeremy here. From the BBC in... Great, thanks. Tell you what it is, Debbie, the series editor, asked me to give you a bell, because sadly we've got something of a-a-a *bottle-neck* in the programme on the day you're coming in. Right, right. So what she's proposing – with your approval, naturally – is not having your discussion at the *top* of the programme but at the *bottom*, right, at the end. Does that sound good? The thing is, with an item like yours, it needs *breathing* space to do it justice, and Debbie thought if we push it back and give it the last twenty minutes, that would be better than kicking things *off* with it. What do you say?'

'So you want me to come into the BBC at...what time?'

'Two-fifteen on Friday would be super.'

'OK.'

'Super. Thanks *very* much – that's cool. By-ee!'

Diarmuid put down the phone and was shuffling towards the dog, which was now sitting on the floor licking its paws, when the phone went again. 'Yes?'

A woman's voice, quiet, like that one in *Casablanca*. 'Who is this?'

Diarmuid sat down. 'Well, now.' Besides the throbbing in his foot he could feel little darts of pain in his right shoulder. 'Since you rang me, why don't you tell me who you are?'

'Is that Mr Monaghan?' A soft voice. Honey and sunlight slanting on to a stiff linen tablecloth.

'Yes, this is Dr Diarmuid Monaghan.' Oh, doctor, I'm in trouble...

'This is Angela – Claire's sister. I—'

Her words were suddenly inaudible as the dog began to bark hysterically again.

'Just a minute, Angela.'

Diarmuid dropped the phone and moved in a series of sideways shuffles across the kitchen. The dog had covered the door in scrape marks, so many it looked like art lattice work. He gripped her collar and dragged her, claws skidding on the tiles, back to the utility room. 'Bad dog. Bad. Bastard. *Dog*.' Pushed her inside and slammed the door. Turned the key. Hobbled back to the phone. 'Sorry. Just had to. Get a dog. Under. Control. But it's all right now.' As he spoke, the dog's whines started up again.

'I rang because I wondered...' A pause. Maybe some velvet mixed with the honey and sunshine. '...if I could meet you.'

'We have met, at the funeral. Remember?' Oh, shite. Why had he said that?

Another pause. 'I'm up in Belfast today getting some of Claire's affairs sorted. Catching the four o'clock train back to Drogheda. Where we live.' The dog was howling now, no longer pornographic, more like a child that's been locked away and deprived of all hope of human love. A-owwwwww-eeeeee.

'I thought your husband worked at the City Hospital, in Belfast,' Diarmuid said.

'He does. Stays up, has a little flat at the hospital, home at the weekends. We tried living in Belfast but I didn't like it.' There was another pause, and an intake of breath. 'I know you're busy with the dog and so forth, but there is...a thing I'd like to talk to you about.'

Diarmuid felt his stomach tighten. This was Claire's sister. What did she want to know? 'Um, this is Saturday.' Oh, Jesus, could you not say you're tied up? 'When would suit you?'

'I'm in the Europa hotel right now. It's just that I'd like to talk to you about...something. We could have a coffee or...would two this afternoon be all right? Even for twenty minutes?' Her voice melted into honey and sunshine and ten trumpets playing the 'Trumpet Voluntary'.

The hotel lobby was so thickly carpeted he had almost reached her armchair before she saw him. Then she stood, smiling, the peach-coloured dress hanging in a refined way over her breasts and stomach. A passing waiter was told to bring coffee and she sat again. Tugged her dress over her knees.

'Nice to see you,' Diarmuid said. 'How's your case against the uni coming?'

It sounded crass but she didn't seem offended. 'Not great. If Tom's cousin wasn't a solicitor, we'd never have been able to manage at all – the expense is ferocious. But now he says – Tom's cousin – our case looks flimsy. Apparently they inspect the lifts regularly, and then it's written up in a report that the inspectors sign. So the university says that, whatever happened, they're in the clear. "An act of God," they claim.'

'That's really too bad.'

She sat back in the sofa. 'How's your friend that got cut with glass doing?'

'OK, I think. I haven't seen him, but his friend Warwick keeps us posted. He hasn't been at work since. Crompton, I mean.' Diarmuid was going to add about Warwick's legal proceedings for the sliver of glass and the name-calling, then decided not to.

'But you got Fido under control anyway.' A warm, fading-up smile.

'Oh right – Princess. She went a bit mad just as you called, I'm afraid.'

'Maybe she was hungry. Or lonely. How did you manage in the end?'

'Just closed the door on her, poured her some more grub and she stopped. It's called tough love.'

'We had a dog once. They're nice, but they take over your life.' She opened a packet of Benson and Hedges and lit one without asking him if he minded. 'What sort of form was she in?'

'She seemed OK. Curled up beside a radiator sleeping when I left.'

129

A thin woman in her fifties with a child of about six walked past, then sat in the couch directly behind them. 'Sure all kinds of superstars come here for their dinner,' the woman said to the little girl. 'It wouldn't surprise me one wee bit – not one *bit* – if Barry McGuigan himself was to come through that door.'

'Who's Barney McQuillan?' the child asked.

Angela blew a plume of smoke towards the ceiling. 'I meant Claire. How was Claire's mood when you last saw her?'

'Oh... She was in, I'd say, yes, she was in a pretty good mood.' Plump upper lip, Diarmuid noticed, sticking out just a tiny bit further than the lower one.

'The thing is.' Pause. 'I haven't said to anybody – not even Tom – but...we had a row, Claire and I. Stupid – of course it was stupid. Julie, my daughter – had been staying with her the weekend before. So on the Sunday, Claire started these comments, how Julie's shorts were a bit casual for Mass. She was very strict about Mass.' Angela frowned and tapped her cigarette hard in the ashtray. 'My mother is seventy-four, lives with us, but even she has the tact to keep her trap shut about things like that. Anyway, what happens is, when Claire started up, Julie ran off and changed into her other outfit, slacks and a white T-shirt, because she's like that, tries to please everyone. And then next thing, when the two of them are in the car on the way to the church, Claire starts on about the *slacks,* were they not a bit tight, and her T-shirt, was it not a bit brash – that's the word she kept using, *brash.*'

'Brash?'

'It said 'French Connection UK' on the front and 'FCUK' on the back. Half the youngsters you see are wearing that these days. But Claire nearly had a fit. Kept talking about how she could see Julie's stomach, and how coarse and vulgar the lettering was. On and on until by the time they got to the church poor Julie was ready to bawl. And when she got home and spilled the beans to me, I was fit to be tied. So I got on the phone to Claire and went through her for a short-cut.'

'But *I* want to see the *clowns!*' the child behind them complained.

'The clowns had to go home, pet. Their mammy is at home waiting for them and fretting about what's keeping them. Put you your head on my lap here.'

'And you didn't see her again?'

Angela shook her head 'I spoke to her briefly the night she died, but that only ended up in argy-bargy as well. It was awful.'

'But I. Want. To see. The clowns!' The child's voice was a half-yell. Suddenly the woman stood and started walking briskly towards the hotel exit. The little girl trotted after her, wailing.

'And then I heard you were the last one who talked to her. So I wondered if – if she'd been in bad form or anything. Or said anything.'

The coffee arrived. Angela paid and poured.

'We were talking about...business...work,' Diarmuid said. 'So bad form or good form didn't really arise, in a way. But if you forced me, I suppose I'd say...good form.'

'And did she say anything?'

'Oh, yes, lots. About this study leave I was supposed to be going on, and... What else? About career paths. That sort of thing. It was a very productive meeting.'

The woman and child came back across the lobby. The child was holding a furry toy.

'But did she say anything about... me? About us and our row?'

Diarmuid hesitated. Angela's face looked like a punchball waiting for the blow. 'Well...now you mention it, she did say something. About feeling guilty.'

Angela leant towards him. 'Guilty?'

'Well, I can't really remember the exact words.' What the hell was he lying for? *Stop.* 'She did talk at one point about the need not to be hasty. She said they'd agreed to let me go on study leave to Boston, after my having applied twice before. She said they'd delayed because they didn't want to make a hasty decision. Because acting hastily often led to, you know, regret in the long run. But now they were OK-ing it.'

Angela lit another cigarette. 'Maybe she was thinking about *me* when she said that. That I'd been the hasty one. Maybe that was what she meant.' She flapped at the smoke.

Her skin, Diarmuid thought. On her neck a red map of excitement, on her mouth a little fat rosebud. If he kissed her, there'd be a smell of tobacco. '"My own worst enemy" – I do remember her saying that. I thought she was talking about her work as department head. "My own worst enemy".'

'Not as long as I'm alive.'

'Sorry?'

Angela waved a hand, dismissing her own words. 'Nothing. Old joke about a Hollywood crowd talking about Judy Garland – you never hear it? Somebody said Judy Garland was her own worst enemy, and Groucho Marx said, "Not as long as I'm alive." Did you not say you couldn't remember what she said?'

'Well, yes, I – I did. Except that while I was listening to you, things started coming back. Like always hurting the one you love – I remember that distinctly. The song.'

'She was *singing*?' The rosebud mouth stayed open.

Jesus. Stop this now. 'Humming. Just this one song. I recognised it immediately.

'But she was in good form?'

'Oh, yes. Good form definitely. Except for the bit where she talked about being hasty and hurting the one she loved.'

Angela pushed back a wisp of hair that had been hanging in front of her face and put out her cigarette. The line in her forehead smoothed and she smiled. 'Thank you very much. I can't begin to tell you how important hearing all this is. It's been preying on my mind ever since Claire died. Sitting about the house on one's own doesn't help either – Tom is in the States at the moment and my mother is down in Kerry staying with her cousin.'

'Do you have a job – I mean, do you work?'

'Not for pay. I edit the parish bulletin. And I'm still on the board of governors where my daughter used to go to school, so I help them with their monthly newspaper. It's quite good, actually – you should see it. Regular profiles and interviews with past pupils.'

'That sounds great – sounds like you have a journalistic flair. Anyway, I just hope our chat was some help.'

'It helped more than you can imagine – honestly. Thank you very, very much.' Then, as he watched, she dipped into her handbag and took out a tissue, which she used to wipe the tears that were spilling down her face and the clear snot that was running from her nose.

Her face was still blotchy when she came back from the toilets.

'Sorry.' She tightened a scarf round her throat. 'My mum sometimes gets weepy – I must have inherited it.'

'You should see my uncle Dan – every Christmas Day, once the movie's over, he boohoos bucketfuls. Always waits to the end of the movie on TV.'

Eyes puffy and red, she squeezed out a smile. 'I've kept you back.'

'No, no, no. Glad to be of help.' Nice legs. Imagine them unsheathed.

'Have you had your lunch? My train for Drogheda isn't until four. Or I could buy you a drink if you've eaten.'

'I'm fine, thanks. Anyway, I need to get back and take Princess out for a walk. I'm dog-sitting her for the weekend.'

'Where will you go?'

'Round the university lake. It's artificial, but they've cleaned up the undergrowth, painted the railings, built dry-stone walls. Quite nice on a day like today, actually.'

'Sounds marvellous.' She blew her nose loudly.

'Would you like to come?' The words seemed to say themselves. 'I could drop you off at the station in time for your train – what time did you say it was? Four o'clock? You'd have plenty of time and it'd give you a chance to get a bit of air, you know, get back your composure. And if Princess goes mad again, you could calm her down. A woman's touch.'

She closed her eyes, gave a long sniff, opened them. 'OK. As long as I don't miss my train.'

At the house Angela sat in the car while he bundled Princess into the boot.

'Does she like being put in the boot like that?' Angela asked anxiously.

'Don't know – she's never been in it before.' All the way to the lake, little whining sounds and the occasional bark came from the back. Diarmuid pretended not to hear them.

At the lake car park he opened the boot carefully, attached the lead to Princess's collar. The dog shivered and jumped out, stump quivering. They walked down the steps to where the water glinted turquoise, then grey and blue nearer the middle of the lake. Diarmuid risked a sideways glance: a strand of blond hair fluttered against her left cheek, touched the edge of her coat. She probably cried a lot, living with that thick-necked bastard husband of hers. A small sailboat caught the breeze and cut a white line across the water. Princess hurried ahead, nose to the ground, stretching her lead.

'I love being near the water. Every July my parents used to rent a house by the sea in Donegal – we'd drive there and we'd be exhausted by the time we arrived. One year Claire was so sound asleep, Daddy carried her into the bed and at three the next day – *three*! – he had to go into the bedroom and literally *push* her eyelids open. Claire started crying because she said a whole day of her holidays had gone past with her asleep and she hadn't even seen the sea!'

When they reached the far side of the lake Diarmuid pointed up the hill to their right. 'They've landscaped that section – torn out a lot of undergrowth, rotovated, put in grass-seed. Used to be full of undesirables. These days…'

The 'Ode to Joy' began to play in her handbag.

'Hello. Yes… Well, don't worry. I'll put something in first

134

thing tomorrow... It'll be OK. Ring me later tonight at home. Any time after eight... No, eight. Talk to you then. Bye.' She rolled her eyes at Diarmuid: 'My daughter Julie from Manchester – not even freshers' week and she's feeling the financial squeeze.'

They didn't speak until they reached the concrete bench with the plaque to the first Vice Chancellor. The inscription read, 'In memory of a scholar and a dedicated leader.'

'Never could understand these things,' Angela said. 'After the person is dead.'

'Maybe the relatives feel better. Actually, they say your man here – the VC – was a brute. Womanising, drinking, you name it. But a financial go-getter, and these days that's what counts. '

Angela turned, looked across the stretch of water. 'Did you get on with Claire?'

He hesitated. 'She was my boss. Of course we got on.'

'She was married for a while – did you know that? Funny that we both married doctors. Tom knew him – they worked in the same hospital. It lasted just over a year and then, when they saw the marriage wasn't working he went back to England and she got an annulment, end of story. Parchment from the Pope and everything, saying, "I hereby annul." That meant a lot to my mother, although I think Claire would have wanted one anyway. She kept it tucked away in a drawer, never talked about it – Claire, I mean.' Angela paused. 'I shouldn't be telling you this.'

'It's all right,' Diarmuid said. He wasn't sure what he meant by that. 'I think she had a happy enough life. At the university.'

'"Intensity," she said to me one time – it was her birthday, we were out for a meal, sank two bottles of wine between us. "That's what I want. Feeling things intensely. Otherwise, what's the point?" She was the same with religion. Went at it hell-for-leather.'

Princess sent her nose quivering along a bench, then the rubbish basket beside it. Satisfied, she glanced back at them, parted her back legs like a weight-lifter, and started a slow, knee-quivering shite on to the grass. Her little docked tail vibrated as she strained.

Diarmuid caught Angela's eye and they laughed.

'Total informality.'

'Animals are amazing. Everything just one big Now.'

'A Buddhist dog,' Diarmuid said.

'Should you not have a plastic bag or something? To...clear up, you know.'

'No. And even if I had, I don't think I could bring myself to use it. Could you?'

'They hadn't started doing that when we had a dog.'

Diarmuid tugged the lead and Princess ended her squat.

Half a mile further along, the path turned between the trees and up on to the street. Angela glanced down at his shoes. 'Hope you don't mind my asking, but is there something wrong with your foot? I noticed it at the Dean's place as well.'

'Just a bruise – nothing serious. Can you hold the lead a second?'

He handed Princess's lead to Angela and bent to loosen his shoelace, pulling the sock up where it had slid down his heel and into his shoe and bunched around his toes. On the other side of the street, a white-haired man with a stick emerged from the newsagent's, a boy by the hand, eating an ice-cream. A passer-by spoke to the man and the two went into earnest conversation. The child, cone to mouth, spotted Princess. He tugged his grandfather's hand. No response. Another tug, harder this time. Then he said something and pointed across the street with his ice-cream at the dog.

Perhaps Princess thought the child was offering her something to eat, because she whined and rocked back on her haunches, then hurled herself forward. The lead whipped out of Angela's hand and two seconds later Princess was on the other side, tongue billowing, jumping to put two big paws on the youngster's shoulders. The ice-cream looped from the child's hand as he disappeared beneath the dog's weight.

'What did you let her go for?' Diarmuid yelled at Angela.

'What kind of a – Christ Almighty. Here!' he called after Princess. 'You damned bitch, come here!' Dodging cars he hurried after the dog. 'Gotcha, you bloody pest!' Diarmuid grabbed the dog's collar and tugged her clear of the screaming child. 'Terribly sorry,' he told the man. 'She got away – from the lady.'

Underlining his apology, Diarmuid aimed a flat-handed blow at the dog's ear, which was a mistake. Princess leapt backwards on the road and, as she did so, a Marks & Spencer truck hit her head with its side bumper. Princess flew back the way she had come and landed on the pavement at Diarmuid's feet where she lay whining, blood coming from a jagged cut in the middle of her head. The driver, oblivious, drove on.

'Could you – could you – could you not keep that – that mongrel under some sort of control?' The grandfather's eyes were bloodshot and his hand trembled as he pointed at Diarmuid. 'Creating *mayhem*.' He bent to help the wailing child to his feet. 'Here shush, shush, shush, we'll get another ice-cream, chocolate and red stuff and the whole works. And we'll keep it a secret from Mammy, won't we? For she'd only be fussing, wouldn't she?'

Angela stood beside Diarmuid, her cheeks burning. 'I'm really sorry, she just… Your little boy wasn't bitten, was he?' she asked the grandfather. 'Poor little angel. Ah, but you're grand now, aren't you, pet?'

'Bad doggy licked my face,' the child said, pulling his sleeve across his mouth. 'Granda, can I get another ic-cream? With chocolate and strawberry stuff?'

Diarmuid pressed a twenty-pound note into the man's hand. 'Here, allow me. Please.'

'No call for that – no, no, no, no. He's right as rain, aren't you ? Aren't you right as rain?'

'Is that for me?' the child asked Diarmuid, looking at the money.

'Of course it is,' Diarmuid said. 'Please,' he told the

grandfather, pressing the note into his breast pocket. 'I'd be grateful.'

The older man removed the note from his pocket, stared at it, then turned to the boy.

'What do you say, Jonathan?'

'Thank you.'

Several people had gathered round Angela, who was now sitting on the pavement with the dog's head in her lap. 'Vet's place just over there, you know,' someone in the group said. 'He'd look at that cut for you.'

It took Diarmuid and a couple of bystanders to carry the dog to the vet's. Twenty minutes later the wound had been washed and a wad of cotton wool applied, held in place by a plaster that Princess tried to scrape off without success.

'Surface wound, better in a week or two,' the vet explained. 'Except it was to turn out to be a fracture of the skull, but I doubt that. Can't tell for sure in the absence of an X-ray. Thirty pounds will do grand.'

It was after half past three by the time they got back to the car, so they decided to leave Angela off before Diarmuid took Princess home. All the way to Central Station she sat in the back, comforting the dog. 'Poor old dote. You'd hardly credit what some human beings do to animals.'

'She was lucky,' Diarmuid said over his shoulder. 'Another metre into the road and we'd have needed shovels to scrape her up.' In the rear-view mirror the afternoon sunshine picked out highlights in Angela's reddy-brown hair. They turned into the street that led to the station entrance.

'What will you say?'

'To who?'

'To whoever owns her – I mean, they're bound to notice the dressing.'

Diarmuid tried to loosen the tension he could feel in his neck and shoulders. 'It's easy. The dog pulled away, ran out in the road, got hit by a truck. That's what happened, that's what I'll tell them.'

'Yes, but it was my fault. I should have held on to her.'

'No, no. These things just…happen.' Or they do if you haven't the wit to hang on to the bloody dog's lead as you were asked to *and said you would*.

'Yes, but I—'

'It's all right.'

They shook hands and he noticed how soft and warm hers felt, just like it had in the graveyard. The calves of her legs went bulge, shrink, bulge, shrink away from him, down the sloping platform towards her train.

Back home, he carried the dog into the utility room, wrapped her in her blanket. She whined and tried to lick his hand. The dressing on her head looked enormous.

Diarmuid went back to the living room, whiskey in hand. Positioned carefully on the footstool, a cushion under it, his foot began to tingle, then hurt. Tingling foot, tingling arm – soon his entire body would be tingling. Outside the light was draining away. On the TV, a man who kept shouting, 'You will, and your auntie Annie!' was organising two teams somewhere to have a water-balloon fight. Clenching his teeth, Diarmuid tried to think of something good – a single unequivocal part of his life that could be described as positive to put in the balance against lonely graveyards, a son who left his mother to rot alone and a wounded dog. He couldn't think of one.

Chapter 8

UNCLE DAN'S DÉCOR

The following morning at half past seven, he was in the shower and had reached the hairwashing stage when the phone rang. Turn off the water and listen. Terry? The cops? *Angela*? He put on the *Sunday Times* special-offer white-towelling dressing-gown and hurried downstairs, leaving damp footprints on the carpet.

'Hello?'

'Rurrp, rurrrp, ruurp, for the last half-hour. What the hell kept you? Were you in the bed getting a bit of—'

The voice broke off and was replaced by a bout of sneezing.

'Uncle Dan – *Uncle Dan*... Thank you. I was in the shower and didn't hear you. I'm now in the kitchen half-naked, dripping water over everything and getting very cold.'

'Getting very cold – isn't it a big pity of you?' There was a sound of nose-blowing. 'If you were tortured with hay-fever like me you'd have something to complain about – I have the head near sneezed off myself. '

'It's dust-mites, Uncle Dan. Nothing to do with hay-fever. Get the carpet taken out of that study room and you'll never sneeze again.'

'Will I not? Anyway, that's not what I'm phoning you about. What I want is to consult you about another thing completely.'

Calm. Speak slowly. 'Well, that's good. We should have consulted, had a proper consultation in fact, the three of us—'

'For the likes of this what you need is one that'd have an eye in his head. Your man Paul now, you'd know looking at him he hasn't the kind of eye that's wanted for this.'

'Yes, well, I'm sure Paul would be happy to be involved. You might be surprised by how much he has to contribute.'

'It's past time this whole thing was settled.' Uncle Dan paused for five more sneezes, followed by a sniff. 'Left lying far too long. Get to my age, postponing a thing makes no sense at all at all. Now's the time to get the use of a kitchen, not five years down the road.'

'A kitchen?'

'A kitchen and a study for my computer and me too. And for to do something like that right, it'd take a bit of help from an up-to-date boy like yourself that would know about tiles and the décor and that.'

'I'm an education lecturer, Uncle Dan, not an interior-décor guide.'

'No need to be smart. If you're going to be smart, you needn't bother yourself. All I'm looking for is a bit of colour advice and that for the room where I have my computer and for the kitchen. And if all you can manage is smart remarks, then we'll manage grand on our own without you, and you can go on to hell.'

It took Diarmuid several minutes to calm him down. Yes, Diarmuid said again, he'd be happy to give any advice he could.

'Right so. How long will it take you getting to the Fine Tile Gallery in Sprucefield Centre?'

'Well, around forty minutes. But this is Sunday, Uncle Dan. The shops are all shut.'

'Are they now? Well it so happens there's none of them shut at Sprucefield. Open every one of them from one o'clock onward – supermarkets and everything. Myself and herself is heading there for half three. So you may leave your house about half two to be on the safe side.'

'The Fine Tile Gallery.'

'Right. At Sprucefield Centre. For to advise us.'

'Right.' Diarmuid forced his voice to sound positive. 'Great. And we could maybe have a chat about Mammy's will while we're at it. Clear up one or two details.'

Uncle Dan sniffed and sighed. 'God be good to poor Katie.'

'Anyway, I'll see you at half past three, all right?'

'Or will we say four?'

'No we'll not say four, Uncle Dan. We'll stick to half three.'

'Right so. Barring acts of God or hangovers, half three!' Uncle Dan shouted. He sneezed a final time, very loud, and hung up.

Acts of God, maybe, but definitely no hangovers – Uncle Dan hadn't touched a serious drink in twenty years. When he'd been in the cattle-lorry business, there'd been enough hangovers for several lifetimes. 'Drinking and carousing,' Mammy used to say, 'with the lowest of the low.' Now that he was over seventy, a half glass of sherry at Christmas was as much as Dan could manage. The old Dan drank and fought over everything, the new Dan abstained and expected everyone to agree with him. Diarmuid thought he maybe preferred the old Dan.

The parking spaces outside the Fine Tile Gallery were all filled, and it was some time before Diarmuid found a spot. When he arrived at the gallery ten minutes later Uncle Dan was sunk in a strawberry-coloured sofa, walking-stick lodged between his knees, pretending to study a brochure.

'Well, Uncle Dan, how's the form?'

'They haven't measured me for the coffin yet.' He took a dark red hanky from his pocket and blew his nose. 'Blackguards down the road after the pub had me awake till near two, and when I miss the sleep, the oul' sneezing starts. And don't start blethering about carpets, whatever you do.'

Diarmuid looked around. The ceiling appeared to be mainly skylight, so brightness and air flooded the room. Cleverly concealed lamps brought out the tiny dimples on the tiles; and looking from one colour to the next – blues, browns, pinks, greens, whites, yellows – your eye felt dizzy, as if you'd been viewing a series of paintings. The honey-coloured maple floor added to the feel of an art gallery.

'Where's Carmel? She'd be a better judge of what way to do your kitchen and computer room than I would.'

'She's shopping – be here in no time.'

'Some lucky boy, your uncle Dan,' Mammy used to say. Lucky to have made money with cattle lorries, lucky to have survived all the drinking when he was younger, lucky now to have a one-third share in the will of the sister he'd always irritated, to add to whatever he'd salted away from the cattle-lorry days.

'Would you like to fill in our book?' She seemed to materialise from behind one of the revolving stacks. Thin face, cropped black hair, the hint of a Clark Gable moustache. She placed a visitors' book bound in leather on a coffee-table. 'Just your name and address would be lovely. And perhaps a phone number, if you wouldn't mind.'

Obediently, Diarmuid took the book from her and filled in his details.

'And yourself, sir,' the woman said.

Uncle Dan looked up from the couch. 'The oul' hands are far too stiff for that class of carry-on.'

'Can I show you something, then, sir?'

'I'd say you could.' Uncle Dan watched her, then stood up, tapping his stick. 'Only it's kitchen tiles we're after.'

The assistant gave an even-teeth smile. 'And did you have a particular colour in mind?'

'Not sure.'

She led them to a display beside the mini-fountain in the opposite corner. Orange tiles in a rectangular shape, glowing and reflecting on her hand as she pointed at them. 'These are on special offer just now – and you get an interesting effect if you interrupt the regular pattern. Like so.' She produced a dark green tile from a long flat drawer, and held it beside the orange ones.

'And the price – is the effect to it interesting too?' Uncle Dan studied the woman's face as he spoke. 'Don't forget it's not millionaires you're talking to here.'

'Was a complete revamp of the house what you had in mind, or just the kitchen?'

'The kitchen and the thinking room – where I have my wee computer. That's all. Only I don't want tiles there. A bit of wallpaper that'd cheer me up when I'd look away from the screen the odd time would be more the line of things.' Uncle Dan moved back to the sofa. 'But you may hold your horses until the woman of the house comes in, for she's the organ-grinder and I'm only the boy with the tail.'

A big woman with a small, breathy voice, Carmel had been Fr Sheedy's housekeeper for years. When the poor man had fallen getting out of his car one night and broken a bone in his wrist, she'd become first his nurse and then his chauffeur. The third day of chauffeuring, when Carmel called at Uncle Dan's to collect the priest after a game of chess, he and Dan were having an argument about what constituted a just war. Fr Sheedy's back had been turned and Carmel had caught Dan's eye, drawn a red fingernail across her throat, then tapped her watch. Dan gave a ghost of a wink and had brought the conversation to a close inside seconds. On the way out he nudged her in the back with his knuckle, rolled his eyes and mouthed, 'Sorry!' It wasn't a word he used too often.

Three days later she rang and said that she'd bought a big tin of pineapple chunks by mistake. Father Sheedy couldn't stand pineapple. Would they be any good to Dan? He took it and soon she began to look in on her way home from work – a packet of biscuits, a tub of Häagen-Dazs, a head of lettuce. Some of it was stuff Fr Sheedy didn't want, others were items she had seen at a special price in the supermarket. 'Useless for the likes of me and maybe they'd fatten you up!' she'd call, moving her bulk across the kitchen in a sideways movement, like a supermarket trolley. A pattern developed where she'd cook a Friday-evening meal for him, sometimes bringing and lighting two red or pink or blue candles on the table beside them. 'Sure I have no dances to be running to!' she'd say, and wink back at him as she served up plates of lasagne and fresh buttered carrots, and the candlelight threw shadows on plates, food and faces.

'The parish priest's bloody woman,' Uncle Dan called her, when her name arose in conversation. But a few weeks later, he and the bloody woman were going for short walks, stopping sometimes for a cup of coffee on the way back. When Diarmuid told Frances she said she didn't believe it. 'His digestive system will collapse under him – she'll have him dead in a fortnight.' But it was Fr Sheedy who took a small stroke and retired to live with his sister in Bangor. The following weekend, Carmel moved out of the parochial house, took a taxi with her suitcases to Uncle Dan's three miles away and moved in as his housekeeper. The house was big, five bedrooms. There was plenty of space for them both.

Now, in the Fine Tile Gallery, Uncle Dan put one hand on top of the other on his walking stick, sighed and looked around him. 'We might be having a general overhaul or we might not. Herself will know the answer.' Beside him Diarmuid shifted his weight from one leg to the other. The moment he did so, a stab of pain shot into his bruised toe. He looked down, half expecting the bulge to show through his shoe.

'She's away buying shoes,' Uncle Dan went on, 'and a bit of meat for the dinner.'

Diarmuid looked at his watch, then at the tile woman. 'Right, then, Uncle Dan, I'll leave you in this good lady's hands. Like her, I think orange is the one you're looking for.'

Uncle Dan stared at him. 'Where are you for? Not much good in coming if you're clearing off after two minutes before Carmel even gets here.'

'I thought you wanted my advice on choosing tiles? I've given you it already. Now, I have an article to write with a deadline—'

The door of the shop ch-chinged and Carmel entered. She was wearing a dark purple suit with a deep-cut neck, a small silver pendant lost in the bra-strain of her breasts. Talking in little gasps she moved across the gallery, a bag of shopping in either hand. The contrast between the big country face and the Marilyn-Monroe voice was unnerving. 'Dear God, my *feet*! Marks & Spencer's is coming down with ladies buying Black Forest gateaux. Well, Diarmuid.' She unbuttoned her jacket and tugged the front of her T-shirt, making her breasts bounce briefly.

'How are you?' Diarmuid asked.

'I could feel worse, I suppose, and I could look better, although we'll not go there, as they say now. We'll not go there, if you don't mind.'

Diarmuid was casting about for a reply when his mobile sounded. He creaked across the floor to a corner.

Paul's tense voice: 'Is he with you – Uncle Dan? If he is, say, "That's right", if he's not, say, "That's odd." That's right for yes, that's odd for no. Have you got that?'

'That's right.' Across the showroom Carmel helped Uncle Dan to his feet. They moved nearer the orange display, the assistant following.

'What do you want?' Diarmuid whispered. 'I'm at the Fine Tile Gallery.'

There was a gulping sound from the other end. *Are you drinking?* 'Is Frances there?'

'That's odd.'

'Good for her – bit of sense. What about her nibs, Mount Carmel?'

'That's right.'

More swallowing sounds. 'Guessed as much. Look, be sure to get him on his own and raise the will thing, won't you?'

'That's right. But,' Diarmuid spoke more quietly, turned his back to Uncle Dan and the two women, 'that's easier said than done.'

'Just *say* something, that's all. Say you'd like him, we'd like him to think if this was really what Mammy would have wanted.'

'That's odd.'

'For God's sake.' Paul sounded impatient. 'This needs

147

resolving. Say that… Wait till we see… Say that there's such a thing as morality. Remind him of that. And that we have to respect the wishes of the dead. I only hope that doesn't remind him to ask you why you didn't go to the funeral.'

'Maybe you should talk to him yourself, then.'

'If he would arrange to see me, I certainly would. Meanwhile you're there, so I suggest you get on with it. Tactful but firm.'

'That's right. OK, Arthur, gotta go now. See you at the staff meeting on Tuesday.'

Breathe deep, think of a wide beach, Portstewart strand on a hot day, the swish of water, the sand without a pebble, the sky a dizzy blue, the water clear. Think dipping a big toe into its sweet chill. Think remedy administered. Think pain-free. Fixing a smile on his face and repeating a silent 'Ooohhhhmmmm,' Diarmuid crossed the floor.

'Bad news?' Uncle Dan asked.

'No, no, no, no. Colleague ringing, thinks I've marked students too easy. Ha-ha.'

'That'd make a change,' Carmel said. 'I did a course in the tech about eight, no, nine years back in psychology. I thought, This is right up my street. I'll enjoy this, learn new things, but do you know, I did not like one minute of it, and that's the truth. It was the attitude of the man teaching us – some of the things he wrote on my essay, well, it wasn't much encouragement to go on learning I can tell you. Too many airs and graces, half these people.'

Uncle Dan tapped Carmel on the shoulder, then left his hand resting there. 'Blue – what sort of a colour for a wall is blue?'

'Blue is a soothing colour,' Carmel told him. 'Better than orange, and it stimulates communication. You could have it on the study wall behind your computer.'

'I want wallpaper in my study, not bloody tiles. And I don't want a kitchen either with a pile of tiles that'd put you in mind of the North Pole.'

'Could I make a suggestion?' The tile woman smiled, all the way to her strong back teeth. 'Why don't you take both colours home and try them out? Putting a colour in context can change everything. Do you have a car nearby?'

Uncle Dan and Carmel didn't have a car nearby, it emerged, because they had taken the bus – Carmel was nervous about driving on the motorway, she said. So when the tile woman heard that the only car nearby was Diarmuid's she looked at him and smiled and asked if he'd get it and drive it round to the front of the Fine Tile Gallery, then bring Uncle Dan and Carmel and the different colour of tiles home together. Carmel began to tell Dan that Diarmuid had to get on, he had all sorts of demands on him, but Diarmuid said it didn't matter, he'd finish the article later.

He'd walked for just one minute in the direction of his car when the rain started. Not light misty rain but fat splashy rain, banging down on him and the pavement. He hurried back to the shelter of the shopping centre entrance, waiting for it to ease. After five minutes there was still no slackening, so he took a newspaper someone had left in the doorway corner and held it over his head. By the time he got to the car his trousers were soaking and his left shoe was squelching. Hadn't the grave-digger in *Hamlet* said something about wet corpses rotting quicker? He drove back and parked the car on a double yellow line near the door of the Fine Tile Gallery.

Inside the door the woman pointed to two boxes. 'These are the orange and these are the blue tiles. There are six tiles in each.'

'Could we take some greens when we're at it?' Carmel asked.

So the tile woman packed six green tiles, and then at the last minute Carmel's eye was caught by a purple, so six of them were included as well. 'Normally we carry materials out to the car for clients. Unfortunately all our men are busy delivering today. We do apologise for that.'

'Sure haven't the three of us arms of our own?' Uncle Dan told her.

But then Carmel reminded Uncle Dan of the way the rain could bring on his sneezing, and she herself had a touch of arthritis in her shoulder, so it was left to Diarmuid and the tile woman to bring the boxes of tiles to the car. The tile woman arranged them in a line at the front of the store and Diarmuid picked them up one by one and carried them out.

He had the engine started, Uncle Dan and Carmel in the back, and was about to pull away when the tile woman darted through the rain and leant in the window, wet strips of hair coiled flat across her forehead. 'Here's my card if you've any queries. And I have a note of the samples issued under your name, Dr Monaghan – hope that's OK.' Her smile seemed to go halfway down his throat. Then she turned and skipped back into the shop, elbows jutting from her sides as she ran.

When they got to the house, the rain had eased. Diarmuid moved from behind the wheel and felt a pain cross his groin and move down his leg, brief but so intense he gasped. And when he opened the rear door of the car and leant in to lift the first box, everything in the car seemed to tilt. He crouched in the back, one knee on the seat, panting, waiting. The pain eased.

Uncle Dan's kitchen door, at the back of the house, swung loose on its hinges. It had still to be painted; there was a round hole where the lock would be fitted, and it had no handle, but it was a strong PVC door. Carmel had pushed the rubbish bin against it, to stop the wind blowing it open.

'The men doing it are to be back on Monday,' she said. 'We may just keep something propped against it until then. Two nights ago I was lying listening to it, my heart in my mouth, the clack-clack-clack of it, I didn't know what it was. In the end I got up and stuck a chair behind it.'

Uncle Dan pointed at Diarmuid. 'Don't you be doing those tiles on your own – we'll give you a hand.' And, ignoring protests from Carmel, he shuffled out to the car and stood, arms open, ready to take the first box.

'You two boys are just the best,' Carmel murmured as Diarmuid and Dan set their boxes in the corner of the kitchen. 'Sure you're half finished already.'

When it was all done Diarmuid followed his uncle into the living room and flopped into an armchair beside him.

Uncle Dan wiped his forehead with a red handkerchief. 'The people are lost for a bit of exercise.'

Diarmuid waited until his heart had stopped thudding. 'Paul and myself, we were over at Mammy's the other day. After we were finished we went to see McAleavy, the solicitor.'

Uncle Dan blew his nose. 'Is there a clean hanky about?' he called to Carmel. 'This one's soaked.'

'And we wondered if the three of us – you, me, Paul and the solicitor, four, the four of us should have a chat some time.' Diarmuid watched Uncle Dan unfold the neatly pressed hanky Carmel brought. 'About the will.'

'Your mother, God be good to her, used to help me collect for the Silver Circle.' His voice was hoarse, probably from the effort of lifting boxes. 'We'd collect money for a raffle every week from all the parishioners, then bring it in a big envelope up to the parochial house, and Maggie Mahon the housekeeper never missed but give us a cream bun apiece when we were leaving. Wee Katie could have ate buns to a band playing.'

'We were wondering,' Diarmuid said carefully. 'If – if you felt that the will – the last version – was what Mammy really wanted. Was it the kind she'd have made when she was herself?'

'Her hair would blow up around her mouth when she was riding along, and there'd be bits of cream from the bun stuck in it.'

Diarmuid nodded. 'The thing is, when she made that last one, it was, what? Four or five days before she died and, of course, there was an awful lot of medication in her system.'

'She used race me once we got as far as the lane on the way home. "Ready, set, *sprint*!" and away she'd go, the spokes on her wheels whirring and whirring. I'd go slow on purpose, so I could watch her pedalling ahead of me on that red bike of hers. Like a wee screeching bird.'

Carmel put her hand on his shoulder. 'Dan, like a decent man, what you do is, go up and throw yourself down for half an hour.

Come on now, upsadaisy. Sure you're great.' Uncle Dan got slowly to his feet and, with her help, ascended the stairs, holding on to the banister.

'We sold more Silver Circle tickets than anyone else in the parish,' he called, without turning. There was a final sneeze as the bedroom door closed behind him and Carmel.

Alone in the living room, Diarmuid stretched his legs until he was rigid from head to toe. The house was quiet. On the mantelpiece the Belleek china clock ticked; beside it stood an Aynsley vase. In the back garden a blackbird sang, bouncing the notes about with random generosity. If a blackbird sang and there was no one to hear, did its song exist? And what about after you died? Did the universe go on existing?

Ten minutes passed. Fifteen. Maybe Carmel had fallen asleep as well, wasn't coming back. Time to get out, leave meeting arrangements with Uncle Dan for another day.

Diarmuid reached in his pocket, tore a page from his notebook, scribbled 'Got to run!' and propped it against a glass paperweight on the table. Behind him, as he went down the path, he could hear the new kitchen door, with a hole where the lock would be inserted, clack-clacking against the rubbish bin.

Chapter 9

PRINCESS GOES HOME

It was after six by the time he got home. There were breadcrumbs on the kitchen floor and flaky bits from the peat briquettes on the living-room floor and two plates and a fork on the sofa and empty mugs in the bedroom. So he lifted all the tableware he could see into the dishwasher, then got out the vacuum cleaner and went round the floor as quickly as he could, sucking up some clanking stuff, but since it was only 5ps and paperclips, he didn't mind. That done, he got the sponge from the downstairs toilet, then a bit of Zip firelighter and set the fire, afterwards sponging clean the marble slab surround. It felt good to look at the brown gleam and sniff the lemony smell of it. Then he rushed in and put the pork chops under the grill, ready to cook them, and the spuds on the hob. Outside the back door a thrush was singing and poking himself with his dart beak.

Anything else? Well, the windows could do with a wash but he was damned if he was going to start that. He considered pouring himself a drink but decided against it too. Drunk and in charge of a dog wouldn't go down well. He approached the utility room, gripped the door-handle and began to open it, then stopped. Leave it. Remain uncertain. That way when he opened the door, he'd be as surprised as she was over Princess's condition. Well, maybe not completely surprised.

Would Frances invite Mairead and Joy in when they dropped

her off, or would they sit sullen in the van and wait for him to bring the dog out? No, they'd sit tight – they'd want to get themselves and their doggy straight home. Or to the vet. Or the mortician.

But in the end it wasn't Joy and Mairead's van that pulled up outside the house. It was a taxi. It sat there, the taxi man twisted round, giving change. Then she stepped out, clutching her purple travel-bag. Her jeans looked more elegant, her blue sweater better filled, and her face...fresher, somehow.

He took the bag from her. 'Dinner's nearly ready. Drink?'

'Thought you'd never ask.'

The old joke. Woman comes into a pub and asks for an innuendo, so the barman gives her one. Diarmuid brought the whisky into the living room and gave it to Frances. 'Nice time?'

'It was...grounded.' She sniffed the drink, then held it to her lips until a third of the contents were gone. 'Not all the time but most of it. Especially the last day.' She licked the tip of her finger. 'What about you and Princess?'

Tell her now and get it over. Or show her the dog, let her draw her own conclusions. His heart began to hammer. 'What?'

'I said how did you and Princess manage?' She began to walk towards the kitchen, glass in hand, as she spoke – like the sheriff moving down the street in *High Noon*, come to seek justice, mete out retribution.

He hurried into step beside her, talking faster as she moved through the kitchen towards the utility-room door. 'Nice and warm and dry in there, and – I had her out for a walk so she could stretch her—'

His words trailed off. Frances was standing absolutely still, so Diarmuid looked over her shoulder. Princess was lying in the corner, chin resting on her left paw. From where they were standing you couldn't see the plaster. Then the dog whined and turned her head and Frances gasped.

'Oh, here. Oh, here now. Dear dear dear. What's this – hmm? *Hmmm*? Did someone *neglect* you?' She put down her drink and patted the dog's head, tugged gently on her left ear, then the right. The dog's mouth trembled.

Speaking very fast, Diarmuid began to explain what had happened, emphasising the suddenness with which the dog had launched into the road and the speed of the oncoming truck. He didn't bother mentioning Angela.

Frances listened, her face expressionless, occasionally stroking Princess's head. 'Why didn't you wrap the lead round your wrist? You're supposed to do that with a dog.'

'Joy didn't mention it,' Diarmuid said.

Frances stroked the dog silently for several seconds. Then: 'Although at the same time it is their own fault, when you think of it. If they were concerned about their dog, they'd have got proper kennels. These things happen because people allow them to happen.'

'Well, I—'

'And half these van drivers think the rules don't apply to them – park on the pavement, ignore lights, do whatever comes in their heads.'

'I'm not sure it was so much the van driver's fault as—'

'He hit the poor dog, didn't he? And drove on without so much as a by-your-leave. Isn't that right? I'd say that was his fault.'

'Well, yes, only—'

'Supposing Princess hadn't moved as quick as she did – she'd have been crushed. Completely.'

'Mmm.' Diarmuid did what he could to look concerned. This wasn't the way he'd expected her to react: she appeared to be annoyed with the van driver. *Not him.*

Frances tugged Princess's head round. 'C'mere till your mammy has a look at you. Oh, dearie me, oh, dearie me. How long's that contraption going to be on her head?'

'Vet said leave it for a week anyway.'

'Vet? How much was he?'

'Thirty pounds.'

'Mm.' Frances straightened, picked up her drink. 'If she'd

been properly looked after, there'd be no need for a vet at all. But sure they've been feeding the poor brute nothing but the cheapest dog-food you could imagine all her life. No wonder the poor thing is in the shape she is.'

Diarmuid lifted the dog's water bowl and emptied it into the sink. Refilled it. 'Did you not get a lift back with Joy and Mairead?'

'They left before me – had to rush off to start some job or other.'

Diarmuid refilled Princess's eating bowl. The dog let her black-strawberry nose quiver over the food a couple of times, then began to gulp it down. 'So how did you get back?'

'Jorg gave me a lift as far as town. Taxi after that.' She patted the dog's back. 'It was the most meaningful car journey I've had in my life. He just…I dunno. It was that feeling you get when you're with someone who's only concerned with, you know, the *essentials*. That's what you miss out on when you're running around all the time – the essentials. There was this sort of *power* coming off him'

She wasn't going mad about the dog. And she was talking to him. *Talking* to him. Diarmuid tried to keep the exuberance out of his voice. 'How did Joy and Mairead get on?'

'Well, their main worry seemed to be could they get the landscaping contract for the body-soul centre. That seemed to be *their* big concern. All the time I was talking to Jorg – he asked me to stay after one of his lectures, wanted to hear more details about my organic gardening – they kept trying to get his attention.'

'Did they?'

'Until in the end they were right beside my elbow, listening to everything Jorg said to me, shuffling their feet. Near the end they even started throwing in comments.'

'You mean heckling?'

'*No*. Just saying that they'd worked with me and that they were the only Catholic-Protestant gardening firm in the Belfast area, and that they brought not just gardening expertise to their work but a philosophy of reconciliation as well, with themselves as a model, Catholic and Protestant. In the end Jorg got sort of fed up.'

'What did he say?'

'He said he'd be happy to respond to their concerns, but for the moment his focus was on issues relating to me, and they should have a fruit juice in the cafeteria and he'd be with them in fifteen minutes.'

'Fair enough.'

'They went off in a bit of a huff. What got them was the way he was giving time to me.'

'So. Did they get the contract?'

Frances laughed. When she put her head back and opened her mouth wide, it reminded him of when they used to go to the pictures, before they were married, and *Woody Woodpecker* came on – she'd laugh and a little gleam from the inside of her mouth would show in the light from the screen. Woodpecker – he hadn't noticed the *double entendre* until this minute: was that why she'd laughed so much at it? 'Jorg is a completely centred man – not self-centred, *centred*. That's why he believes in people running their own business. He told me he would look at Joy and Mairead's plan and see if its aura was one of integrity,' She smiled. 'I think that means they're not getting it. Anyway. We're back. How's your foot?'

'Not so bad. A bit sore.'

'Jorg's office walls are *covered* with testimonials, one from a woman who had cancer. Signed and everything.'

Diarmuid resisted the temptation to shout, 'Bollocks!' 'Amazing,' he said.

'And you know that pain I get between my shoulders sometimes? Well, he took me through a session – a really quick one, just before we left – and it's gone. I was in his car on the way home, and coming through Letterkenny, suddenly, out of nowhere, the pain seemed to go.'

'And did it?'

'Of course. I said it did. And that wasn't...' She trailed off, staring past Diarmuid. 'Would you look at the state of that.' She strode towards the kitchen door and fingered the parallel lines of scratches left by Princess. Several flakes of white paint came away on her finger and fluttered to the ground. 'What happened here?'

'She just came rocketing out of the utility room, and before I could stop her she'd put these big scratches all over the door.'

'Had you got her on a lead?'

'Well, as a matter of fact, I was just about to put it on her when—'

A rattling sound interrupted him, a bit like a lorry loaded with milk crates coming into the cul-de-sac. But it wasn't a lorry. It was Joy and Mairead's van, which pulled up to the pavement, the exhaust pipe dipped at a dangerous angle to the ground, belching black smoke. The two women emerged and walked up the driveway, Joy taking little clockwork steps, Mairead with her head tilted to one side, watchful. Frances opened the door before they could ring.

Joy stared at Diarmuid for a moment, then spoke to Frances. 'Can't stay. Just time to load Princess and run.'

Frances led them towards the utility room. 'She's resting, poor thing. Had a bit of a knock while we were gone, but she'll be grand.'

Behind him Diarmuid could hear the rustle and small panting *whuhs* as Mairead, in her tight runners, came behind them.

'Got in a wee accident when Diarmuid and her were out for a walk,' Frances continued. 'Pulled her head clear of the lead and took a knock off a car.' She opened the utility-room door.

Joy sank to her knees, touching the dog's face with her fingertips. 'Oh, my God, oh, my sweet, suffering Maker.' She patted its head several times, then twisted round to look up at Diarmuid. 'This dog's been lying here in pain. This dog's been neglected.'

'I had a vet look at her yesterday,' Diarmuid said. 'She ate a huge meal yesterday evening and another this morning, and a third about fifteen minutes ago. Hardly neglected.'

'Her eyes look tired,' Mairead said. 'I see a shadow of suffering on them.' The dog whined and tried to lick Joy's hand. 'And hear that? She's moaning with pain. What else would she moan for if she wasn't in pain?'

'Pleasure,' Diarmuid suggested. 'Animals sometimes moan for pleasure. Same as people.'

There was a moment of silence. Oh, shite. He shouldn't have said the thing about people moaning.

Then Frances pushed him aside. 'Diarmuid's right, the dog's grand. If she was in pain she wouldn't be eating. She'd have taken a lump out of you – it's in the nature of an animal that's hurting to try to defend itself. Diarmuid's quite right. Keep the bandage on for another week and she won't know herself.' That was twice she'd said he was right. It was like hearing a stranger talk.

Joy clipped a lead over the dog's head and straightened. She was trembling as she leant her face into Frances's. 'Well, I've been a dog-owner for eight years and *I* say you're talking rubbish and this dog's been abused.' She tugged the lead roughly. Princess's claws clicked uncertainly on the kitchen floor. 'We'll be sending any vet bills here. Just so you know.'

'Don't bother yourself,' Frances said. 'We've enough bills of our own.'

'I've already paid one bill for her,' Diarmuid said. 'The vet said to bring her to your own vet if she was acting funny.'

'What for?' Joy demanded.

'In case she had a hairline fracture.'

Mairead pulled Joy aside and stood red-faced, fists clenched in front of her. 'You two have got some nerve! We left our dog here with him, your bloody husband, and this is the thanks! Our poor wee dog – *mutilated*. And then people saying it's our fault!'

'I'm not sure whose fault it is, but it's not ours,' Frances moved to the door. *Ours,* Diarmuid repeated silently. 'Diarmuid has looked after your dog to the best of his abilities. For nothing, I might add.'

'Well his abilities aren't good enough, then,' Joy said, her head twitching with irritation. 'Miles from it, in fact. Next time we'll—'

'—make other arrangements.' Mairead headed for the door. 'Someone more reliable.'

Diarmuid stood, arms folded, shoulder touching his wife's. 'Face it, ladies. Things happen to dogs, things happen to people, and sometimes – sometimes – nobody at all is to blame.' Nice touch, that. 'Ladies.'

Joy turned at the door. 'No one to blame!' Little flecks of spit made parabolas in the light. 'That poor thing's face is twisted off her with pain, she could have a split skull – and I'll just bet she has – and you've the bare-arsed cheek to stand there and say it just happened!'

'It's "bare-faced" not "bare-arsed".' Frances said. 'And what you need to do instead of insulting people and talking coarse is look after your dog properly. Look at that coat – practically moth-eaten from malnutrition. When you've done your duty by the poor creature – like feeding her properly – then come back and start giving out to the rest of us.'

'I declare to God,' Joy said. 'I can hardly credit this.'

'We do the work, we leave off the dog, and you – *you*,' Mairead jumped forward again to point her finger in Diarmuid's face, 'you inflict or maybe that should be just *allow* grievous bodily harm to be done to her! D'you know what you are? You're a chauvinist bastard!'

'What kind of chauvinist bastard? There's more than one, you know.' Diarmuid said.

'A male chauvinist bastard!'

'Oh, right. Fair enough. '

'Shut up, *please*!' Frances shouted. 'Just take your bloody dog and go! And give us peace.'

'All right. Come on, Princess! *Come on*!' Mairead tugged the dog across the kitchen, its claws skidding on the tiled floor.

'That's what happens, you see,' Joy said to her. 'Some people, it's a waste of time trying to be civil to them, let alone *friendly*.'

'You'll not be hearing from us!' Mairead yelled over her

shoulder. 'You'll be hearing from our solicitor!' She slammed the door behind them.

Frances and Diarmuid watched from the living-room window as the two women struggled to get the dog into the back of their van. When Joy tried to lift on her own she couldn't manage; when the two tried together, one end of the dog kept being lifted too high and the other too low. Eventually women and dog stumbled and squeezed on board. The van engine gulped, wheezed, collapsed. Wheezed once again, collapsed a second time. Joy got out and tried to push from the back. Mairead got out as well and steered and tried to push simultaneously. The van wouldn't start.

'We should help them,' Diarmuid said.

'No, we shouldn't,' Frances told him.

'But they'll never get it started.'

'They should have thought about that before they started giving out.'

'This could go on for the next hour. And end up them having to come back in here to call for a tow-truck.'

Frances tossed her magazine aside. 'Oh, all right. But you're far too soft.'

When Diarmuid, Frances and Joy all pushed at the back, the van began to roll, and once it got onto the gentle slope that ran down from the house, all Joy had to do was scramble on board quickly, then Mairead let out the clutch and the engine coughed, coughed again and started. A flash of tail-lights and they were gone.

'That's half their problem – people can't be sure when they're going to turn up and when they aren't because that old jalopy is stop-start-stop.' Frances turned back into the kitchen. 'But they're too mean to invest. Cutting off their nose to spite their face.'

'How are you feeling?'

'Shaking.' Frances took down the bottle of Jameson and two glasses from the cupboard. 'But good at the same time.' She laughed. 'What about you?'

'Same.'

'How's the foot?'

'A bit sore after that pushing.' He took the half-filled glass from her. 'Maybe I should see Jorg.'

She gestured towards his foot. 'Show us till we have a look.'

In the end the living-room light wasn't clear enough so they went into the bathroom, where Diarmuid sat on the toilet and took off his sock. His heel was normal and so was his ankle. But just past the ankle the colour deepened suddenly, and by the time it reached the tip of his toes three were purple.

Frances rubbed the sole of his foot gently. 'Circulation. The blood is all sitting at the top, you see. Because your toe got hurt, it triggers a chain reaction.'

'I thought poor circulation meant your blood got cut off.'

'It's not so much cut off as not moving fast enough in some places. Needs a bit of a push, that's all.'

In bed that night, Diarmuid lay thinking about the blood going around inside him like in a washing machine, plunging into places where it shouldn't and staying there too long. Maybe going into his head and giving him a stroke. Or lodging permanently in his penis.

'Do you think will Joy and Mairead really get a solicitor?' he whispered.

Frances wriggled herself into the spoon position against him. 'I doubt it. You should have seen them at the centre.' She gave a little shiver and giggled again. 'Every time he talked to me, they'd start inching up behind him. I pretended not to see them but I could just tell they were *livid*.'

'With him? Because he spoke to you?'

'In part. More because of the Sunday-afternoon healing session, though.' She put both her hands flat on his back. 'Everybody on the course had to get in groups of five, you see, and put into practice the movements and withdrawals he'd taught us. The person being practised on told you something that was wrong with them. Everybody had some wee thing – I

162

told them about between my shoulders. So, anyway, I was in the group with Joy and Mairead, and there was this man of about fifty and this woman of about forty. And the man said he had this pain in his ear, he'd had it since his wife died three years earlier, been to all the doctors – hopeless. He had this little squint too – you'd have felt sorry for him. So Mairead and Joy said they'd work on him. That meant I had to do my stuff on a woman who had a rash on her stomach. She didn't even want to show it because it'd involve lifting up her sweater, but eventually we went into a corner and she did. So I worked on her, and Joy and Mairead got the man. This woman is lying back on the mat with her eyes shut, and I'm doing a field-pass over her convergences—'

'A what?'

'It's where you move your hands over the person's energy points without contact.' She lifted her hands from his shoulder-blades for a moment, then put them back. 'That's the way body-soul works. Anyway, I was with this woman and I could hear Joy and Mairead. "Is that any better?" they kept asking him. "It's bound to be a bit better." And he kept saying, "Damn the hair better," and they would try again.'

'What about your one? The woman.'

'I cured her.'

'You *cured* her?' Diarmuid turned round in the bed, got up on one elbow to look at her.

'I was thinking it was time I stopped – my arms were ready to come off; only then her face went sort of pale, and I asked if she was feeling all right, would I get her a glass of water or something. And she opened her eyes and said, "Christ Almighty it's gone."'

'The rash?'

'The rash. Without even lifting her jersey again, she knew it was gone.'

'Completely?'

Frances nodded. 'Joy and Mairead were still working on the man. And then Jorg came round and made us change subjects.

163

So I got their man and they got my woman. Only my woman had nothing wrong with her now, you see, with the rash gone.'

'Did you tell them that?'

'Hadn't the nerve. 'Is your ear painful?' I asked the man. 'It's like some boy's hammering a six-inch nail into it,' he says. So I did the energy passes and that quietened him down a bit. And then when I was thinking we should call it a day, fifty per cent success rate wasn't bad, he sat up. Put his hand on his head, the way you'd do with a radiator you weren't sure what heat it was. And then, in this sleepy voice, he says "Holy Malokey it's gone."'

Diarmuid stared at her. 'You cured him too?'

'He cured himself. Both of them did – opened themselves to the body-soul energy all around and got well. So I think you should go and see Jorg.'

Diarmuid cautiously wiggled the top joint of his toe, which felt like a piece of meat that'd been left in the fridge too long. 'But, couldn't you cure me? If you cured those two, surely you could do something for my foot? Save me all that driving to Inishgorm.'

Frances patted, then began to rub his left hip. 'Sorry, pet. Even Jorg can't explain it, but for some reason energy healing doesn't work with family members. You'll have to get it from the horse's mouth. He charges eighty-five pounds a session.'

Chapter 10

HEAL ME, HEAR ME

Going over Glenshane Pass was always beautiful, no matter what the season or weather. Now, soaked in rain, the hills and rocks and bog were brown and grey and purple bruises through the windscreen. He thought of people who had lived here centuries earlier, herded sheep and trudged along soaking roads, headed for the nearest cave or hovel, to huddle round a fire with steam rising from their scraps of clothing. Had the world made any more sense to them?

From six miles outside Derry, the traffic thickened and buses, lorries and cars crawled forward at fifteen miles an hour. It was warm in the car and the windscreen kept steaming up. Reluctantly he switched on the air conditioning, which cleared the windscreen but gobbled petrol. When he crossed the border he'd fill the tank.

It was a round trip of nearly two hundred miles, and if he could have got out of doing it, he would.

'I have my broadcast in the afternoon. What if I get a puncture?'

'You'll not get a puncture. You'll be finished with him by half past eleven – that gives you tons of time. It'll be well worth it. Jorg is an *amazing* man.'

He didn't want to annoy her, now that they were back on the same side, so he left home at eight on Friday morning. Besides, there was that stuff about her having cured the man and the woman – she was hardly making that up, was she?

Past Altnagelvin Hospital, trying not to think about the pain and sickness inside it – could do with some healing in there. Turn right at the roundabout and down the hill towards the new Foyle Bridge. John Hume Bridge, they called it, the great man's legacy to the city. Only now, unfortunately, it had become a magnet for suicides. Young men, when all hope had gone, would come here and jump off. And the occasional woman. John was upset, they said, since many of those who jumped were SDLP voters, voting not with their heads or hearts but their feet, the soul-freezing sweep of water and countryside the last thing they saw as they tumbled into eternity.

All the way out to the border, big houses occupied by the professional class of Derry, interspersed with some more modest teachers' houses, near to their work in the big convent grammar school, grappling with the minds of hormone-crazed schoolgirls. A new school under construction across the road from the old one, only they'd run into a neolithic site or something, and work had been briefly held up. A month to let archaeologists scurry in and rescue a few relics, then the foundations of modern education thudded back into place, put a concrete overcoat on the wisdom of the past.

And finally, down a hill and round a corner, here we are in Muff. An inoffensive wee place, not looking for trouble, happy to settle for money pouring into its multi-pump service station and shop, northern cars queuing to get cheap southern petrol. After he'd paid, Diarmuid asked one of the attendants for directions to Jorg's house.

The man rubbed his palms on his overalls, then pointed up the main street. 'Do you see yon green Bord Fáilte sign? Well, now, turn you right there and go on, on, on out that road – straight out – couple of mile she'd be. Jorg's place is a yellow bungalow, set a wee bit back off the road, on your right.' He bent lower, peered in the window at Diarmuid. 'You'll be looking for a healing, I suppose.'

'Oh, now. You never know.' And you never will, you nosy bastard.

The rain had given way to uncertain sunshine that made the trees glitter and the damp roadway look greasy. Mostly two-storey houses now, separated from the road by a gravelled drive and a screen of dripping trees. The occasional child kicking a ball in a driveway, an old man at the roadside, finger raised to acknowledge Diarmuid's passing.

And then, with the tripometer saying exactly four miles, he saw it. A tasteless yellow bungalow with white pillars at the door. And, yes, at the side of it, two biggish cars – a BMW 7 series, and beside it, a brand-new fuel-injection turbo Honda Civic. Well, now.

Diarmuid pressed the bell. After a pause a female voice: 'I'll get it.' The door opened and what looked like a girl of eighteen, with a round uncomplicated face and brown eyes, smiled at him.

'He's inside. I'll get him for you.'

There was a rustling behind her and a man of fifty, maybe more, appeared. Corduroy trousers and denim shirt, the sleeves rolled back to mid-forearm. As he smoothed his wiry grey hair with one hand, he eased the girl-woman aside with the other.

'Ah, here you are. Good man. Thanks, Lisa, I'll take over from here.' The girl tossed Diarmuid a sideways glance and disappeared into a room at the end of the hallway.

The man's eyes, the colour of wet slate, moved over Diarmuid. 'Your wife told me you might be coming. I'm Jorg, and that was Lisa. Come in, come in.'

Diarmuid followed him down the hallway, noting how his shirt half hung over his trousers at the back. Was this the man who had got Joy and Mairead jealous of Frances? And could this man in his fifties possibly be married to someone as young as Lisa? *Or maybe they weren't married.*

Jorg led the way into a room with a wicker chair on one side of the fireplace and a tall stool on the other. He gestured Diarmuid towards the chair, climbed onto the stool himself.

'Well, now. Tell me why you have come here.' The voice was rumbling and soft.

So Diarmuid told him, and it felt like confession. Told him about the pain and foolishness of drawing a wheel of a chair – no, not of a wheelchair, a wheel *of* a chair – over his own foot. And how it was OK until he stood on it for more than five minutes, at which point it turned hot and angry. He didn't mention that it had happened in his department head's office and that the department head had died almost immediately after.

'And how are things generally? In your life. In your work, in your leisure. Is there…stress?'

Diarmuid stared at the bookshelf beside Jorg's arm. *T'ai Chi*, it said, and beside it *Meditation*, and beside that *The Seven Storey Mountain*. 'I suppose I'm…stressed enough.'

'Any particular reason?'

'Well, I was hoping for a period of study leave in the States.'

'You'd have liked that.'

'But it doesn't fit in with the university's plans. Or my wife's. Whom you've met.'

'Ah. The university.'

'I teach there. North-Eastern University.'

'Very good. And beyond that, what things preoccupy you?'

'Beyond that, there's a radio discussion coming up and I'm involved in it. Good bit of stress there, really. The Dean himself has told me he's depending on me.'

'I see.'

'If I do well, it'll be good for me and the faculty.'

'And if you do less well?'

'Not sure… I'm keen to have a change. Been doing my present work for so long. And then there's my mother.' He felt himself blush. Jorg waited. 'She died some months ago and I…couldn't get to her funeral. I was sick.'

'That is sad. When did you recover?'

Diarmuid hesitated again. 'The day after her funeral.'

'It sometimes happens. Grief can paralyse us temporarily. Have you had an opportunity to…?' He waited.

'To what?'

'To visit her resting place.'

'Oh yes, I've had several opportunities to do that. Over the past few months.'

'That's good.' He paused. 'Did you take them?'

Diarmuid looked at the way the material of his trousers formed little ridges along his thighs, felt his face grow hot. 'No.'

'You've never been to the grave? At all?' Diarmuid shook his head, miserable. 'In my line of work, this is something that happens fairly frequently, so whatever else, you are not unique. You have it in mind to move forward, but forces hold you back. Perhaps a link with the foot there. It hurts when you stand still. What about when you walk?'

'OK when I walk. It's when I stop it hurts.'

'I hear what you say. Did you know you have a strong blue aura? You seek to master the airwaves, walk on them, which of course is miraculous, walking on waves. But your discontent with your present position links to your foot, which aches when rooted, when you are held back from doing what you want to do, what you feel you should. As always, body and soul are united in one egg, white and yolk conjoined as we move forward on our journey of life.'

Nodding agreement with his own words, Jorg took off his shoes, then stood silent on the rug in the middle of the polished wooden floor. Behind him a pair of wooden praying hands held a lit candle. On the wall above it were three pictures, all featuring fire: one a log fire in a stately home, another what looked like a bush fire, the last a smelting furnace.

'Slip off the shoes, now, and the socks. Good man. Now. What's happened here is, the knock on the toe has blocked the energy that would normally get out at the top of your foot. And because it's blocked, it's like someone stuck in a room hammering at the door – damaging the wallpaper, the door-frame, doing all sorts of destruction. Same with your foot and that's why your poor old tootsy is getting a bit of a hiding. So we'll have to see if we can't help find it a channel out or around or something, and let you go about your business and your daily duties.'

He touched a button on a black hi-fi system. There was click, then a moment of silence in which the sound of sheep bleating in the distance could be heard. Then a guitar and flute came floating into the room, speaking of islands, water, trees, sunsets.

'Slip off the watch too. Sometimes the energy can knock the stuffing out of a watch's mechanism.'

Then Jorg reached up towards Diarmuid's right shoulder and, keeping both his hands some three inches from him, moved them down either side of Diarmuid's arm. It was as if he were removing an invisible cobweb clinging to the sleeve. When he reached Diarmuid's fingertips his hand movement continued on into mid-air, shoulder height; then he rubbed his palms together and made a flicking motion, depositing the unwanted cobweb a decent distance off.

He did the same with Diarmuid's other arm, and then again with his front, from Adam's apple to mickey. Fingers gliding through the air, always close, never touching. Diarmuid didn't know whether he should look down or not, and finally opted for eyes straight ahead.

'Right foot forward a bit... Good man. Lovely job.'

Now he was doing the same thing to Diarmuid's right leg, the palms of his hands moving slowly, always a careful three inches from Diarmuid's thigh, calf, foot.

The voice, coming through the music, was calm, comforting. 'You're wondering what I'm doing so I'll tell you. I'm getting rid of the charged particles, that's what I'm doing. You've a lot of charged particles – in fact they're backed up like in a traffic jam, so many cars, none of them can move. And it may take us a wee bit of time to get the traffic flowing again. That's what we're working at now. Seeing can we get the cars at the front of you moving, and then the others should be able to start moving after them.'

He resumed the movement of his hands, more energetically now, crouching his big body into it, leaning away from

Diarmuid, legs flexed and well apart, rubbing and flicking his hands over his shoulder like a man digging, as he dispatched the unwanted particles. And all the time the guitar and flute played, and Enya sang of floating away to a magical island where all was dreaming and delight.

Then he disappeared behind Diarmuid, and Diarmuid could see his outline reflected in the glass of the biggest fire painting. He seemed to be just standing there, directly behind, not moving.

Then, without warning, all the energy in Diarmuid rushed from the rest of his body and congregated at the back of his neck *because Jorg had laid his hand on Diarmuid's neck*. And now, breathing in little rasps, he was putting his other hand on the small of Diarmuid's back. Touching him. Two hands. Both of them hot. The breathing began to grow more audible – *haark, haark*. Easy now, steady – you don't want to annoy or insult people, swinging round and accusing them of things they weren't doing at all, Diarmuid told himself. At the same time you don't want to stand there until some healing bastard's dick is halfway up your arse either.

But now Jorg's hands had lifted from Diarmuid's neck and back, as softly as two birds taking flight, and both were skimming the air and rubbing again, getting the particles shooed off into some outer darkness. And now Jorg was swaying, and as he swayed he brought the palm closer to Diarmuid, closer still. Diarmuid found himself tilting back on his heels, a little further, a little more, then was forced to do a sudden shuffle to recover his balance.

'D'you feel the tug? Some of my clients can actually feel the particles tugging and I thought maybe you could... No matter, not a bit of odds. Either way a sign the treatment is beginning to work.'

For another five minutes he stood behind Diarmuid, breathing like Boris Karloff. On three occasions one of Jorg's hands appeared in front of Diarmuid's face, as if he was playing an invisible harp. Then Diarmuid felt a clap on his back – a comradely clap.

'Now, if you could have a seat over in the armchair for me.' The recliner had been upholstered in check cloth that made Diarmuid think of the Bay City Rollers. 'And I'll tilt you back... There we are.'

It was like being in the dentist's chair, looking at the ceiling, legs relaxed and pampered, the weight catching his calves. And the same problem of whether or not to look at the face that was peering down at him, get a close-up of the pitted skin, the little white dots clustered round the edge of the nostrils, the grey curl of nose-hair, the broken veins on cheeks and chin. Or look beyond him to the window, to the curtains hung on a brass rod the shape of a spear, the point slicing out at the top. Or watch the hands.

Now the movement had change, Jorg's left hand travelling parallel to Diarmuid's leg, starting at his mickey and working down, palm cupped the way you'd do to gather crumbs from a table after a meal. At the same time the right hand hovered, waiting for something interesting to come along, and just when it seemed nothing much was going to turn up, *SMAAACK!* The two hands clapped together, as if squashing a mosquito. *SMAAAAAACKK* again. Then the left went back to get some more particles and cajole them down to the bottom of Diarmuid's foot, and once more *SMAAACK*. He worked the length of the right leg several times, always from waist to toe. Then the left.

'Right now. Give me a tick to get things reorganised here.'

He pulled over a little wooden stool and sat with Diarmuid's soles inches from his chest. Then he took Diarmuid's right foot, sandwiched it between his palms and sat, eyes closed. The head was bent in what looked like prayer, except the lips weren't moving and there was no sound other than harsh breathing. Diarmuid wanted to ask him if holding his foot wasn't trapping the particles into him rather than drawing them out, but was afraid to.

Eventually Jorg looked up. 'Right so. Feel anything?'

'Your hands are hot.'

'That's exactly what they are. I'm not one bit surprised to hear you say that. Good.' He lowered his head again, eyes closed, hands clasped warm and tight over Diarmuid's other foot.

Three minutes later the eyes opened: 'Righty-ho.' He rose and placed the stool against the wall. 'Let's see if we can't create some movement.'

He bent over Diarmuid's chest, like a doctor about to ask for deep breaths. But instead he formed two fists with his hands – an Elastoplast on his thumbnail, what had he done to it? – and began to pump them up and down, stopping inches from Diarmuid's body. Rightdownleftuprightupleftdown, the moving fists a blur. And as Jorg moved down towards his knee, Diarmuid suddenly became aware that something was happening. Before he could decide what it was or where it was happening, Jorg had stopped the air hammering, moved behind him and placed both his palms on Diarmuid's head. Warm again, intimate, holding the skull like an egg that's cracked and might spill. Then the hands were lifted and the dancing hammers moved once more above his legs.

And then he felt it. It was as if a breeze, except it wasn't a breeze because everything was perfectly still except the two whirling fists, as if a *coolness* was moving down his leg with the fists. And the nearer they got to the bottom of his leg – to the knee, the calf, now the ankle – the deeper the coolness became. If he closed his eyes he could imagine his right foot encased in ice.

'Feel anything?' The slate-grey eyes were staring at him, the untidy eyebrows raised.

'I feel as if – my leg is cold. I think.'

'Aha! Now we're getting somewhere!'

He repeated the exercise on Diarmuid's left leg. Except this time, as the wave of coolness moved down and deeper into his skin, through the muscle, into the bone and the marrow, it seemed to cross over and envelop the right leg. Two for the price of one, Diarmuid thought. It took a huge effort of the will to stop himself saying it aloud.

Then Jorg moved to Diarmuid's shoulder, which he clapped in a manly way 'That's you done. Now how are you feeling?'

'Well,' Diarmuid said, steadying himself as the recliner was raised to the upright position. 'Rested, I think. And my feet feel cool – like ice, really.'

'And is the bad leg any better?'

Diarmuid hesitated. 'It feels – relaxed. Not sure if it's changed. But definitely relaxed.'

'That's good to hear, because that's one of the classic signs. If you told me there was no difference, that would be bad. But the coldness and the relaxed feeling – that's good. One of the signs, you see. You've heard of the *yang* and the *yin* – well, our job is to get the particles organised so the balance comes back between the *yang* and the *yin*. It's a condition an awful lot of people, a *shocking* lot, suffer from. Young girl only a week ago, going to get married to her fiancé, came to me miserable, the colour of her cheeks was that ugly, she said. It wasn't ugly at all, of course, all they were was a wee bit rosy, but she *thought* it was ugly, and she was so worried she wouldn't be right for the wedding photos. And after not the first but the second session there was a bit of change, actually for the worse. They turned a wee bit of a purply colour, and of course that worried her terribly. Worried me a bit too, to tell you God's truth, ha-ha-ha. And then with the third, there she was, her two cheeks this lovely pink. Perfect balance, you see, *yang* and *yin*. If I'd put five thousand pounds in her hand, she couldn't have been more pleased.'

'I can imagine.' Diarmuid took ninety pounds out of his wallet. Jorg murmured something, took the money and opened a diary with a red tassel in the middle. 'Well, let's see what way you get on after this. No good rushing your fences looking for instant results. The traffic doesn't just vanish, it sometimes takes a bit of time for to loosen up. Could be a week or a month, even. Although, having said that, a man from Galway last week was here, and it was in the car on the way home. "Good gracious me," he said to himself, just outside Clonmany. "My back is *better*." Nearly crashed the car he was that pleased. These things can happen every way and any day.'

In the hallway Jorg turned suddenly. 'What am I thinking of?' 'Thinking?'

'I'm sure you must want – before you leave, quite a long journey...' He pointed down the hallway...

Diarmuid locked the door, lifted the toilet seat. The bath held a snorkel and a man's bathing trunks. Over the shower-head hung a pair of woman's tights.

When he had washed his hands, the only towel to be seen lay half in and half out of a wickerwork laundry basket inside the door. He used the end of it, then lifted the towel inside the basket and closed the lid. Glimpsed something just before it closed. Was halfway to the bathroom door when the temptation became too much. No one watching. He turned and lifted the lid again. A sea of shirts, towels, hankies...and, yes, there it was. Underneath a man's navy T-shirt, a shy little edge of something pink and shiny. Diarmuid lifted the T-shirt clear: satin knickers, slightly soiled, a large red heart surrounded by exclamation marks decorating the crotch.

'Do remember to give my regards to your good lady, won't you?' Diarmuid nodded and tucked the five pounds' change deep down in his breast pocket. 'God bless, then.' Jorg unlocked the front door and patted his shoulder as he went out.

It was nearly one-thirty when he arrived home and the place was empty. Diarmuid had a ham sandwich, then showered and cleaned his teeth, checking them in the magnifying mirror. Avoid addressing large audiences with a piece of ham stuck between your front teeth. Going down the stairs and out to the car he walked slowly and thought hard: let the good work Jorg had done filter into the legs, the body, the being. And not just Jorg's work but his attitude.

He parked the nine-year-old Renault in the car park directly underneath the BBC security cameras. Before he got out he sat for a moment, eyes closed, concentrating. I *will* embrace this broadcast. I *will* make the words stop bottle-necking. I *will* take the discussion by the throat. The revolving door at the front of the building opened as he approached.

When he said who he was, the woman behind the reception desk sighed through her nose, ticked off his name on a clipboard, then typed stuff onto the computer. A cardboard pass clattered from the printer. 'Wear this at all times.' She passed him a necklace with a label that said Dr Diarmuid Monaghan was a VISITOR. 'And have a seat if you would.'

He sat in an armchair across from the desk. A thin, sallow-faced man in a pinstripe suit sat on the sofa. When their eyes met, the man picked at his teeth with a small piece of cardboard, making sucking sounds as he did so. Then the lift behind them pinged and a plump woman with bouncy brown hair was striding towards them.

'Hello! Great to see you – I'm Debbie Watkins, the series producer!' It was as if she'd just found this out herself. Eyes shining, touching their elbows in turn with her left hand. 'So then – right, well, Professor Norman Tiedt from GUD, Guinness University, Dublin,' she addressed the man with the teeth. 'Do you know each other? This is Diarmuid – Dr Diarmuid Monaghan from NEU, North-Eastern University.' She stood back from them, hands clasped tight in front of her discus breasts. 'We really are excited about this week's programme, having two such eminent people on! And the one next week as well – improving school experience! Such a practical topic, and a central area today too, definitely, I agree. But now, look, the show is going out live, as you know, so it's a matter of smuggling you into the studio without disturbing our presenter too much. OK? And check all mobiles, please – we'd prefer *not* to have "Dixie" playing half-way through a question!'

As they tiptoed into the studio, the presenter, a woman with coal-black hair and a chunky red necklace, waved and went on speaking into a microphone. 'After the news, we'll be back with today's discussion question, "Are we getting our money's worth from our universities?" Ring us and tell us what *you* think. And don't *dare* go away.' She punched a button, put her hands above her head and yawned loudly. 'Oh, excuuuuuse me. Too many late nights or is it middle age? No, no, no, *no,* don't tell me. Good to see you – I'm Rosemary Farquhar.' She shook hands without getting up, then bent forward and began to scribble furiously on her pad. Diarmuid and Professor Tiedt slipped into seats opposite her.

'I was wondering,' Professor Tiedt said, leaning forward, 'could you tell us what sort of questions you—'

'Fifteen seconds to air,' Debbie's voice said, through a speaker. Diarmuid could see her dimly through a huge glass window behind a bank of instruments.

Rosemary blew her nose, made a deep hawking noise in her throat. 'No time to tell you, I'm afraid, but it'll be OK, promise. OK, here we go. Keep her peppy.'

A green light lit up beside her.

'Welcome *back*. And with me now, to consider *whither* universities in this post-conflict, post-war, really – period, we have both of today's guests, and I'm delighted to have them, Professor Norman Tiedt from Guinness University Dublin, GUD, and Dr Diarmuid Monaghan from North-Eastern University, NEU. Gentlemen, you're both *very* welcome *to* the programme. Professor Tiedt, let me come to *you* first. Would you describe GUD as a truly *international institution?*'

Professor Tiedt put his elbows on the table, smiled and said he felt GUD had become emphatically international in recent years. 'Walk through our quadrangle, Rosemary, and you'll see the faces, forms and costumes of at least a dozen nationalities. We have registered – *full*-time, remember – over a thousand international students, representing more than ten different countries. That's registered. A veritable melting pot. So we at GUD are proud of that – and rightly so, I would argue.'

Diarmuid checked the figures on the little card he had placed on the desk in front of him. Seventeen different nationalities –

and *one and a half thousand* students in NEU. Suck on that, dirt-bag.

'Dr Diarmuid *Monaghan*, can I turn to *you*? What is it that international students bring to a university such as *yours*?'

For a couple of seconds it was as if Rosemary was in a film that had stuck. Why hadn't she asked him about NEU numbers? And what did her words mean? How did people take in what others had to say? What did they do with their mouths and tongues to make them form words and send them croaking into the air? Then, mercifully, the words came.

'I'm not sure what you mean by "bring". Can you tell me what you're getting at a little more, um, clearly?'

'Well, I'm sorry if you find a word like "bring" confusing, ha-ha, but let me try *this* and see if you understand any better. Do our home students benefit from the presence of these students from *overseas*, or would it be better, as *some* might argue, if NEU was exclusively for *Ulster* students?'

Oh, thank God. The machinery had unfrozen. Words formed in Diarmuid's brain, went spinning out into the world. 'Well, our students at North-Eastern don't care much what colour a student's skin is. Nor, to be honest, do staff. The student who comes to us must bring the requisite level of ability and the requisite fees. Those given, we are content. We have students from at least seventeen different countries.'

Rosemary didn't return his smile. 'So are you saying that, as far as you are concerned, international students are essentially a *money-making venture*?'

'I didn't say that.'

'But money is an element, clearly,' Rosemary insisted. 'From what you say, Dr Monaghan, it appears to be right at the top of your university's priorities. Whereas I always thought universities were supposed to be primarily places of learning.'

Professor Tiedt leant forward, smiling apologetically. 'A word here perhaps? The fact is, whether he likes it or not, or anyone does, Dr Monaghan's university lives in a commercial world. When decisions are made at his university, money always –

always – comes into the reckoning. This is equally true of GUD, where money again is a factor – *one* factor. That's the real world.' He turned to Diarmuid. 'Does that summarise your position accurately, Dr Monaghan?'

'Well…yes. That's what I was saying. I mean, that's what it's all about, really, when the whole equation is—' He kept trying to get a sentence going, but the pain had started up in his foot, coming in jagged waves that sawed into his nerves.

'An example.' Professor Tiedt raised his hand, looked at Diarmuid and Rosemary in turn. 'GUD has plans for a major upgrade of its video-conference suite. An investment. Early next year, 2002, some staff members – your humble servant among them – will visit Argentina to share with people there GUD's experience of technology and the contribution of ICT to global learning. Because, you see, one thing all institutions know – including the BBC, ha-ha – is that to achieve anything of worth, you must have a sound economic base and a going-out-to-the-world philosophy. Without both, nothing happens.'

'Dr Monaghan?' Rosemary, fingers tucking raven hair back, then repositioning the big red beads on her front, swivelled back to him.

'Yes?'

'Has NEU got similar overseas links?'

'Well, yes. Although we believe it's important – important to start close to…home. That's why we were the…were the first institution to establish – establish form-, form-, formal *links* with the…the south of Ireland in, oh, in, in, in 1989. Not with Professor Tiedt's institution, as it happens.'

'That's not strictly the case,' Professor Tiedt said. 'Just to set the record straight.'

'Well, the record. The record will show. Show that certainly our institution—' Diarmuid's voice stumbled forward in bursts.

'No, sorry. It's important to have key facts right.'

'Can I finish? Can I *finish*?'

'Certainly, indeed, but—'

'*I didn't interrupt you so why are you interrupting me?*'

'Of course, certainly, agreed – but it is important to—'

'Gentlemen – *gentlemen*!' Rosemary rapped her pencil on the table. 'I'm in charge here.' She gave a little chuckle. 'Keep this up and I may have to put you in detention afterwards… Now.' She pointed at Diarmuid. 'Dr Monaghan. You have the floor.'

Diarmuid tried to smile but his cheeks hurt. 'Thank you. I was just saying. We've had an external examiner. In fact we were one of the first – for…' He paused. Swallowed. Tried to ignore the pain that had now reached his knee. 'As far back as…1989… we—'

Suddenly it seemed as if a floodlight had been switched on in his mind, illuminating every corner, chasing away every tiny shadow of thought. If someone had offered to kill him, he could not have repeated a single one of the words he had uttered in the last twenty seconds. Then the light faded and his mind felt ordered and what he had been planning to say became crisp and clear. Except that he couldn't say it. When he opened his mouth, no sound came out. A column of ants or maybe a string of sausages or a pillow or even a bolster had somehow got into his throat – swallow, swallow again, oh, God – cough then – *but lean away from the microphone first* – oh, God, no good either, tickling still there—'

Diarmuid half rose, swivelled violently away from the table so that his chair rose with him, then rattled back down again. Dizzy, he took two paces towards the corner of the studio and coughed.

It started as a nearly acceptable, closed-mouth cough, thin and strangled, something you hear on air from time to time, Diarmuid's hand almost smothering it. But then another, bigger and hairier, started at his right big toe and came powering up his leg, scraping his windpipe as it went, tugging all the air from his system and erupting in a hooting *haaaarrrrghh*. Then a second, equally hooting but more painful, shuddering up to explode in his throat and mouth, *haarraarrrarrrghh*.

Somewhere, far away, he could hear Rosemary's voice. 'Are you all right, Dr Monaghan? Do have a glass of water and, and

– uhm, catch your breath. Meanwhile let me come back to you, Professor Tiedt. Can third-level education offer anything to address social problems? Racism, sectarianism, whatever. Or is what you do simply a matter of individual achievement, without social relevance?'

And as Professor Tiedt began to speak, Debbie and somebody else – a sound engineer, maybe – were hooking their arms under Diarmuid's oxters, lifting him towards the door, miming, 'Come this way, quietly, *quietly.*' Fingers to lips: *Don't cough whatever you do!* Outside the studio they supported him down a corridor to an empty room where they told him to stretch out on a couch.

He lay there gasping for nearly ten minutes, clearing his throat from time to time, opening his eyes to stare at the pale green ceiling, which had in it a crack the shape of a witch's tit. Then his coughing stopped but his left foot felt as if it had been encased in cement, and his skull as if someone had filled it with very hot soup.

Debbie's arm was round his shoulders. 'It's *terribly* unfortunate – and when you were doing so well, too. Still, could have been worse – could have been TV!'

But if it had been TV, the viewers would have seen what an ugly, hairy-eared pompous little *bastard* Tiedt was and they'd have sided with Diarmuid. If it had been TV they would have seen he was a normal, honest and unpretentious human being, not a posturing prick like Tiedt. Why weren't things ever the way they should be?

Debbie patted his back. 'Don't worry – you'll be marvellous next week – I just know it! Improving school experience for students! Now *there*'s a topic you can get your teeth into! Super!'

Professor Tiedt didn't say anything on the way down in the lift, but as they made for the revolving door he put his hand on Diarmuid's shoulder and said it had been a pity about the coughing and he hoped he was feeling better now. Broadcasters came and went but you were stuck with your health, and he felt sure things would go better in a week's time.

'You do look a good deal rosier now,' Debbie told Diarmuid. 'Would you like us to order you a taxi?'

'Yes… No, no, it's all right. My car's in the car park. I'm fine.'

'Well, if you're sure. Take care, won't you?'

As he walked to the car park, unlocked his car, got into it, rolled down the window, started the engine, Diarmuid kept seeing himself staggering around the studio. A Mr Bean figure, going from mental white-out to coughing his guts out to mental white-out, on and on until he collapsed in a corner in a coma, with Professor Tiedt's little browny-yellow face bent over him, mouth open as he prepared to give Diarmuid the kiss of life. Diarmuid felt the vomit come up his throat.

'What'd you say?' the security man at the barrier said, peering in the window at him.

'Nothing,' Diarmuid said. 'Just "*Oh, Jesus.*" Sort of praying, that's all.'

Chapter 11

IN DENIAL

She must have heard him as he came in the back door but she didn't squeal delight, run to him and wrap her arms around his neck. Or turn his way and whisper, 'I missed you terribly, Diarmuidy, my big-balled seed-bearer!' She just went on sitting at the little desk with the curved legs and the pull-down writing part, not looking up. Diarmuid stood in the doorway taking off his coat, trying not to feel gloomy. Finally, pen in mid-air, she swivelled round. 'We've been sent a bill for tiles.' She held up a docket. 'This says you owe the Fine Tile Gallery for four boxes of tiles. Different colours. Ninety-eight pounds.'

'Uncle Dan got samples to see if they'd be the right colour.'

'Then why are we getting his bill for ninety-eight pounds? They're his tiles – why is the bill for ninety-eight pounds in your name?'

'It was raining when we went there, so—'

'So that's the arrangement, is it? Every time it rains, we pay for Uncle Dan's tiles. And him stinking with money.' She swung away again. 'I'm bringing this over to him, and I'm going to tell him that he's to cut out these cute little manoeuvres or there'll be trouble. I bet your woman is behind it.'

Diarmuid thought of just ignoring her and going upstairs. Instead he said, 'Your healer man was older than I thought he'd be.'

She put down her pen, sat back in the chair. 'Oh, God Almighty, I forgot! Was he good? Did it work? How's your foot now?'

Diarmuid tested his right foot against the carpeted floor. 'About the same.'

'Sometimes they get worse before they get better. That's how these things are. You get a dip before the improvement graph starts going up.'

Diarmuid went into the kitchen, poured himself a whiskey, brought it back to the doorway. 'In a way it feels worse. Little stabs of pain.'

'That's a sign it could be going to get better.'

Diarmuid tried to keep the irritation out of his voice. 'I think I've stopped expecting miracles.'

'Well maybe you should start again. Maybe if you don't expect miracles, you're making a big mistake.'

She turned away and continued writing, the whisper of her pen drowned from time to time by a cla-cla-clacking magpie in the garden. He was turning to go when she looked up. 'Your friend Warwick rang – I swear he has a screw loose. Or several. Anyway, he told me to tell you that... What did he say? I wrote it down because he was coming out with so much old guff...' She rummaged through the sheets of paper on the desk. 'Ah, here we are. His friend Crompton won't be back at work for another week at least. Suffering from post-traumatic stress. That's the message.'

Diarmuid considered the profusion of papers piled up on the tiny desk, several lying on the floor beside it. 'If you used the computer instead of writing on scraps, you'd have stuff properly organised.'

'Except that writing by hand happens to be more... authentic. *And* it suits my style of doing business.'

'So what are you working on anyway?'

'A plan.' Pause. 'An integrated business plan.' She swung back to the desk.

Diarmuid went into the living room and switched on the TV.

As he leant back in the chair he could feel his foot throb, like a heart beating inside his shoe. Maybe that bugger Jorg had actually damaged his leg. Set something going that could end in – oh, my God – *amputation*... He headed quietly for the kitchen, got a refill and drank it quickly. The pain seemed to fade. He listened to the news headlines and, at five past ten, he put his head round the living-room door again. 'I'm for bed.'

She didn't look up. But as he began to leave she called after him: 'You didn't mention your broadcast. I heard it was a cock-up.'

No 'Oh, you poor baby, come upstairs.' No 'I bet you were terrific and they're jealous.' Just 'I heard it was a cock-up.'

'Where did you hear that?'

'Joy and Mairead caught it.'

Suddenly the fatigue of the day filled him, from the roots of his hair to the soles of his feet. Her talk of miracles, Jorg pulling the cobwebs, the giving away of eighty-five pounds, the coughing, Joy and Mairead *catching* it – it was as if all this had hardened into a feeling of leaden exhaustion that had invaded his body. Damn, damn, *damn*.

'Joy and Mairead said you got sick on air.'

'Did they now? That makes it sound as if I was throwing up all over the microphone.'

'No, it doesn't. Joy and Mairead said you were coughing and had to stop halfway through the discussion. That's all.'

'It was nowhere near halfway. In fact there were about three minutes left. But naturally it was a much better story to say I was choking on my own vomit for the whole programme, wasn't it? Well done, Joy and Mairead.'

'They didn't say that. Anyway, there doesn't seem to be much wrong with you now.'

Diarmuid looked at the way she sat, head to one side, little wrinkle lines running north and south of her mouth. Hen's arse. 'As it happens,' he said, through clenched teeth, 'I have a ferocious pain in my leg.'

'Good sign. The dark before the dawn.'

'So you said at least once already. Well, your friend may have cured lots of other people but he hasn't cured me.'

'Well, no. Of course. If you decide to block it out, obviously no one can reach you.' She swivelled around to the desk again.

He lay in bed with the light out, his foot sticking clear of the duvet. Beyond it what resembled moonlight, but was in fact the streetlight, cut across the chair where they stacked their clothes at night. From downstairs, silence. For all he knew, she was down there this minute pretending to work but in reality plucking her eyebrows or shaving her legs. Was this what people everywhere were doing? Lying in bed thinking about stuff that affected them, like did they have split ends or was their foot sore, not really giving a damn about other people's worries or world hunger or anything, only wrapped up in themselves and at the same time being tugged in different directions and making a balls of their lives? He looked at the bar of light and the way it sliced across the floor, then mounted the chair and the clothes, and then slid on back down to the floor again. Light didn't let anything get between it and where it wanted to go. Your wife could be bankrupting you with some half-cocked business plan and a pair of lesbians could be waiting in the shadows, your foot could be turning black and festering before being amputated, but the light didn't care – it just went where it wanted to go. Single-minded. Fuck you, said the light.

He closed his eyes and saw himself in space, his leg hanging on only by the skin. And then, out of nowhere, Angela appeared and put her thin soft arms around him. 'My big-balled seed-bearer,' she told him. 'Amputation is bad for you.' And she reached down and pushed the bits of his leg together again. Then as his flesh knitted without even a scar, he and Angela, holding hands, dipped over the hill like swallows into a valley full of greens and yellows and sunshine.

He was asleep long before Frances came to bed.

The first thing he heard in the morning was the oil lorry. It was reversing up to the house in the other corner of the cul-de-sac, and it had an in-built thing that went bleep-bleep-bleep to warn dogs, kids and anybody else bone-brain enough to stand behind it that it was coming. A glow of daylight was filling the room, which turned yellow when he looked up at the drawn curtains. Frances was gone. Her place felt cold, the sheets twisted, pulled out of position. She must have risen early.

He moved his head a little lower under the duvet and closed his eyes. Put his hand on his mickey and felt its warmth. Grateful to God for it, he should be and was, even if it got few opportunities to show its horsepower. Grateful to God for a hand to hold it, for shoulders to lean against the mattress, for legs to move under the duvet, for feet...

He stopped breathing. Closed his eyes and said the first half of a Hail Mary. Moved his left leg very slowly so that it wasn't touching the right. The undersheet felt cool and pleasant as his leg slid up, then down. Slowly, fearful that rushing it would upset everything, he let his mind move down from his knee, to his calf, to his ankle, and then slowly, with infinite care, up along his foot, past the heel, past the instep, along the ball of the foot, then ever so lightly along each of the toes.

It was better.

Not just less bad, but better. Completely better. It felt as if a casing of pain, a plaster-of-paris casing, had been slipped off it. He scrunched his toes together, let them release like the petals of a flower. They felt perfect. He moved his foot in a small circle from the ankle, ten times one way, ten times the other. Still perfect. He pulled aside the duvet, put his foot in the air. It looked pale and normal. Lifted his left foot in the air beside it. A perfect pair.

He lay back, panting. Downstairs, Frances was running water into the sink, moving in and out of the living room, using the Hoover, clattering plates. If he didn't get up soon she'd be up running the Hoover round the bed, maybe inside it, catch his mickey-hammer in the suction.

He got up, moved cautiously to the bathroom. Showered and shaved. Descended the stairs. At each step, his right foot took the strain, pushed back, sent waves of – dammit, that was what it was – *pulsating energy* up into his body.

He poured himself a bowl of Fruit Loops, propped yesterday's paper against the milk bottle. His mind was racing like a car on a hoist, wheels spinning but going nowhere. He couldn't tell her bloody Jorg had cured him. *He couldn't.*

'Are you going into your office?'

'At some point. Why?'

She began to unload the dishwasher. 'Just that I'm going into town and you could give me a lift, save me the bother of parking. I can get a taxi back.' She banged several dinner plates together, put them into a cupboard. 'What about your leg this morning?'

Diarmuid took a quick bite of toast. 'Oh, well.'

'Well, what? Well it's well?'

'Not worse. Definitely not worse.'

'Then it's better. You said it was worse yesterday. If it was worse yesterday, and it's not worse today, it must be better.'

Diarmuid felt anger ripple across his chest. Sudden, violent rage. It made his voice shake. 'What I mean is, it's not worse. Which is another way of saying, and I am saying it, that it's not better. It's. Not. Fucking. Better. Let's leave it now. *OK*?'

She lifted two cups from the table beside him and banged them into the dishwasher. He buttered and marmaladed another slice of toast, noted that she was wearing her pinstripe trouser suit. 'What are you going into town for?'

Silence for several seconds. Then: 'The bank.'

Oh, God. Speak slowly. 'Look, Frances. We took out two hundred pounds only the other day. Once you get into the red, they start charging you for—'

'I know that. I know when they start charging you – for God's *sake*. I'm not going to get money out. I'm going to talk to the *bank manager*.'

She stood in the middle of the floor, arms folded across her crisp white blouse. It was her breasts that had attracted him originally. Then when she'd said something that annoyed him, he would look at her breasts and they forgave him for feeling annoyed and he forgave her for whatever she'd said. Breasts, the twin soothers. But not this time.

'I'm going to ask him for a loan. And what is the loan for? Well, actually I told you several days ago but as usual, *quelle surprise*, you appear not to have been listening. I'm going. To set up. A business.' She put her finger into the middle of her hair so as not to disturb it, and scratched. 'Not planning to set one up, *going* to set one up.'

'In organic gardening?'

She shook her head. 'That's all right if you've plenty of time and plenty of help. I always have to rely on Joy and Mairead, and the truth is they're not terribly reliable. Anyway, after the weekend with Jorg I now see that my growth potential is in another direction.'

He carried his dishes to the dishwasher. Put the milk back into the fridge, ran the dishcloth over the table. Dried his hands on the towel. 'I'll just do my teeth, then. Ready in a minute.'

He had intended – planned, been *going* – to say nothing more about it. She obviously wanted him to, expected him to quiz her. What business? How will you do it? Where are we going to get the money? But that would be to satisfy her. There would only be so much she could do – their money was in a joint bank account and he'd have to countersign for any serious withdrawals.

At the lights he glanced across at her. 'What do you plan – are you *going* to set up in business doing?'

She scratched her knee. 'Three guesses.'

'For fuck's sake, Frances! *What.* Are you going. To *do*?'

'No need to shout. I'm going to set up as a body-soul therapist.'

Diarmuid drove, eyes fixed straight ahead. She was going to put his money – all right, their money, but in fact *his* – into a New Age therapy? He checked his foot on the accelerator. It was cured. Felt like the foot of a fifteen-year-old. How in God's name had that halfwit child-molesting chancer in Inishgorm managed it? Or maybe he'd just been around when it happened, like a bystander at a miracle, nothing to do with him... Except it was a hell of a coincidence. But even if Jorg had done it, *that didn't mean Frances could set up in business*. Jorg wasn't going to give courses so that his pupils could hit the street and take a share of his clients after they were finished.

'You think this carry-on of Jorg's actually works?'

She pretended to look out her window. 'I *know* it works.'

'Didn't work for me.' He felt uneasy saying that. Bad luck. 'And if it didn't work for me, you may be sure there are lots like me.'

'Well, there certainly *aren't* lots like you. Thank God for *that*. But I bet it has worked for you. Or soon will. Look at the way you're driving.'

'He didn't cure me, Frances. The man's a chancer.'

'No he's not. He's an amazing man. Did you see the newspaper clipping about how he'd healed a woman who had cancer?'

Diarmuid started to count to ten but gave up at three. 'No, I didn't see the cancer testimonial. But I'll tell you what I did see – I saw Lisa. Did you see Lisa? No? She's about fourteen – sixteen tops. "My partner Lisa," he called her. And do you know what else I saw? In the bathroom? I went for a pee and there, lying on a chair for anyone to see – a pair of Lisa's pink knickers with a red heart on the crotch, and round the edge in blue fancy writing "My heart belongs to Daddy". Nice, eh? This is your amazing man, you see – "My heart belongs to Daddy". Around a big come-and-get-me heart on her you-know-what. Fourteen years old.'

Frances pressed the button to open her window, then pressed it again to close it. Flipped down the sun shield and checked her appearance in its mirror. 'Well, whatever about this Lisa person – if she exists – she can't be any less grown-up than you, for you sound most of the time like a schoolboy of about twelve. I mean, for God's sake, Diarmuid – looking at women's underwear in people's bathrooms! What's going to be next? Dressing up in it? Is that your next project? I sometimes think one side of your brain got overdeveloped – loads of qualifications – and the other side, the commonsense, grown-up side, was left to shrink to the size of a pea. I mean, look at this – this – this sniffing at knickers like some sort of pervert, and at the same time you have the nerve to stand there badmouthing a real, grown-up, mature man like Jorg!'

Diarmuid didn't respond. He just drove on for the next five minutes without speaking. That always got to her if he kept it up long enough. Bitch. Bloody clueless *bitch*. And she had the nerve to call him immature!

'Look.' Her voice was quieter now. 'If I can't do it – this business, the body-soul therapy – people won't come. All right? If I can do it, they'll be lining round the block. But *I have to find out*. I'm going to give the first session free to get them interested. All I need is a start.'

Diarmuid drew into the pavement, pulled on the handbrake with a savage grawwwwk. 'You need a start *and* a pile of money. Anybody would think we were millionaires.'

She tapped the *Irish News* she was carrying. 'Know what the base rate is this morning? Four per cent. Hasn't been as low since the early 1980s. Besides which, this isn't a million I'm looking for, it's a measly watery skimpy oul' eight K to do up the living room.'

'Christ Almighty! You're going to do these – these – these *therapy sessions* in the *living room*? What are the rest of us supposed to do?'

She smiled. 'Well, if you mean what are *you* supposed to do, you can watch TV in the kitchen. Or the spare bedroom.'

'So I'm to stay upstairs, lie on the bed in my own house watching telly?'

'You're a scream, d'you know that? A scream beyond belief.' She opened the passenger door, then squeezed his forearm. 'Wait until this business takes off – you'll whistle a quare different tune then.'

' "The Poor House Blues!" he shouted after her, and imagined himself slamming the door on her head. 'That's the tune both of us will be whistling – "The Poor House Bloody Blues"!'

She gave him a mock-wave, moved on to the pedestrian crossing, turned right towards the glass door of the bank. Even from the car he could see her hips moving inside the pinstripe suit, and it was like watching a strange sexy woman he'd spotted in the street.

The morning was spent in his office preparing lectures and reading Hazel's dissertation. At eleven o'clock he rang Warwick's office, but his voicemail was still on. 'I hear you're internal examiner for Hazel,' he told the machine. 'I've just finished reading her work and it's good, I think. Surprisingly good.' He got a sandwich and ate it at his desk, and in the mid-afternoon went home.

Nobody there. He opened the back door and stepped out onto the patio. Stood looking at the different coloured plastic clothes pegs: were they multicoloured to cheer up depressed housewives? And did they work? Carefully, slowly, with arms extended, he raised his right foot, letting his entire weight rest on the left.

Nothing. Not a twitch, not a tremor of pain. If anything, it seemed stronger than it had been before he'd hurt it. He checked over his shoulder to be sure there was no face at a window of the house next door, then did a series of small hops round the circular clothes line and back to where he started. Still nothing. He felt as if he could run a mile without breaking sweat.

Four o'clock. He sat at the kitchen counter with a cup of tea. How had the bugger done it? Even if we were a bundle of particles, how did a clown like Jorg manage to work out the way to manipulate them so that he was able to heal – *completely heal* – somebody's foot? He lifted one of the stools and put it beside the counter. Stood on it, then on the counter. Cautiously opened the top cupboard, reached in as far as he could and took out some cigarettes. Extracted one, put the packet back as far as he could and closed the door. Went out to the patio again and lit the cigarette. Watched the smoke drift over the grass, curl between the branches of the pear tree. Telling her the truth now would be a bad idea, because she'd get mad that he had pretended not to be cured earlier *and* it would encourage her in this stupid business venture.

The phone in the kitchen rang. He stood on his cigarette butt, dropped the dead end in the wheelie-bin – Frances could spot the smallest clues – and hurried indoors, noticing as he did that there was no twinge or even tiny limp in his movement. It was all he could do to stop himself punching the air.

'I suppose I have you woke from your *mañana* or whatever it's called.' Uncle Dan, shouting into the phone. 'Some of us has half a day's work over.' Diarmuid heard a background voice call something. 'I am not sitting at my computer looking at pornographic sites, ha-ha. Hold your tongue, woman... Now. What was I ringing about? Oh, aye, that meeting with yourself and myself and Paul and that solicitor boy.' He cleared his throat noisily. 'When're you for having it?'

'I've nothing arranged yet.'

'Didn't I say I was agreeable? Your own flesh and blood – I'm agreeable surely.'

'OK, I'll get one set up for...the weekend? Not sure about the solicitor, but Paul and I should be OK. Will that do?'

'Do grand. Have you herself there?'

'Frances? She's gone...out. Did you want her?'

'Only to tell her there's not a woman in the country could touch her. Up and down the length of me for a full half-hour. Up and down and smack and round.'

'She did a healing session – with you?'

'Isn't that what I'm saying? Not a trace of a snifter or snot left.'

'She cured your sneezing?'

'You're like a bloody cuckoo. Sure amn't I telling you? It's a born miracle is what it is. Since Thursday last and your good lady, every tube in me is as clear as a whistle.'

Diarmuid looked out the kitchen window at a blackbird. It was pulling a worm from the ground, leaning back on its heels, the worm stretching and trying to resist. As he watched, the worm snapped in half. The blackbird tilted its head to gulp down the top part, went stabbing into the grass after the remains. 'But – but she told me it didn't work on relatives.'

'Well, she's no relation of mine, is she? She's married to you, God help her, but she's not my relation.'

'What did she do?' His voice sounded shrill.

'What difference to you what she done? Listen to this.' There was a sound of heavy breathing at the other end of the line. 'The best-quality oxygen rattling in and out. And me plagued half my life! That's some smart wee woman you have. Anyway, get you that meeting set up, and don't forget to tell us what time it's at. We're not all clairvoyants.'

Diarmuid took an apple out of the fridge, cut it in half, ate the first piece, thinking. Then he dialled Paul. 'Uncle Dan rang.'

'Oh?'

'He's agreed to have a chat with us.'

'Well, now… Did he say what about?'

'No, but it's obvious.'

'Nothing's obvious about Uncle Dan. We'd need to watch. Make a meeting inside the next day or two before he changes his mind.'

'No go. He says it has to be the weekend some time.' Well, if he doesn't, I do. 'Will we make it Saturday morning?'

'OK. Let's meet him at his place. Take the old so-and-so for his lunch afterwards, maybe, if it works out. Even treat Mount Carmel if we have to.'

'His sneezing's cured, you know. He's had a cure.'

'Glad to hear it. You collect me about eleven and we'll drive over.'

Didn't say, 'Would that suit you, Diarmuid?' Didn't say, 'Thanks for going to this bother, Diarmuid.' Just orders. Do this, phone him, be there. Bastard.

At ten to five Frances still wasn't back. Maybe she'd been

refused a loan and gone off to Joy and Mairead for a cry. Or got one and gone celebrating. Suddenly, he felt the need to phone Angela. Didn't want to sit and think about it, didn't want to analyse was it good or bad, just wanted to phone her. Not from here – Frances might walk in, and if he hung up Angela would know he felt guilty, and it would be bad at both ends. He checked that he'd got change, then drove to a phone-box and rang directory enquiries.

'Hello.' He'd forgotten how nice her voice sounded. 'It's me,' he said. 'Diarmuid. Again. I was over in Inishgorm yesterday getting a body-soul guy to look at my foot. Remember my foot? He, mmh, he cured me.'

There was a pause. 'He cured your foot? That you had the bother with?'

'You've no idea the difference it makes.'

'Are you *sure* he cured it?'

'Well, certainly, after he looked at it, it happened. This morning, in bed, I woke up and it felt...perfect.' He took a breath. 'How are things?'

A little laugh-sigh. 'Nothing as dramatic, I'm afraid. We've decided to drop the case against the university. It was costing too much and these big institutions always win in the end. Aaaaand, let's see... Tom says the intellectual life in Harvard is heady.'

'Heady?'

A knowing laugh this time, as if she'd read his thoughts. 'That's what he said. Heady.'

'It must be lonely. For both of you, I mean.'

'Not really – I'm used to it by now. Actually, I was thinking of registering for a course at the leisure centre here – the Alexander Technique. How to walk and stand and sit and so on.' Didn't she know how to do those already? 'What about you?'

'I'm going to be meeting my uncle on Saturday. My brother and I are going to talk to him about my – our mother's will. I mean, he's in it but my brother thinks he shouldn't be. My uncle, that is. They didn't get along, you see – my uncle and mother, I mean – and she didn't want to leave him anything, and yet it ended up he conned her into giving him stuff. Long story.' He felt hot, stupid and pointless. Why had he spilled out that information to her? Why the hell had he rung her anyway?

'Well, I hope you get whatever it is you want.' A doorbell sounded in the background. 'Somebody at the door. I'd better go.'

'Yes.' Diarmuid hesitated, opened his mouth to say something, then closed it. She was gone. He sat staring at the phone for a full minute. What now?

Chapter 12

A CONSTABLE CALLS

He'd just begun a morning pee when he thought he heard the front-door bell ring. Swearing, he stopped splashing into the toilet-bowl water and switched to a quiet hiss against the porcelain. Yes, it was the bell. Some bastard was leaning on it, waiting for a couple of seconds, then starting again. Not loud enough to waken Frances, of course, but loud.

He pulled his dressing-gown around him and hurried downstairs, two at a time. Probably the postman with something to sign for. Why couldn't he leave the damned thing at the door, get it signed tomorrow? 'Jobsworth moron,' Diarmuid muttered, as he stepped on the swinging belt of his dressing-gown, pitched forward and hit his head on the wall at the turn of the stairs. Suppressing a moan, he cupped his hand over the bruise and stood for a moment. Then he hurried down and opened the door. A uniformed figure with a folder, yes. But not a postman – a policeman. And not just a policeman but Constable Sonovadic. Staring at him, unblinking. *Christ.*

'Morning, sir. Could I come in and have a wee chat? Shouldn't take long.'

'No, no.' Diarmuid touched his forehead where it was throbbing. Glanced at his fingers, this time a dab of blood, omiGod. He wiped it on the side of his dressing-gown. 'I mean, yes, that's fine, that's fine.'

Sonovadic raised his eyebrows. 'Bit of a wound you took there, sir.'

As he entered, the cop's eyes left Diarmuid and looked around – at the ceiling, at the slightly sideways painting in the hall, at the small burn-mark on the carpet beside the kitchen. As though it was a house he, Sonovadic, had toyed with the idea of buying but hadn't yet made up his mind about. 'Here?' he asked, pushing open the living-room door. Before Diarmuid could say or even think that he'd prefer it if he, Diarmuid, was the one who decided what room they'd sit and talk in, since it was his house, not Sonovadic's, before there was time for any of that, the policeman had sat down in the armchair and put his clipboard in the middle of the coffee table.

Diarmuid held his dressing-gown lapels across his chest. This must be how it was for women – naked bits popping out while pig-dumb men like Sonovadic stared at them. 'Would you like a cup of tea?'

A big hand raised, the light glinting off pale-gold hair. 'No. No time for tea or carry-on of that nature. I just need to have a word with you, if you don't mind. Sir.'

'Well, I've already given a full statement, Officer. But certainly I'll—'

Sonovadic picked up his clipboard. 'Start with details confirmation. You are, ah, Dr ... Dr Darren Monaghan, lecturer at North-Eastern University?'

'Yes. That's Diarmuid, actually.'

Sonovadic took out a pen. 'That'd be the Christian name.'

'Yes.'

'Not Darren.'

'No. Diarmuid.'

'Dermot.'

'No, not Dermot – Diarmuid.' He spelt it out for the policeman.

'I see. And that's the official name.'

'It's my official name.'

The policeman completed the change on the clipboard. 'The

purpose of my visit is not to discuss the recent fatality of the professor, as I think maybe you suggested a while back.' Diarmuid hoped the cop couldn't hear the thud of his heart. He watched as Sonovadic removed the sheet from the clipboard, held it up and flicked it with his middle finger. 'This here is a different matter entirely. This is a matter of what could well be adjudged a criminal nature.'

With a massive effort, Diarmuid stopped himself shrieking. This was about taking the file – *his* file – from Claire's office! Terry must have decided to abandon all efforts at pressuring Diarmuid to give Hazel good marks, gone straight for the nuclear option... Or maybe not. Maybe—

'I have some bad news for you, I'm afraid, sir. All right?'

All right? How would bad news be all right, you bone-headed ape?

'Yes, yes. Grand.'

Behind Sonavadic, the living-room door opened and Frances came in. She had on her black dressing-gown with the salmon of knowledge on the back, and her hair looked a bit like Cherie Blair's the morning after she and Tony had been celebrating the 1997 election win. Her feet were bare. 'What's going on?'

Diarmuid, who didn't need to, stood up, while Sonovadic, who should have, sat where he was. 'Frances, this is Constable, ah, Dixon. You remember he took statements from me about Cl– Professor Thompson.'

'No,' Frances said.

Sonovadic laced his fingers and made them crack, nodded to Frances. 'Morning.'

Frances looked at her watch. 'It's not half past seven yet. What's up?'

Diarmuid began to speak but Sonovadic held up his hand. 'I'm on a mission that I'm not that fond of, madam, I may tell you, for it's one that involves breaking a bit of bad news.' He waited until Frances had settled on the arm of the couch beside Diarmuid, her thigh touching his shoulder. Then he reached into the breast pocket of his tunic and took out a piece of paper. 'It's in connection with Mr Daniel Costello, who would be a relation of yours.'

'Is something wrong?' Diarmuid asked. Thinking that maybe stuff about Uncle Dan waking up at night and worrying about death had triggered something in the universe, something that had now come back into Uncle Dan's life as...

'At two ten a.m. this morning, two officers were called to the home of Mr Daniel Costello, 6 Durham Close.' Sonovadic looked up from the sheet. 'This would be the residence of your uncle – yes?' Diarmuid nodded. 'There they found the owner-occupier in a semi-conscious state. He had a wound to the head...' Sonovadic paused to glance at the lump on Diarmuid's forehead. 'And he was in a state of some agitation. This mental confusion or semi-consciousness was due to the fact that some two hours earlier, according to his account, his premises were forcibly entered and he was attacked by an assailant or assailants unknown.'

'God Almighty,' Frances said. 'You're joking.' She looked at Diarmuid. 'What happened your forehead?'

'Slipped.'

The policeman looked at her reprovingly, then went on. 'At oh-three-hundred hours an ambulance was called, and Mr Costello was taken to hospital. He is at present in...' The constable licked his thumb and checked briefly through his file. 'He is at present in Ward M4 of the Royal Victoria Hospital, where his condition is described as comfortable.'

'Jesus, Mary and Joseph protect us,' Frances said. 'The poor creature. He's not going to die on us, is he?'

'My notes here just say, "comfortable". That's all I have to go on.'

'Is he conscious?'

'It doesn't say he's *un*conscious, so that probably means he is. Although I wouldn't want to swear to it.'

'What happened?' Frances asked.

Sonovadic sighed and looked out the window, scratching his chin with his nail, which made a rasping sound. 'From what the gentleman has reported to us, there appears to have been something of an altercation. The intruder or intruders effected entry and an altercation ensued between your uncle and him. Or them.'

'What are you saying?' Frances demanded. 'I can't understand you. Are you saying there was a fight?'

'A disturbance, ma'am, might be a better way to put it. A physical disturbance and the theft of some property – that's all it says in my notes. Maybe the gentleman himself – your relative – can shed more light, when his injuries are recovered and he's up for more sustained questioning.'

Sonovadic asked them to sign a sheet saying he'd told them what he'd told them, then stood up. Diarmuid saw him to the door, promised he'd get in touch with his uncle as soon as possible. 'Ward M4, you say?'

'That was the exact place I mentioned, sir.' Sonovadic adjusted his cap, moved his head upwards to create more room at the collar of his shirt. 'I can't say what would be the case about visiting hours.'

'Hospitals don't bother with visiting hours any more,' Frances said, from behind Diarmuid. 'You can visit people any time you like.'

Sonovadic closed the brass clip on his file with a snap. 'I'm sure there's truth in that. Although they'd need some order about the place, I'm sure.'

Frances went upstairs as Diarmuid saw the policeman to the door. He said his duty had been to inform the next of kin, which he'd now done, and he'd be in touch in the near future. He gave Diarmuid a half-salute as he left.

Frances was standing at the bathroom door in her flesh-toned pants and bra when he came up the stairs. 'What were you up to?' she asked him. Her skin, which once glowed, had a greyish tinge.

'Seeing that prying bastard out.'

'I meant your forehead – there.'

He winced as she put her hand on the bruise. 'Does it look bad? Hit my head on the wall going down the stairs.'

'First thing struck me the minute I saw you. No pun intended.' She turned back into the bathroom, took a pair of tweezers from the cabinet and began to tug at her eyebrows. He'd asked her to close the door before doing that kind of thing but she never did. 'So, what do you think?'

'About Uncle Dan? I think he got off lightly. There was a thing in the papers the other week where they tied up and burned a pensioner with cigarettes, and before that, an old woman who had a heart attack a week after hoods broke in and threatened to rape her.'

'Better not tell Dan that when you visit him.'

'I'm also raging that I didn't bring him the bill for those tiles before he got mugged. It'll look mean, doing it now.'

He was drying his feet after a shower and thinking about the smell burning flesh would give off when the phone rang downstairs. He could hear Frances's voice: 'No. Really? I don't believe it. No, that can't be. There's a mistake, obviously.'

When he came downstairs she was putting a lot of butter and marmalade onto a piece of toast. The jacket of her pinstripe suit was draped over the back of her chair. 'That was Carmel. She's in a bit of a bad way,' she said.

'Not surprised.'

Frances took a huge mouthful of toast. 'Not what you think. The old so-and-so won't let her see him in the hospital.'

'Why not?'

'She says she doesn't know why. She wondered if we were going to see him, and if we were, could she come in with us and talk to him?'

'But didn't he say he doesn't want to see her?'

'Yes, but she sounds desperate to talk to him.'

'But he doesn't want to talk to her.'

'I know, I know – stop it, for God's sake. The poor woman just wants to make sure he's all right, or find out what's wrong anyway. Besides, I could maybe give her the tiles bill, get her to bring it into him.'

'Except that Uncle Dan doesn't want her to. God Almighty, why did this have to happen now?'

'You know, no matter what happens, you always bring it round to how it affects you. Say you were the one lying in a hospital bed, how would you like that? Or say you were poor old Carmel, barred from seeing him, just because Uncle Dan decides that's the way he wants it. Anyway, when are you going to see him?'

'I suppose I'd better.'

'I said *when?*'

'You don't have to shout. This afternoon. OK? But I'm certainly not taking bloody Carmel with me.'

Immediately after lunch Diarmuid drove to the Royal Victoria Hospital. It was a mild, slightly foggy day, and the moisture in the air drew a halo of mist around the lights that lined the motorway.

Propped up by at least five pillows, Uncle Dan looked like a maharajah. He had a blob of cotton-wool on his forehead, held in place by two strips of sticking plaster, and his neck was in a brace. 'I'm like a bloody porpoise stuck on the rocks and not one of my own to look next or near me. Don't sit on the bed – you'll have my leg murdered.'

'Here – take the weight off your ankles,' a nurse with black hair and red lipstick said, bringing a chair from beside the next bed. She turned to Uncle Dan. 'Did someone take your temperature recently?'

'Sure what would be the point? It'd only be going through the roof, with you smasher nurses every road a fellah looks.'

'Would you listen to him,' the nurse said. 'Romeo's come to town.'

Uncle Dan's eyes followed her down the ward.

'How are you feeling?' Diarmuid asked.

'Three bruised ribs and this thing on my neck torturing me,

and you want to know how I feel? It takes two of them to get me set on a bedpan.'

'How long are they going to keep you in?'

'How would I know? Until I get my legs under me.'

'What happened?'

'What happened to you? On your head?'

Diarmuid touched the Elastoplast on his forehead. 'I hit my head off a wall.'

'That was smart. God putting penance on you, I dare say, for letting the likes of this happen to me.'

'What did happen to you?'

'Two blackguards broke into the house and tried robbing it, and when they seen me they tried to murder me. That's all. That's the whole shin-ding.'

'When was this? When did it happen?'

'Twenty minutes to one in the morning. And the reason I know when it was is that the bedside clock stopped then. The pair of them smashed the good clock at twenty minutes to one in the morning.'

'Were you asleep?'

'I was and I wasn't. I was lying on my back sort of thinking and sort of sleeping at the same time, you know the way you be half and half, and next I hear this cracking or splintering down the stairs, thought maybe it was the fire, something burning and crackling. And then the next thing was the back door opening as slow as slow, an inch an hour, but I could hear it just the same. All that was keeping it shut was a lump of board up against the back, no big job getting it open, I may tell you. And then next thing there's a scream, and the front door's opened, and then it slams shut again powerful quick, and next, what do I hear but your woman going whoo-hoo, whoo-hoo, down the road with her feet like a Zulu.'

'You mean Carmel?'

'Who the hell else would I mean?'

'What was she doing?'

'Amn't I telling you? Woo-hooing down the road.'

'But before that.'

'Sitting on her arse in the front room, watching one of these oul' films of hers. Only the minute she heard your two scumbags coming in at the back door, she skedaddled out the front.'

'So did the – the intruders come up the stairs?'

Uncle Dan tapped his index finger on the bedside locker. 'They did not, for I went down to them first. Pair of boyos, standing at the hall table going through your woman's bag, with wee woolly caps and scarves across their mouths. So I gave a roar out of me. "Hey, youse blaggards, what're youse at?"'

'Did they not know you were in the house?'

'Well, if they didn't know before I roared, they knew after. Not that it took one fidge out of them. One of them comes to the foot of the stairs with his gob hid behind a Rangers scarf. "Where have you the money hid?" says he. "We're the UDA." "There's no money here," says I. "And if there was, by Christ, the UDA would be whistling awhile before they got it. Just you two buckos stay there," says I, "till I get the police for you." And I turned to go up the stairs to the phone.'

'You told them you were going to phone the police?'

Before he could answer, the nurse with the black hair and red lipstick appeared. 'Open,' she said, and Uncle Dan did as he was told. She inserted a thermometer and stood tapping her foot, her finger on his pulse. Rolled her eyes at Diarmuid. 'This is the only time we can keep him quiet, you know. Shove a thermometer in his mouth.' She looked at her watch, dropped his wrist. 'You'll live.'

Uncle Dan watched her retreating back until it was out of sight.

'So you went upstairs to phone,' Diarmuid reminded him.

'I did. Only the two blackguards come running after me. Next thing I'm on the ground and the pair of them is sitting on top of me. "Where's the fucking money? Give you us your fucking money!" Screaming at me. Pardon my French.'

'How did they know you had money?'

'They didn't – that's the thing, only chancing their arm. And when they seen I wasn't going to cough up, they tried to get away.'

'And you tried to stop them.'

'I got a hoult of the first one and pulled his head back as hard as I could. Took the hat and scarf off him. And then the two of us rolled against the bedside table and knocked the clock over. And next the other boy produces an iron bar and starts hammering at my back and shoulders. I don't know how long he was at it for the next I knew I was in here.'

'You're a lucky man to be alive.'

'If you could feel my legs and back you mightn't say that.' Uncle Dan groaned and shifted under the clothes. 'Attempted murder, that's what should be the charge. Not burglary at all.'

'But have they caught them? I thought—'

'Didn't I pull the scarf off one of them? Put that boy in an identity parade and I'll soon stick my pin in him.'

'Yes, but…this could have been the UDA or somebody.'

'Damn the UDA. Just a pair of wee skitters looking for money.'

'But if – if it was the UDA—'

'If it was Gusty bloody Spence, it wouldn't matter. As soon as the peelers put him on parade I'll settle his hash for him.'

'You could be opening a can of worms, Uncle Dan. And it's got nothing to do with your case. Not one thing.'

'So that's it, then – you want me to sit and never say a word? By God, I'd be in a right pickle if I was relying on you for my law and order.'

There was silence for a few moments. Then Diarmuid said, 'Is it true you won't let Carmel see you?'

'Don't mention that name.'

'I'm only asking if Carmel—'

'I said, don't mention that bloody woman's name! Did you not hear me?' Uncle Dan's face had gone slightly purple.

'I'd have thought you'd be glad to see another visitor.'

'What did she do?' Uncle Dan was sitting up in bed, eyes hot. 'Tell us that – what did she do?'

'Well, to be honest, if I'd been in her shoes, I'm not sure I wouldn't—'

'She ran like a bloody hare, the minute she heard them coming in. Ran the length of the street, looking after her own skin. I could have been murdered in my house for all she cared – do you know that? When I think of all the things I done for that one, and then, the first peep of danger, she hightails it out. There'll be two blue moons in the sky and a third in the lavatory the day she darkens my door again.'

Diarmuid looked at him. Uncle Dan's face was blotchy and his eyes pink-rimmed. 'What did you expect her to do? Jump on the two boys and pin them to the floor?'

'No, but she could have lifted the phone. Called the peelers. Set off the alarm. Couldn't she? Something itself. Bloody woman. Let her go, then, if that's what she wants, grab her goods and chattels and clear off to hell.'

Then the dark-haired nurse started putting up screens and saying it was time for Dan to have a bed bath. He pretended to be annoyed, said he was as clean as a born-again Christian, but Diarmuid could tell he quite liked the attention.

Frances was standing in the middle of the kitchen with the phone to her ear and saying 'Oh dear. That's *terrible*. Oh dear... *Car-mel*!' she mouthed, pointing at the phone. Then, with no further warning, she handed him the receiver.

'Oh Diarmuid.' The little breathy voice was shaky with tears. 'Isn't he a terrible man? Isn't he an awful terrible man altogether?'

'Well now,' Diarmuid said.

'It's the shock. The staff nurse said that that kind of thing happens all the time – somebody gets a shock and next thing they don't even recognise their nearest and dearest but they come round in the end. Did he know you?'

'He did.'

'Did he say anything, you know, about me?'

Why were women always asking him that question? 'Well – yes.'

'What did he say? Tell us, Diarmuid, or—'

'He said – well, he said he never wanted to see you about the place again, and that you were to move out. Actually, that's what he said.'

At first he thought Carmel had begun to laugh, but then, as he listened, he realised she was crying. It was the same sound, really – like water leaving a sink. *Uik-uik-uik-eeaaaghhk.*

'I know if I could ta-ta-talk to him, that he'd see re-ee-ee-eason, and that we could get – get the whole affair ss-ss-ssorted out. But I caaaan't. *Uik-uik-uik-eeaaaghhk.*'

'Well now,' Diarmuid said. 'There you are.' He made a couple of desperate attempts to pass the phone back to Frances, but when he held it out Frances moved away. Eventually Diarmuid started to say, 'The thing that bothers me about all this, Carmel, is that—' And in mid-sentence he pressed firmly on the cut-off button. When he'd done that he lifted the phone clear of its cradle, just a little, so that it'd be off the hook if she tried ringing back. You could see why Uncle Dan wanted a get-out clause from somebody as nuts as Carmel.

Chapter 13

NOISES OFF

Dr Fr David was standing at the window of the boardroom, talking to a porter who was positioning a vase of flowers on a small table. When he saw Diarmuid the priest came over, little eyes round with pleasure behind his glasses. 'Ah, Diarmuid. Let me get you a cup of tea – the cup that cheers, ha-ha. Professor Tiedt should be here any minute.'

Something electrical crackled in Diarmuid's head. He put down the cup and saucer Dr Fr David had passed him. 'I thought it was Wilkinson. The man from Bath – Wilkinson. That's what it said on my form.'

'Oh dear – were you not told? Quentin Wilkinson stood on his child's toy, poor man, a miniature train, I believe, fractured his collarbone, so we had to draft in Professor Tiedt. Fortunately he's a friend of the Dean's, which meant a phone call from that quarter provided encouragement – and then Dublin's not as far as Bath, and that's good. I thought you'd been told.'

The door opened noisily and Warwick bustled in. He was wearing a blue shirt with a white collar. The collar made him look vaguely clerical.

'Good afternoon, Billy,' Dr Fr David said. 'We've got tea or coffee, if you would—'

'Fish copulate in it – that's what W.C. Fields said about water. Except he didn't say 'copulate'. In the absence of hard evidence,

I'll give his hypothesis the benefit of the doubt.' Warwick peeled off his overcoat. 'Our friend from across the fish-shagging water arrived yet?'

'Well. actually...' Dr Fr David said. He explained Dr Wilkinson's absence again.

'The bastard,' Warwick said. 'What a supremely stupid thing to do. Who's standing in for him?'

'Professor Tiedt of GUD.'

Warwick removed the chocolate-chip cookie he had inserted in his mouth. 'My God. What moron suggested him? He's a menace.'

'Well, the Dean did – he's a friend of Professor Tiedt's. Funny enough, Professor Tiedt had been trying to contact the Dean, to ask *him* to act as external examiner down *there*, in Dublin, except the Dean has been working from home for the past week, and the Saddingtons have mislaid their phone or it's gone missing or something – but I gather the Dean doesn't want to invest in a new one when there's still a chance the old one will turn up. Because then he'd have two phones, ha-ha. Which is why Professor Tiedt couldn't contact him. But, as I say, the Dean came into college and contacted him, so it worked out.'

'Has he read the dissertation? Tiedt, I mean.'

'We sent it to GUD by special delivery on the Enterprise yesterday morning – only way to be sure he'd get it in time.'

'It's over three hundred pages. He couldn't possibly read it in that time.'

Dr Fr David chuckled. 'I think you underestimate the concentration and intellect of a man like—'

He broke off as the door to the room shook violently. Then when it seemed that the handle must break, there was a babble of voices and it opened.

'Very good. No need of further assistance,' Professor Tiedt said, over his shoulder. He closed the door in the boardroom secretary's face and strode in with quick little steps.

Dr Fr David held out his hand. 'Hello, Professor Tiedt. I'm

David – yes, nice to see you again too... Let's get you a coffee. Much traffic on the drive up?'

Tiedt put down his briefcase, dropped three spoonfuls of sugar into his coffee and sipped noisily. 'Greater part of the journey passed in a preoccupied state. Only the vaguest recollection of traffic lights and speed limits and so forth. Busy doing a mental draft of a conference paper for Cape Town.'

'You got your copy of the candidate's dissertation, then.'

'Well...yes. A copy was received.'

'You know Dr Billy Warwick, I think' Dr Fr David said, 'our internal examiner. And this is Dr Diarmuid Monaghan, the candidate's supervisor. Diarmuid will be sitting in as an observer, if that's acceptable.'

'Certainly. Feeling better now, are you?' Tiedt asked Diarmuid. He turned back to Dr Fr David. 'This poor chap was seized by the most unfortunate coughing fit during our radio interview last Friday. At one point it appeared he might have to have the Heimlich manoeuvre administered.'

'Heimlich?'

'When someone is choking, you know – grab them from behind and squeeze like fury. Makes whatever is in their windpipe pop out. Fortunately wasn't necessary with our friend here, but still, an embarrassing experience. Better luck with the second leg, eh? Do you know, I cannot think what is scheduled for discussion at the return fixture. Perhaps you might refresh?'

Diarmuid thought about saying, 'Fuck off,' but instead muttered, 'Improving school experience for student teachers.'

'Of course, of course. Really must give it some thought one of these days.'

Dr Fr David looked at his watch. 'Perhaps if we have a short preliminary chat, and then we'll have the candidate in.' They arranged themselves behind the table. 'Would you like to start, Billy?'

Warwick took off his jacket and draped it over the back of his chair. His shirt was short-sleeved and his arms looked pudgy and tanned. He took out a single sheet of paper, cleared his throat

211

and looked at each of the others in turn. He said he'd read Hazel's dissertation and he would say at once that it was impressive – very impressive, in fact. Signs of wide reading, topic thoughtfully chosen and of interest to a wide audience. And well organised. Warwick gave a number of instances of good organisation, said the choice of books in the literature review section was particularly impressive, and finished by saying that while there were weaknesses – the *conclusion*, for example, might have been strengthened, and there were points where the *phrasing* could have been less clumsy – he felt this was of Master's level and he would recommend acceptance. Provisional, of course, on minor amendments and a successful viva.

'Thank you, Billy, for that,' Dr Fr David said, writing briefly in his pad. 'That's been very helpful. Professor Tiedt?'

Professor Tiedt looked at his notes and sighed. Then he took off his glasses, rubbed his eyes with his knuckles, blinked vigorously and put on his glasses again. It was always a pleasure, he said, to come north like this. He believed that a great deal of research emanating from NEU was of a high calibre, and the institution had every reason to be proud of the work it was doing. On the other hand it had to be said that this particular dissertation raised a number of issues. Problems, even.

'Yes?' Dr Fr David smiled, as if pleased to hear this.

'Like our friend here' – Tiedt gestured towards Warwick – 'Initial reaction—'

'Warwick,' Warwick said. 'Billy Warwick.'

'Initial reaction, after careful reading, is positive, to a point. Further reading, however, yields an element of depression rather than encouragement. First, the topic. There is an argument for saying this topic is one of contemporary significance. But in another sense, of course, it is overworked. Nor is a completely happy state of mind possible about the organisation of the thesis. What exactly, one wonders, is the link between Chapter One, which ends with identification of the research issue, and Chapter Two, which blithely ignores that issue and provides a

Cook's Tour of some books the candidate appears to have flicked through in a somwhat desultory manner? In one respect it's easy to agree with our friend—'

'Warwick. W.S. Warwick. Should I perhaps make out a placard?'

'Total agreement with Mr Warwick is possible – '

'Dr Warwick.'

'– about the quality of some of the writing. It really does get pretty scratchy at points. In fact pretty well throughout, to be frank.'

'So would it be fair to say,' Dr Fr David said, glancing at his watch, 'if I could summarise and with one eye on the time, you have reservations about some aspects of the work?'

'More than a few.'

'All right. Very good. Next, will we say your reservations are relatively minor, or relatively major?'

'Major. Definitely major.'

'Whereas you, Billy, your concern would be considerably more—'

'It certainly would. Minor. Very minor. To the point where I'm beginning to wonder if Professor Titt and myself have been given the same dissertation.'

'Oh, I think you have.' Dr Fr David chuckled, touched the little silver cross in his lapel. 'Could I suggest at this point that we invite the candidate in? If that's acceptable to you, Billy, and to you, Professor? It may well be that we will see the way ahead more clearly after we've talked to her about her work.'

Hazel was ushered in. She was wearing an orange trouser suit and black high-heeled shoes. She sat bolt upright in the chair, her hands laced tightly together, head tilted to the left, so that you hardly noticed the tilt of her nose.

'Welcome,' Dr Fr David said. 'I hope the wait hasn't made you apprehensive.'

'Not at all.'

'Good, good. As you know, while the viva is an important and integral part of the examination process, it isn't something

213

that we want or feel should be a daunting experience. Essentially it's an opportunity for your examiners – Dr Warwick and Professor Tiedt – to get you to expand on or explain the occasional issue that may have caught their eye in your work. So, if you'd like to start, Dr Warwick?'

Warwick got Hazel to tell him why she had chosen this area as a topic, what she had learned from her reading, what major conclusions she had drawn from the work, and what degree of satisfaction she felt with it. Hazel responded, smiling and speaking rather quickly, which might have been nerves or perhaps enthusiasm for her topic. 'I won't pretend I'm completely satisfied,' she concluded. 'I never am, probably because I'm a bit of a perfectionist, actually. But I'm reasonably proud of what I've done. Flaws, don't I know it, but reasonably happy.'

Dr Fr David glanced along the table. 'Professor Tiedt?'

Professor Tiedt said he was glad Hazel had a sense of dissatisfaction with her dissertation. People who were content with work they'd done, he found, were often people with little critical awareness. Professor Tiedt said he'd read through the dissertation carefully and there were a number of points he'd like to raise with Hazel, if she didn't mind.

Hazel said she didn't mind at all.

Professor Tiedt said first of all he'd like to suggest that maybe the selection of topic wasn't as important as Hazel indicated. He then gave three reasons why it might be considered unoriginal, including the fact that a book with a similar title had come out the year before. 'That particular publication was called *Journey towards Light*. It does not appear to be in your bibliography.' Hazel said as far as she knew it wasn't. 'Your dissertation is called' – he flicked back to the title page – "Journey towards Daybreak". Have you read that particular work – *Journey towards Light*?'

Hazel blushed and said she hadn't.

'I see.' Professor Tiedt then went on to talk about some other aspects of her work, such as structure and proofreading. 'On page forty-two, you have "I there is an extended parallel here." On page sixty-six you have "The note of world-weariness is admixtured" – *admixtured?* – "with the feeling of." And then there's a full stop. Had you some reason for doing that?'

Hazel went red. 'I'd need to sit down and look at it and, you know… I'm sure it's just a matter of a detail.'

Professor Tiedt looked at her quite hard when she said that. Then he went on to point out things about the way chapters were organised, the way the dissertation didn't look at the ideas of Heinrich and Edel Fossenberg who, of course, were a *seminal influence* on most of those who followed them in this field. There appeared to be the use of the same quotation twice – once in the second chapter, and again in the final chapter – quite a long quotation at that, occupying well over half a page. And then there was the methodology chapter, which, apart from being rather short on references, didn't really address the issue of *why* the research model that had been adopted was a fitting one in the circumstances.

As the professor spoke, Hazel's smile got smaller and the knuckles on her hands, clenched in her lap, grew whiter and bonier-looking. Oh, Jesus, Diarmuid thought.

'If I might come in there,' Warwick said. He told the panel that he had some sympathy with the points the professor was making – there could be no denying their validity – but at the same time it seemed to him they were essentially minor matters.

'The choice of research method?' Professor Tiedt said loudly. 'No, research method cannot be classified as a minor matter. Granted, the – the *spine* of the dissertation is relatively acceptable; but there *are* matters of some import that *do* require attention. It is owed to the candidate and to the quality of this award and to the university *itself* to draw such matters to the attention of the candidate and the institution.'

'Sorry,' Warwick said, 'I don't think that's quite accurate. What we owe the candidate is a balanced examination of her work. That's all we owe her.'

'Well, indeed. Assuming it's one that takes in all the features and qualities of the work presented. *All.*' The skin on Professor Tiedt's face seemed to have tightened and he leant forward in his seat as he spoke. Hazel, Diarmuid noticed, was looking at her knees, occasionally slipping her laced hands between them. She seemed to have shrunk, except for her nose, which had expanded and looked more bent than usual now.

'Well, then, let's see.' Dr Fr David tapped his pen against his teeth. 'We have an agreed view that much of what is here is worthwhile. Correct? Now, I have a sheet that requires me to classify the candidate as, one, "Satisfactory, recommend award." Two, "Satisfactory with reservations; minor amendments before submission." Three, "Unsatisfactory, recommend fail, possible resubmission within a twelve-month period."'

At the word 'fail' Hazel began to sob.

'Now, now, now,' Dr Fr David told her. 'We are merely discussing details. We're all agreed on that.'

'With respect,' Professor Tiedt said, 'the point has already been made – these are central issues, not details. It's pointless to pretend that they are.' He looked at his watch.

'Correct me if I've got you wrong, Professor – are you saying that there are matters of central importance that are deficient in the work?' Dr Fr David asked.

'That's precisely what is being said. Has been articulated over several minutes. For example, where are the research questions? They do not appear. Can someone point them out?'

'She has hypotheses,' Warwick said. 'There's no practical difference between hypotheses and research questions.'

Professor Tiedt sighed and tapped his index finger a number of times on the polished table top. 'Really. Let's not stretch academic integrity beyond recovery point. What confronts this panel is an honest piece of work. Signs of effort, granted, no argument. But there are matters in it that give cause for real concern. Should have thought that was crushingly obvious.'

At that moment there was a shout from outside the room and the door-handle began to rattle violently.

'Oh, for pity's sake.' Dr Fr David stood up and hurried

towards the door. 'My apologies, Professor Tiedt – and to you, Diarmuid, and you, Billy,' he called over his shoulder. 'This kind of interruption is—' Passing Hazel, he touched her arm, lowered his voice: 'Sorry, Hazel – I feel badly about—'

His hand was inches from the doorknob when the door sprang open and the Dean burst into the room. He was panting heavily and his forehead above the pink glasses shone with sweat. He gripped Dr Fr David's shoulder. 'Something – Something terrible.'

'It's a bomb!' Hazel jumped to her feet. 'There's a bomb in the building. Oh, my God Almighty, Terry, where's Terry?'

The Dean moved his arms like a man swimming underwater. 'No, no – no bomb. Not here.'

'Please!' Professor Tiedt stood, arms folded on his little chest. 'Please, then! A viva is in progress – a Master's viva.'

The Dean gave the ghost of a smile. 'Oh. Well. Could have been worse – could have been a doctorate. Ha-ha.' Then he slumped into a chair and covered his face with both hands.

Professor Tiedt came out from behind the table. 'For God's sake, Basil, get a grip on yourself. *What is the matter?*'

'I can hardly credit it but – I saw it. On the television. It's like a dream.'

'Saw *what*?'

'A plane – several planes have flown into skyscrapers in New York. Exploded against them. Thirty thousand people may be dead. That's what's the matter.'

'Oh, good heavens!' Dr Fr David said. 'Oh, good God! Eternal rest grant unto them, O Lord. My heavens!'

The Dean's voice was a hoarse rasp. 'They say other planes may have attacked other American cities as well.'

'How many?' Professor Tiedt asked.

Warwick came from behind the table. 'Is it the Russians?'

'We don't really know. We don't really know who anyone is, for sure. Is your viva nearly complete?'

Dr Fr David looked towards the others.' Well, we were nearing a point of closure, I think, Dean. Do sit down for just one moment, Hazel, if you would. Thank you. Professor Tiedt, have you any final thoughts on…?'

Professor Tiedt glanced back at the table, blinking rapidly. 'What did you say?'

'I was wondering, as chair,' Dr Fr David said, 'if you had thoughts on the viva. Should we postpone or—'

The professor began to laugh like one of the Goons. 'Did you say *postpone*? For Christ's sake! Didn't you hear what he said? They've attacked America!'

Dr Fr David looked towards Hazel, who had straightened in her chair but still had a handkerchief pressed to her face. 'So Billy, Professor Tiedt, can we register a consensus decision, then?'

Warwick began to collect his papers. 'I would like to register my judgement that the dissertation has reached the requisite Master's standard.'

Dr Fr David's voice was anxious. 'And Professor Tiedt?'

The professor was on his feet, ramming his file back into its bag, face white. 'Yes. Yes, yes yes.'

'Is that yes that—'

'Yes, pass her, pass her, if that's the desired outcome, if—' The professor stopped and fixed Dr Fr David with his bulging eyes. 'This is beyond belief. Can you not grasp the significance of what has happened?'

'Well, yes, I think so.' Dr Fr David wrote his name carefully on a sheet, ticked a couple of boxes, filled in a blank, and put the document in front of both men to sign.

Hazel's face was mottled white and red as she shuffled towards the door. 'Congratulations,' Dr Fr David called after her. 'You're now an MCont. Ed.'

Hazel gave a tiny smile and hurried out.

Dr Fr David turned to Diarmuid. 'Incidentally, Brother Ambrose, speaking to him after Mass this morning. He said to tell you he needs your material urgently for Friday.'

Diarmuid followed the priest into the corridor. It was filled with people. The door of the audio-visual viewing room was open and inside half a dozen TVs were switched on, all showing news. The commentators kept replaying the wobbly pictures of the first plane disappearing behind the tower before flames and smoke belched out into the New York morning sky. 'Jesus!' several people said. 'Holy Christ.' A couple of women were weeping.

'You ain't seen nothin',' one of the technicians said, taking a drink from a plastic bottle. 'There are ten other planes, all over America. Carrying nuclear bombs. It's the eve of destruction.'

Warwick pointed at the technician. 'People like you should be muzzled – *neutered*, better still. You know nothing, not a thing, *damn all*, but you still come out with these stupid, *brain-dead* remarks.' He pointed at the screen. 'Things happen. Random, meaningless. There doesn't have to be a conspiracy or big plan, you know.'

'We'll see!' the technician said. 'We'll soon see whether it's meaningless and who knows damn all or not. Soon see who's smart and who's not!'

'Keep quiet, please' Professor Tiedt's voice was high and tremulous. It reminded Diarmuid of Feargal Sharkey singing. 'We have a duty to witness these events as they unfold. There is an historical imperative that we do.'

'*Historical imperative?*' Warwick laughed loudly. 'Unfold? As if it was the plot of an opera! Can you believe him? *Unfold* !'

'Ssssh – shut up, you bastard!' several voices called.

Silence fell as the second plane was shown coming in – you could feel people willing it to pull out of its dive, willing it to miss the skyscraper and bring about the proper happy ending. Instead it tilted at an angle, so it was coming in from above AND sideways when it hit the building, and you could see the bulge coming out the other side.

'Oh, sweet fucking Jesus.'

'Oh, the dirty animals.'

Some people stood, moved towards the screen, as if they'd take the TV and smash it to pieces. But some other people called, 'Easy, easy – hold it, sit down there, hold it.'

It was only when they were watching the collapse of the towers and the guys running for their lives, and the cameraman repeating, 'I hope I don't die, I hope I don't die,' that Diarmuid realised Hazel was standing beside him. 'Did you find Terry?' he whispered. He didn't know why he was whispering or even asking.

'I'm here,' said a voice, and when Diarmuid looked to his right, Terry was there, eyes shining as if he might be about to cry.

'This is the real stuff,' Diarmuid heard Warwick call, like someone at a football game. 'The real stuff.'

'Shut up!'

'Stitch your hole, prick!' someone called.

'This is probably the most momentous event in television history!' Warwick yelled back. 'History before our eyes – *Bonfire of the Vanities* meets *Towering Inferno*!'

His voice trailed off because now on the screen there were shots of people covered completely with dust. A black woman, like a statue but walking bathed in dust – every detail, including her big lips and nose and eyes – as if on her way to work.

'I was so lucky!' Hazel whispered to Terry. 'In the middle of the viva, I started to pray to St Jude, and guess what? Inside *two minutes*, the professor, Tiedt, is saying, yes, he'll go along with a pass, and a minute before that he was all set to fail me. That's a miracle, you know. I know you don't believe in them, hon-comb, but that's a miracle, can't say it isn't.' Her happy face shone out among the faces of fear and bewilderment.

As Diarmuid drove home, Mark Carruthers was reminding listeners on the car radio why there was no Hugo Duncan that day to play people's favourite music. Instead Mark was talking on the phone to people in New York, who kept telling him where they had been when they heard about the planes crashing. Diarmuid glanced in the rear-view mirror and was shocked to see his own face, fresh and smiling, looking back at him.

He stopped for petrol at the service station a mile from home.

'Terrible business, these planes, isn't it?' he said to the girl with the earring through the top of her ear as they waited for his credit card to be accepted on the machine.

'They've had it on the television for the last three hours,' she said, flattening the payment slip on the counter for him to sign. 'It'll be the same for the next three weeks as well, wait till you see. Like the time Princess Di died – cancelling *Eastenders* and everything – ones coming on and giving out about it all over the place. This'll be the same only twice as bad.'

Frances was in the living room, standing by the window, a glass of whiskey in her hand.

'You mean you didn't see it on the TV?' he asked her. 'Or listen to the radio?'

'Heard them going on and on but I couldn't be bothered. Tell you what I did do though – I got my first body-soul customer this morning! A woman who works in the water service signed up for three sessions! I'm giving her the first one free, and the next two at a reduced rate. And she's going to tell all her friends at work if she's happy with it, she says, and I just *know* she will be... What about Uncle Dan? Did you see him today?'

'For God's sake, I had more to think of.'

She finished her whiskey, shook her head. 'Don't know what more you'd have to think about than your own flesh and blood.'

'You may be right.' It was the easiest thing to say. He stood looking at her – cheeks hot with excitement, body thick and untidy, the skin on her arms starting to hang loose. Tell her the truth, so. Now, before the world spins off into total confusion. 'Frances. Remember I said my visit to your friend – the body-soul guy – was useless?' His wife stopped, her gloved hand on the oven door. 'Well, actually, it wasn't. The pain in my foot is gone. Happened when I visited him, or rather the day after I visited him. I assumed it was coincidence and would come back again, so I didn't mention it to you, but the fact is it worked, the treatment worked. I don't know why I didn't tell you – pride or something. Anyway, I'm telling you now. It's better. And I'm sorry – that I didn't tell you before, I mean.' It felt like confession used to feel.

Frances washed her hands and dried them on the tea towel. Stood facing him, her rear resting against the counter.

'I knew your foot was better. It was obvious in your face. And, frankly, I don't care. All I want to know is can we use it to promote my business? Or does you being my husband mean you'd be no good for an endorsement – it'd look too like a set-up? Actually, it should be better because it's you, not worse – a professional man, a university lecturer. Shows that we're putting into operation in our *own* lives the service we're selling to them. Authentic and that sort of thing. I think we should use it.'

Diarmuid went into the living room and switched on the TV. President Bush was at a podium, his eyes small and skittery, saying the US was going to hunt down and smoke out whoever had committed this foul deed.

Frances stood behind him. 'You could even mention how you pooh-poohed the idea in the first place, and it was only when it happened to you that you acknowledged it and now you know for sure that body-soul works because you've gone through it yourself and experienced the benefits. Do you think would that work? I know I'll have to go out and grab the customers still – but what a start, eh? What – a – start!' She put her arms above her head and did a little tango foot-stamp towards the cupboard where the whiskey was kept.

'*Frances*!' She turned slowly towards him. He could feel sweat on his face, but whether from embarrassment or excitement he didn't want to think. 'Look. There are thousands of people dead – people jumping out windows, *appalling* stuff. And now Bush says he's going to get the culprits. The man's fucking half-wit enough to try anything – he could be getting ready to bomb Russia or the Middle East this minute – and you're standing here talking about how to advertise a bloody course in body-soul!'

She didn't say anything. Just poured two whiskeys. Gave him one, sat in the armchair by the window and drank a quarter of her glass's contents. When she spoke her voice was slow and calm.

'Diarmuidy, my sweetie. Remember in the Eighties? The Russians were going to attack, they had us all wetting ourselves. And then? Oops. Soviet Union fell apart, the Berlin Wall came down, contest over, no nuclear war, Armageddon postponed. So now, here they go again, telling us to worry about something else. Well bugger them. George Bush and company mean nothing to me. What matters is a woman I'm meeting tomorrow who's going to pay for a body-soul session and might put me in the way of a couple more customers. That's what matters to me – paying customers, not some eejits in an aeroplane in New York.'

Diarmuid took a sip of the whiskey, increased the volume on the TV. The leap from the window, the air rushing past your face and ears as you fall, the end of all puzzlement and effort only seconds away.

She stood behind him and put her hand on his shoulder. 'All this TV stuff, it's voyaging, that's all. Pure voyaging.' She swirled her whiskey and began to sing the first verse of 'Blue Velvet'.

'Voyeuring.'

Frances laughed. 'Aren't you the great man for the right word?'

Diarmuid took another sip of his whiskey and thought about his wife's argument. He searched the front, the back, round the sides of it, but he couldn't find a point where he could get in and defuse it.

Frances tapped the side of her glass with her nail. 'Anyway, we all know what most people are thinking. Poetic justice. The Yanks deserved this – bossing people around wherever you look, had to happen sooner or later. But, frankly, I don't give a twopenny damn. I've a business to get going and there just isn't room in my head for this stuff. The Yanks and those ones in the aeroplane and all the rest can scratch each other's eyes out or slice each other's mickeys off, if that's what they enjoy doing. And the same goes for the bloody IRA and the bloody UFF and

223

all the others here... Speaking of which, you should visit your uncle. Seriously. That poor man is lying up in hospital with not a sinner to look near him.'

Diarmuid stared at her. Not for the first time it struck him that his wife was maybe a bit mad.

Chapter 14

THREE CRISES

'Pleased?' Warwick said. 'No, I wasn't pleased. I was orgasmically delighted.' He opened his office door and tossed in a copy of *Conflicting Concepts of Curriculum*. It landed on top of a pile of papers, books, catalogues for more books and the lid of a tin, which clearly doubled as an ashtray, despite rules about smoking. 'I'm two-thirds of the way through a Communication Skills and Reflective Living day, and if it hadn't been for the memory of our viva, when I awoke, I'd have called in to declare myself indisposed. Let's get a coffee.'

Hundreds of students were emerging from classrooms and mingling in the central concourse area. At the cafeteria counter a long queue had formed for the dinner section. They joined a shorter line for coffee.

'What made it particularly sweet was that it just *happened*,' Warwick went on, adding a Snickers to their tray. 'The lesser-spotted Tiedt on his high horse, convinced the rest of us would fall into line...and then, at the last moment, the door rattles and wheeeoooo, there's our lovely Dean, the colour of a newly flushed toilet bowl. I mean, who could have predicted that?'

They found a table in the corner near the window.

'My main worry was, would the lovely Hazel hold up?' Warwick slipped his hand beneath the table and appeared to give his balls a tug. 'All I could see was her head sinking lower on her bosom as Tiedt's verbal mugging continued. And then, shazam! That...*unmanned* look on Tiedt's professorial face – I shall treasure it until death dims these poor eyes. Too bad the twin towers had to fall, but omelettes don't get made without stretching a hen's intimate parts.'

'What did you actually think of her dissertation?'

'After a quickish read, a pass. The problem with excrescences like Tiedt, when they hear the word "Pass", a little button clicks in their head and they start shouting "Fail!" As if being negative were some token of academic virility. Personally, my question invariably is, "Will I be happy to see this person get their degree?" If the answer is yes, then they pass, unless evidence that they're illiterate becomes mountainous. Besides which, early judgements need to be sifted in the light of later evidence. I mean, I'd been led to believe Hazel the Nut was illiterate, which she isn't. Sexually handicapped probably, *virgo intacta* possibly, but not illiterate.'

They watched a girl wearing a black T-shirt with the American flag on it stand in line at the counter. She had red lipstick and the flag on her chest wobbled as she moved along the queue.

'Well, I was happy for her, too,' Diarmuid said. 'But I'm not sure it's right to give people marks depending on how you feel about them.'

'Why not, for pity's sake? Where there is sorrow, let me bring joy. Speaking of which, when have they scheduled your on-air rematch with Tiedt?'

'Tomorrow afternoon. Talking about school experience for student teachers.'

'That'll be nice. Got a battle plan?'

'I think I'll play it more by ear this time. Maybe it was a bit too...structured last time.'

'Yes, but what are you going to say?'

'I have to make the case for the *Teaching Practice File* and its articulation of the hundred and fifty essential skills.'

'By thunder. And how are you going to do that?'

Diarmuid studied his nails for a minute. 'I'm not sure, really. What would you suggest?'

'Well, you must be careful not to suggest that the *Teaching Practice File* has only a hundred and forty-nine skills – that would be seen as a diminution of standards. Nor that a hundred and fifty-one skills are within its scope, for that would be arrogant and the gods would punish you. My own option would be to describe it as a vomit-inducing insult to intelligence, and the hundred and fifty essential skills as compacted manure produced by cretins.' Warwick tugged his balls again and yawned. 'Does that seem a fairly fair synopsis to you?'

'It does.'

'Well, then. *QED*.'

'Except all that stuff is department policy and I'm expected to defend it.'

'I shouldn't worry. Tiedt will do that for you. He's a hundred and fifty essential skills man if ever I saw one.'

'Yes, but if he starts arguing in favour of it, the presenter woman will expect me to be against it – it's supposed to be a debate. But at the same time I can't go against department policy, simply to keep a discussion-programme woman happy.'

Warwick inserted three fingers into his beard and scratched vigorously. 'You're much too anxious about too many things, old boy. Get nowhere being that way. Why not try something new and simply say what you think? Meanwhile, refresh your soul by feasting your eyes on an ornament from my Communication and Reflective Living. She does carry her bits with pride, doesn't she?'

They sat in silence watching the American-flag girl make her way to a table, her tray held some inches from her front. 'It's all a cod, isn't it?' Diarmuid said, when she sat down. 'I mean, Hazel's degree, the radio broadcast, your Cont Psych Communication and Reflection course – the whole thing. Is a cod. *Has* to be. There was a guy waving a towel from one of the windows, you know. You sort of assumed he'd be saved, felt sure he would, only next thing the whole skyscraper collapsed. Not a bit like the movies.'

Warwick wiped the edge of the table carefully with his napkin, then placed both elbows on it. 'Quite right. Not at all like the movies, because in the movies things follow a pattern. A causes B, B causes C, and C ties the knot in the plot with a neat conclusion. Life's not like that. Life's one damn thing after another, no order, no pattern, nothing – a tale told by an idiot indeed. Anyway, here's an interesting statistic for you – got it on the Internet this morning. More people were killed in car accidents in the states of New York and New Jersey last year than died in the twin towers. Now, have you noticed anyone wailing about them? Indeed you have not. There is something about the twin towers that everyone is scared to say, and that is, the Americans don't know what to think that so few people were killed. At first it was to be thirty thousand, then it went down to fifteen and now it's three or four. Any lower and the Yanks will need counselling to cope with their disappointment.' He leant back, laced his hands behind his head. 'Ah, there she is. The sweet cherry on top of my Communication Skills and Reflective Living cake. Directly behind you, to the left. Her husband may be a pain in the prostate but she is a gem beyond price.'

When he turned, all Diarmuid could see was the young woman with the American flag on her chest, drinking soup and frowning at *Cosmo*. Then he looked several tables to the right and there, wearing a pale brown sweater with a high neck, was Angela.

Warwick pushed back his chair and stood. 'You know anything about body space and African tribal ceremonies? Thought not. Which means I have' – he checked his watch – 'twenty-two minutes to find out about it before I resume lecturing. *Ciao, bambino.*'

Diarmuid drank his coffee quickly, kept his eyes on the bowl containing sachets of sugar and salt. Should he go over and talk to her? The walk along the lake had been nice, and he'd enjoyed having someone smile and sound interested in the things he said.

But…he wasn't going to ask her to take her clothes off, was he? Because if he did, it'd start a whole train of things – did he love her, when and where would they next take off their clothes, had he told Frances about them yet… Risks. Demands. Her dead sister – if she'd taken her clothes off, while still alive, of course – that *would* have been something. Worth a risk or two. That's probably why he'd written the Little Known Facts about her – giving flesh to fantasy he knew could never become real. He jumped when he felt a hand on his arm.

'I thought it was you.' Her eyes looking down at him, taking him in – his hair, his shirt, his jacket. Both blue, both eager.

'Well, for goodness' sake!' Diarmuid tried to sound surprised. 'I believe you're on this Communication Skills and Reflective Living thing. Enjoying it?'

She slid into the seat opposite him. 'Definitely. Dr Warwick was, well, a bit crazy-looking at the Dean's place, I thought, but he's actually quite a good lecturer. He was telling us this morning about the body-language customs in different countries.'

'Oh, very good.'

'Why people stand in the corners of a lift, why Japanese women put their hand in front of their mouths when they laugh… How did you get on at that meeting with your uncle?'

Diarmuid felt his ears get hot. 'He had – he had a little accident, so we had to postpone it. Long story, really… That's Whatshisname, isn't it? The comb-over man – Desmond Morris – that stuff about hand in front of mouth. Billy's very good on him. I have his *The Naked Ape* in my office, actually. His book – Desmond Morris's, I mean. He used to be very big. Morris. Famous, that is.'

'You have a book about all this? Could I borrow it?'

'Well, it's a bit dog-eared, and in the library they've probably—'

'If we went past your office on my way back to class, you could get it then. Would you mind? I'd love it, and there's fifteen minutes before we start again. By the way, I dreamt about

229

Princess the other night – in the dream she'd lost an eye in a fight with another dog. I'm always having dreams. How is she, poor pet?'

He told her briefly about Joy and Mairead and their threats of legal action, which had fizzled out at the threat stage ('Thank goodness!') And then as he stood up, and as they left the cafeteria and as she said, 'You're really good, going to this bother for me', he thought that he should have kept his trap shut or, if he had opened it, have Just Said No. Should never have mentioned *The Naked Ape*, and if he'd *had* to mention it, which he didn't, to have said, 'Oh, *The Naked Ape*, sorry, I used to have it, but I lent it to someone and never got it back.' Or have told her it was at home. Or… But here, now, walking down this dimly lit corridor towards his office, it was too late.

Speak. Be casual. 'Did you come up all this way from Dublin for the one-day course?'

'Not Dublin – Drogheda. Well, actually three miles this side of Drogheda. Julie's in Manchester – I think I told you that. And Tom – my husband – he's over in Harvard for five weeks since yesterday. So I was on my own and just decided last minute to come up in the train for this course – going back this evening.'

'What's in Harvard?'

'He's teaching part of a six-week course to pre-meds – Trauma and Caring is his module. The City Hospital is great that way – always have been. They give him time off, no fuss. He does quite a bit of that sort of thing in different places. Two years ago he spent time in South Africa.' Trying to revive apartheid, no doubt. 'Tom feels strongly after what happened in New York, he wanted to make a contribution, so when Harvard offered…'

'I can imagine.' Diarmuid turned the key in his office door and led the way in. He tried to leave the door open but she used her heel to nudge it closed behind her. Stood looking round the room.

'I love seeing where people work. It's like getting a glimpse into the real person, not the façade. Reveals their soul.' She ran her finger over some student photographs on the noticeboard. 'Something...warm about this office. Emotionally, I mean. Self-contained.'

Diarmuid moved behind his desk, checked his bookshelf. Where was the bloody book? 'Well, I do occasionally sally forth to meet students. And this Boston conference paper I have coming up – I'm doing it on Gaelic games in Irish Protestant schools – will keep me busy. It's going to be a comparative study between north and south – very time-consuming. Up and down to Dublin looking at archives.'

Why had he said that? She didn't need to know that – that he went down to Dublin *through Dundalk and then Drogheda where she lived*. Fuck. And here was the stupid book, half hidden behind *Deschooling Society*.

'That's what I'd really like – to be involved in something interesting, find ways to push it forward... You must stop off with us anytime you're stuck – we've *always* got a spare bed. Oh, *super*!' She took *The Naked Ape* from him, then rummaged in her bag and produced a card. 'That's my address and phone number. My mum stays with us, but a lot of the time she's over in Galway with an aged cousin of hers. I think she'd move there only the cousin wouldn't have her.'

The business card had pale blue writing on a cream background. Expensive. All funded by Mr Tom, probably. He was still staring at it when he felt her two hands – small hands – circling his wrist and lifting his arm in the air. She pushed back his shirt cuff, kept her middle finger on his wrist. On his pulse. Her hair brushing his shoulder. 'My watch is stopped – what time is it with you?'

Little tanned fingers touching hairy wrist. Could she feel his blood hammering? Should he pull his hand clear? Before he could move she had tightened her grip and pressed her cheek against the back of his hand. Her perfume corkscrewed into his brain.

Christ Almighty... 'Look, Angela. The– the– the– thing is, I find you you– you– a– a– a– what? Attractive, I suppose, really, yes – who wouldn't? But, to be honest, I'm not sure this is that wise. Honestly.'

There was a long pause. Then her face came up and looked at him steadily. 'What are you talking about?'

It was as if a new person had replaced Angela in the room. Someone with a voice they used for boring holes in metal sheeting.

'You know – getting emotionally involved. I mean it'd be great, but—'

She laughed, the hiss of an acetylene torch. 'What on *earth* are you talking about?'

'It was just – when we had that walk, and then when you had your, you know, hands on my arm just now, looking at the watch, with your hair – and then your cheek – I mean it was more the way you—'

'Are you trying to say that because I wanted to know the time I was making a *pass* at you? Is *that* what you're saying?' She laughed again, a gasp of blue-white flame. 'Well, excuse me.' *The Naked Ape* sailed through the air, bounced off Diarmuid's desk, slapped onto the floor. 'I don't think I'll take this with me after all. Great book, no doubt, but not really me.' At the door she turned and stared at him. 'I'll say one thing for you, though. You. Have got. A nerve.' The door closed loudly behind her and a notice about overdue books from the library fluttered from the noticeboard to the floor.

He sat at his desk. Images of the man waving the towel at the window of the twin tower. Images of Angela on her doorstep outside Drogheda. 'Well, hello, Diarmuid! Mum has gone to stay in Tuam and Tom's still in Harvard and my daughter's safe in Manchester, so here, give me your bag and come in, you big fucking sex pistol you.'

There were three cats sitting in the middle of the service tunnel as Diarmuid made his way down it the next morning. As he approached, they scattered silently into the shadows. Warwick emerged from the doorway to Block A, smoking.

'It's at half ten, isn't it?' Diarmuid asked. 'The meeting.'

Warwick let smoke leak from his nose and mouth. 'To look at you, nobody would guess that you're quite an operator.'

'What?'

'What not, what pish-posh. Butter wouldn't melt in your rectal area, I suppose, not in a thousand years.'

'I can't think who would be so absent-minded as to put it there in the first place. Let alone wait that length of time.' Even as he spoke, tried to smile, Diarmuid could feel a space opening in the bottom of his stomach and the contents sliding through it.

'She said nothing during the class, mercifully, because I wouldn't have begun to know how to handle it. Bad enough having to cope with her sitting there throughout my entire lecture, afflicted grief drawing all eyes.' Warwick looked at his watch. 'Here, it's time. We'd better ascend to the heights.'

'So what does she say? Angela, I mean.' Diarmuid's legs felt shaky as they made their way up.

'When the lecture ended I kept shuffling papers, in the hope that she'd remove herself. But she sat on, face in her hands, insisting she had a headache. So I said, "Oh dear, how unfortunate," and moved towards the door. "He made a pass at me," she said then. "A pass? Who made a pass?" "Your friend Monaghan." I misheard her, of course. Thought at first she'd said Crompton, because that particular donkey does that kind of thing regularly, says it helps him forget his life-threatening illnesses. Anyway, she said it again, louder this time: "Your friend Dr Monaghan."'

'My God. The lying bloody *tart*.'

'Diarmuid – please. I've built you up in my mind – Shagger Monaghan, the corrupter of the young. Or early middle-aged, in this case. Anyway, she said she went with you to get a book you said you'd lend her, only when you got to the office you locked the door, and then you put one hand over her mouth and another on her "private part" and held it there in a lascivious manner. Irritatingly vague, given that women have at least three private parts. Which did you in fact go for? I'd have asked her but it didn't seem the right time.'

'None. None at all. Of *course* none at all.' It felt as if a rag had got stuck in the cogs of his brain. 'Did you tell her she was talking rubbish? And lies?'

'I said I was shocked to hear what she said, shocked to the core. Then I gave her my handkerchief, patted her shoulder. In my experience, if you provide a comforting father figure when they get in that kind of state, nine times out of ten the tears dry up and next you know they're whipping off intimate garments to display the depth of their gratitude to you. Not this one, I'm sorry to say. "Volatile", I think, is the word.'

'How do you mean?'

'Unpredictable. Female loose cannon – although of course the cannon is a male image, according to Freud. Hard to predict anything about her type.'

'What type? What are you *saying*?'

'Well, she talked at some length about reporting you to the Dean, lodging a formal complaint, but my guess is she won't.' Warwick smiled, patted Diarmuid's arm. 'All talk and no action, that type. Most of the time anyway.'

'Talk and documentaries, T and D,' the security man behind the desk at Broadcasting House said on Friday afternoon. 'Take a seat on the couch over there and I'll have a TD pass ready for the pair of you in two shakes.'

When he'd seen Diarmuid crossing the street, Professor Tiedt had waited outside the BBC's revolving glass door. He was wearing a pair of beige trousers and a polo-necked sweater. In some vague way Diarmuid thought he looked thinner.

Wintry smile. 'Hello.'

'Hello to you,' Diarmuid said. 'Must have been a pleasant drive from Dublin.'

They took their seats on the couch as directed. Professor Tiedt folded his arms and stared at the patch of carpet between his feet. 'Travelled by bus.'

'Ah.' Diarmuid struggled to think of something to say. 'My Master's candidate, Hazel, was very pleased to have succeeded in her viva. She sends her thanks.' She hadn't, but what harm? Tiedt glanced up, forehead wrinkled, gave a little nod, then back at the floor without speaking.

The phone rang. 'BBC Reception.' There was a pause as the security man switched the receiver to his left ear. 'How's about you, Trevor?... Mmm. No, quiet enough... Yes. Right, they're here. Right. Windsor fifteenth.' He pressed the phone against his chest. 'Just to be sure – are youse Dr Tiedt and Professor Monaghan?' Diarmuid and Tiedt nodded – it didn't seem worth correcting the title error. 'OK, I'll pass the word on. They'll be along in five minutes.'

The security man hung up and came out from behind the desk. 'It appears youse are in the wrong building, gentlemen.'

Tiedt thumbed a card from his breast pocket. 'It says here Broadcasting House.'

'There's been a change of plan, well. They're going to broadcast youse from Windsor House instead.'

He led them through the revolving door and pointed up the street. 'See there? That's it – with the green glass. Go in there and they'll call Debbie the producer down. Or she might be waiting.'

She was waiting, beside a reception desk even bigger and shinier than the one in Broadcasting House. 'Welcome, welcome! Good to see you again! Sorry about all this musical chairs, but you know how things are nowadays – and we have a free studio here at the moment. Now, here are your passes – just pin them on your lapel. No, the other way round, Professor Tiedt. No, sorry, you've—'

Eventually Debbie had to fix the professor's pass on to his lapel. Then all three made their way across to the lift. Debbie pressed the Down button to summon it. 'It's funny, you know,' she said, smiling at each in turn, 'but since that attack in New York, I've noticed people, I don't know if it's me or maybe I'm more on the look-out now than I would have been, but they seem to be just that bit—'

She broke off as the lift pinged and the door slid open. She entered and put her thumb on the Open button, waved the two men to join her. Diarmuid stepped in and stood with his back to the far wall.

'If you just want to hop in, Professor,' Debbie said.

The professor took a step towards the lift, then stopped, looked around.

'Did you forget something?'

'No, no...'

'Oh, good! All set, then?'

Professor Tiedt turned his head towards the revolving door by which he'd entered, his right hand massaging the back of his neck.

'Is there a problem, Professor? It's just that we're pressed for time – not that long until the programme starts and...'

Tiedt stopped massaging with his right hand and sent the left up to pull at his ear. Then he turned towards the open door of the lift, where Diarmuid and Debbie were waiting, raised both fists to shoulder height, and shouted.

It was a very loud shout. Diarmuid could detect no word inside it, although when he thought about the incident afterwards it seemed possible that the professor might have used the word 'tower!' But it might equally have been 'power!' or even 'flower!' The noise of it filled the reception area, making the glass display case containing pictures of smiling Sony Award winners along with a smiling Controller for the Region shiver. The security man called, 'Oh, here, here, HERE!', jumped out from behind his desk and approached the professor. Diarmuid and Debbie came out of the lift and moved towards him from the other side.

Sensing a pincer movement, Tiedt's eyes rolled from Diarmuid to Debbie, then to the security man. Two more quick checks and then, teeth clenched, he had darted towards the revolving door, was pushing vigorously with both hands flat against its glass surface. But the revolving door had stopped revolving: somehow the security man had immobilised it. Tiedt turned back, panting, his glasses tilted sideways on his face, and ran straight into Diarmuid's arms.

'Easy, easy,' Diarmuid said. The professor gave a small moan and slid to his knees.

'Would you look at that?' the security man said. 'Are we all right here, do you think?'

'Professor,' Debbie said, 'we need to go up – programme starts in five minutes. Are you feeling well enough to join in? We're on the fifteenth floor, but you really can't tell—'

At the words 'fifteenth floor' the professor sat back on his heels, covered his head with his hands and began to rock backwards and forwards, saying, 'Aaaagh' in a muffled voice.

Debbie leant into Diarmuid, and beckoned the security man before she spoke. 'I think this gentleman – Professor Tiedt – is a little distressed. Heights – a fear of heights, I'd say. Especially after that plane crash in...' She glanced quickly over her shoulder. 'The thing is...' She put her hand on the security man's shoulder. 'I've a programme starting in four minutes, Clive pet. Do you think could you take the professor in the back and give him a wee cup of tea? Then ring the medical room on the eighteenth and tell them Professor Tiedt isn't feeling the best, and would they send someone down to have a little look. OK?' She turned to Tiedt, who had got shakily to his feet. 'You'll have to excuse me, Professor. I must dash now – programme deadline looms, like a great mouth about to masticate us all, ha-ha. Clive here will look after you. I'll check post-programme.' She let go of Tiedt's elbow and turned to Diarmuid. 'OK – into the lift. Not a second to lose.'

The lift doors whispered shut and they ascended so smoothly it was impossible to tell they were moving. The discussion with Rosemary went almost as smoothly, Diarmuid explained to Warwick later, partly because Tiedt wasn't involved, and partly because Rosemary asked him such easy questions and agreed with just about everything he said.

'This programme has such an *effect* on people!' Debbie said afterwards, as they shook hands at the entrance. 'Last week you were unwell, this week it's him! But I must say I loved that interview – you handled the whole thing beautifully. *Many* thanks!'

On the following Monday, Dr Fr David rang Diarmuid and asked him if he could step down and see him, if he had a minute. The priest's desk had what looked like a Foxford rug over it. On the wall behind his head was a Salvador Dali painting of the crucified Christ, pictured from above.

'This one's a little ticklish and that's why I didn't really want to raise it while others were around,' Dr Fr David said, smiling and then not smiling almost immediately at Diarmuid. 'I had a call from Angela Passmore this morning. You know, Claire's sister, from where is it? Drogheda.' Diarmuid nodded, uneasy. 'Quite a long call, as it turned out. She appeared to be suggesting that you invited her to your office where you then, um...' He looked down at his desk. '...acted inappropriately.' Diarmuid said nothing. 'By initiating overtures.'

'Is that what she said? Overtures?'

'Behind a locked office door.' Dr Fr David's face was pink. 'She is urging me to bring the incident to the attention of the Dean.'

'What incident to the attention of the Dean? There was no incident!'

'The alleged incident then – the matter, let's call it the matter. Bring the matter to the attention of the Dean, and if necessary higher. She seemed quite determined.' He leant closer to Diarmuid. 'Naturally the university would be keen to avoid controversy. These things get out of hand once the media step in, as you know yourself.' Dr Fr David polished his glasses with his white handkerchief, nodding as he did so. Then put his hanky away and sat up straight in his head-of-department chair. Looked at Diarmuid, waited for him to speak.

'This woman is crackers,' Diarmuid said eventually. 'It's obvious.'

'Well, now. You may be right, you may be wrong. But I do

think you might be best avoid contact with her, until matters are a little more...settled. Meanwhile the Dean and I will use what channels we have to see if we can resolve the matter.' He put on his glasses again. 'By the way, might I say – a most professional performance from yourself the other day. Most enjoyable listening. No mishaps at all.'

'Thank you.'

'I understood Professor Tiedt was to have been a participant in both programmes – did he miss his train maybe?'

At that point Diarmuid told his department head that Professor Tiedt had not been a well man when last seen. The wrinkles in Dr Fr David's forehead deepened as the details emerged. 'Oh dear, oh dear,' he said. 'I should inform the Dean of this. They're good friends, you know.'

Diarmuid was passing the door of Claire's old office when Terry came out and grabbed him by both shoulders. Pointed down the corridor towards the communication centre. 'I warned them. I said "Are we happy with these installations, are they what we need, are they reliable?" Those were my exact words – "Are they reliable?" Three little words. And DH thought about it and she said in the end she thought they were reliable. And I took her at her word. But then something like this happens which she couldn't have foreseen, and it's obvious that what *she* thought was totally misguided because they *are totally and completely and utterly unreliable*!' His voice was a lot louder than normal and his eyes red-rimmed.

Diarmuid guided him back into his office, eased him into a seat. 'Something like what happens?'

Terry's hands shook on the desk. 'I've already told the Dean – well, I haven't yet told but when I do I will tell the Dean – that it's my opinion, backed up by experience, that this is sabotage and something should be done. Deliberate, wilful, probably insider sabotage of our system.'

'What is?'

'Any of the machines that were left switched on. All right, that's regrettable, these things happen. But, then, when they switched *theirs* on again – all the computers in the offices along this corridor – they worked perfectly. But when they switched *mine* on again – blank screen. *Blank screen!* You can tell when something's dead.' He gestured helplessly towards the computer on his desk. 'Terminal wipe-out.'

'I thought you had a new zip-drive system. Don't you have back-up disks? '

'I have. The zip drive arrived some weeks ago. Excellent system and I spent all of Friday transferring my floppies to it. Over sixty back-up floppy disks fitted on a single 256MB zip disk. But then, because my zip-drive disk was still in the machine, it got hit too. Obliterated, from start to finish. Can you believe that?'

'What did you do with the back-up floppies you transferred from?'

'I put them in the corridor wheelie-bin. It was emptied last Friday.'

Terry's shoulder twitched under Diarmuid's hand. Glints of white scalp beneath the black hair. 'That's too bad,' Diarmuid said in a slow, sad voice. 'How did the virus get into the system in the first place?'

Terry paused for a moment with closed eyes. 'An email. The title on it said, 'Rally In Sympathy', so I assumed it was about New York and, without thinking, I opened it. All there was was this note, 'Goodbye, sunshine', then the computer gave a hum and the zip drive rattled and the screen did a starburst and went blank. Everybody's screen along the corridor went blank at the same time. Only when I unplugged and tried to start up again, nothing. The electricity was getting through but nothing on the screen. It *must* have been sabotage.'

'But you can't have lost everything?' Diarmuid prayed that his voice was the proper mix of concern and casualness.

'Every single last thing. Internet access, all the systems, every email that's come through the department in the past quarter, all the files for the last six months – everything. It feels like a violation.' He sucked air into his mouth. 'Teeth. Aching.'

Diarmuid pictured himself, hands in pockets, walking towards the window. He would keep his face turned away for a couple of moments before swinging round. 'So are you saying you haven't got my Little Known Facts on disk or elsewhere any more, Terry?' he would say. And Terry's little skittery eyes would bulge and he'd say 'Yes, that's exactly what I'm saying, Diarmuid – the LKF file is gone along with everything else.' And if he did say that, how would he, Diarmuid, feel? Partly ecstatic, of course – a huge boulder weight rolling off his mind. At last, no more LKF. But at the same time, a tinge of regret for all those words, all that wit, vaporised, etherised, gone.

'It's as if it had all been sort of pre-ordained. As if the attack on the twin towers had been ... allowed to happen,' Diarmuid said. 'So we could all appreciate how, how, how *fragile* we are, how fragile *everything* is. At least that's the feeling *I* get.' But even as he said it, Diarmuid knew that wasn't the feeling he got at all, nothing remotely like it. 9/11 had changed damn all in his life, but his foot getting better most definitely had changed things. Hijacked planes meant little, a hijacked file meant everything. But now, finally, thanks to some mad hacker – or was it God or both? – things were different. The crooked ways had been made straight, the rugged path smooth, the hijacked file had been destroyed, Diarmuid had completed a more-or-less triumphant broadcast, and Professor Tiedt was in bed somewhere, heavily sedated, having a nervous breakdown.

Turned away from Terry, Diarmuid closed his eyes and did a very short mental handstand. *Carpe diem*, he told himself. Squeeze the last delicious drop out of this moment of cosmic harmony. Because in the shadows ahead, grinding its teeth and adjusting its knuckle-duster, an anonymous bad thing is almost certainly getting ready to knock your pan in.

The thought had barely time to register when he remembered Uncle Dan.

Chapter 15

LAID UP

He watched the lights above the lift door change, listened as the electronic voice said, 'fourth floor, fifth floor, sixth floor,' and 'doors closing, doors opening, doors closing.' Mirrors in the walls, on the ceiling: watch yourself comb your hair, straighten your tie, have sex between floors. Anything to stop you thinking about the pain and death outside this moving box.

Uncle Dan was in the corner bed, barely visible above the bedclothes. Diarmuid set the grapes on the locker. 'Didn't mean to disturb you.' Uncle Dan opened his eyes, then closed them again without speaking. 'I got your message and came as soon as I could.'

The nurse with black hair and red lipstick approached the bed with a tray. She put a mug of tea on Uncle Dan's locker. 'Know something? We have this man spoiled. He'd be away home long ago only he has such a cushy number. Don't you? He'll be away by Thursday next,' she said quietly to Diarmuid.

Blinking, Uncle Dan struggled into a sitting position. 'Wait until I'm gone – youse'll be sorry for the dog's abuse!' The nurse swatted the air with her hand and bustled off, Uncle Dan's eyes following her. 'They're powerful good to me. Only they're not always there and then the oul' thoughts start buzzing about in my brain.'

Diarmuid smiled. 'When we were small you used to have a

riddle. Remember? You would ask, "What did thought do?" And we would yell, "Peed the bed and thought he was sweating!" and run away because we'd shouted a bad word. Remember that?'

Uncle Dan sipped his tea and sighed. 'You look at these boys hitting aeroplanes against the skyscrapers, and you know then you're not going to be around forever.'

'None of us is, Uncle Dan.'

'Then the oul' thoughts start their buzzing. What's the whole thing for anyway? What way was it those ones in the skyscrapers was picked? Or the ones in the planes? Why them and not some other ones?'

Diarmuid shrugged. 'People get killed on the roads every day. More people died in road accidents in the states of New York and New Jersey last month than died in the twin towers. Did you know that?'

Uncle Dan massaged his chest under the sheet. 'Ones lepping out the window, to get away from the fire.'

They sat without speaking. The sound of nurses calling and characters on *Eastenders* shouting at each other from the other end of the ward filled the background.

'That's true,' Diarmuid said at last. 'We all felt that a bit.'

'And then when I get to sleep the dreams start. Dreamt last night about a hayshed on fire with horses in it. And about your mother as well.'

They said nothing until the nurse came back with her trolley. 'Whatever about spoiling him, Nurse,' Diarmuid said, passing his uncle's empty mug. 'You've definitely made him seriously philosophical.'

'Sure he'd be that way anyway. He has a head on him that's only bursting with brains.'

Uncle Dan fingered each ear in turn, as if checking for something. 'It was like she was there in front of me, riding her bike, the wee legs whirling like a fan. "Once round the house! Once round the house!"' Dan gripped Diarmuid's sleeve, drew him in close. 'And then when she'd rode round three times, she hopped off and started walking and she didn't stop till she was as close to me as you are this minute.' His mouth trembled briefly. 'She took a hold of my shirt: "Give and you shall receive." That's what she said to me, as sure as you're sitting where you're sitting. "Give and you shall receive."' He lifted a small metal bowl from the locker top, cleared his throat and spat into it. 'I was sweating when I woke. Pyjama bottoms sticking to my legs, and every time I tried to turn in the bed, whatever way the pyjama top was it twisted under me like a rope... There was something powerful queer about her voice. Like a wee sparrow's, and at the same time you'd have thought she was over a hundred.' He closed his eyes and continued speaking. 'D'you know what wouldn't surprise me? This could be the end of the world coming. Wouldn't surprise me one bit. Now.'

'For God's sake, Uncle Dan—'

'Two big skyscrapers flattened to the ground in seconds. The towers of Babel.'

'It wasn't seconds. It was nearer half an hour.'

'They came down just the same. And that's only the start of it.'

'Uncle Dan, this is a handful of Arabs – not exactly the Red Army with nuclear weapons.'

Uncle Dan shook his head. 'Your mother was put into a dream to me whether you like it or not. "Give and you shall receive." That's what the whole shebang is about. We're being given time to get ourselves right, and if we let it go, by God, we'll have time and plenty to repent during eternity.'

Diarmuid took four grapes from the bunch on his uncle's locker and began to eat them. 'So what are we supposed to do, then?'

'You know rightly.'

'I know nothing of the sort.'

'You know rightly.'

Diarmuid spat a pip under the bed. 'Uncle Dan. I do *not* know rightly.'

'You do surely. Consider the swallows.'

245

'The whats?'

'Consider the swallows – no knitting and less sewing do they do. That's the only way to look at money – don't bother your head one bit about it.'

Diarmuid laughed. 'I don't believe this.'

'What?'

'Weren't you the man who was insisting – you *were* insisting – on your right to a share of Mammy's estate?'

'Go on – put words in my mouth. I wanted what I was left, that's all. I wanted what *she* wanted. Only when you see them aeroplanes going in and killing that many, and next thing you have a dream with your mother, poor Katie, in it, a saint of the first class, and her coming down especially to you, you begin to see the codology money and all the rest of it is.'

Diarmuid tried to keep his voice level. 'What about the hood who attacked you – are you still on for identifying him? '

'Life's too short. Let Our Lord on Judgement Day identify those boyos.'

'Good thinking,' Diarmuid said.

'Not one of us knows how long we have. That's the thing.' Uncle Dan sank back on the pillows, eyes closed. 'Angels,' he said quietly. 'That's what they call the nurses, you know. Angels.' There was silence for several minutes. Then, just as Diarmuid was wondering if he shouldn't tiptoe away, Uncle Dan opened both eyes again. 'I'll tell you another thing I've decided. If you have the time to listen. About poor Katie's place.'

For the next fifteen minutes, Uncle Dan did nearly all the talking.

At the end of the M1, instead of going straight ahead, Diarmuid turned right and up towards Malone Road. Waiting at the lights beside the King's Hall, he plugged in his hands-free mobile, pressed the earpiece into place and dialled. At the other end, what sounded like a desk being overturned was followed by throat-clearing. 'Yes?'

'Brother Ambrose, it's Diarmuid. Just called to let you know this week's column will be with you tomorrow afternoon at the latest – OK? I want to submit it as late as I can in case there are new developments.'

'Ah, Diarmuid – yes. How exactly do you mean, now, developments?'

'Well, you don't know. There could be other attacks. Or the Americans do a retaliatory strike. I'd want to comment on whatever happens.'

There was silence. Then: 'Oh, right. Surely… Mind you, we do have Fr Gerard in New York. He'll be watching things and faxing us an eyewitness account.' There was a sigh. 'The one thing we always have to be careful about is overkilling a story – and God forgive me for using that word now. People need a bit of a boost at a time like this as well. Maybe something like how they could reach out to the man next door, how beautiful the world is, the sense of God in everything and everybody – the kind of thing you write about so well week in and week out. And if we don't give the readers the things they're interested in, we won't have readers. Isn't that the long, short and middle of it?'

'Well, yes, but the column needs to have some meaning at the same time. Some integrity to it.'

'Indeed and it does. Meaning. And integrity. You're a hundred per cent right. And what could have more meaning than that piece you did about the eight-year-old who prayed that God would raise her granda from the dead? Remember that one? Ah, except you become like unto little children… But sure I'll leave it to your judgement what you write, Diarmuid. You know well yourself. God bless.'

Anne answered the door even quicker than usual. There were two dots of colour in her cheeks that Diarmuid had never seen before. 'It's you! Come in, come in. I hope you're not going to go tearing off like a mad thing, way you did last time… No, no excuses. I get enough excuses from him, without you too. *No excuses*!' She laughed, her earrings twinkling, little chuckling sounds coming from deep in her throat.

'He's not interested in it any more,' Diarmuid said, as Paul's study door closed behind him. 'His share, that is. If anything, he's in a hurry to get rid of it.'

Paul took off his glasses, sucked one arm. 'Are you sure? He's a tricky old bugger, don't forget. Did he actually say he didn't want his share?'

'Not in so many words. But he clearly has been badly shaken by this New York thing. That coming so quick after the mugging. And then when I was getting ready to leave, he said, "Hold on a minute, I've decided it'd be wrong to cash in on Katie's death."'

'Well, now. It's not like him to feel for anyone beyond himself.'

'And he said he had this dream where he saw Mammy and she spoke to him.'

'Of course, he would never have been in the will in the first place if she hadn't been half gone in the head near her end.' Paul rubbed his hands energetically. 'So anyway. Has he made any new arrangements – contacted McAleavy, put something in writing?'

Before Diarmuid could answer, the door of the study was shouldered open and Anne entered with three mugs of tea and a plate of custard creams. 'Don't touch yet!' she said, put the tray down and left the room again. A couple of minutes later she was back with a smaller tray, on which sat three wine glasses half filled with Bailey's Irish Cream. 'Normally I wouldn't dream, but I'd say this calls for a teeny-weeny toast. Don't you think?' She passed them each a glass.

'How did you know what Uncle Dan said?' Diarmuid asked her.

'Woman's intuition!' Anne said, smiling. 'When I opened the door and you were standing there, I just knew.'

'I was wondering, dear,' Paul said softly, 'would there be a danger that the alcohol in that might interact with your, you know, drugs? Because the last thing we want is—'

'Paul!' Anne's voice was a shrill shout. 'Could you this once try not to sound like a slack-snatched ninety-year-old *woman*?' She turned from him, held her glass level with her face and peeped round it at Diarmuid. 'To the master negotiator!'

Paul joined his wife, put an arm round her shoulders. 'Let's say that you were in the right place at the right time, Diarmuid, and that's what counts. If you hadn't been there, we'd still be at square one with his lordship – *and* the insurmountable Mount Carmel.' He gave his wife's shoulders a squeeze, then raised his glass. 'To Diarmuid, and to the successful development of our heritage.' He lowered the glass and frowned. 'Although one does feel a little...uneasy, celebrating. In the light of the recent tragedy, I mean.'

Anne shook her head until her earrings quivered. 'Rubbish! The thing is, do we know these people? And since the answer is, no, we don't, then we simply put them out of our minds. The people nearest and dearest to me, I know them all right. I care about *them*. But that's as far as it goes, I'm afraid.' Smiling, she put both arms round Diarmuid's neck and gave him a kiss, then a hug, her breath warm on the side of his face.

'I'll contact McAleavy first thing tomorrow,' Paul said. 'The sooner we get this thing tied up the better.'

Frances was trying to attach a picture hook to the wall. Diarmuid was holding a large framed painting of a mountain stream, with a stag dipping its nose into the black-and-white waters. Pieces of cardboard packing, in which the painting had come, were scattered on the floor.

'What do you mean, he doesn't want it?' she asked. Diarmuid said nothing, because he was concentrating on holding the picture at different heights along the wall for her. 'There, that'll do. Stop there.' She crossed to him, put a pencilled X where the nail was to go.

Diarmuid took the hammer from her. 'I told you. He's worried about dying. Wants to make amends. No pockets in a shroud and all that.'

'But I thought you said he's getting better.'

Diarmuid hung the picture, then joined her at the opposite side of the room to look at it. 'So he is. As healthy as you or me – healthier, probably. But the plane hijacking shook up his conscience. A stop-gathering-rosebuds-and-start-organising-repentance moment, it seems.' Diarmuid put his head to one side and closed one eye. 'I *think* that's about right.'

'It'll do.' Frances was gathering the pieces of cardboard. 'At the same time you'd feel sorry for him, wouldn't you? Stuck in hospital on his own.'

'He's not on his own. He's got the nurses dancing attention on him – *and* he's due home on Thursday.'

'But he's dumped Whatshername, his housekeeper, Mount Carmel, hasn't he? It'd be a right pig's ear if he goes home and he's broken into again, and him on his own.'

'I don't think Carmel was much help last time. Besides, he says he got a warning from Mammy.' Diarmuid recounted Uncle Dan's dream. 'You never know with him, of course. Paul's right on that at least – if there's a possibility of manipulating someone, Dan'll be at it.'

Frances crammed the cardboard, piece by piece, into the bulging bin outside the back door. Then she pulled down the kitchen blind, peeled off her hat and T-shirt and stood in her bra and jeans, wiping her hands on an old cloth. He could see the bulge of her nipples, giant prawns, through the silky material. 'Maybe if you'd been broken into and the woman that was supposed to be looking after you had gone running off, you might want to manipulate a bit yourself. Take that ladder back to the garage for me, would you?'

When he came back she had changed into a fresh lime-green T-shirt and a pair of navy blue trousers. He watched her cross and recross the kitchen, carrying cups from the dishwasher to the shelves. A shaft of sunlight lit up the hairs on her arm as she made the journey. 'When did you say he's getting home?' she asked.

'Next Thursday.'

'I'll put my head round the door to him tomorrow maybe and say hello. Bound to be lonely enough for him.'

'If he barred Carmel from visiting him he can't be too lonely.'

She put the stack of plates on the shelf, turned, watched him lift out the cutlery container. 'As it happens, that's the very time people *do* appreciate a bit of support – after a break-up. If you weren't so wrapped up in yourself you'd see that. And don't put the knives in with the forks, please.'

Diarmuid thought of the ceiling above her collapsing, a huge beam pinning her broken body to the kitchen floor. 'But why should somebody who has arranged for people *not* to visit him, suddenly be someone we should go around feeling pity for when he then feels lonely? That doesn't make sense.'

She wrung out the dishcloth, draped it over the tap, shook her head slowly as she dried her hands. 'Men just don't get it. They do. Not. Get it. That's all I can say.' She took out the sharp knife and began peeling spuds. 'Reach me down that Pyrex dish from the top shelf, please.'

Chapter 16

MONEY CAN'T BUY ME LOVE

The following evening, the voicemail light was flickering on the phone when Diarmuid got back from evening class. Beside it was a note from Frances saying she'd gone shopping, she might call with Joy and Mairead on the way back. Diarmuid reread it, trying to decide if its tone indicated that she was no longer fed up with him for being a man. It was impossible to say. He pressed the button for new messages and Warwick's voice sounded. 'Diarmuid my boy, could you drop in and see me for twenty minutes? Tonight would be good. Sixty-nine Ailesbury Avenue in case you've forgotten – first left after the Devon Centre roundabout. Like a word with you about a matter.'

The front door opened within seconds of Diarmuid touching the bell. Warwick, wearing a T-shirt that said 'Read' on the front and 'You Won't Go Blind' on the back, led him into the kitchen. 'Beer?'

Diarmuid declined.

Warwick sat back in an armchair and hissed open a can of Stella for himself. 'Should be champagne, only it's hard to break the frugal habits of a lifetime. Even on a high-point occasion like this.' He drank with real purpose for several seconds, not bothering to wipe the damp on his beard when he lowered the can. 'Shall I tell you the nature of this particular lifetime high-point occasion?'

'That might be helpful.'

'I'll take that as an encouraging yes. Only Crompton, myself and one or two other select souls know what I'm going to tell you, so I trust you're appreciative. Fact is, I've recently received some extraordinary information. Knock-me-down-and-drag-me-out information, you might say.'

'That makes two of us – no, no, I'll explain mine later. What's your big story?'

Warwick tapped his thumb against the middle of his chest. 'Not just my story, mine and Crompton's jointly. Remember at the Dean's place – the glass-in-the-dessert affair? Well. We took a case against them, you probably heard, which looked as if it might deliver the compensation goods, because we had a certificate from our local GP saying Crompton could have been scarred for life by that sliver of glass – that's mentally as well as physically. And in parallel we took a second, linked case against the homophobic rantings of our good Dean's wife. Guess what? We were four days from appearing in court when the university's solicitor called our solicitor, and then our solicitor called theirs back, and the two went into a four-hour huddle. Yesterday my phone rings – it's my solicitor with news. And guess what?'

'Stop saying that, would you? It's irritating. Get on.'

'They struck a settlement. Case abandoned, compensation delivered, end of story.'

'The university coughed up? I don't believe it.'

'I promise you they did. To the sweet tune of twenty K. Ten thousand pounds each.'

'I don't believe... But why are they paying the two of you? Crompton was the one got the glass in his mouth.'

'Because Crompton and I are a team. That's how we operate. Anyway, if it hadn't been for me, Mr Tom would have flushed the offending shard down a sink and there'd have been no case, so I judge I've earned my share there. Plus the lovely Mrs Saddington didn't merely call Crompton a pervert, it was both of us – "a pair of ineffable perverts" was her actual phrase, as I remember. If that's not homophobia in a public place, before witnesses, from a dean's tightly buttocked wife, then I'm a monkey's toy-boy.'

Diarmuid stared at him 'The university actually gave you – him – twenty grand because somebody said you were bent? Anyway, why would they pay out for her? She's the Dean's wife, not the university.'

Warwick grinned. 'It happened at the Dean's, where we'd all gathered on official university business, so apparently the Dean's wife counted as temporary university catering staff. Something like that. Anyway, it wasn't so much the prospect of court costs and damages that made the university play ball – it was the headlines the case might have attracted. In reality, of course, we could have afforded a court case even less – these lawyers would take your assets *and* your testicles if you weren't watchful. Anyway, the two sides, their lawyer and ours, went into this eyeballing contest and, whoopdedoopey, they blinked first.' He smiled and gave the crotch of his trousers a brief tug. 'The thing is – *entre nous* – I now have a substantial nest-egg in search of a suitable nest. The question is, where? Stock market? Hopeless since 9/11... O God of language corruption, my apologies. *Mea culpa*. I swore I'd never say 9/11 and now look. Or listen, rather.'

'Why not?'

'For a start, because it's a deeply silly phrase. For another, people often think you mean the ninth of November instead of the eleventh of September.'

'I assumed people said 9/11 to make it easier for the computers.'

'So let's accommodate the computers, and to deepest Hades with human beings – is that your recommendation?'

'Look. Forget that, would you? This nest-egg – what about it?'

'The position is, I can lodge my guilty gains in the post office, safe but minimal to non-existent profit, or I can put them in shares, slightly less safe but a tiny bit more promising, profit-wise. Only now, however and aha, I hear on the wind and a certain little birdie tells me, you have inherited property from your late mother. So I took a little walk around it a couple of days ago – just the outside, hope you don't mind – and more and more I'm convinced this may be the answer to my investment prayers.'

Diarmuid felt a tweak of irritation. 'Some birdies have big beaks. And if you're going to go tramping around my mother's property, consult me first next time, OK?'

'Steady, champ. No slight intended. All that is being suggested is a business venture. Nothing more.'

'With ten thousand? You're not going to screw much luxury out of that.'

'Plus, of course, what I'll get from the sale of the house in Spain.'

'What house in Spain? Who has a house in Spain?'

'Crompton *et moi*. Bought it ten years ago, in a burst of sun-worshipping enthusiasm. Since then it has had its share of naughty and fun-filled moments, I do confess, and I've the photographs to prove it. Lately, though, it's fallen into something approaching disuse. Sobriety setting in with age, perhaps. And, of course, Crompton has been so anally obsessed of late that Dublin's about his limit for travel. Even though he's been examined from bottom to top, as it were, certified that all parts are clean as a whistle, he is, as the great Brian Friel put it, tethered by the arse. Anyway, point is, we've sold the south of Spain *hacienda*, for which we paid a hundred and twenty grand, and at the time, yes, indeed, it was steep, steep, steep. Only now we've been offered over three hundred and fifty for it, which is even steep, steep, steeper, and which does my inner being gigantic good every time I think about it. "And then my heart with pleasure fills/ And dances with six-figure bills". Anyway. I want to launch a business venture with my half, and you appear to have a promising property, so what I'm thinking is, can we maybe tango on this one?'

'Tango?'

'Establish a joint enterprise. Strictly business, of course – as in

The Godfather. No room for sentiment, personal feelings. What we have here is your property, my capital, your vision, my expertise. A killer duo, combining to squeeze the development world by its softer parts to our mutual enrichment.'

'Well, for a start, this property we're talking about, it's not just mine – my brother owns part of it. And my uncle, although we think that may be going to change.'

'Oh.'

'Uncle Dan is getting on and he's begun to think he's not really entitled to it. But that'd still leave my brother owning half.'

Warwick read the ingredients information on the side of his beer. 'I hope your brother is a man of good sense, because people who come into land almost always make the same mistake – they get excited at this sudden infusion of wealth and they sell their inheritance on to the damned property developers. And, of course, the damned property developers then make a ten-fold profit. So what I'm proposing is, *don't* sell your mum's house and grounds. Develop it yourself. Develop it with *me*. Build – what? Let's say twelve upmarket – and I mean up*market* – apartments. For sale or more likely rent. Set in mature grounds, catering for the discerning customer. Professionals, retired folk, people who've had a bellyful of lawn-mowing and gutter-cleaning and other maintenance nightmares and just can't wait to move into a stress-free existence.'

'My mother's place is four acres maximum. There wouldn't be room for a development like that, even if we wanted it.'

Warwick tapped a lower lip with his thumb, looked at Diarmuid. 'But the fact that your mother's house is *in situ* means getting planning is unlikely to be complicated. In fact, I've checked with a certain party and I know it would be a carefree breeze.'

'Are you for building these apartments at the front or the back of my mother's place?'

'Neither, actually.' Warwick smiled. 'On top of it.'

On top of it. His mother in the doorway, arms wide to hug

him and Paul when they came in from school. His mother ironing lace curtains, singing 'White Christmas' along with Bing Crosby on the radio. 'Forget it, Billy. Shove your bulldozers.'

'Whoa, whoa, whoa.' Warwick got to his feet, pushed Diarmuid back into the chair. 'Sit tight, Tonto. Let me show you something.'

He left the room and came back with a large white cardboard rectangle, which he laid carefully on the coffee table. It was an artist's watercolour impression of two buildings that contained, according to the text at the bottom, twelve apartments each. The brick in the buildings was honey-coloured, the lawn a soft green, trees and flowers sprouted all around.

'What do you think?'

'Where'd you get that?'

'An architect I know had them left over from another development, did an adaptation for me. This is what our venture might look like.'

'Well…it looks…stylish, I suppose.'

'But…? Come on, spit it out.'

'It still means building on my mother's house. Obliterating everything she cared about.'

'Cared about. That's what you said, isn't it? Cared – past tense. How long has your mother been dead?'

'Four months, roughly.'

'And how long were you planning to keep this domestic monument to her in place – five years? Ten? Twenty? It'll go eventually, you know. And whether it goes in a year or in fifty years, it won't matter to her. Because the dead. Don't. Care. The dead *can't* care.' He produced an envelope and extracted several sheets of typed paper. There were figures on it. 'Have a look at these.'

'Yes, but some bugger with tattoos in a bulldozer – the wallpaper torn, the ceiling pulled in. It's like building on her grave.'

'It does seem kind of brutal, put like that. Look at the sheet, though.' Warwick turned it towards Diarmuid. 'Now what do you say?'

The sheet had a five-paragraph description of the two proposed apartment blocks; underneath a listing of the expected construction costs and the expected rentals/sales. Diarmuid pointed to the bottom line. 'Who did these calculations?'

'A business associate.'

'He says here the projected profit *after mortgage repayment* is three hundred pounds per apartment per month. That means if you had twelve multiplied by two, that would be...over seven thousand two hundred pounds a month. Eighty-six grand a year *profit*.' Diarmuid smiled, shook his head. 'Sorry to bear bad news, Billy, but your friend appears to have stuck an extra nought on.'

'No, actually. The figures are completely accurate. I've checked them. His noughts are exactly right.'

'Eighty-six thousand? Are you sure? But...you could live off that, and still have your capital.'

'Divided by two we could both live off it. Not to mention property appreciation. And our university pensions.'

And, as Warwick said the words, Diarmuid saw himself sitting at his kitchen table with the sun streaming in the window onto the white oak table, sipping a second cup of excellent coffee, warm in the knowledge that he'd never again have to mark and return student essays or try to keep awake at department meetings or lick the Dean's arse when he'd rather attach electrodes to the old goat's balls and flick the switch.

'The fact is,' Warwick said, standing up and stretching, 'this is my chance to get out. And yours, if you want to take it. If I can find a satisfactory income source – and this place of yours looks like the real McCoy – I won't have to keep going cap in hand to the nuclear barons and their ilk, on my knees begging for another research grant. You'd like me to tell the nuclear barons where to put their plutonium rods, wouldn't you?'

'Of course.'

Warwick stood up. 'Anyway, thought I'd show you the

possibilities. Got to go now. Got a dinner date at La Bella Figura: pricey but she tells me the grub is good. So you'll give my modest proposal a think, won't you?'

'When do you want to know?'

'A week, say. That should be adequate reflection space, don't you think?'

'I'll talk to my brother – I'm meeting him this evening. See what he says.'

'She tells me you went there several times.'

Diarmuid felt a coldness move up his middle, from his stomach to his neck. Like at the body-soul man's place. 'Who? Went where?'

'La Bella Figura. And that you were always pleased with what you got.'

'Who says?'

'Frances,' Warwick said. There was a pause. 'We'll be talking some business as well, of course, but it's mainly a nice meal we're after.'

'You and Frances.'

'Yes. No objections, I trust?'

'What objections would I have? None of my business.'

'Well, indeed. My thoughts exactly.'

Warwick passed a copy of the brochure to Diarmuid. 'Anyway, converse with your sibling, sleep on what I've said, keep an open mind. And let two matters be central to your thinking. One, that eighty-six K is a conservative figure and, two, this is business. We are serious commercial associates, fifty-fifty all the way, our testicles brass-plated, our eyes fixed unblinking on the financial prize. Sentiment, positive or negative, plays no part in our calculations.'

As Diarmuid drove towards his mother's house, clouds loaded with lakefuls of rain were lumbering into place in the sky. They were the colour of ripe bruises, except for the cloud edge where the sunlight gave a yellow rim.

Paul was sitting in his car at the front of the house, reading *Time* magazine. Diarmuid pulled up and got out as the rain started to fall, hammering down, thudding onto the roofs of the two cars, hissing into the gravel of the drive. He tumbled into the passenger seat beside his brother.

'For heaven's sake, you're dripping like a dog.' Paul pulled the edge of his coat away. 'Do you want to go inside and dry off? You've got my good car soaking.'

'That's OK. We'll stay where we are for the moment.' They sat side by side, not speaking. Paul closed *Time* but kept looking at the face of Osama Bin Laden on the cover, smoothing down a corner of the magazine where it had turned up.

'What's up?' Diarmuid asked. 'And what d'you want to meet here for anyway?'

Paul gave him a sideways glance. 'Somewhere we could talk without Anne knowing. It's Uncle Dan.'

'What about him?'

Paul pinched his lower lip in silence for a few moments. Then: 'Six months ago, if you'd told me I'd be sorry to see Carmel gone, I'd have said you were certifiable. But do you know what? I am – sorry, that is. When she was around, you at least had some idea what was coming next. Not now. Last night I visited him and it was like talking to one of these pinball machines – going off at the weirdest angles every two minutes.'

'Well, he's in his mid-seventies. At least.'

'"Only a wee while to do good in the world" – and then a load of guff about giving a leg-up to "small people" – "the last shall be first". If he said that once he said it five times. The damned old buzzard! And in the same breath he says he's not ready to sign anything. He's "not up to it." He's going to withdraw his claim for his share of Mammy's place but he needs rest now, the signing will keep. And then the nurse said I'd have to go, he was tired. I got the impression he wished I hadn't come to see him, because he knew I'd see through him. Because know what? I don't think he's going to sign away his share. The guy's a snake – a twisted, slimy snake. Mammy was right.'

The rain had eased. Diarmuid could hear the drip from the

trees and the sound of rainwater coughing into the barrel at the back of the house. He opened the car door. 'I need a pee.'

Inside, the house seemed darker but warmer than usual. The smell of ointment had faded. Diarmuid went to the toilet, came back to the living room. The recliner still stood tilted towards the fireplace, its foot-rest extended. He sat into the chair, felt the rough texture of its arms, closed his eyes and listened to the clock on the mantelpiece ticking the seconds away. Where she'd sat like a condemned woman, waiting for the weeks and months to go by until it was time to die. Waiting for her two sons to help carry her out to the hearse for fixing, one shaking with the fear of parting.

He must have sat for several minutes with his eyes closed when the front door opened and Paul came in. 'I thought you said you were going to the toilet.'

'So I was.'

'But you're sitting here.'

'I know. I went to the toilet and now I'm sitting here.'

Paul stood, arms folded, by the door. 'Well, I need to get on. Anne's at home on her own. Waiting for me.'

There's a wee wifey waiting... 'She'll survive without you for once.'

'Even to say that shows just how little you know.' Paul looked around the room. 'Anyway, at the risk of repeating myself, this place *has* to be sold. The messing about has to end. Just put it to him – we want to sell, and we want him to sign over his portion to us. Look at the corner of that ceiling – damp appearing already. I think we should try for another meeting with him the minute he gets out of hospital.'

For a moment Diarmuid thought he saw something behind Paul in the doorway. Then it flickered and was gone. 'How much do you think we'd get if we sold?' he asked.

Paul turned towards the front door. 'Well, McAleavy says he wouldn't be surprised by anything up to a hundred and fifty.'

'Let's say a hundred and forty then. That's seventy thousand each. No, no, no – skip Uncle Dan for the moment. Let's assume

– let's just assume it's the two of us, and you had seventy thousand. Would that be enough? Would it do you?'

Paul stared at him. 'What do you mean, would it do me? Of course it would do me. Only it's not going to be that way because Uncle Dan—'

'Yes, it is. It's yours.'

'It's mine?'

'I'll buy you out – buy your share – for seventy thousand.'

Paul's arms unfolded. 'Where will you get that kind of money?'

'That's my problem. Well, actually, it's not a problem, it's my concern. My matter for attention.'

'You'd have to let the house be knocked down, though, wouldn't you? Last time this came up, you were the one wouldn't hear of it.' Paul put his head to one side. 'What's going on? Are you and Uncle Dan up to something together?'

'Up to nothing. The fact is, you need the money for Anne's hospital bills, surgery, all the rest of it. Right? That's what you said. Well, this'll give you the wherewithal.'

'What about Uncle Dan?'

'I think he'll come round. The important thing is not to rush him. If we rush him he'll do the opposite for spite.'

'I don't think he will. And I'm tired waiting,' Paul said. 'Anne is *sick*, sore and tired waiting.'

'That's what I'm saying. Sell your interest in the place to me for seventy thousand.'

Outside, the rain had stopped. Paul glanced back, eyes shining, at Diarmuid as he got into the car. 'I'll talk to Anne. Ring you tomorrow.'

He's more alive now, Diarmuid thought, as he followed his brother's car down the driveway. Funny how the thought of money got people's adrenaline pumping. He looked at his hands on the steering wheel, clamped and white-knuckled, turned his gaze back to the traffic around him. Suddenly he realised that, as each car passed, he was smiling broadly at its driver.

Chapter 17

SURPRISE, SURPRISE

Paul rang him as he was driving through the university gates the following morning. He'd drawn up a little document, he said. He'd bring it over to Diarmuid's office on his way to work.

'I've talked it over with Anne,' he said, putting two copies of a typed sheet on Diarmuid's desk. 'We're happy to go with your offer.' After they'd both signed the documents, which said Diarmuid would lodge seventy thousand pounds in Paul's account within an eight-week period, they shook hands. Paul said it was better to have these things formalised – that was the problem with Uncle Dan: he couldn't bring himself to formalise things. Diarmuid said they should really have had a drink to seal the transfer, but Paul laughed and said he was in a rush to see a client and, anyway, the absence of a drink was unlikely to affect the document's legality.

The next two days were a work-whirl, with things changing from second gear to sudden, surging overdrive. There were ten emails waiting for Diarmuid when he booted up his computer, including one from the Welsh bastard in the Research Office wanting to know why he hadn't submitted his five-year plan a week ago, and three from the Examinations Office bastards telling him about three different dates when he was due to invigilate examinations. His pigeon hole in the main office was blocked with a huge envelope containing thirty-six assignments from the new PGCE students, with a note from the Assignments Office bastard telling him they were to be marked and returned to his office within two days.

Diarmuid locked his office door, cleared the desk, lifted the phone from its cradle and started on the pile of assignments. After the first seven he groaned; by the twelfth he'd was waving his fists in the air; by five o'clock that afternoon he'd begun to address the writer of each assignment, commenting in detail on their IQ, physique and the smell given off by their mother's body. Even if it had been work that had some point to it, which it wasn't, or work that showed signs of intelligence, which it didn't, marking the assignments was so crotch-achingly, heart-attack-givingly *boring*, he felt like crying. At six o'clock he bought a double beef sandwich and a paper cup of coffee at the university cafeteria. When he got home at five past ten Frances was out. A note on the table said she'd gone to meet a contact in connection with her new business. At quarter past one Diarmuid heard the front door open, her feet on the stairs, the door of the spare bedroom closing behind her.

Next day he was in his office, at his desk, before eight o'clock. He resisted the temptation to read emails and began marking immediately. At lunch time he took a twenty-minute break, another sandwich and a can of Diet Coke, then started marking again. Finally, at three thirty, eyes hot and hand aching, he scribbled the last comment on the last essay and tossed it into a box, which he carried down to the Assignments Office and set, very gently, on the desk of the secretary. Then he went home.

His dinner was on a covered plate in the microwave but there was no note explaining where Frances was. Near dinner's end, as he sat with two biggish glasses of wine glowing in his gut, she came in the front door. He watched as she reheated her own dinner and ate it quickly, bending her head to snap the food from her fork, straightening to read the business section of *The Irish Times*. Her hair was freshly styled and little shadows came and went in her face as she chewed.

'Talking to Paul a few days back.' His voice sounded

uncertain. 'He says Dan's capable of anything, really, once he takes a notion in his head. Erratic. I'm beginning to think he's right.'

Frances poured the remainder of the wine into her glass. 'Well, he couldn't have been nicer when I did the session with him. Your brother rubs him up the wrong way.'

'Of course he was nice to you – you're a woman. And you cured his sneezing for him. Dan can ooze charm if he thinks it's worth the effort. Anyway, Paul says we should have got him tied down in writing.'

'Paul should have been a lawyer – he's got that nasty quality really successful lawyers have. Anyway, all I know is, he was in grand form last night.'

'You met Paul last night?'

'Don't be ridiculous – *Dan,* not Paul. I brought the bill for the tiles into the hospital and showed it to him – I'm sick looking at it. Only then when he saw it he got this frightened look on his face, like a wee boy that's been caught stealing sweets, and I hadn't the heart to push for it. Ninety-eight quid's not the end of the world.'

Diarmuid put down the wine bottle. 'You were in seeing Uncle Dan last night? What time was this?'

'I can't remember. Nine o'clock. Maybe later.'

'Can you remember if you met someone after you came out? Maybe they'd remember what time it was.'

Frances pushed back her chair and stood up slowly. 'Do you think you're talking to a child or something? I don't have to account to you for my movements and who I was with or what time.'

'No, I don't think I'm talking to a child. We don't have a child.' As soon as he'd said it, Diarmuid wished he hadn't.

'I hope you're not suggesting that's my fault.'

'I didn't say it was.'

'Round half the consultants in the country, poking and peering until I could have screamed.'

'I know that.' They sat in silence for a minute. 'All I meant

was, you might have told me you were going to see Uncle Dan.'
It wasn't all Diarmuid meant – what he'd really meant was,
she'd been out with Warwick, and part of him felt crackling rage
at the thought and part of him didn't give a damn.

'I did tell you I was thinking of going, but you weren't
listening, that's all.' Frances stood up to clear the table. 'He's
getting out tomorrow, by the way.'

'Who is?'

'Your uncle Dan. Mother of God, do you listen to a word
anybody says?'

'But tomorrow's Wednesday. He's supposed to be getting out
on Thursday.'

'Well, they've changed it, then. Tomorrow. Wednesday.'

'Brilliant.' Diarmuid put his feet into his shoes. 'I'll have to go
and see him this evening, that's all. If you'd told me earlier I'd
have gone last night.'

He went upstairs and splashed water on his face. Doing
something was better than doing nothing. In the magnifying
mirror he could see the wrinkles at the sides of his eyes, he could
see the way his hair was turning grey not just at the sideburns
but also on top, he could see…a middle-aged man. A man whose
wife went out and had a meal with a small garden-gnome
bastard with a ginger beard. A bastard who had offered an
attractive financial deal. A really, really attractive financial deal.
He splashed more cold water, rubbed hard at his face with a
towel. He thought he could hear Frances talking quietly on the
phone downstairs.

There was a surprising number of people visiting the hospital,
considering that it was after seven on a Tuesday night. Shapeless
women huddled with their grandchildren inside the entrance;
younger women with blond hair and hard faces outside the front
entrance, pulling on cigarettes. When he went up to Uncle Dan's
ward, an elderly man with wispy grey hair was in his bed. A fat
Filipino nurse suggested he check at Reception, they had the
records.

The receptionist sniffed as she scanned the computer screen, dabbed at her nose with the back of her hand. 'Ward eleven. He's been moved to Ward eleven. You take the lift to it.'

The lift was full of people, so close he could smell their breath, their clothes, their bodies. After what seemed a year it stopped at the eleventh floor.

'Ward eleven?' he asked a man in overalls sweeping the corridor.

'Wrong floor, mate. Ward eleven is on the floor beneath this.'

'On the tenth floor? Ward eleven is on the tenth floor?'

The man leant on his brush, closed his eyes. 'Right.'

'I was told Ward eleven was on the eleventh floor.'

'Told a lie, then, mate. Tenth floor.'

Diarmuid pushed the button to summon the lift. The light winked up to floor eight, then went down again. Then to floor five and down again. When it went to Floor nine and started descending, Diarmuid said, 'God pity anybody sick or in a hurry,' to no one in particular, found the stairs and walked down a flight.

A corridor stretched ahead of him; to his right a door marked 'Ward 11'. He pushed it open and found himself in what looked like a small kitchen area. There was a kettle boiling, two mugs with teabags waiting to be filled. One of the mugs said, 'One day, you will meet a goal so beautiful, you will want to marry it and have its children.' As his eye caught a sign saying 'Authorised Personnel Only' a broad-shouldered nurse with thin, honey-coloured hair appeared. She stared. 'Can I help you? What are you doing here?'

'The lift was stuck, so I came down the stairs. I think I'm lost.'

'The lift is stuck? I heard nothing about any stuck lift. I work on the floor above and I'd be bound to have heard.'

'Well, it was a long time in coming, seemed to be stopping at lower storeys and then—'

'Oh *stopping* – I thought you said stuck. That's just wheelchair day. The wheelchair patients at ground level slow things up. But sure you wouldn't begrudge them. Not everyone is lucky enough to have the use of their limbs, you know.' She looked at him, her head to one side. 'Anyway, who is it you're looking for?'

'Dan Costello. He's my uncle. Ward eleven.'

'Better try the desk on this floor. I'm from the floor above – we just share the kitchen here. Straight down the corridor on your right, they'll look after you.' She turned away to fill the two cups from the kettle.

There were arches the length of the corridor, off which lay small wards containing six beds each. In some of the wards families and friends stood or sat; in others, a lone man or woman slumped in a chair, glancing up each time they heard footsteps. From an office a short distance ahead – or was it another ward? – came a muddle of urgent voices.

In front of a small reception desk a tall man with fair hair stood facing Diarmuid. He had a stethoscope circling his neck and was chatting to a man in a pinstripe suit, who was turned away. Something about the shoulders of the second man seemed familiar. Then he turned and looked straight at Diarmuid, and it was McAleavy the solicitor. He approached, both hands extended. 'It's yourself – glad to see you. You didn't waste time.'

'Well, I intended to come yesterday but... How is the invalid? Dressed and hot to trot tomorrow, I suppose.'

There was a pause. Then McAleavy glanced at the doctor, who was fingering his stethoscope, and touched his elbow. 'Ah, Doctor, this is Dr Diarmuid Monaghan – no, no, not medical. Diarmuid is – he's Dan Monaghan's nephew, is what he is.'

The doctor looked surprised, said, 'Oh, I see.' He nodded twice and his voice was soft. 'In that case, there's a bit of bad news, I'm afraid, and I'm more than sorry to be its, its harbinger.' He put his hand under Diarmuid's elbow and his voice sank to a whisper. 'Just over an hour ago, your uncle had a relapse. At seven thirty-eight I'm afraid we lost him. My sincere condolences.'

Diarmuid stared at the little petrol-rainbow gloss on the man's glasses, at the way his lower lip stuck out and glistened, at the hair that wisped forward on his forehead. Had he taken much time this morning making himself nice? Did he think it was worthwhile tending this body of his so carefully when, one day, a thunderbolt would hit it and it would lie down somewhere and die? He wondered a lot of things, about the doctor and Uncle Dan and McAleavy, all at breakneck speed, and even as the images were colliding and stumbling in his brain, he heard his own voice say, 'Can I see him?'

The doctor hesitated, then spoke to a nurse who had emerged from one of the wards. She looked along the corridor, said something, pointed. The doctor hurried back to them. 'Nurse says you can, if you feel you would like to.'

McAleavy touched the small of Diarmuid's back. 'Go on, you, and pay your last respects to the poor man.'

A screen had been put in place around the bed nearest the arch, and the nurse moved a section aside so that Diarmuid could enter. A man lay in the bed on his back, his face a candle-white colour. Around the top of his head and under his chin a wad of bandage was tied, as though he was suffering from gumboil or toothache. It was like no face Diarmuid had ever seen, and at the same time it was a face he had seen all his life. It was Uncle Dan and he was irretrievably dead.

Someone moved beside him. It was the dark-haired nurse who had joked with Dan about malingering. Her eyes brimmed. 'His heart couldn't take the strain, that was the problem. Doing grand up to then, getting on the best. Then out of nowhere after lunch, this fit of sneezing and coughing, sneezing and coughing. I've never heard anything like it. Once he got started on it there was no stopping him. We tried everything we could think of – even stuck cold spoons down his back – but it was hopeless. Every single one of us was dying about him, you know.'

Over an hour later, when the fussing began to die down, after an undertaker had been contacted and a priest contacted to give the last rites, even though Uncle Dan was already dead, and a hotel contacted for lunch after the funeral, McAleavy nudged Diarmuid and spoke in a whisper. 'Do you know what the pair of us will do the first chance we get? We'll slip across the road and throw a jar into us. God knows, we've earned it after this night's work.'

The different-coloured bottles behind the bar, the cigarette smoke, the TV screen, the clink of glasses and the shouts of laughter from a table – there was something heartless and yet comforting in all this.

McAleavy stood, called above the noise. 'What is it? A whiskey? Good man. My shout.' He headed for the bar.

Diarmuid watched the other drinkers. Not one of them had this day been touched by death. Maybe in the past, certainly coming up later, but not tonight, not tonight, Josephine, and tonight was the only night that mattered... He should phone Frances and tell her. Although coping with her being upset was the last thing he wanted right now. On the opposite side of the pub a man and a woman stood up and headed for the side exit. For a heart-pounding second he was sure they were Warwick and Frances. Then they turned towards him and he saw there was no resemblance to either.

'Now,' McAleavy said, putting a double whiskey on the table in front of Diarmuid, 'get that into you as quick as you're fit.'

Diarmuid felt the whiskey tingle through his system, felt his lips part and swell slightly. McAleavy downed half his Guinness in one go and wiped his mouth. 'I know it comes to all of us – I know that, sure we all know it – but it can be some knock when it comes close. Ha? By Jesus, I'm not worth tuppence.' He drank again.

Diarmuid tried to think of something to say but couldn't. McAleavy reached across the table, put a hand on his arm. 'The thing was, I thought you knew. I thought somebody had contacted you. I mean, Christ Almighty, if for one instant I'd even *suspected*, I'd have found a way to break the thing easier to you. Could have had the doctor find a quiet place, call you in for a private word. *Something*. You may be sure of that.'

'Thanks.' Immediately he said it, Diarmuid tried to think why he was saying it. *Thanks.* McAleavy had done nothing. Maybe for Uncle Dan but certainly not for him. *Warwick and Frances.* He stared at the solicitor, who was raising his finger and calling to the barman 'We'll go again,' and went to fetch the drinks. When he got back, Diarmuid remembered what it was he'd meant to say. 'How did you know Uncle Dan was critical? I mean, how come you were there before anybody else?'

McAleavy drank most of the second half of his pint before he replied. 'They rang me from the hospital before lunch, about paperwork they said he wanted done. Says I to myself, it's just some sort of a clause or comma he wants, and he might even have his mind re-changed by the time I get there. He could be that way, as you know yourself.'

'Like a pinball. That's what my brother said he was like.'

'Not far off the mark, I may tell you. So I came into the hospital a while before lunchtime, and there's your uncle Dan sitting up in the bed, looking...in charge, that's the word. In charge. And erratic too. They're giving this man painkillers, that's what's they're doing, says I to myself. He was as pale as pale, but at the same time like a dynamo. In charge.'

'What paperwork did he want done?'

McAleavy brushed invisible crumbs, first, from his left knee and then the right. Glanced at Diarmuid from under his eyebrows. 'He wanted to make a change to his will. So, says I to myself, this is just some wee clause he wants inserted. And sure enough, that was what it was. Had to take a sum out of his account and earmark it for a particular party. Party X, he called this person – didn't want even me to know who it was. 'A person of my acquaintance,' he kept saying. And he has a letter written and sealed, to be opened after his death, which will say who X is. I know one sure thing – whoever they are, they'll be right and pleased when they're told, for they'll be picking up a cool ten thousand pounds.'

The solicitor looked around the pub, as though checking for someone who might be eavesdropping, then reached over and gripped Diarmuid's arm, almost whispered the question.

'He had a sort of a *grá* for your wife too, hadn't he?'

Diarmuid studied the solicitor's face. The teddy-bear brown eyes, the damp, thin fringe of hair combed across the forehead, the nose with tiny red veins that hinted at purple.

'He had, hadn't he?'

Diarmuid looked into his whiskey. 'He thought a lot of her after she cured him of sneezing.'

'The only pity is that it had to come back again. And come back that bad too.' McAleavy sighed and sat for a moment, head bent. 'And then your missus paid some bill for him too.'

Diarmuid felt a stab of pain in his left ball. 'It was for his tiles that came to us – she was going to make him pay. Then she saw the look on his face and she couldn't do it.'

McAleavy nodded. 'That'd be it then. That'd explain the thing.'

'What thing?'

'Why he did what he did.'

'Would you mind not talking like some fortune teller's dummy? I'm too tired for guessing games.'

'Well, now, I shouldn't really be going into these things – they should be done sitting round a table in an office officially. But sure I won't tell if you don't.' McAleavy laced his hands and spread them on his stomach, leant back and looked at Diarmuid. 'Maybe you should order up another double or take a nerve tablet or something before I lay this next bit out for you. Because your uncle Dan...' He puckered his mouth into a pout. '...did a very funny thing. He left *his* bit of your mother's place to *you*. One-third.'

'What about Paul?'

The solicitor shook his head. 'Just you. And he did something else as well, which is even more of a turn-up, in my estimation. He left his own house *and* a portfolio of stocks and shares to – no, *not* to Paul, I don't think there was ever a pile of love lost there, to tell you the truth. No, the house and portfolio is what he left... to your good lady.'

The noises of the pub – the shouted orders, the faint thunder of traffic, the ching of the cash register – faded, as if an unseen hand had turned down the volume on everything.

'To Frances? He left his house and all his shares to *Frances*?'

'The very thing. And I can tell you this as well: that man had some way with shares. I don't know where he learnt investment or how he learnt it, but by God, he had. Some. Knack. With. Shares.'

'Is the portfolio worth much, then?'

'He never forgot a favour, your uncle. D'you know what he said to me? He said your missus – this is as near his actual words as I can remember – your missus, he said, was as decent a woman as he'd come across, ever. "Up there with Kate." That was your mother, wasn't it? Kate. And his sister, I suppose. "That wee woman is up there with Kate and the angels." Kept repeating that.'

The pain moved across to Diarmuid's right ball, where it began a whirling motion. 'The shares. How much…are they worth?'

'It depends on the markets and so on, that goes without saying. But if you threw me on the ground and sat on my chest and put a knife against my throat, I'd say they'd be worth, oh, what? Three hundred, three hundred and fifty thousand pounds. Give or take a bit.'

Chapter 18

GUARDIAN ANGELS

On a Friday afternoon three months later Diarmuid sat alone in his office, waiting for a taxi. It was odd, looking for the last time at the bookcases and filing cabinets and Venetian blinds that had knitted themselves into his eyeballs and brain for some twenty years.

'Are you sure?' the Dean had said, standing in the office door two days earlier as Diarmuid lifted a selection of books into a cardboard box. 'We can have the entire office packed into a container and delivered to your home address – it's standard procedure, really. Or at least we can deliver the contents of the office, can't actually move the room, ha-ha-ha-ha, we'll need that.'

'No thanks, Dean. I'm not actually living at home, these days. And to tell you the truth, my interest in education went up something of a siding about ten years ago and never quite came down. You can dump anything I leave behind with my blessing. Or torch it.'

'Oh dear,' the Dean chuckled. 'We'll miss that dry tongue of yours, Diarmuid. Now, what was the other thing I meant to... Oh, yes. Have you heard anything from Mrs Angela Passmore – Claire's sister?'

'I have.'

The Dean cupped his hands in front of his breastbone, as if

holding a small bird. 'My reason for asking – my office received a letter from her three days ago, requesting that we disregard an earlier letter she sent us, which was in the nature of an, um, complaint about an, eh, unpleasant incident. In this latest communication, happily, she explains that the incident in question arose from a simple misunderstanding, and that, in changed circumstances, she now has "a happy working relationship" with you. Is that a fair description of the current circumstances?'

'"Working", yes – not sure about the "happy". All I've done is provide a bit of funding for a small religious magazine, which then was able to appoint her as its marketing manager. Brother Ambrose – the editor – thinks she might bring in a wider audience for the magazine. Not sure if he's right but for now it's an arrangement that suits both parties.'

'Splendid, very good. That's the one for which you write a religious column – am I correct?'

'You are. Although I'm thinking of calling it a day.'

'Well, indeed. So many possibilities are now open to you.' The Dean uncupped his hands and put one under Diarmuid's elbow. 'And you're certain I cannot persuade you to the smallest of farewell presentations? Even something quite informal?'

But Diarmuid said no, kept saying no, in the end said it rather loudly. Then the Dean made a soothing motion with his hands and said, well, if that was how he felt, so be it; at the same time if he changed his mind to ring him at home that evening, the household telephone system was finally up and running again, at last, the insurance people had been tardy but in the end had reimbursed the theft of their handset, quite generous ultimately, but it was just a pity that it had to happen in the first instance and when it did happen that it took such an unconscionably long time to resolve. But, then, that was the way with so many things in life, wasn't it, the Dean said.

Now, staring out the window at several crows throwing themselves around against a fresh breeze, Diarmuid searched for an emotion that he could take from this room with him.

Sadness? No, there was nothing here he felt sad to leave. The memory of young faces looking up in admiration at his lectures over twenty years? Ha – looking at their watches, more likely. A stab of regret, then, that he'd no longer be a part of this big, clanking, chattering institution? Hardly. Two afternoons ago, during class time, he'd walked along a corridor, paused outside each door in turn. Voices explaining, voices instructing, voices debating. The blind energy of the speakers, each convinced that what he or she had to say would make a difference. Deaf to the fact that, once the course was over, nine-tenths of the knowledge poured into young brains would evaporate or get tipped down the nearest drain. All of them part of a giant wheel that kept on turning, nobody able to remember what its function was other than to keep turning.

At five past three a 'Kabs4U' taxi drew up outside the main entrance. Diarmuid left the office, locked the door for the last time. It was as he turned away from dropping his keys off at the porter's office and stood lighting a cigarette outside the main entrance that he was able suddenly to put a name to the feeling that had taken possession of him, was filling the air around him, was swelling every part of his mind and heart. Odd that he hadn't been able to identify it earlier. It was of anticipation.

He told the cabby to head for his new apartment on Laganside. Sixth floor, nine hundred a month. Painfully expensive, you bet, even after you'd allowed for the view of the Lagan and the refined nature of the other tenants. He'd have a shower and then two, maybe three cold beers with Gilbert and Sullivan in the background. Ring Warwick and arrange a meeting. Let the evening drift past with the river below. But a mile up the road, panting a little, he was surprised to find himself leaning forward and asking: 'Do you know where Ardclogher is?'

The man glanced in the rear-view mirror. 'Should do. I was reared less than a mile from it.'

'Take me to the chapel there.' As they left the main road, Diarmuid sat back and squeezed his eyes tight shut. No need to make a drama of this: it was a journey he'd taken mentally a dozen times over the past five months. Had pictured himself driving up to the gates, felt the soft jolt as the car stopped outside. The gravel crunching underfoot, birds shouting their alarm as he moved through the graves checking each until he found her... Face your fear, face your fear, face your fear.

The taxi drew up outside the chapel, parked alongside a Mercedes van. 'When will you be heading back?' the driver asked.

'Hard to say. Ten, fifteen minutes.'

'I'll have my crossword done by then.' The driver produced a copy of the *Irish News* from under his seat and drew a biro from an inner pocket.

At first Diarmuid thought the metal gate to the cemetery might be locked, but when he held down the latch and leant hard, it groaned open. Inside, a noticeboard protected by a glass panel listed the occupants of the graves, with a letter and number beside each. He had to read through it several times before he located his mother. 'M-o-n-i-c-a-n': they had spelt her name. 'Katherine Dolores Monican'. The last of the Monicans. Her grave was B7: Row B, seventh grave.

It had rained the day of the funeral, heavily from dawn until nearly ten in the morning. Diarmuid had turned in the bed and stared past the little rain-worms on the window, heard the feet of the coffin-carriers shuffling on the chapel floor, imagined the chocolate earth piled beside the grave. Now, no rain, no mud, and underfoot a concrete path with a slight ripple in it. Afternoon sunshine, birds rustling and calling from the rhododendron bushes by the cemetery wall.

A small typed notice in a metal stand marked her grave and the five new graves after hers. No headstone yet – the earth must settle first or any stone would tilt at a drunken angle, maybe collapse. On the grave beside hers a vase lay on its side, flowers scattered all around. Lager louts? Drug addicts? Grass (sown by good son Paul?) had begun to grow on her grave, a tender green crew cut above her remains. What an apt word: remains.

Nothing remaining of her but a coffinful of jelly and bone. And maggots. He looked quickly away at the sky, listened as a lamb bleated somewhere. Life calling, singing a song of hope above a green hill.

He blessed himself, stared at the dust on his toecaps. What was the point in coming here, apart from proving he had the courage to do it? People are buried because they can't stay above ground – if they weren't buried, disease would spread and more people would die. Just as living people can't stay below ground: they need to come up for air. So a hole gets dug and the dead are pitched in, covered up. They're below ground, we're above ground, and never the twain shall meet.

Except that, as he stood here now, they seemed to. The hillside was packed with funeral rags and bones, barely out of sight under a skin of earth, but the air around him was alive. An electrical current seemed to flicker from headstone to headstone, grave to grave, filling the air, touching him and the birds and, yes, probably the maggots and worms too, galvanising them all. The ground beneath his feet seemed to vibrate with the presence of his mother, dark and smiling as in the passport photograph. Mammy outside the front door after school, arms wide, hugging two small boys, the smell of her apron, the comfort of her stomach. He could feel his heart thumping as he opened his eyes.

Mammy – it's me. Yes, late as usual. I couldn't come before, or at least thought I couldn't. But all that day of your funeral I was in bed thinking of you. And when I got up the next day and people looked at me and said they were sorry for my trouble, and even when they didn't say it I thought about you. And every day for the next two months you were the first thing came into my mind when I woke up and the last thing I thought of at night. It was just that coming here that day – I thought that if I saw the open grave, saw you put deep into its dark, stood looking down at you, it would end everything. Even carrying you out to the hearse with Paul – your legs felt like a girl's or a bird's, so small and fragile, and here we were carrying you away to stick you in a hole forever. I didn't want to bring you out of your bedroom and into a hearse and then a coffin and then into a trench cut in the ground to be completely dead forever. If I'd known how you would be able to do this – stay alive even though you're dead – I'd have come sooner. Gone to the funeral, visited every month. Honestly.

He left me his share, Uncle Dan... Yes, I know he had no use for it any more, but at the same time... And he left Frances his house and shares. McAleavy says the shares alone are worth over three hundred thousand. No, Frances didn't trick him – she cured his sneezing and he liked her, that's all. Yes, I know you didn't like her, but... Anyway, that means I now own two-thirds of your place so I've decided to leave the university... Well it wouldn't make sense when I can make a better living doing something else... Myself and another lecturer are going to build some flats, and if we get them sold OK, we'll invest in another apartment block, or even... No, it's not Paul I'll be working with, it's another lecturer – a colleague... Well, he is annoyed, Paul, of course, understandable, really. He was on the phone to me doing a bit of shouting because he thought we should scrap the seventy-thousand pound deal, where I bought him out, but I didn't see it that way. Then when he saw there was no progress there, I think he thought at the very least he would be the X that the ten thousand was earmarked for, but then it turned out that X was a woman in the Fine Tile Gallery, the one who served us the day I went down to advise uncle Dan about what to select. He said in the letter that he'd liked the way she'd talked and gone about her business – brave and a real go-getter, he called her, and if there were more like her the country would be in a better state. That *really* got to Paul when McAleavy told him that. Anyway, I told him I'd cover the cost of Anne's operation, and he cooled down a bit, although not completely. But, you know, he was the one drew up the legal document, not me; and it was Uncle Dan who wrote the will, not me... No I would *not* have knocked down the house to build flats if you were still living in it... No, you're wrong there... Well, actually, I've moved out of our house for the time being, which gives Frances more room to develop her body-soul business... No, just the reverse, actually – my living in a flat has meant we get on far better. Yes, I know, I know, I shouldn't have written that stuff in Little Known Facts, bad thoughts, you're right, but it was meant as more of a joke than... Anyway, it's sorted now. End of story. Except...except that some nights I wake up and have this feeling. It's not so much a pain, as, well, as if somebody had scooped me out – if I knocked on myself there'd be an echo. Don't know what it is. Once I'm up in the morning and have the newspaper bought and the radio going, I'm OK, but sometimes at night it's... Yes, I'll go to the doctor – if it gets worse... Yes, the foot's better. Completely better, indeed. Thank God. Or should that be thank Jorg?

He closed his eyes again and watched the blobs of green and red behind his eyes float through the darkness. It was like when he used to hide under the stairs as a child, with a bar of chocolate or a piece of cake, feeling his hands and mouth become moist with its pleasure, the darkness deepening the sense of being a transgressor, stained in sweet stuff and sin.

At first the noise was a pinpoint of sound, mixing with the blobs, swirling in a pattern along with them. Then it grew bigger, insistent, with pauses for other sounds. He couldn't make out what they were, maybe sounds of the timpani in an orchestra, clank, thud, rat-a-tat-tat. He opened his eyes, breathing quickly.

Two dots of blue and grey about a hundred metres away, distinct against the green of the graveyard. Then the dots moved, two figures, bending, lifting, working. A realisation of who they were came up slowly, like using a dimmer switch on a light. Joy and Mairead, a metal wheelbarrow to their right, hunkered down in front of a headstone.

Leave. Get away. Quick! Diarmuid bent his head, clasped his hands together. Come with me, Mammy. Guide and protect me, save me from life. Amen.

Walking briskly, he was halfway to the cemetery gate when the call came. 'Hi! Wait!'

Look casually at the trees on either side. Whistle softly in a preoccupied way. Nobody could be expected to hear from that distance.

'Diarmuid! Hang on!'

The shout seemed to bounce off the side of the chapel. Before it had died down the sound of feet running, slapping off the concrete path. As they grew near he had no choice, had to turn and look.

Joy panted to a stop, pointed dramatically at him. She was wearing a pair of black jeans, the bottom of the legs plump with fold-ups. 'I thought it was you! I said to Mairead, "That's your man Diarmuid, Frances's husband," but she said you were taller and what would you be doing in a cemetery? Wrong as usual.' Joy looked at the scrubbing brush in her hand, which was dripping onto the path, then back at Diarmuid. 'We're in charge of maintenance here, seeing that everything's kept shipshape – a total tip it was, before we started. What are you doing here?'

'Visiting my mother's grave.'

'I said that. I said, "I bet you he has someone buried here." Just *knew* it. Joy gets it right again. Your mother, is that what you said?'

'Yes.'

'Have we done her? How long is she dead?'

Diarmuid paused. Sisters Do The Dead. Saying her name aloud would somehow link his mother with Joy and Mairead, people she would not have understood had she been alive but would certainly have disapproved of.

'When did she die?' Joy's voice was insistent, a bright, cheerful wire burrowing through his ear to the middle of his brain.

'Over eight months ago.'

'I bet you we've done her, then – we've done all the recent ones. What's her number? It'll be on our new noticeboard, just inside the entrance. Did you know we did that noticeboard ourselves? Typed the whole thing up. We gave everybody a number.'

'She's B7.' He felt ashamed saying it.

'In that case we've definitely done her.'

He wanted to lift something – a stick, a stone, the scrubbing brush, his fist – and hit her with it. Again and again and again. Instead he heard himself say, 'What do you mean, "done her"?'

'Done up her grave. We have this contract with Fr Lonegan. The day we met him we told him about us being a cross-community gardening firm – working together and Mairead coming to the Twelfth marches with me and me going to Gaelic games with her. He seemed to like hearing about that kind of thing. In fact, I've a notion that's what got us the contract.'

'So what do you actually do for him?'

'First we cut the grass on all the graves. Then we clean the headstones – your mother wouldn't have a headstone yet, but if she did we'd spruce it up. Not just soap and water either. The older ones we do with a sand-blaster, it takes that to get the dirt off and bring up the colour of the headstone. Most of them are light grey but some are a kind of honey colour when they've been cleaned. They look gorgeous, good enough to eat, after Mairead's finished with her blaster... I'm telling him about the way you clean the headstones,' she said to Mairead, who had appeared beside her, carrying a strimmer. She, too, was wearing black jeans, although hers had a series of small pockets down the legs. They flared at the bottom, so only the tips of her pink Nike trainers were visible.

Mairead nodded, wrinkles forming and vanishing on her neck and cheeks. 'You have to watch out for the lettering, though. The blaster can be very sore on the lettering.'

'She practically wiped out the name and everything on one headstone,' Joy said. 'Lucky for her it was an old one that nobody really looked at, so it wasn't so bad. After we've cut the grass and weeds we clean the stones. Rake it and take away dead flowers and things like that.'

'Somebody knocked over the flowers on a grave near my mother's,' Diarmuid said. 'Some Grade-A morons in action.'

Joy smiled. 'Morons didn't do that.'

'Morons – that's a good one,' Mairead said.

'In my book they're morons. The whole grave is a mess – flowers ripped apart, the lot. I'll show you what they did.'

'No need,' Mairead said. 'There are loads of graves like that. That's why we've started putting down poison.'

'Did you say—'

'To control them.'

'Poison?'

'Rabbits,' Joy said. 'That's what did your flowers. They're all over the cemetery. Come out at night and chew up any flowers put on the graves. Or, rather, the stems – they eat the stems. Can't be bothered with the flower part but they go mad for the stems. Chew and chew and then scatter them left, centre and right. And then they leave their wee black-ball calling-cards all over. We even found some burrows, didn't we?'

'They're the worst,' Mairead said. 'Burrows. Once they start burrowing, the only thing is the poison. Your mother's OK because she's recent. But if she had died, say, ten years ago, she'd probably have a rabbit warren down there scurrying all over her by now.'

'In her grave?'

Mairead nodded.

'I – never thought about that,' Diarmuid said. He tried not to think about it now.

'How many of them did you gather in that bag the other day?' Joy asked.

Mairead closed her eyes, pinched the skin above her throat. 'Five.'

'We take them to a mink farmer near Ballymena,' Joy said. 'He has a place in London he sells the furs on to. Give us thirty per cent.'

'Should have seen on Tuesday morning,' Mairead said, patting the pockets of her jeans as if they might contain another furry body. 'I came out here first thing – know how many I got? Eight. Just flopped there, on three graves, one beside the other. There'd been a really heavy dew and their fur was soaked. Eight of them, lying there dead. Only, with the poison, you can't eat them.'

'Are you full-time...grave-tenders?'

Joy looked around. 'Mondays, Tuesdays and Fridays – those are the days we work here.'

'I'd find it depressing, I think,' Diarmuid said.

'That's a good one,' Mairead said. 'Depressing. That's the last thing we feel.' She waved her arm in a near-circle. 'See when the sun starts to go down? You look at those headstones – the shadows on them, getting longer and longer, all of them pointing the same way, like big javelins or arrows or signposts or something. I really like that. Depressed is the last thing I feel when I see something as nice as that. I say, "The tombstones point the way."'

'Anyway, when you're working that hard, you don't have time to think about depressing,' Joy said. 'The important thing is, the spirits here know our work is to honour them.'

'Honour them and their memory.' Mairead gestured towards Joy's jeans and her own. 'We dress in black jeans to show respect for the place we're working in and the memory of the dead people.' She nudged Joy and dropped her voice. 'Would he like some of those flowers, maybe?'

Joy nodded. 'We have a wheelbarrow full of fresh flowers up there for putting on a selection of graves,' she told Diarmuid. 'Father Lonegan supplies them – his congregation is all old people, so they're keen on looking after the dead. Have you got something to put them in – a vase or that? Don't worry, no problem – we'll check around. B7, you say? We'll put them on it for you.'

'Put some poison on it, too,' Mairead said. 'To be on the safe side.'

'That's kind of you.'

'No skin off our nose,' Mairead told him, raising her eyebrows and hunching her shoulders. 'We're not paying for it.'

Joy tapped her glove against her thigh, twisted each finger of the glove in turn. 'Frances rings us sometimes.' It sounded like a half-challenge. 'Your wife, I mean. She's starting a healing centre upstairs in Dufferin House.'

Diarmuid looked away. 'I'd heard that.'

'The university is going to use the ground floor for its classes. Asians and that, the students are going to be, apparently.'

'The place is huge now, since they knocked down all those inside walls,' Mairead said. 'Do it all up, full of all sorts of equipment for training doctors. She's going to pay for half of it, you know. Frances. Your wife. It'll cost her a fortune.'

'Yes, but the whole first floor is going to be for herself and her clients, don't forget,' Joy said. 'No rent or anything. And see that body-soul business? Absolutely booming – they'll be hanging out the windows. She was saying she'll have to take on two certified assistants next term or she won't be able to cope. Half the staff in the university has applied to her already. Fair few students as well.'

'They can thank the Dean's daughter for that,' Mairead said. 'You see her on the TV and in the papers? He didn't see her!' She turned to Joy. 'He hasn't even heard about the Dean's daughter! Tell him about it.'

'Mrs Saddington was the one brought her to Frances,' Joy said. 'The Dean's wife. Wanted to know if there was anything she could do with the daughter's arm – you know, the way it's all curled up and everything. Been like that since she was a baby. Anyway, they did a session and after it the girl said it was no different. But then two days later, after the follow-up session apparently, she could reach it up to her shoulder, and then the next one up, above her head.'

'They got a big photograph took after the arm got better and the Dean's wife signed it,' Mairead said, face thrust forward, eyes bulging. 'It has the girl with her two hands in the air and her mother and father on either side of her. "Forever in your debt – Professor and Mrs Saddington." The Dean's wife wrote that on the photograph. They have it hung up on the stairs of Dufferin House, so anyone going up to Frances sees it. One of the cleaners told me the Dean is for giving her a degree for nothing – Frances, I mean – he was that pleased.'

'If you look in really close at the photograph, where it was took at the front of Dufferin House, you can see the garden in the background,' Joy said. 'That's our work. We got the contract for it after your wife recommended us, you know. She's been really good to us.'

'So things have worked out for you.'

'Well, more that we made them work out!' Joy said, slapping her glove again. 'Once we got the opening and the bit of help, we made good and sure that it worked out.'

'You see our van out at the gate?' Mairead said. 'It's a Mercedes – haven't even had time to get our sign painted on it. You'll not see us having to push that van, I can tell you.'

'We pick our jobs now,' Joy said. 'Pick and choose. The one we really have our eye on at the moment is the contract for the garden behind the clubhouse at the Morton Golf Club.'

'The men-only place?'

'We don't make the golf-club rules,' Mairead told him. 'That's their business. We're only doing the garden – if we get the contract.'

Diarmuid was trying to think of something to say to that when his mobile started to ring.

'B7, did you say?' Joy mouthed. He nodded and watched as the two trudged up the path. The evening sun made a halo of the fine hair frizzing out from Joy's head and gleamed on the steel handle of Mairead's rake. On the horizon beyond, thin strips of cloud glowed pink; in the cemetery, the tombstone shadows pointed towards the cemetery gate.

'Hello?'

'Der-mott my son.' Warwick, with a background of chatter and music. 'Can you talk? Where are you?'

'In a cemetery.'

'Have you decided if your stay there will be permanent or temporary?'

'I'm leaving this minute. Was visiting my mother's grave.'

'Ah, indeed. Mine is buried in Berkshire, so I grieve for her from my living room. More convenient for both parties.'

'I was talking to her – my mother,' Diarmuid said before he could stop himself. 'I sometimes think she can hear me.'

There was silence at the other end of the line for a moment. Then, 'Listen to me, Diarmuid. Jump on a bus and meet me in the Bodhrán Room at the Ashgrove Hotel. I'll be in a corner looking thoughtful.'

And he was. Hunched forward, his elbows protecting a double Scotch. 'Ah, the man from the place of shadows. Let me get you something.'

'No, thanks.'

Warwick signalled to the waiter. 'Two double Scotches and water, please.' He finished the drink in front of him and when the new ones arrived he bent and sniffed carefully at his. 'Be here now. That's what the Buddhists say – did you know that? Opinions vary as to what they mean. My interpretation is, should you get lucky enough for a drink to land in front of you, it is your moral duty to smell it, taste it, feel delight as it goes head-over-heels down your gullet. Similarly with all physical and mental pleasures. Looking beyond the moment is a snare and deception, as is talking to your dead mother but as is not, repeat *not*, planning for property development. *À la carte* Buddhism, you might say. Anyway, anyway, anyway – did I tell you? I've been talking to a local company. Smallish building outfit, prepared to start in the spring, planning permission permitting. I'll show you the figures back at my place after. If I can still read at that stage.'

They stayed there until five o'clock, at which point they crossed the road, looking both ways first, and had a meal in a restaurant called Sauve Qui Peut that had opened a couple of weeks earlier. It had thick tablecloths and fresh wild salmon and an Australian sauvignon blanc that cost thirty pounds and did a delicious Chinese burn on your tastebuds but was worth every penny because, Warwick and Diarmuid agreed, it was the best wine with the nicest fish they'd ever had in their lives, even better than La Bella Figura. After that they had brandy, and exchanged views about the incestuousness of academia, and the fresh air that was business, and the high that came from a successful investment. They also exchanged stories about their mothers, and Diarmuid said that his visit to his mother's grave that afternoon had been liberating in many ways, and Warwick said he could see how that might be the case, although he preferred to remember his mother as she was, which was in a rocking chair with a big glass of brandy in her hand.

But at no point in the meal did Warwick mention that on most Friday evenings in recent weeks, he had liked to take a taxi to the house in which Diarmuid used to live, where he would collect Diarmuid's wife and go with her to a half-decent restaurant, often La Bella Figura, and afterwards take another taxi back to the house in which Diarmuid used to live, where he and Diarmuid's wife would sit in the living room drinking Bailey's Irish Cream, or sometimes a coffee, before going upstairs to enjoy prolonged sexual intercourse in the bed where Diarmuid used to sleep, but not before Frances had spread a large bath towel on top of the sheets and pulled the curtains. Nor did Diarmuid ask him if he was doing any of these things, although he suspected Warwick was doing at least some of them.

On the way home in the taxi from the restaurant, Warwick told Diarmuid that this had proved a good ending to what had started out as a gloomy afternoon, and Diarmuid said it had proved to be a very, very good ending, better than he could have believed possible when he took the taxi to the cemetery, and that he, Diarmuid, was grateful to him, Warwick, for recommending Sauve Qui Peut and for calling this taxi in which they were now travelling and for persuading him to leave the university and take up a business career and for tipping the waiter so generously and for understanding about his mother. 'You have taken the hinges off my prison door, Billy my friend,' he kept saying. 'Your wind of freedom blows in my face.'

He was still saying these words, or something close to them, as he put the chain-lock on his apartment door. When he switched on the television, Tom Paulin was telling Mark Lawson how TV soaps consisted of philosophical narratives that addressed modern life and its relationship to ordinary people. Diarmuid put the sound to mute and had a pee in the bathroom. Then he knelt by his bed and tried to say a prayer for the happy repose of his mother's soul, but he kept nodding off, so in the end he crawled into bed in his underpants and socks, the flickering TV in the living room forgotten. From the street below the honks and shouts of Belfast life drifted up six storeys, the brief silences filled in by the cluck and gurgle of the river Lagan. But Dr Diarmuid Monaghan heard none of it. He lay curled in a ball on the bed in his new apartment, his breath rasping against the pillow, sunk in a dreamless sleep.